A Song for Chloe

ISBN#978-1-943-789-52-8

Cover design and layout by: WhiteRabbitgraphix.com

Photographic elements by Donnez Cardoza, used with permission.

This is a work of fiction. Any characters, names and incidents appearing in this work are entirely fictitious. Any resemblance to real persons, living or dead, is purely coincidental.

This book may be purchased through:

Amazon.com and Amazon Kindle
Taylor and Seale Publishing.com
www.taylorandsealeeducation.com
Barnes and Noble
Books-A-Million

Taylor and Seale Publishing, LLC.
Daytona Beach, Florida 32118
Phone: 1-386-760-8987
www.taylorandseale.com

Dedication

Five of Hearts
A tear on my knee

.

A Song for Chloe

Bob Bickford

Prelude

There was a flower, just one. It grew in a small patch of sun on the forest floor, a tiny splash of pink in last year's dead leaves, quietly soaking up the spring morning and radiating it back.

"This is how it all begins," Chloe said. "Once upon a time starts like this."

Her face was clean and clear.

"Look."

She raised a hand and swept it out slowly, tossing light and color into the sky. As it spread, the dirt and woods were warmed, and the wintertime graves melted. Leaves and grass showed new green, and the sky caught fire and bled blue into the lake below. The water burst into sparkles and obliterated the far shore. When the glow faded, it left dark sky behind. It was night time, just like that.

"Can you hear it?" she asked. "Listen."

I heard the sound of a train, far off but coming closer. Air caressed my face, and soft wind carried the voices of everyone I had ever lost. They were brought back to me on music, and I knew that nothing is ever really gone.

She leaned in close. I smelled the promise on her skin and hair. The flower behind her made a small colored puddle of light.

"Heartbeats are only where it begins," she whispered. "It's all just starting. Do you understand?"

Part One

"Things That Get Lost"

-One-

Hollow Lake, Canada
Tuesday, June 17, 1980

Out on the water, a boat engine backfired. Nick Horan looked at the lake, and set the cold bottle of soda onto the cement beside him. He lifted a hand to shield his eyes against the glare. In counterpoint, the door to the marina building banged open behind him. A girl, one he had seen at the snack bar, came down the steps. She glanced at him as she passed.

"Hi," he blurted.

She glanced back, surprised, and didn't answer.

"It's a nice day," he said, and felt his face burn at the stupidity of it.

She nodded slowly, regarding him warily. Color flushed her cheeks and she turned away. He saw dark eyes, long sandy hair, smooth skin painted with a hint of dusky rose, and then she was gone. He watched her as she crossed the expanse of green lawn and disappeared into the covered boat slips lining the water's edge. She left behind a trace of her fragrance, coconut suntan oil and a sweet something else he couldn't identify.

The sun was hot, but a breeze stirred from the lake, cooling the sweat on his forehead. He wished that he had worn short pants, but the morning had been cool when he left his house. He picked up his bottle, stood up and walked down toward the docks. At the edge of the marina clearing, several picnic tables were scattered beneath the trees, and he headed for one in the shade. The table's dark green paint curled up in peels, revealing gray wood beneath, and he picked at them while he finished his soda.

A Chris-Craft boat, fitted for water-skiing, burbled its way out from the berths and moved slowly through the no-wake zone in front of the marina. The boat gleamed bright red, with chrome fittings and white trim. A blond boy about Nick's age lounged at the controls. Golden and confident, he surveyed the picnic area as he floated past. The sun glinted off his dark glasses. In his sweaty dungarees, his canvas high-top shoes, his awkwardness and his poverty, Nick wished, absurdly, that he could be invisible.

His breath caught. The light-haired girl bent over in the back of the boat, busy with skis and lines. She had stripped to a one-piece swimsuit. The pink fabric was bright against her tan. She moved back and forth, confident and competent.

As the craft approached the buoys marking the entrance to the marina, Nick saw "A Letter" painted on her stern. He thought it was an odd name for a boat, and wondered what it meant. The girl tossed varnished wooden skis into the frothy wake, and dove cleanly after them.

"Cold!" she shouted happily when she bobbed up. "So cold. I just love it!"

The boy in the cockpit turned in his seat to watch her as she lay back in the water to slip the skis on. When she raised one hand, the Hercules engine roared and the rear end of the boat buried itself in the water. The girl came up behind it, rising like a magician's trick in pink. She leapt the boat's wake and got lost in the sparkles, reappearing and then disappearing again in the brilliant spray. She danced in the waves as if she were a part of them, a creature made from sun and water and summer.

The boat moved into the distance, its sound growing faint as it headed toward the islands in the east. When it had finally gone from sight, Nick looked down at his feet, surprised. He stood at the water's edge; he had moved down to the shore without realizing it. He dropped his hand to his side, unaware he had been reaching toward the blue horizon. A part of him was gone for good, pulled away by the red boat, dancing with the light-haired girl in pink.

~ * ~

Present Day:

I stood on my dock and listened to the loons call, far out on the black water. It's a sound that I have always hated. Their spooky warbles sound like lost ghosts, crying because they'll never be found. They were going to leave here soon, and migrate to the ocean for the winter. They don't leave to find warmth. They just want deep water that doesn't freeze.

I lived here, on an island in the middle of Hollow Lake, which is deep enough and cold enough to suit the loons most of the year. I grew up around here. In fact, I had drowned in this water as a teenager. Passing Samaritans had pumped out my lungs, started my breathing again and gotten me to a hospital. The coma afterwards had pretty much erased any memory of the event, but dying even for a little while probably bonded me to the lake. It had sunk the place deep inside me, and I didn't hold a grudge against the water that had once killed me.

I had grown up, drifted away and into being a writer. When I had some money in the bank and my fill of the city, I moved back and bought a summer home on Duck Island. I had the idea of living simple and trying my hand at a novel. I thought fiction might offer more truth than the free-lance stuff I had been paid to write.

My old cabin looked pretty much the way it had a hundred years ago, if you ignored the electric light in the windows and the powerboat tied up at the floating dock in front of it. I'd forced most of the necessary amenities on the place. I had hot and cold running water, an air conditioner in the bedroom window, and a washing machine in the small addition at the back.

It could all seem fragile, though, this civilization that I'd imposed. There have been summer nights when I stood on my dock and been overwhelmed by the vast blackness above me. The stars appeared alien, and close enough to touch. The woods behind me were silent, and the lake in front of me seemed bottomless. I felt like I was the only spark of life on the planet. My securities and routines, the money in my bank account, and all of my electronic gizmos and gadgets were impossibly frail. The coming of ice forced me to move to temporary quarters on shore for the two months that it locked the lake. Remaining on the island was simply too isolated and too dangerous, without a boat.

The loneliness was never deeper than on near-winter evenings like this one, when the water gave off the smell of coming ice, and the wind promised me I would soon have snow.

My dog, Kuba, nosed the wet pebbles at the water's edge. He lifted his head, listened, and then took off into the dark trees, likely chasing something he had imagined. I let him go.

Across the lake, I could see the light on Nora Martin's dock. She left it on for me, a signal that she was never far away. Seeing it at night made me loved, somehow, and I loved it back. She was my lover, my best friend, and the soon-to-be mother of my baby. Dark-haired, blue-eyed, she was almost ten years younger than me. It hadn't been love-at-first-sight for either of us, but she

4

was level-headed and generous. Trim and tidy, she jogged and read good books. I thought she was beautiful, inside and out. She lived in a small white house on shore, a mile away across the reach. I liked to look across the water at her light while I talked to her on the phone.

"What do you have left to do, Nick?" she asked.

I thought about it. "Not much, really. I've pretty much packed up what I'll need for a month or two and put away the rest. Winterize the plumbing—that'll be the last thing. I'm shuttering the windows this year. Remember we found two broken ones this spring. I'll take a last walk around the shoreline, all the way around sometime in the next couple days, and then I'll pull the dock in and be on my way."

"Do you want a hand? With the dock, at least?" She sounded worried. "I can come over."

"How? Your boat's put away already."

"I can run to the marina and borrow one from Bill. He's still got a couple in the water."

"No way." I shook her off. "You're not running a block and tackle when you're pregnant. I'll get hold of Bill if I have trouble."

"I'm not incapacitated, Nick." She sounded mildly offended, and I smiled.

"No, I can't imagine anything slowing you down, Nora. I'll let you know if I get into trouble."

"I'll bet."

We were quiet for a moment. Something unseen on the lake created a wash, and the small wave lifted the dock fractionally beneath me and lapped at the rocks on the shore. When she spoke again, her voice got quiet.

"Are you scared?"

"Scared of what, Nora?"

"Moving in with me. The baby. All of it."

"A little," I said. "Are you?"

"Maybe," she admitted.

5

"You've been married, and it didn't last. I've never been married. Didn't even wonder about it anymore. I guess I figured alone worked best for me."

"You aren't alone," she said. "There are two of us with you now. There might be times you'll wish you were alone, but it's too late. You're stuck with us."

"I don't know if I'll make much of a father, at my age."

"Every man who's worth anything worries about that, no matter how old he is. Nobody is ever the right age, or ready."

The wind picked up. I felt frozen. "I'm going inside, Nora. It's getting unbearable out here."

We said goodnight. I knew she would leave her dock light on until morning, my talisman, though she'd never say so. I imagined I could see its reflection in the water all the way across the mile that separated us.

The autumn moon came up pale orange, and the surface of the lake brightened with its glow. Waves shimmered as the wind picked up. I was turning to go inside when I saw a tiny spot of black on the water, a loon, making its way across the reach toward me. Usually they stayed close in the lee of one of the islands at night. It was unusual to see one moving on open water in the dark. I pocketed my phone and stood, watching.

I repeatedly lost sight of it in the waves, and then found it again as it came closer.

My floating dock was anchored to a finger of rock that jutted out from the island. This natural stone pier sloped down, into the lake, and the water beneath me wasn't much more than four or five feet deep. As the loon came closer, I saw it wasn't a bird at all, but rather the top of a ball, floating low in the waves. It didn't make sense. Instinctively, I moved slowly backward and onto the rock behind the dock.

When the ball floated and bobbed to within a dozen yards, it splashed strangely, and then a woman stood up in the shallows. I had been seeing the top of her head.

She stood still, staring at me. In the moonlight, hair plastered to her cheeks, she was simply beautiful. She crossed her arms

6

across her breasts, clutched her shoulders, and waded into shore. I inched back, not breathing.

She wore a one-piece bathing suit. I couldn't tell the color in the strange light, but it seemed pink. Completely out of the water now, she picked her way up the rock slope. As she passed, she stopped and gave me a sidelong look. Somehow, she was familiar. I knew the posture, I knew the face, and I knew the walk; I just didn't know from where. Her eyes were illuminated, not by the single bulb on my dock light, and not by the rising moon, but rather by a dark light within her. None of her features were in shadow.

"It's so cold," she said. "So cold."

Her voice was soft. I could hear the music and shiver in her words, the air bitter enough to see her breath. She stood huddled, and although I was terrified, I wanted to pull off my coat and drape it over her shoulders. Her teeth gleamed.

She smiled. "I'm always so cold. I love it. I just love it."

She glanced back over her shoulder at the lake for a moment, and then turned to stare at me.

"Do you remember me?" she asked.

I had no breath, let alone words. When I didn't answer, she laughed once, a sound like old silver. She turned and walked quietly, gracefully into the trees. I heard a tiny jingle, a faint chime that moved with her steps as she disappeared. A tiny glimmer followed her up the path, and then darkness enveloped her.

I listened, but there were no more sounds. No rustling or snapping of twigs marked her progress. The wind gasped, and rattled the bare branches above me, stirring the few remaining dry leaves. She was gone.

Another loon called, out on the lake behind me, and I nearly jumped out of my skin. My hands were shaking.

I looked across the darkness to where Nora's dock light burned. Though I had been completely unnerved by the apparition that had emerged from the lake, the lamp shining

7

across the water calmed me. Bare moments later, it felt like a dream.

I could see her in my mind, my Nora, now gone to bed, her book left open on the living room chair, her empty tea mug in the sink. The cell phone in my hand stayed warm from our conversation. I wanted to call her back, but I didn't want to steal her sleep.

My hands and face were numb. Kuba reappeared at the water's edge. If the stranger who had waded in to shore troubled him, he didn't show it. I pocketed my phone and whistled for him, then walked slowly up the path through the trees to my cabin and my bed.

-Two-

Hollow Lake, Canada
Saturday, June 21, 1980

The marina property had been nearly deserted because it was raining, the kind of warm summer downpour that makes even the air seem green. Nick looked up from the boat he was painting, and out the door of the old drying shed. The brush in his right hand stayed poised, forgotten. A single drop of white landed on the packed dirt floor, and then one more on the toe of his sneaker.

The light-haired girl walked toward him. She didn't hurry, and she didn't shield herself from the wet. He had the absurd thought that she owned the rain; she was completely at ease in it because it belonged to her and she had been made from it.

When she reached the door, she wiped the water from her face and smiled; a little bit shy, just a girl. He put the paintbrush down across the top of the can.

"They said I could find you here," she said. "They told me you know how to drive a boat."

He nodded, but he couldn't find his voice.

She was a girl who spent most of her time alone. She loved Shakespeare, but when she tried to say so, her schoolteachers thought her impertinent. Girls her age just didn't. She adored ballet, but was dismissed as a dancer because she moved with the music, and not the way she had been told to move. Social conventions were foreign and bewildering. She had to memorize them like mathematical equations. The politics of being a popular girl were conducted in a language she didn't speak. She wore no masks, because she didn't have any to wear.

Being beautiful made things much worse, because people were drawn to her and then disappointed by her strangeness. When they left her alone, it hurt more than having been shunned in the first place. Her honesty seen as unkindness, she got repaid in whispers—but she was profoundly kind. Creatures who didn't

9

*speak, butterflies and bears, toads and crows and trout, knew it
and accepted her as a secret sister. The beasts loved her, and
she moved with them perfectly. No one ever saw it, though.*

*She was more than a little bit magic, although she would
never have used the word aloud, or even thought it. She saw
movement and colors where nobody else did. She had been born
knowing a little of how the universe danced. She felt the secret
vibrations in music, and she knew about the Moon. She never
told anyone a thing about it any of it, but she wanted to tell this
boy everything.*

"I can drive a boat," he finally managed.

*"Yes, you can," she agreed. "They said your name is Nick,
and you know how to do it better than practically anyone else
around here. The last boy who drove my boat started a fight with
me, and he left. I need someone. I'll pay you, of course. I have
money."*

*He felt a quick flash of resentment. She was the rich summer
girl, and he was the poor local.*

*"I don't need your money," he said. "I'd do it because I
want to."*

*He started to say more, but she laughed at him, a silvery
sound that made her seem older than she was. She sounded like
a movie star.*

*"I knew you would say that," she said. "I wouldn't have
asked you, otherwise."*

*He was a boy who spent most of his time alone. He could
have been an artist, a painter or a sculptor . . . or a writer,
though he didn't have the patience for poetry. He dreamt when
he was awake, so he had learned to be useful, instead. He saw
ghosts, the beings that flitted through dark air, and hid behind
trees and beneath rocks. They had haunted him before he could
walk. Afraid of everything, he worked to make himself fearless.
He waited, without knowing he waited, and he looked west from
time to time, unaware that he did so.*

*He saw what wasn't there, and he did his best to see nothing
at all. The girl embodied all the light and color and sweetness*

he had thought were only his imagination, and his relief was so fundamental it couldn't be explained.

"The guy who left," he said. "The one you had a fight with. Is he your boyfriend?"

"I don't believe in boyfriends," she said. "That's what we fought about."

She bent and dipped a fingertip in a drop of paint, and drew a careful figure eight on the lid of the can. He thought that even the smallest things she did seemed exactly right.

"What's your name?" he asked.

She stopped painting and watched his face, reading him. Her eyes were dark, and very still.

"Chloe," she said.

When she spoke, the winds of Faraway began to blow, and took him for good and always.

~ * ~

In the morning, I opened the kitchen door to let the dog out. I picked up my coffee cup and followed him onto the veranda. I stopped short. The world was covered in white. Winter had come during the night, while I slept, evicting summer and autumn so completely that they might never have been. I leaned in the open door and finished my cup, and then pulled on my boots and went out, pulling the door shut behind me. The woods were hushed; the birds and squirrels had foregone their morning squabbles to gaze, like me, at the change the gray sunrise had brought.

I walked down to the dock. On the water, outside the shelter of the forest, the wind blew wild and insistent. My boat strained and creaked against its lines, windshield staring blindly under the new coating of snow. The pines on the far shores disappeared behind curtains of blowing white. The lake water, in contrast, was utterly black. It heaved and broke against the shore on either side of the dock.

I checked my watch, and called Nora. She answered on the first ring.

"Don't you love it?" she asked. "The first snow of the year is the best, it really is. I can feel Christmas. Come pick me up. I'll help you today."

"Not much to help with in this weather. I'm probably just going to spend the day in front of the fire."

"There's a fire here," she said. "Weather guy says there's freezing rain coming in, on top of the snow. Come quick, before the storm really gets going."

"Sold. I'll come over right now."

I called to the dog, and he followed me to the boat.

The wheel was freezing, and I piloted away from the dock with one hand in my coat pocket. As I left the lee of the island, the wind slammed into the boat. The deck rocked and pitched beneath me, and I kept busy with both hands. I misjudged a quartering wave; it lifted the stern and nearly drenched me with icy spray. The dog skidded and scrabbled on the slippery surface. I cursed bitterly.

Long, clean, cold, and averaging almost a hundred-foot depth, Hollow Lake can seem like the ocean when a storm has it, especially in autumn. This piece of wooded paradise, a playground for water-skiers and fishermen, can quickly turn into a very frightening place, and more than a few drowned boats and drowned people had come to rest on the lake bottom because they didn't seek shelter fast enough in a storm. This late in the year, the place was deserted, and if I ran into trouble the help had to come from the marina, at the farthest end.

Starting across the reach, the boat bucked and slammed its bottom before I found a rhythm in the surge. I crossed the mile of water as fast as I could. The wind sang, full of icy particles that stung my face and numbed my hands. As the opposite shore came close, I saw Nora walk down from her small white bungalow and cross the yard to her dock. Bundled into a winter coat, she waved to me. I cut the throttle as I came in, and saw at once that I was going to have trouble.

The waves began to turn the boat around. No pattern revealed itself in the water; it came and pushed from every

12

direction. I moved on a floor filled with murderous dancers, swirling black skirts and spinning on stiletto heels, completely given to the music of the storm. Furious, they crashed into me, and each other, in an awful tango. My feet on the rolling deck and my hands on the wheel moved in time with them, dancing against my will.

I pushed the lever all the way forward. The sound of the engine rose above the general din and I bulled forward toward the dock, which suddenly rushed at me. I threw it into reverse. From the corner of my vision, I saw Nora waving frantically as she backed away. The bow shuddered when it hit the wooden pilings. The boat wallowed, wounded, until the propeller got purchase and pulled me back and away.

Nora stood fifty feet from me. It might as well have been fifty miles. She held up her cell phone, and then turned away from the wind. I fumbled my own out. When it rang, I could hardly feel the vibration in my cold hand. I cupped it to my ear.

"Holy crap. Who taught you to drive a boat?" she shouted, over the wind.

I could hear the laughter in her voice. She sounded exhilarated.

"I've been running boats since I was a kid," I answered. "I taught you, remember?"

"Don't tell anyone. Listen, you're not going to dock in this! Go to the marina and get to shelter. I'll take the truck and meet you there."

Instinctively, I checked my fuel gauge. "That's thirteen miles of this, Nora," I yelled. "I'll freeze to death before I get there. The passage between Duck and Long Duck is going to be brutal. The current will be crazy. I'm going back home."

"Going to the marina is safer than trying to dock back at the island!"

I thought quickly, and nodded. "Race you there," I said.

She waved, and ran for the house. I looked west, shook my head, and got going. The boat porpoised and fought to come up onto plane. I huddled behind the windshield glass, and wished

I'd taken the time to completely fit the boat's canvas top. Bumpers and lines flapped in the wind stream. The noise deafened me. Darkened cottages, closed for the season, peered at me from the trees as I flashed past. An occasional permanent dock like Nora's stuck out from the shoreline, but most people used floaters that could be dragged onto land, which avoided ice damage.

Large lakes are like bathtubs, with all the faucets turned on and the drain open. They may appear placid and tideless, but there is a lot of movement down deep. Hollow Lake is fed and emptied by two small rivers and probably countless streams. The amount of current under the surface varies depending on where you are.

Across from my own Duck Island lay the much larger Long Duck Island, home to a dozen or more cottages. To the west lay tiny Echo Island, which had only one long-abandoned cabin. Privately owned, the place was rarely visited, probably because the locals claimed it was haunted.

The deep water between Duck and Long Duck got turbulent in bad weather. The channel had claimed more than one vessel over the years, and I approached it nervously. A massive underwater stream flowed deep and silent, but came insanely close to the surface when it stormed. I passed by the first cottages on Long Duck, and then the bow slammed sideways, and I plunged into it.

The channel sucked the boat in, twisting and heaving. I was drenched by a wave, from behind. Once or twice the propeller came clear of the current and the engine screamed until the stern buried itself again. Eventually, I cleared the islands and the channel spit me out into calmer water. I had a ten-mile run through blowing chop to the marina. The channel buoys leading in to the red and yellow Shell sign at the main dock had been pulled in for the winter, but I knew the way.

Nora's truck waited at the water's edge, facing away from me, its exhaust steaming. The prospect of heat made me realize how numb I was. I cut my engine to idle, and as I drifted in, the driver's door opened and she got out. She walked onto the dock, ready to catch my line.

"You're soaked," she called, concerned.

"Freezing," I agreed.

"Get in. Let's get you home."

We left my boat tied at the dock, and took the shore road back to her house. The dog huddled miserably between us. Wind buffeted the truck. Watching the gray lake heave, I knew I was lucky to have made it to shore.

Inside Nora's front hall, I started to shiver as she helped me off with my coat. We moved through the kitchen to the living room, and then up the hall to her bedroom. I lost my saturated shirt and pants along the way. She pushed me down to sit on the edge of the bed. The wet socks resisted, but finally yielded to her.

"You're just about blue, Nick. I'm going to towel off the dog. Be right back."

She disappeared up the hall, bending to collect soaked clothing as she went. I sat at the window and watched the storm. When she came back, she put me between clean sheets and spread a comforter over me. I could hardly feel them. I watched her undress. Her belly was beginning to visibly swell with the child she carried. Our child.

Impossibly warm, nearly hot to touch, she enfolded me, from head to feet. I buried my face in her hair and breathed in the smell of her. Somehow Nora always smelled like summer to me, alive and essential.

After a long time, she began to move against me, and the cold fled completely. When we were done, we lay and looked out the bedroom window at the lake. Sheets of snow blew like curtains across the gray morning. I couldn't see my dock on Duck Island through the sheets of white, but tiny Echo Island disappeared and then reappeared at the farthest edge of visibility. It appeared impossibly lonely, out by itself on the frigid lake.

15

The dog padded in from the hall, his nails clicking, and settled himself on the wooden floor by Nora's side of the bed. Eventually, we all slept.

-Three-

Hollow Lake, Canada
Saturday, June 21, 1980

At the small desk in his bedroom, the boy sat and stared out the window, at the street below. There was nothing to see; it was too dark. A pencil and a sheet of lined notebook paper filled the pool of lamp light in front of him, and he sketched idly. He was a fair artist, and the boat curled across the surface of the paper, throwing up a wave and drawing the water skier behind it. The girl in the pink bathing suit leapt across the wake, a dancer made of sun and music and cold sparkles.

He wrote the words, 'Best Day Ever' in the watery spray that trailed behind her, and after reflecting for a minute, underlined them twice.

He dropped the pencil on the desk, leaned back, and contemplated the Red Sox pennant on the wall. If he had been older, he would have recognized falling-in-love, but he only knew he felt a little bit sick, and so it was that his happily-ever-after was marked for good and always.

There came a tap at the open door. His mother ducked her head in from the darkened hall.

"Tired, Nick?"

"Not really," he answered. "Can't sleep."

She came in and sat on the bed. The room's dimness was kind, softening her weariness. An echo of the pretty young woman she had once been floated in the amber light.

"First day of a summer job's always pretty exciting, I guess," she remarked. "The first time I got paid my own money I felt like the richest girl in the whole world."

"I don't get my pay for almost a week. I can't wait to see what it feels like, being the richest guy in the world."

Mother and son regarded each other quietly.

"What else?" she asked.

17

"What else?" he echoed, puzzled.

"What else aren't you telling me?"

"I met a girl today."

She smiled.

Later, Nick turned his pillow to the cool side, closed his eyes, and willed the dark room away, reached for light and color. He wanted to sleep. He could only hear the girl's voice, see her eyes, and smell her hair when the wishing was so profound it carried him away to dreams.

He thought about Time, and wondered what would become of them if their time never came at all. They would be timeless then, forever and always possible, and he didn't know if that comforted him or sharpened the pain.

Slow as slow, his consciousness toppled and he fell asleep. Night air waved the curtains in the window and moved shadows softly across his face, but he didn't stir.

~ * ~

We slept until mid-afternoon. I stood at the stove, making us a late lunch. Nora sat at the table with both hands around her coffee cup, staring out the kitchen window. The snow had stopped.

"This'll be melted by morning," I said. "Just an autumn trick."

"Probably. Winter's still going to be here, Nick, and getting the island buttoned up is going to get more and more unpleasant. You keep putting it off, and you're going to wake up one morning soon and find your boat locked in the ice. Your insurance won't cover it."

"We'll get it done. Next couple of days, I promise. Week at the most."

"If you don't want to move in here," she said peevishly, "at least get yourself an apartment in town."

I slid a plate in front of her and kissed the top of her head. I needed to change the subject.

"I had a visitor last night, after I hung up with you."

Her expression cleared and she looked up, interested. "Visitor?"

"You won't believe it," I nodded. "I think I saw a ghost."

She watched my face, uncertain if I was joking. I told her about the young woman who had waded to the shore of my island and disappeared into the trees.

"Are you serious?" she asked. "You don't seem very—shocked, or disturbed."

"I didn't have time to be anything at all," I said. "I just stood there. She was there and then she wasn't. Maybe you have to believe in something to be shocked by it, and I don't really believe in ghosts. I just don't have any other explanation."

"I would run screaming," she said. "I'm not sure you ought to sleep alone on that island anymore."

"There might be a story in it," I said. "I haven't made much progress on getting a novel written."

"A ghost story?" She appeared dubious. "You don't know anything about ghosts."

"I think I saw one last night, Nora." I smiled. "That puts me ahead of most of the planet when it comes to ghosts."

She blew a wisp of hair from her eye. "Seriously?"

"I've made a career out of writing about less interesting things than ghosts."

We were interrupted by her phone. She glanced at the display and took the call into the living room.

I stood in the kitchen and looked out at the lake. Everything dripped with the melting. These early harbingers of winter always vanished in a few hours, but the wet heavy snow tended to strip the trees of their changed foliage, and take autumn away. We were going to go back to warmer temperatures, but the last pretenses of summer would be gone.

I looked in on Nora. She sat curled in an armchair, feet tucked beneath her, hand to ear. Head down, a wing of hair hid her face. Her voice pitched too low for me to hear what she said.

I went back to the kitchen. I considered putting her plate in the refrigerator, and left it alone.

I thought about making coffee, and rejected the idea. I sat at the table and thought about starting dinner instead. Finally, call finished, she appeared in the doorway and stood with her hand on the jamb, watching me.

"Sorry," she said.

It seemed like an odd thing to say.

"Sorry for what?" I asked.

She looked flustered. "I don't know. Interrupting lunch, I guess."

"Anything wrong?"

"Not really, no. Just Esteban."

"Esteban?" It surprised me. "What'd he want?"

Esteban Martin was Nora's estranged husband. A good-looking man, he boasted exclusive taste in everything but women. She had finally given up on his promises to keep his hands to himself. He lived in Toronto, and she hadn't heard from him in months.

"Nothing," she said. "Just catching up."

"That's nice, I guess."

"Actually, he's having some trouble with a client. Some guy lost a lot of money, and decided it's Esteban's fault, so now he hates him. Financial advisors are supposed to have crystal balls, and call winners every time."

"He's an easy guy to hate."

She gave me a warning frown, and then came in and helped me clear up from lunch. My ghost story had been interrupted by Esteban's call. I told Nora more about the woman who had emerged from the lake.

"It was hard to tell in the dark," I said, "but her bathing suit looked pink."

Her expression became disturbed. "This is ringings bells for me. I've heard stories. How old was this woman?"

"Hard to say. She moved like a dancer. Sort of an exotic face—she could have been twenty, or forty. No idea."

"I know who this is. Did she seem unhappy?"

"Unhappy? I don't know, really. Why?"

"Sometimes I wonder if she's unhappy, that's all. She has a bad reputation—but I'm not sure if she's really that bad."

She turned to look out the window, and I crossed to sit beside her.

"You aren't the first person to see her," she said slowly. "Her name is Chloe. Her last name—let me think—Hunter. She committed suicide, about thirty years ago. She's a campfire story. A lot of people claim to have seen her. She's a ghost story I've heard since I was a little girl."

It startled me. I had heard the stories, too, over the years. I had never paid much attention, and didn't think much about ghosts, so the connection hadn't occurred to me.

"I know the stories," I said. "I even knew her, I guess—at least a little. She ran in a group of kids I hung out with before my accident. I don't remember her."

The year I turned seventeen was mostly blank, after I had fallen from a boat and nearly drowned. Some passing fishermen had pulled me from the water and done some amateur resuscitation while they got me to the marina. They carried me in the bed of a pickup truck to the hospital. I had stayed in a coma for weeks, and woken up with a memory so full of holes it could never be rebuilt. The doctors were astonished I had come back at all. They had advised my mother to do her crying and move on.

"You knew her?" Nora asked, curious. "You never said anything. She's probably the most famous thing around here."

"There's nothing around here but trees and water," I said. "Not hard to be famous."

"All of it happened a long time before we moved here," she said. "When I was a tween, I was fascinated with her for a whole summer. I even went out in a canoe at night, to try to spot her. I wanted to find out everything I could. She's buried in the Huntsville cemetery."

"What else did you uncover?" I smiled. "If you're the expert, is she my ghost?"

"She was kind of famous when she was alive, too, at least around here. She won a bunch of water-skiing championships, and performed at Wasaga Beach. She was American, though, so she only came for the summers. Her parents had a cottage on Long Duck. That's her old boat, the red one Bill keeps in the marina shed."

"The red Chris Craft?"

"Yes, it used to be her ski boat. Bill probably knows some history, too."

I knew the boat. The marina owner had an antique mahogany inboard, painted bright red, and lettered white. I didn't remember the boat's name, if it had one. Mostly, it stayed under a tarp in a dim corner of a marina outbuilding. Bill launched it a couple of times a year, for a ceremonial tour of the lake.

"The Letter," Nora murmured, as though she was reading my thoughts. "That's the boat's name."

Bill had spent a small fortune in time and money to restore it, but if he'd ever mentioned the boat's history to me, I didn't remember it.

"Did she have some connection to my island?"

"Not at all, that I know of. Why? I think she's been seen all over the lake, at one time or another."

I thought about it for a moment before I spoke. "It didn't seem random, somehow," I said. "She seemed to be engaged with me, specifically. Talking to me."

Nora stared at me, perplexed. "Why would she? She doesn't have a connection to you. You don't even remember her."

"I think she came to see me," I insisted. "She knew me."

"I imagine it was random, Nick. Assuming we believe in this, it's still a bit weird. I haven't heard her mentioned in years. You seem awfully comfortable with this. Do you plan to see a lot of ghosts? Develop some kind of psychic voodoo abilities?" Her smile was affectionate.

"If I get a book out of this, I'll become a huge believer," I said. "I hope I see her again."

"Be careful what you wish for."

I considered Kuba, stretched out on his side, asleep on the kitchen floor.

"Poor guy," I said. "I think I'll leave him here with you tonight. He's had enough cold water for one day. No point in dragging him back and forth. We'll be here for good, soon enough."

"Darn straight, mister."

She smiled, but her eyes were absent.

After dinner, Nora dropped me off at the marina to collect the boat and head back to the island. With the storm over, the dark water was utterly calm.

"Are you sure about this?" she asked, for the fifth time. "You got seriously chilled today. I don't want you in that cabin sick, by yourself. I don't even have a boat in the water to get to you if you need me."

"I'll be fine," I said, and kissed her goodnight. "I have a lot to do, still. I'll call you in the morning."

I started the boat's engine, and floated quietly past the locked-up fuel pumps and empty slips, over a surface like black glass. The storm's passing had left the lake unnaturally still, as though it was exhausted. The sun had gone down, but I knew the way. I could see the glow of Nora's headlights for a little while, along the south shore, but I moved slowly and she left me behind.

Hollow Lake is curious, come autumn. With the onset of winter, as first the dark and then the ice cover her, the wolves have her to themselves. The snow echoes, empty except for their songs. In the spring, she belongs to the bears; she is green, muddy, and smells vital. Summertime, she carries the permanent flavor of holiday. She is decorated with barbeques, water skis, and the always-wet bathing suits that are hung on the docks at night.

23

The fall, though, is different. The cottagers have gone, boats are stored in racks, and the bears are finding beds. The birds have fled, and the frogs and turtles have settled deep into the mud at her bottom.

That's when the place seems pensive to me. Leaves crunch, branches look like skeletons, and the ground is wet and cold. The water is too deep to understand, and shadows move through the woods. Daylight is gray, and the trees on her shores watch and wait, watch and whisper, whisper, whisper:

Autumn is for ghosts.

There's a deep crevasse in the lakebed off the western shore of my island. A few hundred yards long and half again as wide, it's a crack, a dark, cold fissure about four hundred feet deep. The locals have called it the 'Hole' for as long as anyone can remember.

In World War Two, the nearby Muskoka Air Base served as a training field for Allied pilots, since the skies were safe, and the terrain resembled the parts of Europe that were most threatened. In 1943, a heavy bomber went down at night into Hollow. The plane and its crew of three Norwegian airmen were never recovered, and are still resting down in the Hole.

They are not alone. There are other boats down there, sitting too deep for salvage to be practical. There have also been accidents over the years, swimmers who went in and never came out, and people who have disappeared for one reason or another, sometimes not accidentally. They keep each other company down in the deep and the dark, without currents to disturb their sleep.

The water stirred as I made my way to the wide reach and through the channel to Duck Island. The surface over the Hole was like black glass, and I throttled my engine back, reluctant to disturb the hush. I navigated to my dock by moonlight. When I had left that morning, I expected to return immediately, so my dock light was off.

I jumped out and tied off the boat. The dog usually scrambled out as soon as we were at the dock, and I looked for him before remembering he had stayed behind with Nora. I missed him. At the end of the path leading through the trees, the cabin windows were dark. The interior of the island was pitch black.

Before I went up, I turned and looked back. The surface yawned, huge and black. I shivered, just a little. Although I had chosen a home in the middle of a huge lake, I had always been afraid of water. I could swim comfortably in well-lit municipal pools, but deep water stirred a fundamental dread in me. Dark water was worse.

Across the reach, Nora's dock light twinkled at me. A sudden, inexplicable loneliness stabbed my chest.

I shook my head, and headed for the path. The clearing in front of the cabin still showed a dusting of the morning's snowfall, scantily illuminated by the stars overhead. I saw footprints in the snow, leading toward the porch steps. They weren't mine. I went inside, got a flashlight from a kitchen drawer, and came back out.

I snapped the light on and pointed it at the ground. Definite footprints, smaller than the marks I had left with my own boots, led away from my door toward the woods. Heel, ball, and five toes, the delicate marks in the snow had been made by bare feet.

A voice whispered in my ear, no more than a puff of air.

"I'm not real."

I jumped, and spun around. There was no one there.

-Four-

Hollow Lake, Canada
Monday, June 23, 1980

The red-and-white ski boat, The Letter, *moved beneath them at the dock, as if it was a horse reined in and impatient to be underway.*

"Look for the button," Chloe said. "Most things start with a button. Are you sure you know what you're doing, Nick?"

He fumbled, embarrassed. He found the starter button, and the massive old Hercules engine fired up, vibrating the steering wheel. He glanced back at her. She sat on the transom, smiling at him.

"I'll try to remember that," he said. "Everything starts with a button."

She laughed. It was musical and infectious, a lovely sound that made him laugh, too. The propeller shaft reversed with a heavy clunking sound, and he eased the red boat back and away from its slip. The idling engine sent bubbles up through the green water; they burst beside him. As they moved slowly through the marina, the boat started to feel good to him, heavy and natural, bigger than what he was used to.

"Time to get ready," she said from behind him.

He left the no-wake zone, and eased the throttle forward. The deck vibrated beneath his feet, and the craft began a steady, powerful, forward surge. The wind ruffled his hair, cooling the sun on his face. He felt the first stirrings of exhilaration. Behind him, the girl bent and straightened, tanned and glorious. She removed shorts and top to reveal the pink swimsuit underneath.

She leaned her water skis against the stern and came forward to join him. Standing in the slipstream, she held the windshield frame with one hand.

"How well do you know the lake?" she asked.

"Well enough," he said. "Lived here my whole life, year-round. Ought to know it."

26

She smiled gently, removing the offense from her remark.
"I know I'm just a summer person," she said. "That isn't
what I meant. We have to learn together—wind and currents and
chop. It isn't just the skier dancing, the boat does, too. If you
travel with me this summer, we'll be in waters we've never been
in before, and that won't be the time to learn to dance with each
other. If we both know this lake, it's the right place to learn, and
now's the time."

She held her light-colored hair away from her face in the
wind, and kept her eyes on his.

"That's all I meant," she finished. "So there. Stop the boat."

He eased the throttle lever all the way back. The boat came
down off its plane, and pushed a wall of water in front of itself
as it slowed to a stop. They rocked gently.

"Why do you water ski?" he asked. "I mean, why this, and
not something else?"

She thought about it, just for a second. "You've seen my ski
jump? You know where we're going?"

He nodded.

"We had it built in front of our cottage for a reason, not just
because it's where we live," she said. "The channel between
Duck and Long Duck islands is tricky—treacherous currents
that run fast. It's hard to make the boat do what you need it to.
You can't be too slow or too fast, and you have to put me in a
place where I can line the jump up. If I can jump in the channel,
then everything else I do is easy. There's nothing at Wasaga or
anywhere else that seems intimidating."

She smiled thinking about it, and when she spoke again, her
voice glowed.

"For me, it can be hard enough just to stay on my skis, let
alone make the jump work. It all comes up so fast that when I
catch air, it's always a surprise, and I almost forget how I got
there. It's just flying."

"You want to fly?" he asked.

She laughed delightedly. "I can fly! I can fly. When I was
little, I used to write it, over and over. It became my mantra. I

wrote it as one word-'IcanFly'. I wrote it everywhere, because it was true."

"Could you really fly?"

"I could," she said, suddenly sad. "Then I got older, and I forgot how. When I water ski and jump, I'm trying to remember—that I can fly."

She began to ready the towrope, checking it carefully. When she moved, a tiny bell on her ankle jingled faintly.

"I like the bell," he said. "It's different."

She appeared confused for a moment. Then her face cleared, and she lifted her foot for him to see.

"I've had it since I was a baby. My mom put it on me when I started to crawl, so she could hear me move. Then it stayed, when I started to toddle. She always knew where I had gotten to. By the time I could walk, it got to be my signature. The anklet has changed a couple of times, but not the bell. I don't even notice it anymore."

"But you'd notice if it was gone," he said. "It's perfect."

"Perfectly perfect." She smiled, pleased. The lake was quiet, except for a small airplane-buzzing overhead.

"Do you want to do something tonight?" he blurted, and was instantly aghast. The unplanned words had escaped him.

"Like what?" she asked.

"Do you like bears?"

He wondered what insanity had control of his mouth. She smiled at him. It was genuine, lovely, and she looked more like a little girl than a young woman.

"I love bears," she said. "Take me."

Without taking her eyes from him, she rolled backwards off the stern, entering the water with hardly a splash. When she surfaced, she pointed at a sign, posted on shore beside the channel. Black letters on white-painted wood, it read: Danger: Unseen Currents

"That," she said, "isn't necessarily a bad thing."

~ * ~

One of the huge sheds at the back of the marina property housed the repair shop. Inside, the wood stove in the corner popped and pinged. Fluorescent bulbs lit the work area, but the corners were shadowed, and the rafters high overhead were dark. The warm air smelled of old wood and even older motor oil.

Writing a novel didn't pay the bills. I had spent my life around boats, and catching odd jobs at the marina brought in enough that I didn't have to dip into what was in the bank.

I was still curious about Chloe Hunter. The woman who had walked out of the lake seemed less real after a night's sleep, but almost anything I had been connected with before my coma had the taste of buried treasure, and it intrigued me that I once had a slight acquaintance with a girl who was now a ghost story. I wanted a better look at her old ski boat.

Most of the boats on the lake were wrapped and racked, like books on shelves, in open sheds outside. A few prized vessels, mostly antiques, spent the winter inside, beside the boats that were being worked on. Bill's red Chris Craft slept on a trailer in a quiet corner of the work shed. Its red paint gleamed. The white script on the stern said 'A Letter'.

I pulled the door closed behind me. "Morning, Bill."

He stood bent, hands on his knees, peering at an outboard motor mounted on an engine stand.

"Junk," he pronounced. "But we'll see what we can do."

"Why don't you leave that one for me?" I asked.

"I can't," he said. "I never know when you'll be around. Nothing would get finished."

"I'm around as much as you need me. Part time is the deal, but I'll never say no if you fall behind."

"Oh, I know," he said. "I'm just bitching. So far, I've pulled eighty-some boats from the water and racked them, and you were there for every one of them. Don't think I don't appreciate it, Nick. This time of year—I'm just getting too old for it."

Running the marina made a mostly pleasant past- time for my friend, but I knew it wasn't the semi-retirement he had envisioned when he bought the place.

"You off the island yet?" he asked.

"Not yet. Soon. Starting to get things closed down. Had a bit of a scare yesterday."

I told him about getting caught on the lake in the storm. He straightened, and crossed his arms.

"Better start being a bit less casual about this, so you should. That's a dangerous place you live on, this time of year. You haven't seen it, but I have. Winter creeps up on you—one night you go to bed and it's water outside, and in the morning the shoreline's iced up."

"We're at least a month away from that, Bill. Relax."

We were silent for a moment, facing each other. The shop got so quiet I could hear the buzz of the light over our heads.

"Point is, the shoreline is where you'll be, with an eighteen-foot fiberglass boat tied to your dock. A steel hull will break loose from light ice, no problem, but you're starting behind the eight ball."

He cuffed me gently. "If you have trouble getting away from your dock, you'll walk around deciding what to do, and maybe call someone, if your lousy cell reception out there lets you get through, and the whole time, the ice is spreading and spreading."

"I know all this," I said.

"No, you don't, because no one does. Every year it's different. I've seen years the whole thing freezes in forty-eight hours, and I've seen years it never completely ices over. If there's too much ice to get a boat in or out, and not enough to walk across, you better have enough food, and you better not get sick or hurt, because you're going to be stranded out there, on that island of yours."

"Came by to ask you something," I said, changing the subject. "About your boat."

I nodded at the red ski boat. "Nora says there's a story behind it. The girl who originally owned it killed herself on the

30

lake. I knew her a little, but I don't remember her or anything about her."

He looked at his red boat, silent for a moment, then shook his head. "It's the ghost story that you want to hear, I guess," he said. "Every time I think I've heard the last of it . . ."

He turned back to the outboard motor. I held the light while he pulled off a fuel line and set it on the bench. "What's the interest?" he asked. "You never wondered about it before."

"Didn't occur to me," I said. "Might be a story in it. I tug at what might be interesting, one of these days I'll pull out a book."

"Had this boat a while now," he mused.

"*A Letter?*" I asked. "Why did you name it that?"

"That was her name for it," he shrugged. "I never saw a reason to change it."

"When did all this happen?"

"Early '80s, I guess," he said. "I didn't know her or the family—no reason I would have. I was working for the town then, a few years before I bought this place. They were Americans. Had a cottage on Long Duck. Brightmans own it now. The brown one with the big deck on the western side. Nice place."

"I know the one," I said. "Their dock is still in the water, by the way. Heard from them?"

"They usually come up late, I think, for Thanksgiving some years. I'll get hold of them. We'll pull it in this week if something's come up and they can't make it."

"And the girl. Her name was Hunter?"

"Think so, yes. Kate at the coffee shop knows more than I do. I mostly know about the boat itself. You said 'the girl who originally owned it'. She wasn't the original owner, not by a long shot. It's a 1955, so it was already an antique when she had it. She's the one painted it red, though, far as I know."

"What color was it, before that?"

He grimaced at the boat. "It wasn't any color," he said. "It's mahogany. Shame it ever got painted at all. It came from the builder varnished natural, and should have stayed that way. I

31

guess she wanted it painted bright red for her water-skiing. She was something of a free spirit, from what I hear."

"Her suicide was connected with the boat?" I asked.

"No," he answered, thoughtfully. "I don't think I would've wanted it, if it had been. She didn't go off the boat when she drowned. It was winter. Anyway, the boat had been pulled from the water and put away because of an earlier skiing accident. She left her car in the lot right outside here. She went into the water off my dock, although her body got pulled out quite some way from here."

"Any idea why she did it?"

He put his tools down, and leaned back against the bench. "Depressed, maybe," he said. "She lost a boyfriend. I think I heard he died, but I don't know for sure."

I felt like the proverbial goose had walked over my grave. "I wonder if I knew him," I said. "That's the year I drowned. I woke up with no memory of the months before it happened. Not much of it has ever come back. I try sometimes, and feel like I get glimpses. I figure whatever I remember is just imagination."

"You never talked to your mother about it?"

"Any mention of that summer upsets her, Bill. I learned a long time ago to let it rest. She never talked about it again— acted like none of it ever happened."

"Nearly losing a kid would be hard." He nodded. "I can see wanting to put it away."

"I took a boat out on an evening by myself," I said. "I went overboard without a life jacket, and couldn't get back in. I don't know what happened, or why I was there. My mom didn't talk about it, and neither did my friends. I suppose everyone was trying to protect me."

"Natural way to react, I guess," he said. "I don't remember hearing about it, at the time. Probably be different if you'd died."

He picked up a clean cloth and ran it lightly over an invisible spot on the paint. The red hull gleamed in the low light.

"Strange thing about the girl's drowning," he said. "They found her body on shore the next morning after she went in. A lot of times they don't recover a drowner for six or eight months."

"Not recover for six, eight months? That has to be pretty rare. I thought everyone floated up in a day or two."

"Happens more when the water's cold, I think they're slower to float up. Sometimes they never come up. There's a mother and daughter, not that long ago, went overboard in a storm in the island channel. Father survived, but neither one of them ever turned up. Currents take them deep and they stay there."

"So what happened with her? The girl—Chloe?"

"Like I said, she left her car one night in the lot. November or early December. Water wasn't frozen yet, but plenty cold enough to kill you right quick. She went in the lake, off the gas pump dock. For sure she wouldn't have made it far. Even if she changed her mind and tried to get back out of the water, she wouldn't have made it. Done for as soon as she went in."

"Were they sure she committed suicide? It could have been an accident, couldn't it?"

He peered at me strangely. "They were sure, all right. Sure as could be, so they were."

"Did she leave a note?"

"She didn't have to," he said. "She was wearing her bathing suit."

He let that sink in, and shook his head sadly. "A bathing suit, in December. Better than any note. Can't be any clearer than that."

I thought about a teenage girl facing the lake alone, in the cold and at night. I was all at once terribly sad for her. I wondered if she was indeed the phantom on my island.

"And the boat?"

"Cops pulled it in to the municipal yard. It sat there for a year or two. Eventually we moved it into the town garage. No reason, except it seemed like a shame to leave a nice thing out in the weather. I ran the plow for a few years and used to park right beside it."

"And it just sat—forgotten?"

33

"More'n twenty years. Family wouldn't claim it, and township didn't want to go through the legal stuff to impound it. We talked about junking it from time to time, when we needed space, but we didn't. Mostly, it sat there and people walked by it for so many years they didn't see it any more. When I retired from the municipal and bought this place, I got the idea to salvage it. Her folks were still alive in New York City. I hunted them down and they took a hundred bucks for the title."

"A hundred dollars for a mahogany Chris-Craft? Pretty good deal."

He grinned wryly. "She was pretty rotten, so she was. If you had any idea of the time and money I've got in her, you wouldn't think I got such a good deal."

He wiped his hands briskly on a blue rag. "Well, I've got to get into town. Pick up some things. I'll be back this afternoon."

"I'll stick around for a while," I said. "I'll see if I can do anything with this outboard while you're gone."

He considered briefly, then nodded once and went out. I stood for a while contemplating the red boat in the corner before I turned to the bench and got to work. The door creaked open and Bill stuck his head back in.

"You saw her, didn't you?" he asked. He nodded toward the red boat. "The girl?"

"I saw something." I thought about it. "I don't know what I saw, but it got my curiosity up. I saw something."

"Figured you did." He nodded, satisfied. "You wouldn't be asking, otherwise. Lot of people have, especially near Echo Island. Might have seen something myself, once or twice."

He closed the door harder than he needed to on his way out.

Later, I walked down to the dock. Bill had returned from his errand, and stood at the end, over the water, with his back to me. He was smoking one of the surreptitious cigarettes that he imagined he kept secret from his wife. Seeing him from far away, it struck me how elderly my friend looked. I never thought of him as an old man.

34

"Those things'll kill you," I said, coming up beside him. "Unless Diane catches you smoking one, and beats you to death first."

He laughed. "She knows, I imagine," he said. "She won't beat me. She threatens to leave me every once in a while, but she never does."

Silver rain approached us, blowing across the water in sheets. The surface of the lake was silver and choppy, and the air was silver, too. Only the pines on shores, so deep a green they were almost black, intruded on all the silver.

"I was glad when we got old," he said, suddenly serious. "I worried less about that."

"Worried less about what?" I asked.

The rain reached us, at first a few dark spatters on the old gray wood we stood on. Then, with a gust of wind, came a drenching torrent. In seconds, we were wet through.

"Her leaving me," he said.

His cigarette was soaked, and he threw it away. He had to raise his voice to be heard over the deluge. "She's the most beautiful woman in the world. When she put on some weight, got gray, had to wear glasses, I was glad—so glad. I could still see how perfect she was, but I figured other people wouldn't. No one would come along anymore and want to take her away from me."

He huddled in the rain, utterly miserable. He glanced at me, and quickly away. Water ran down his face. "That's an awful thing to say, isn't it?" he asked. "An awful way to be. Shameful."

I thought about it. The downpour began to lessen.

"It's forgivable, Bill," I said. "You're wrong about her being the most beautiful woman in the world, though."

He gave me a sharp look. "You don't say."

"In the top five or six in the whole world, sure. Not the most beautiful, though."

His smile lit up the lake.

"We going to stand out in the storm all day?" I asked.

"You got something better to do?"

35

I shook my head. Dripping wet, we stood together and watched the rain.

-Five-

Ansett, Ontario, Canada
Monday, June 23, 1980

The springs and shocks on his mother's car complained loudly about every bump on the dirt road, and there were plenty of them. Nick wondered at his own audacity in asking this girl for a date, and felt the first stirrings of embarrassed regret. He had gotten in over his head. She lounged against the open window on her side, cool as ice cream.

When she had gotten into the car, she handed him a small pink flower.

"What's this for?" he asked.

"I picked it for you," she said. "To remember this."

He didn't know how to react. He had never given a girl flowers, and receiving one was outside of anything he had ever thought about. His surprise went deep enough he didn't thank her, which was entirely unlike him. He set it in his lap, and glanced down at it from time to time when he shifted gears.

"What kind of car is this?" Chloe asked. "It looks like a turtle."

Nick blushed down to his collar. "It's a Corvair," he said. "It's my mom's car. We don't have a lot of money."

"It's perfect. Why have I never seen one of these before?"

She traced the dashboard with her fingers, and then quickly braced her hand against the roof, as a particularly deep hole in the road rocked her sideways.

"All the rest of them are probably in the junkyard," he said.

"Oh, I hope not. I want one. Turtles are my favorite thing. Did you know a Turtle watches over us?"

He glanced sideways at her. "The business about the world balanced on a turtle's back?"

"Well, it's simpler than that," she said. "The world spins through space, and the Turtle—watches."

37

Nick turned the car through a break in the trees. The lane
that went to the dump rose sharply upward and then into the
right-hand hairpin turn, and he gunned the little engine and
struggled with the gears.

"There's a bad man. He watches us, too. He wants to kill
the Turtle."

Around a final curve the dump came into view, a red clay
wound scraped into the forest, kept fresh by a rusty yellow
bulldozer. A shack presided over all of it. The caretaker usually
sat in its shade during the hot part of the day, but it was
padlocked now. It was well past the supper hour, and he had left
for home.

There was one other car parked by the largest mound of
refuse, a new sedan. A man in tinted glasses looked over his
shoulder at them. He slammed the trunk lid down, got behind the
wheel, and drove back down the hill.

"You brought me to the dump?" Chloe asked, seeming
unperturbed.

"Bears. We have to wait a little while."

He drove the green Corvair to the far side of the cleared
area, and backed it in, against the forest. He shut off the engine.
They had a good view of most of the trash. He reached into the
back seat, brought a paper bag forward, and drew out a couple
of squat brown beer bottles. The paper labels read 'Molson
Golden' in blue and gold. He offered her one of them.

"I can't," she said. "I got in some trouble when I was away
at school. I'm not supposed to, anymore."

He put the beer away, a little bit relieved. "I borrowed it
from my mom," he said. "Be just as glad to put it back."

The sun stayed busy with its sinking, falling below the tops
of the pines. The light over the dump flashed amber, apricot, and
then quickly began to fade into the green-blue that colored
summer dusk.

"I have a real turtle," she said. "I've always had one, since
I was little."

"What do you call it?"

38

"*I call it a turtle,*" *she said, puzzled, and then suddenly gripped his arm, the subject of turtles forgotten. "Look," she breathed.*

He glanced sideways at her, and smiled at the delight on her face. In front of the car, a line of bears made its way out of the trees. Five, seven, and then eight bulky black shapes waddled toward them, stopping now and then to test the air with raised snouts. They moved forward, paused, and then shuffled sideways, perfectly synchronized.

"They're dancing!" Chloe cried. "It's a tango, can't you see it?"

"I don't know about that. They're just bears. They come here when the dump's deserted, to eat. It's like a free buffet."

She opened her door, and got out of the car. Instinctively, he reached across for her, but she was gone.

"I want to move with them," she called back, over her shoulder. "I want to dance."

He thought she was a little bit crazy, and loved her more. He followed and stood beside her, watching.

"They're yours, I think," she said. "My totem is the Turtle, yours is the Bear. Our totems: Turtle and Bear."

Impulsively, gently, he touched her face. She turned into him. Her mouth tasted of oranges. At first, the sense of her tongue startled him, but then it became as natural as the breath they shared. They kissed for centuries, and the bears stopped what they were doing and watched them.

Finally, she moved her face away and smiled, though she kept her arms around him.

"Want to see my favorite bear?" he asked.

She nodded. He touched her chin and turned her eyes toward the sleuth of bears, which had resumed hunting for edibles in the mounds of refuse. He pointed.

"That one," he said. "The female, off by herself. Watch her carefully."

The sow found something to her liking and lifted it toward her face. Her tongue curled down obscenely, impossibly long,

39

and caressed what she held in her paw. Then she lifted her head skyward, appearing to choke down whatever she had been holding.

"What's wrong with her, Nick?" Chloe asked.

"She has no jaw. She can't bite or chew. She'd probably die if it weren't for what she finds in here."

"What happened to her?"

"No one knows. She probably wasn't born that way. It might have been a fight with another bear, but I doubt it. A hunter hurt her, I expect."

The black bear had been maimed by a shotgun blast in the face when she was seven months old. Normally unconcerned with humans, she had been foraging through the garbage when the behavior of two men had struck her as somehow wrong. They had approached her cautiously, and come too close. Some instinct had caused her to wheel and run, and that had saved her life. The close proximity of the discharge also played a part. The heavy pellets had not fully dispersed when they hit her and took off her lower jaw, cleanly at the hinge.

She had loped nearly a hundred yards and reached the tree line before she collapsed, spewing a torrent of bright red from her mouth. She had aspirated a considerable quantity of blood while running, and her breathing was desperately labored as her body threatened to convulse. The two men stood and watched her for a time before heading back to their truck, feeling vaguely justified. They had protected their garbage from one who needed it.

Years later, after his death, the shooter returned to the dump from time to time in his dreams, though no one ever saw him. The dead do dream, and they go back to things that held sway over them in life. The bear was his totem, and he could not let her go.

"Whatever happened, she survived," Nick said. "She's been here since I was a little kid. I always look for her, like good luck or something."

"I knew it! She's a talisman. She's here to take care of you."

"I don't need taking care of," he said, and kissed her again, and then again.

"This is like a fairy tale," she said. "Someday, that's what I'm going to do. I'll tell you a perfectly perfect story, a fairy tale—one that you'll still have, even if I'm not here."

"You'll always be here," he said. "I won't lose you, no matter what."

Then she kissed him, and it all was exactly that: A perfectly perfect fairy tale.

~ * ~

From the marina's main entrance, a wide dirt and gravel road winds its way generally northwest, up and down, around natural obstructions for eleven miles. It finally dumps onto two-lane Highway 60, which runs into town.

Ansett bursts at its seams during the warm months with the summer swarm of cottagers from Hollow Lake to its west, and the more populous Bays Lake just to the north. Parking downtown is nearly impossible to find in July and August, and traffic moves up and down its main street at a crawl. The Bear River wanders through, and everything comes to an absolute stop when the single-lane drawbridge in the middle of town is raised to allow the occasional sailboat to pass. Every business in town is lined-up busy from early morning until evening.

Now, it was autumn, and the windshield wipers of my old yellow jeep worked against a cold drizzle that seemed to be tinted, a watercolor washing everything gray. The street was nearly empty, and the lone stoplight at the drawbridge stayed green for me. The pizza parlor and the ice cream places were shut tight for the season. The grocery store, tarted up like a rustic trading post, had only a few cars in the parking lot. Only the liquor store, fluorescently bright on the corner, did some early business.

At the western end of the main street, in the last block before it left town and returned to the forest, Kate Bean's coffee shop, the *Echo Island Pie Company*, nestled between a perpetually empty storefront and a seasonal outfit that sold beachwear until Labor Day. Kate's store did double duty as the Ansett postal outlet, which carried it through the lean months. I pulled the jeep into the curb right in front, and hustled through the rain to the door.

The inside smelled, as it always did, of nutmeg, baking apples, and old wood, overlaid by the fragrance of very good coffee. My eyes took a few moments to adjust to the dimness. A long counter fronted the serving area on the right, and mismatched tables and chairs filled the rest. Two older men in plaid were the only customers. They paused, and glanced up at me. I nodded at them, and they returned to their coffee and conversation.

Kate Bean emerged from the kitchen, wiping her hands. At nearly seventy, her gray hair stayed tinged with auburn. Slender and blue-eyed, she moved well. She spotted me, and came to the front.

"Blueberry's good today," she said, "Frozen berries, but local." She thought for a moment. "Not much business today, and I baked too much. The pie's on the house today."

"You've never charged me for my pie." I smiled. "Not once."

"So, this time you don't need to feel guilty after you eat it," she said over her shoulder.

While she got my coffee, I pulled out a chair and sat down. A local girl who helped on the weekends was busy wiping down tables. I nodded to her, and looked around. Shelves on the walls held antiques and curiosities, spice tins and glass bottles in no particular order. The walls were dark with age.

"How's impending fatherhood agreeing with you?" Kate asked, sitting down and pushing a plate and cup across to me. "You and Nora settled in?"

"Getting there, and I'm excited about the baby. I'm buttoning up my place for the season, and then I'll be staying on shore."

"You ought to think about selling the property," she said. "Island's not a place for a baby—or you, either, not in the winter."

I stirred cream and sugar into my coffee, killing a moment before I brought up the reason for my visit. "I wonder about something, and Bill at the marina said you might know. Do you remember a girl named Chloe Hunter?"

She gazed at me, puzzled. "Chloe Hunter? Good heavens, it's been a long time since I've heard that name. Why do you ask?"

"I bumped into the story," I said. "If it's interesting enough to be a sort of local legend, there might be a novel in it, or at least an idea for one. I need a project."

"It was a sad, horrible thing," she said. "Why dredge it up after so long? Why not let the girl sleep?"

I didn't think Chloe Hunter was sleeping, but decided not to say so.

"What do you remember about her?" I asked, ignoring her question. "Did you know her?"

"Been thirty years ago, Nick, hard as that is to believe. Sure, I knew her to see. Everyone around here did. She became something of a local celebrity. She wasn't truly local, of course, but her family summered here for years and years."

She paused to give a small wave to two women who were finding seats.

"She was a water-skier," she said. "A good one."

"Why is that special?"

"It probably isn't, these days," she said. "Back then, it was big entertainment. Jumps and so on. They had a big show at Wasaga Beach every summer, at the Playland. Human pyramids

43

and barefoot jumpers, pretty girls and whatnot. It was even on the television."

"I think I remember seeing some of it, when I was small. People still do it. I wonder why you don't see shows."

"Why don't you see circuses like you used to?" she asked. "Tastes change. Such things can't amaze people anymore. They've all seen too much."

"Maybe so," I said. I tried my pie. It tasted perfect.

"It was an odd hobby for her, maybe. She was a doctor's daughter. Wealthy family, private girl's school in New England, that sort of thing. I think her daddy decided if she were going to do a thing, she'd be the best. Bought her that flashy boat, built her a big wooden ski jump in the channel between the Duck Islands."

"Hell of a place to put a ski jump. It can be hard to just get a boat through there in one piece, if the current's running."

"I suppose," she said. "She had a local boy driving for her, at the end. Rumor was, they wanted to get married, which would have about killed her parents."

"Really?" I asked, interested. "Is he still around?"

"I don't remember who it was, if I ever knew. Just remembering the gossip."

"It happened the same year I had my accident," I said. "I missed the whole year of school, remember? I was supposed to go away to college, and I went to the hospital instead."

Kate nodded. She had taught locally for years before she retired and opened the coffee shop.

"Two nice kids, lost on the lake within a few months of each other," she said. "It broke some hearts, I can tell you. Her parents, for sure—as they say, no parent wants to outlive a child."

Her face paled slightly, and I knew she was remembering that my mother had developed some problems of her own. "Your mother . . ."

"That's true," I said. "I didn't die though—just came close. Go on."

"Two good kids, probably headed for bright futures, and it changed in a heartbeat. I didn't know the girl well, another rich American here for the summer, but I gather she was—promising. You were an especially good boy—one of those young people everyone likes on sight."

She reached across and patted my hand. "You still are, and you did fine for yourself. Probably the only writer to ever come out of an Ansett school."

She paused, studying the curios on her shelves, deep in thought, remembering.

"Her mother went out of her mind, that whole summer. She never came all the way back, I don't think. No parent ever completely recovers from a child's death."

She looked at me directly, and I nodded. She was talking about Chloe, but I knew she was talking about my mother, too.

"I'll never forget them dragging the lake in front of the marina, calling to each other on bullhorns. I think everyone in town came, either to help or watch. The divers coming up, and we'd watch to see if they had her. Awful. Then they found the poor thing on shore, laying half out of the water like she had been sleeping through it all."

She shook her head.

"I had Charlotte Hunter in my kitchen that day, trying to drink tea, while they hunted for her daughter's body. She blamed some boy—wished her daughter had never met him. I didn't make much sense out of it. Just a mother grieving."

"No one saw the suicide coming?" I asked. "Not her family?"

"There was talk later that she was a little bit crazy," she said. "I have no idea. They said she acted odd—said she heard voices out on the water at night. She obsessed about the lake, and might have gone swimming to find the voices."

The girl made the rounds with the coffee pot. Kate and I both nodded.

"Chloe Hunter sat at the end of her dock in the evenings— as if she were waiting for something."

"Maybe she was," I said.

"She's buried in Huntsville. The cemetery beside St. Margaret's church, right downtown."

"Why Huntsville?" I interrupted. "Why not back in New York? Why did they put her body so far from home?"

She peered at me, over her glasses. "If I ever heard, I don't remember. She may have left them a note and asked for that. I have no idea. Want more pie?"

I shook my head.

"Are her parents still alive?"

"As far as I know," she said. "Her mother Charlotte and I are still friendly. We were neighbors, of a sort, for a long time. We didn't have a friendship that would have translated into her social circle in New York, but up here we had lunch once in a while. I send them a card at Christmas. They're retired in Brooklyn. Bill's the last to see them. He looked them up, I think, to get the title for his boat."

"They don't come here anymore?"

She appeared shocked. "With those kind of memories? They never set foot on their summer place again. They sold it as fast as they could. It still looks the same from the lake, but it used to stand out because the doctor built that fancy ski jump in front of the place. The jump's been gone for years, of course. I don't think I've ever met the people who own it now. It's changed hands several times since the Hunters were there. No one's kept it very long."

"Haunted," I said.

"Don't even joke about it."

An older couple stopped to banter with Kate for a moment, on their way to a table in the back. When they left us, her face got serious.

"I'll tell you something disturbing," she said. "I have the sight. It runs through the women in my family—my mother had it, and my grandmother before her. We see things other people don't."

46

"Maybe you should let me write a book about you, then." I kept my tone light, but I was only half-joking. I was interested.

"One afternoon, I went out in my boat. I saw her, Chloe, sitting in a pink bathing suit at the end of her family's dock. She watched me as I went by. Her hair was wet, like she'd just been swimming, and her eyes were—dark. Even from a hundred feet away, they were so, so dark. I could feel them."

She shook her head, and almost visibly shuddered.

"How long before she killed herself was that?"

Her face was blank. "It happened just a few summers ago, Nick. Chloe Hunter had been dead for decades when I saw her sitting by the lake, watching me."

Over Kate's shoulder, I saw through the front window that the rain had gotten heavy. Cars splashing along the street outside had their headlights on. I stirred my coffee. I didn't really want it. We sat in silence for several minutes.

"I saw her too," I finally said.

"I thought you must have." She sighed. "No other reason you'd be asking about her. Want to tell me about it?"

I told her about the woman in pink who had waded in from the lake and disappeared into the dark forest, and about the prints from bare feet that I had found the next day, in the snow.

"She's been seen from time to time over the years," Kate said. "There was a period of time when she was frequently seen by swimmers—in the water. Think about how frightening that would be, to go swimming and see an apparition in the water with you. Of course, it led to the usual wild stories, that she was going to drag swimmers under and drown them."

"Do you think she's dangerous?"

She picked up her cup and tilted it slightly toward her, as though it held answers.

"I think she's probably furious," she finally said. "She died so young. She's been cheated out of life, and out of love. I imagine that could stay fresh for a long, long time."

"Poor thing," I said. "Poor girl."

"Poor thing, yes. Remember, though, I've told you there are two kinds of spirits who come back here. The first kind is the most common. There are souls who dream of what they've left behind—things they haven't quite moved on from. The dreamers are harmless. They can't see us any more clearly than we see them."

"The second kind is different."

"Yes," she said. "Very different. Ghosts who have willed their way back, or somehow found a way to cross over to us. It isn't natural. They're here for a reason, they're forceful and aware, and as a rule you don't want to get in their way."

"And you think Chloe is the second kind of ghost?"

"I do, Nick. I think she could be very dangerous. She's been hanging around the lake for a long time, and she may be very frustrated and angry. If she's focused on you, an island in the middle of an empty lake in autumn isn't where you should be spending your time."

I finished my coffee, and stood up to go. She sat, looking up at me.

"I'll keep it in mind, Kate. Thanks for the pie."

"Alone," she said, "is the last thing you want to be. Don't get caught alone with her again."

I nodded, but didn't say what I really thought. Chloe Hunter's story felt more and more like the start of a book. It was what I had been waiting for. I had retired to the island to write a novel, and so far nothing had come of it. I wanted to know all about her.

Even more, I wanted to see her ghost again.

~ * ~

I lay in Nora's bedroom. The morning was still dark, and I sat up slowly and pulled on a t-shirt. Behind the closed bathroom door, the shower ran. She was getting ready for her day at work. I liked to get up and see her off when I stayed on shore. She tended to take a long time in the bathroom, so I still had a while before I needed to go in and get the coffee ready. I picked up the book from her bedside table and read a few pages by the light of a small lamp.

I heard the faucets being turned off. I stepped over the dog, asleep on the floor, and started up the hall to the kitchen. Halfway there, I heard Nora cry out. The bathroom door opened.

"Nick! Come here!"

The baby, I thought, for no reason at all, and felt a pang of fear. I hurried back into the bedroom. She stood in the bathroom door, holding a towel.

"What the hell is this? Explain this."

She stood aside in the doorway, and I went into the bathroom. It was warm, humid, and fragrant with her soap. The mirror over the sink was steamed over, and written across it, presumably with the tip of a finger, I saw:

IcanFly

"I didn't write that," I protested.

I glanced at the partially open shower curtain, and then involuntarily, over my shoulder. Nora stood beside me, hands on her hips, towel dropped. Her face got red.

"Someone wrote it," she said. "Chloe—Chloe Hunter. If this has anything to do with what you're seeing on the island, I don't want it following you into my house."

"Why would you even think that?"

She put her index finger on my chest, and pushed me backwards, out of the bathroom.

"Because you draw this crap to yourself, Nick. Don't draw it here. Leave it on your island."

The bathroom door shut behind me, firmly. I stared at it, trying to ignore the trapped feeling that welled up. I loved Nora, but I wondered how I could spend the rest of my life with her. A part of me thought I had been alone for too long, and I would never adjust to a wife and baby, to the constant compromises and adjustments, to another person's whims and moods.

Worse, I wondered if I was leaving behind the thing I was really supposed to do. I had lived my whole life with the barely-hidden notion that some hidden thing would be revealed to me, if I just waited a little longer. I shrugged it off. If so, I would have found it by now. If anyone had gotten a bad deal, it was Nora.

I wondered what it meant . . . "icanFly."

-Seven-

Huntsville, Ontario, Canada
Saturday, June 28, 1980

"Squeeze play!" a voice shouted.

The batter leaned into the pitch with his entire body. The bunt was perfect, and the ball lay ten feet in front of the plate, spinning slowly. The Monsters' catcher took a step toward it, and then stopped and retreated, seeing the runner coming from third. The white ball sat on the dirt, too far for either the pitcher or the third baseman to reach it, so he bolted forward, snatched it up and fired to first. The batter was out.

The runner from third scored standing up, and the Bulldogs took the lead.

"Squeeze play?" Chloe asked.

He nodded. "Squeeze play is when there's a runner at third. You'd only use it when the game is on the line. The batter puts down a bunt. He has no chance. He's going to be out, no matter what."

"I don't get it," she said. "He does it deliberately?"

"Yes," he said. "Deliberately. The ball is rolling very slowly, and the defense has a mad scramble to get to it. A play at home plate is usually too difficult, so while they're busy throwing him out at first, the runner at third scores."

"That's so sad. It's like suicide, but he dies so his friend can get home."

He smiled, and waved to a vendor coming up the aisle. He fished a bill from the pocket of his jeans, and took a bag of popcorn.

"Baseball isn't that romantic."

"I think it is," she disagreed. "I think it's very romantic. All of the Monsters looked confused when he did that. It's like they were paralyzed. They didn't know what to do."

"They knew what they were doing," he said. "If the bunt isn't perfect, and it rolls too far, then one of the other players

51

can grab it and throw home. The catcher has to wait until he's sure. If he commits too soon, everyone could be safe."

She took the popcorn from him and studied it, before popping a single kernel onto her tongue.

"Good," she pronounced.

The Bulldogs' next batter bounced one to the mound, an easy out to end the inning. The crowd stirred.

"That's what I would do," she said. "I'd die in a way so confusing to the bad guys that everyone got home safe."

"You probably would."

"Of course I would. Do you like baseball?"

He nodded. "I've been coming to this park since I was a little kid. My dad used to take me. It isn't like the pros, but the Bulldogs are a pretty good team, most years. I want to get down to Toronto to see the Blue Jays, but I haven't done it yet."

"Daddy takes me to Yankees' games sometimes. My mother won't go with him. She says the crowd is too crude."

Below them, the first of the Monsters came to the plate. He tapped his cleats with the bat, and looked around at the crowd, confident. He bowed to the scattering of boos. Chloe handed the bag of popcorn Nick's way, and he took a handful.

"I should take you to a game," she said. "Have you ever been to New York?"

He shook his head, and stared at the field, lost in thought.

"You know what I'd really like?" he said. "I'd like to go back in time—see a famous game in one of those old-time ballparks. Something with the Babe, or Jackie Robinson. I know—Bobby Thomson's walk-off homer, The Shot Heard 'Round the World. Think you can arrange that?"

They smiled at each other, and he felt the first stirrings of always. Forever was coming, like a familiar, forgotten song, the kind where the original words don't matter because you'll make up new ones as you go along.

"I'll see what I can do," she said, softly.

The batter lashed a curveball to the infield. The Bulldog shortstop came across in a blur, tumbling as he fired the ball. It snapped into the first baseman's glove, well in time.
Inning over.

~ * ~

I spent that night back on the island, in my own cabin. The storm returned with a vengeance, although the temperature had risen into the forties, so it brought hard rain instead of snow. The electrical cable from the mainland ran through the woods and then underwater, so it was unreliable in any kind of bad weather. I lit a lantern, and started a fire in the old iron stove.

The main room stayed unchanged from a hundred years before, although smoke and age had given the bare pine walls a honeyed patina. The dog turned around and settled himself on the floor. I pulled a book from the shelves built across one wall and found my chair. As dusk fell into night, I read and listened to the rain hurl itself against my windows. After a while, I realized I was dozing. I banked the fire and went to bed.

I lay in the dark and listened to the water pound the wooden roof. The old cabin shifted, sighed and told me stories about people who had lived within these walls, people long dead. It insisted softly that all pale ghosts had lived in the certainty their days would last forever.

Hours later, I opened my eyes and listened for whatever it was that had awakened me. Whatever it was, it hadn't disturbed Kuba, who sprawled on the floor next to me. The storm had stopped, and the windows showed pale illumination from clear night sky outside. Whatever I had been dreaming lingered.

I was still dreaming, or else I was reading an image into the shapes I saw in the half-light of my bedroom. A woman sat across from me, very still. I waited for my eyes to adjust, for the shape to resolve itself into a pile of discarded clothing, or something else equally familiar. When it didn't, the sour taste of fear began in my mouth.

53

She lounged in a chair in the corner. Her face was in shadow, but the moon caught her bare legs, tucked beneath her. Pooled water made a dark puddle on the floor under the chair. I smelled the cold, metallic odor of the lake, and something else on top, mango or citrus.

The taste of terror in my mouth got stronger. I wondered vaguely if I would be sick. She wore something white, with a design printed on the chest. Absurdly, I recognized it as the T-shirt I had worn that day.

"Are you wearing my shirt?" I asked, not expecting an answer.

"I was cold. Do you mind?"

I jumped, and came completely awake. This was no dream.

"Not at all," I managed. "I thought you loved being cold."

She stayed perfectly still, motionless for so long I began to doubt that I still saw her. Finally, she spoke from her shadows. "I like being warm, too. I like all of it. I'm summer—so I get hungry for winter."

I propped myself on one elbow. "You look real," I said.

"I am real. As real as you are."

"If you're Chloe Hunter, you've been dead for a long time. That means you're not—real."

"No—I'm not real." Her voice was slow and sweet, a little teasing. "I'm not a ghost, though, at least not the way you think of them. I see ghosts, sometimes. They always get the proportions wrong. Things are exaggerated, with noses too big and stomachs impossibly fat."

I heard her take a deep breath.

"It might be a good idea not to make me mad, though."

"I'm not trying to," I said.

We were quiet for a moment or two. Outside, I heard the rain start up again. It blew against the window.

"I came to talk to you," she finally said. "I need to show you something."

Clouds moved across the moon. The cabin went completely dark, and then lit silver again.

"We have a train to catch, and this will mostly work better if you dream it," she said. "I can show you things better if you think you're dreaming, and you won't feel as crazy at first. I'm not supposed to be here . . . it breaks the rules."

"What rules?"

"The rules of the universe, mainly."

"What do you want from me?" I asked gently.

She didn't answer, just sat quietly. After a moment, she began to shake, and I realized she was laughing. "What do I— *want* from you?"

She kicked her bare feet out and lost herself in gales of laughter. She drummed her heels, arched her back, and clapped her hands, convulsed with hilarity. As quickly as it started, the laughter stopped, and there was silence again. She stood up, lit gray. Her face was solemn, and severely beautiful. Wet hair was plastered to her neck.

"That's the most arrogant thing anyone's said to me in a very, very long time. Have you gotten arrogant? Is this what getting old does to people?"

"I didn't mean it to sound that way," I protested. "And I'm not old."

She walked across the room, headed to the door that led to the kitchen, and outside.

"See you later—maybe."

The cabin became quiet again. I heard the dog stir in his sleep, and the wind outside.

She stuck her head back into the room. "I'm keeping your shirt, by the way."

I waited for the screen door to open and bang shut, but it didn't. Still, this time she was gone.

-Eight-

"Come on," she said, and pulled him up the path.

The red ski boat bobbed at the ruined dock on Echo Island, in the western part of Hollow Lake. The white July moon lit the shore and glimmered off the water, but the island's interior was black. A campfire sparked yellow on the far shore. Occasional lights from summer cottages, electric or kerosene, glinted from across the sound.

"We should have brought flashlights or something," Nick said. "Think there might be a lantern inside?"

"Maybe," she said. "No one comes here anymore. The owners are too old. They haven't been around in years. Even my parents barely remember them."

"Are we allowed to be here?"

He sensed her, turning to look at him in the dark.

"I hate rules," she said. "It's the first thing you should know about me."

They went through a screen of trees, into a clearing. The cabin swam up out of the dark, long, low and pale, with a covered porch across the front of it. They felt their way up the steps, eyes adjusting to the dark. The door was open, and they went inside, to the smell of old wood and dry darkness. A back window faced the dark forest, but the branches allowed the barest of moonshine inside, which illuminated the ghostly shapes of an antique icebox and sink.

Chloe went across the room, and began to feel her way through drawers and cabinets.

"I hope there aren't any spiders," she said. "I'm probably scaring them to death if there are."

She finally turned, triumphant, with a box of candles in her hand. He saw the shine of her teeth when she smiled at him.

56

Arching her back, she slid something from the hip pocket of her jeans and held it out to him.

"Matches. I didn't forget everything."

In the main room, she put lit candles on the dresser, beside an old bed with an iron frame. Without any ceremony beyond her own grace, she undressed, and stood there in the guttering light, slender, perfect. He felt as though he had fallen down a well, and stood on wet stones at the bottom, looking up through the opening at a circle of stars in night sky.

The cover on the bed smelled musty and curious, like spice and desiccated grasses. It felt cold at first, beneath his back, and then he felt the warmth of her, and could feel nothing else. Over her shoulders, the exposed rafters pulsated in the flickering candlelight, yellow against the deeper gloom of the roof beams above them. Her breasts, her arms and her face swam in and out of shadow, alternating dusk and gold. Above them, everything moved and shifted. Bright-and-dim turned and fell, like kaleidoscope glass.

Only her eyes were motionless, liquid, fixed on his, dark and for always.

The old cabin nestled among the island's tall trees. It had seen a hundred calendars.

Spring after spring, it had watched the boats land, filled with coolers and lifejackets. The generations of mothers, fathers and children ever came back, bringing wet bathing suits and happy dogs and paperback books. The hottest hits of all the summers played from their radios. Long days were fragrant with warm rain, and tasted like barbeque and beer. When autumn took them all away, and winter came again, it felt the ice and snow, and smelled the cold, minty fragrance of the evergreens. It sang with the wolves at night, songs to the stars about loneliness and fear.

Tonight, though, as the two it sheltered danced to the candles beneath its roof, it sensed something different, something new. On the lake, tinted lights began to move across the surface. Two, ten, and then a hundred of them were reflected in the water. On shore, rocks turned to fine white sand, and the

*cold, washing waves turned salty and warm. The jack pines lost
their shape and changed to towering palms. Their fronds rattled
in the balmy breeze.*

*The Moon grew large in the sky. It was something from a
storybook. It changed color, from white to yellow, and then to
peach, but it was the same Moon. Deep in the island's heart, a
waterfall thundered softly. Bougainvillea flowered pink in the
dark, and the perfumed air blew soft and warm.*

Inside, they were quiet again, until Chloe spoke.

*"This is sanctuary," she said. "Shangri-La—a perfectly
perfect fairy-tale.*

"Sanctuary?" he asked.

*"When we were little, I saw you," she said. "I had a fever,
and you were there."*

He watched at the candlelight on her face.

*"We didn't know each other when we were little," he said.
"You were in New York, and I've always been here."*

*She glanced at him, dark, and he pictured a memory from
the corner of his eye. It came and left before he could seize it
completely. She was very young, and her light hair was even
lighter. She sat in the bow of a little boat, her small hand resting
on the dog beside her. Up high, birds wheeled against the cliffs
towering above them. Everything was hushed, shrouded in mist.*

*"Fever," she murmured against his chest. "The silence was
outstanding."*

"Sanctuary?" he asked again.

Chloe didn't answer. She was asleep.

*He lay there, warm, and felt her breath. He listened for a
while to the waterfall that wasn't really there tumbling behind
the cabin, and smelled the orange flowers blossoming outside
the open window, without understanding any of it.*

Then he slept, too.

~ * ~

My cabin on Duck Island had been standing for more than a century, mostly unchanged. A long wooden rectangle with a shallow sloping roof, it had a veranda across the entire front. It struck me as ironic that for most of its years, winterizing it had simply required shutting the front door and leaving. Most of the challenges and problems came with the conveniences I'd added. The electrical wiring, hot and cold water pipes, and septic system all required preparation to survive the winter months unattended.

I had done most of the upgrades on the cabin with the idea of wintering on the island, but so far I hadn't attempted it. The isolation the ice imposed appealed and frightened in equal measure. The same lake that became a busy community in the warm months was abandoned in the cold. Staying behind could be dangerous. I had grown tired of moving onto shore for the two or three months each winter while the ice was in, though, and I considered Kate's advice to sell the place. Sharing Nora's house on shore would afford me all the same things that I loved about living on the lake, without the drawbacks of being ice-bound from December until March.

I hadn't considered it when I bought the place. I didn't know if I'd found the island two years previously, or if the island had found me. I was tired of writing about the things other people paid me to write. I wanted to tell stories, and I had been distracted from it by the necessity of a paycheck. Since I was a fair marine mechanic and didn't mind living simply, I could work part time for Bill and focus on writing a novel. Trouble was, no novel had emerged.

Electricity came to the island by underwater cable. The previous winter's ice had caused a problem where the wire left the water to come on shore, and I was working on a solution. I stood calf-deep in the shallows just to the east of my dock. The cold seeped through my rubber boots. The shadows were getting long, and I had just about had enough for the day when the phone vibrated in my pocket. It was Nora.

"Are you off again today?" I asked, surprised.

"I'm not going in," she said shortly. "I let them know I'm starting my maternity leave a bit early."

"I thought you were still months away from that."

"I thought so, too."

She stayed quiet on the other end. I could sense her distress.

"What's wrong, Nora?"

No answer.

"You there?"

"I'm here," she finally said. "Nick, I've been doing some thinking—about us, and more importantly, about the baby. We need to talk."

I fought down my alarm. "You're not thinking . . .?"

"Nothing like that, no. I want the baby—desperately."

"Then what's wrong?" I asked. "Look, I'll be there in a few minutes. Hang tight."

"No!" she nearly shouted.

I stood there, in the water, stunned. We were silent for nearly a full minute. I imagined I could see the smoke from her chimney, rising in the clear air across the sound.

"What's wrong?" I repeated, barely above a whisper.

"I'll talk to you tomorrow," she said. "Come in the morning. I'll make coffee—it'll be better than drinking yours. Come in the morning."

She babbled, trying to inject some brightness, some normalcy, into her voice. She was crying, though, and I could sense that she wanted me off the line so she could let the tears have their way.

"Okay," I said. "See you in the morning."

I disconnected without saying goodbye, and instantly regretted it. I left my tools on the shore and walked to my empty cabin. I went inside, looked blankly around the kitchen, and then went to the bedroom to lie down. I forgot to take off my boots.

~ * ~

I opened my eyes. The cabin was illuminated only by the night outside the window.

I checked the clock beside the bed. The display flashed three times, and then went dark. I swung my feet over the side of the bed. In the gloom, I sensed as much as saw the dog lift his head from the floor.

"Go back to sleep," I told him.

I walked through the shadows of familiar things. The kitchen screen swung closed behind me as I went out, onto the veranda. The night was warm and overcast, which made no sense. It felt like summer. A few scattered lights flickered among the trees across the reach from the island, cast by night owls, people sitting up late over drinks, parents waiting for teenagers to get back from town.

"You've always loved the summers here," a voice said from the darkness. "Haven't you?"

She sat in one of the canvas chairs that were lined up along the porch, the furthest one from me. She was hard to see, but I knew she smiled, and that it was lovely. Her voice was soft, music I was already starting to need.

"Sit down—or are you scared of me?"

I folded myself into the closest chair. She rose gracefully and padded down the porch to sit next to me. Even in the dark, I could see the wet footprints she left on the boards. Up close, I could smell her fragrance, summer and lake water, coconut suntan oil and a vague, sweet essence of ginger and limes.

"I'm not afraid of you," I said. "I'll never get used to you, though."

"You better not ever get used to me," she said. "I can't think of anything worse. Want some light?"

The moon broke through the cloud cover, and the clearing in front of the cabin flooded with a pearlescent glow. Through the tree branches over us, I saw the stars revealed, one by one, glimmering in the vast blackness.

"Are you afraid of forever?" she asked.

I didn't answer, and she reached over and took my hand. When she touched me, I saw sunlight and green, felt warm water and the mild winds of far, far away.

"When I was a little girl," she said, "I rode in the back of my father's car. On long trips at night, I lay and looked up through the back window at the stars. It was like flying through space, all huge and infinite. It terrified me, but I couldn't look away."

"Forever?"

"The stars?" she smiled. "Not even close. Look at me."

She leaned in close. The beads of water on her skin glistened.

"You've fallen down a well. You really, really have. Do you know that? Sleep, and I'll take you with me."

I nodded, and closed my eyes.

"Dream with me now." She blew a breath into my ear, cold-and-warm, like lake currents.

She led me through the trees along the shore. The wintry moon shone on the lake to our left. I glanced up at it once, and it had a face that I had never seen before. I didn't look at it again.

Her barefoot steps were sure, even when the rocky beach forced her to veer into the forest. Her pink bathing suit glimmered, showing me the way, and somehow I never lost my own footing. Several hundred yards south of my cabin, I saw dim lights in the window of another cottage. There were no other buildings on the island except for mine, but this one nestled against the shoreline, quite real, contradicting what I knew. A small dock jutted out, silhouetted against the moonlit surface of the lake.

When we reached it, I saw my own cabin, but subtly different. It was missing the new addition at the rear, and the porch had been painted a dark color.

"What?" I stammered.

"This is your place, a long time ago," she said. "Time is a map. You just have to know your way around."

I followed her up the wooden steps. She held the door for me, almost formally, and closed it behind me. It was warm inside. I recognized my own kitchen, but everything inside was different.

"Want tea?" she asked. "Sit down. The kettle's hot."

I sat at a linoleum-covered table, with a lantern on it that bathed the interior with shaky illumination. The chair I chose rocked unsteadily beneath me. She got a couple of mismatched cups from a crude cabinet, and then reached higher for a box of tea. The muscles in the backs of her legs flexed. She was perfect. Her swimsuit dripped water on the floor beneath her, and she left wet footprints when she moved to the stove.

"Don't you want a towel?" I asked. "You must be freezing."

She looked over her shoulder at me for a moment, surprised, and then laughed, a lovely musical sound that chilled me. "Of course I am," she said, bringing me my tea. "I'm always cold. That's the best part of winter, don't you think? Do you hear music? I can hear music outside."

"There's nothing out there. Maybe the wind."

She set her cup on the table beside her, and stared at me. Her eyes were black, and reflected none of the lantern light.

"You aren't real," I said. "None of this is—it's all smoke and mirrors."

"Smoke and mirrors?" she asked. "You think that's all this is? Why do you think you can only see ghosts from the corners of your eyes? Why do you only understand everything when you're drifting off to sleep? Why do dreams make perfect sense when you're dreaming, and none when you wake up? Smoke and mirrors is where the truth is. It's the only place you can find forever."

Suddenly, the lights went out. I was sitting outside in the dark, on one of the large rocks along the shoreline. A cold wind blew against my face, whispering threats of snow and ice. In the pale illumination, I looked down at the cup I held. It was filled with dirt.

"This is real," Chloe said.

She sat on a rock across from me, a featureless black shape, blacker than the woods behind her.

"Do you like real better?" she asked. "Do you?"

I shook my head no, and we were back in the cottage again. The lantern hissed yellow. Across the table from me, she brushed the wet hair back from her face and smiled. Her teeth were even and very white. She was absolutely beautiful. When she spoke softly, I could see her breath in the cold air.

"Now then," she said, dark eyes intent. "Where were we? Drink up. I need to show you something."

We went back out. The night was oh-so-quiet, and the deep, dark blue that is only possible in stories.

The island's south shore was littered with large rocks. They seemed to have been tumbled out of the pine forest and into the lake, where they stuck up above the surface, bleached white by the strange moon. This late, there was no boat traffic, and the water was glassy, broken only by the small ripples following the tide.

I stepped out, onto the first of the rocks, and then the next. The spaces between them were deeply shadowed, and the water in them chuckled and gurgled at me from the blackness. I hopped my way to where the rubble met the reach.

Then I stopped dead and stared.

A skeleton lay on its side in the shallows. The skull turned toward me, smiling gently. The bones were moldered dark, and I caught the delicate glint of a bracelet around one ankle.

"Shhhh."

Startled, I turned and looked back. Chloe sat behind me, cross-legged on a rock.

"She's sleeping," she said softly. "Don't wake her. She's beautiful, isn't she?"

Her pink swimsuit shone silver in the light. She idly squeezed the wetness from her braid, gazing at the remains of the girl in the water.

"Lost love. It never goes away, you know. It only sleeps."

"What do you want, Chloe?"

She ignored my question. "Only sleeps," she sang softly to herself. "Sleeps and dreams, always."

She rose gracefully. The muscles in her bare legs flexed, lithe, and as ever, she seemed to dance as she made her way across to me. We stood together and looked down. The skeleton rested at our feet, her head on a stone pillow, a watery blanket pulled over one bony shoulder.

"What do you want?" I asked again. "Why are you haunting me?"

"Haunting you?" She laughed. "I'm not haunting you. You haunt yourself. You're searching for what you never lost in the first place. You only forgot, and now the remembering scares you."

She brought her face close to mine. Her eyes were lit from inside, and I breathed her in, citrus and spice.

"You talk in riddles," I said.

She took my face in both her hands. I saw sunset, heard waterfalls and drums from distant beaches. The wind blew, rustling the palms overhead, and I tasted cinnamon and smelled the smoke from unseen fires.

"You've been bitten, and it hurts," she said, between kisses. "You've gone and fallen down a well."

-Nine-

Echo Island, Canada
Saturday, July 12, 1980

In the morning, they went out, onto the porch, into a soft, blue early sun. The clearing in front of the cabin shimmered. The ground, rocks, and trees were painted gold. The color was alive, and moved by itself. Gentle wings stirred, barely, by the thousands.

"Butterflies," Chloe breathed.

"They must be migrating. I never saw anything like it."

Both of them hoped that if they stayed absolutely still, the moment would stay still, too. The sun would rise no higher than right now, and the magic would hold them in final, perfect balance.

"Letters are written," she whispered. "They wait to be read—and when the shadows don't seem quite right, then you know—"

"—that love has come to visit," he finished.

They understood, at exactly the same time, that it never ends, not really.

"Perfectly perfect," she said. "A fairy tale."

~ * ~

I waited to cross the road to my truck, a heavy bag of groceries under each arm. A black and white cruiser pulled to the curb on the other side and stopped. The driver's window lowered, and I saw Sergeant John Park's smiling face.

"Let me guess," he called. "A whole bunch of cans and one loaf of bread."

Park's parents had immigrated to Canada from Korea in the seventies and then opened the first Chinese restaurant in Ansett, a fact that caused him endless amusement. He had gone to school with Nora, and I sometimes wondered if they shared a past.

Neither of them said a word about it, if they had. John Park was one of the few I counted as a friend.

"Nope. No bread."

He shook his head, delighted. "Moving in with Nora's going to kill you," he said. "She'll try to feed you real food."

"The cans aren't just for me. I have a dog, don't forget."

"Might as well open one can for the two of you, and split it. His probably tastes better."

He got out, and followed me to the jeep. I dropped the tailgate and slid the bags in.

"I went by Nora's last night. Saw the dog. Didn't see you. She said you're still on the island."

"Finishing up some things," I said. "I'll move on shore in a few days. What were you doing at Nora's?"

"Social visit." He looked uncomfortable. "She wanted my advice on something. You know her ex is staying with her?"

I was stunned. "Since when?"

"Last night, far as I know. They called me just a little while after he got there."

"What's going on?"

"Can't tell you much," he said. "Nora should fill you in herself, if she wants to. Guess Esteban's working financial these days. He got himself a client who feels he got screwed on an investment. Guy's getting ugly about it, to the point Esteban wanted to get out of Toronto for a few days."

"He's a creep," I said. "About time someone cleaned his clock for him."

"He can be a bit much—always has been."

"I'm supposed to be moving in there. Why would she let him in now, for pete's sake?"

Esteban and Nora were an unlikely couple. He talked smooth, and had a taste for expensive things, late nights, and fast cars. Somehow, he had fixed on stable, small-town Nora, and put a ring on her finger. He had kept her attention, and never completely lost her heart, to my great chagrin. He had largely lost interest in married life in a matter of weeks, and they were separated before their first anniversary.

Periodically, he turned up when things were going badly for him, and she always took him back. He stayed for a little while, and then left again. She was always devastated, and promised herself, and lately me, not to do it again.

Park cuffed my shoulder and smiled. "He won't be around long," he said. "He never is. She's just got a good heart, our Nora. Giving him a couch to sleep on while things blow over. There's nothing going on between the two of them anymore."

"So, what did they want to see you about?"

He waved me off. "Nothing, really. Advice, reassurance—restraining orders, stuff like that. I have to get going." He sketched a wave, and started back to his cruiser. Halfway there, he turned around.

"Been meaning to ask you," he said. "We have men's hockey at the rink in town. Couple of nights a week. You're welcome to join us. It's nothing serious—a little exercise, a few beers and some chatter after."

"I'm no good," I said. "Never spent a lot of time on ice skates as a kid. I'm not much of a hockey player."

"I'm no good either," he laughed. "I play anyway. Half the guys are over sixty, Nick. It's just for fun. You'll pick it up as you go along. Get some stress out, and you might smile once in a while. Come out on Wednesday."

"I'll think about it, and let you know."

"Think about nothing. Wednesday at six. I'll bring extra equipment that should fit you okay. We'll eat after."

I laughed and signaled my surrender.

"One more thing, Nick," he said, and his face grew serious. "Get off the freaking island. The ice is coming."

"I know, I know." I raised my hands in mock surrender. "I'm packing and closing, now."

"The last couple years we've had this conversation, and you still leave it until the last minute. You have a place to go this year. You aren't hunting for some crappy winter rental in town. If I were moving in with Nora, I'd be off the island in a second."

"Preaching to the choir," I said.

"One last thing we never talked about," he said. "Last year, you made a bad habit of walking across the ice to check your cabin. Homesick, or something. It's stupid."

I began to get irritated, and tried not to show it.

"The lake's a bitch, Nick. It can kill you in the summer, but it can kill you in the winter, too. It's never still, and you can never trust the ice. Ever. The currents underneath are alive, and they'll put open water in places you'd never expect. Every winter, at least one local asshole who thinks he knows the lake puts a snowmobile into a hole and dies. You know that."

"Heard and understood, John. Promise. I'll be leaving in a matter of a few days, and staying off until spring."

"You have a baby to think about now. Congratulations, by the way."

I thanked him, and he went to his car. He waved again. His exhaust steamed in the cold air as he pulled off. I was happy about his pick-up hockey offer. It made me feel like I was becoming a local again, growing back some roots.

My good mood faded as I started up the road toward Nora's house.

I wheeled the old yellow jeep along the south shore road. Through bare branches, the lake was more visible on my left than it had been when the leaves were on. The water reflected steel gray, darker than the sky. I crested a grade and saw Nora's small white house. A silver BMW sat in the driveway, squeezed in behind her truck. I felt the first real tug of jealousy. I pulled to the edge of the road and set the brake, feeling like an outsider.

Nora came to the back door and opened it before I made it halfway up the drive. When I reached her, she ran her hands though her hair, and stood aside to let me in. There was no hello kiss.

"What's he doing here?" I asked.

"Later." She shook her head. "I'll tell you—after."

I glanced over my shoulder at her. Her face was so bereft that I felt a surge of panic.

"What's wrong?" I asked. "The baby's okay?"

"The baby's fine," she said, but I could see the threat of tears. "Nothing like that, Nick. Sit. I'll get you coffee."

She went to the counter and reached into the cabinet for what she needed. I sat, feeling like an imposition. A day or two previously, I would have been the one making the coffee. I had been relegated to guest status, and I had no idea why. I could see the short hallway from where I sat. The bathroom door was closed, and I heard the shower running.

"I saw John Park today," I said, just to be saying something. "There's a problem—with him?"

She turned around and leaned, arms crossed. The pipes rattled a little bit as the sound of the shower stopped. She shook her head.

"Nothing serious, I don't think," she said. "I'll let him tell you, if he wants to."

The bathroom door opened, and Esteban came out. He came into the kitchen, and appeared momentarily startled. He recovered quickly, flashed a smile and offered his hand. He smelled of expensive soap.

"How you keeping, Nick? Good?"

His damp hair had been artfully tousled, and his teeth were very white. His summer tan had faded just enough to be convincing. He pulled out a chair, and held up a finger to Nora for coffee.

"Almost ready," she said.

He smiled at her, and then turned to me. "You wouldn't believe, Nick, the nonsense I've been going through the last couple of weeks."

Same old Esteban, always right to the point, and the point was always himself.

"Tell me about it," I said politely. You will anyway, I thought.

"You might have some ideas," he said, glancing at Nora. She shrugged. "It's a hell of a thing. I'm with Diamond Investments, now, in the city. We're on Bay Street, on the twentieth floor—the view, it's a wonder I get anything done."

"I can imagine."

"We handle a lot of big accounts, every day. Millions of dollars. Small accounts, too, but it can get hard to keep up, and sometimes people don't understand that. I can't take every single phone call and email on the spot—there has to be some priority, you know?"

Nora brought his coffee to the table. I noticed she had added cream, not sugar, without asking. She turned back to get mine.

"Not for me, thanks," I said. "I'm good. Had coffee with Bill."

I immediately regretted the ungraciousness of my words, but they were out. She held my eyes for a long moment, and then we went back to Esteban's story.

"There's a guy named Risa—Sonny Risa. He was one of my first new clients with Diamond. He has a big car dealership in Thornhill, so I got excited when I landed him. He hasn't been worth much to me, though, mainly a few phone calls every week about some new offering he saw online, or something like that. I think he just plays stocks a little when he gets bored."

"This is the guy you have the problem with?" I asked.

"Yes. He left a message on my phone with a buy order, a week or so ago. I was in and out of the office, and I didn't pick up the message right away. He wanted to buy a few thousand shares at about eight bucks. By the time I got the message, they were trading at almost twelve."

"So, he lost some money?"

Esteban sipped his coffee, and blotted his mouth with a paper napkin. I would probably have used my sleeve, and caught myself feeling inferior, again.

"Hypothetically, about fifteen thousand dollars," he said. "Not a fortune, and anyway I couldn't have executed the buy order with just a phone message."

"You could have called him back, though."

His expression became instantly annoyed.

"Are you on our side on this?" he asked.

I wondered why he said 'our', but let it pass. I spread my hands. "I'm just trying to get a picture of what happened."

"It's garbage—anyway, he got threatening. Things have been up and down for me at Diamond, but I'm making good money, for them and for me. I didn't need the trouble. I offered to make up the difference, and he refused."

"You offered to give him fifteen thousand bucks?"

He shrugged, and nodded.

"He got threatening—how, exactly?"

Esteban sipped his coffee, and thought about it. Outside the window, the sky got darker, and I wondered if I faced another unpleasant boat ride back to the island. I felt the first stirrings of impatience.

"What did he say to threaten you?" I repeated.

"I'm not so sure at first. I thought the implication was he would go to management and make a complaint about me. Technically, he was wrong, but it was the kind of accusation that had been made a couple of times, recently. I just didn't need the grief. Also, he has a way of talking that's a little bit freaky."

"Freaky how?"

"He makes remarks that are borderline inappropriate— insinuating, a little bit nasty. Like asking me if I stayed too busy partying to pick up my messages. He mentioned a couple of places I've been. I'd never seen him there, or anyone like him. I'm not stupid enough to relax where clients might hang out. Then he laughs, like it's all a joke."

Nora straightened, and walked up the hall to the bedroom.

"He laughs and smiles—but it's kind of scary. He smiles a lot. I can't describe it."

We were both silent for a moment, and listened to the door close and latch.

"Anyway," Esteban went on, "he finally made an appointment to see me. I felt better about that—I mean who the hell makes an appointment if they're planning to beat someone up? He already refused my offer to make up the difference buying the stocks he wanted, so I figured he was after something bigger—inside information."

"Be good to have a trader in your pocket," I commented.

"If that were true," he protested, "all traders would be rich."

"I haven't met a poor one. Anyway, go on. Did he show up for the appointment?"

"He did, yes. He sat down across from my desk and told me that I could pay him back by dying in less than three months. It was the only thing he'd accept. He sat and smirked at me while he said it."

"Dying in three months?" I asked. "How are you supposed to do that?"

"Beats me." He shrugged. "Kill myself, I guess."

"Simple," I said immediately. "Go to the police."

"I did," he said. "Nora called a cop here, who she's friends with. Won't do any good. He didn't threaten to kill me. He said I needed to die to pay him back. He didn't care if I got hit by a train, had a heart attack, or hung myself. Means and method—he said he didn't care. Just die within ninety days."

"Or else?" I asked softly.

"He said he'd be very, very unhappy. Very unhappy."

"That's all? Tell him to go play in traffic, and forget it." *And get the hell out of my house*, I added silently to myself. *Go home.*

"It isn't that simple," Esteban said, miserably. "If you'd seen his smile, you'd know that. On his way out, he said he had every confidence I would stay alive, and make him unhappy. He was looking forward to it."

"How long ago was this?"

"A month, maybe a bit more."

"You get threatened like that, and you lose track of the time?" I wanted to laugh.

"I thought he was joking at first," he said. "I didn't pay much attention."

"So, you have something more than a month left. Six weeks? Until Christmas? New Years?"

He stood up, and walked to the back door, leaving his empty coffee cup on the table.

"Guess so. Tell Nora I went for a walk," he said, and went out.

From where I sat, I could see through the big picture window in the living room. After a moment, I saw his back. He was headed down the drive toward the lakeshore. I finished my coffee. The Betty Boop clock on the wall ticked in the complete silence, until the refrigerator clicked on and hummed.

"New Years, I bet," I said to myself.

The bedroom door opened. Nora sat down, across from me.

"How long is he going to be here?" I complained. "We were just talking about me dragging my heels getting off the island, and now I find another guy in the house." I tried to keep my tone light.

She shook her head. "What do you think?"

"About his story? I don't know what to think," I said. I started to shrug, and stopped myself. "Seems like more of his stupidity to me."

"It isn't stupid. He's terrified—and Esteban doesn't drop his self-assurance easily. It's real. I think he's too proud to tell all of it."

She held Esteban's empty cup in both her hands, turning it over. She ran a thumb lightly along the rim. I felt the first stirring of something dark inside of me, jealousy perhaps. I did my best to shake it off.

"He's pretty rattled," I said. "I guess I see things differently. I'd confront the guy—I don't do well with vague threats."

"You're different than him."

"Want me to talk to the guy?"

"No, absolutely not. You care more about some things, but you're careless about yourself. Sometimes, I think you've been through too much. I don't want to add to it."

74

She looked suddenly small, sitting across from me, dark-haired and neat. I saw tears starting again, and something moved inside of me. I had loved Nora for a long time. Even if I could never be sure she returned it without reservation, she was my anchor. I moved around the table to hold her, and was startled when she waved me off.

"I'm exhausted, Nick. I need to lie down."

"I thought you needed to talk to me," I said. "Isn't that why I'm here?"

"I can't," she shook her head. "I can't, now. It's all too much."

She put the cup down, and rubbed her face. She tried to smile. "I'll buy you breakfast at Kate's tomorrow. Does that sound okay?"

"Has to be, I suppose," I said. "Get some rest. I'll call you tomorrow when I get to the marina."

Nora and I spoke almost every night on the phone when we were apart. I hoped she'd contradict me, but she didn't. I kissed the top of her head, and let myself out. As I crunched down the gravel drive to my truck, I thought the day looked grayer than ever.

-Ten-

Huntsville, Ontario, Canada
Friday, August 1, 1980

"*It wasn't your fault,*" she said. "*I need you to stop thinking that.*"

They stood on the platform, waiting for the train to take her to Union Station in Toronto, and then down to the big one in New York City. Chloe balanced herself on crutches, as naturally as if she had been born with them under her arms. Her mother stood a few feet away, cool as ice cream, made-up and composed, reluctantly giving them some privacy. She wanted no part of Canadian doctors, and was taking Chloe's knee to a specialist in the City.

She was very, very angry with the small-town boy, who had imposed himself on their nicely ordered family summer, and whose carelessness had injured her daughter.

"*It was my fault.*" Nick said. "*Who else's fault would this be?*"

"*We weren't dancing together. That's all. We need to learn to think like one person when we're out on the water. You did one thing when I thought we were going to do something else, that's all. Blame both of us.*"

"*She doesn't blame both of us,*" he said, jerking his chin at her mother. "*She blames me.*"

"*No one blames you for the missed jump. I do blame you for losing my ski, though.*"

"*I had to get you in to shore. We couldn't chase after a ski.*"

"*I've been hurt before,*" she said, a little bit petulantly. "*The darn current's taken my best ski to the end of the lake and over Bear Falls by now. I can't replace it. They don't make those anymore.*"

"*I'll find it while you're gone, don't worry.*"

"*You'll search the whole lake, Nicky? That's how you'll spend the rest of your summer. It's gone. Forget it.*"

The train's air horn sounded in the distance minutes before the headlight appeared, far up the track. The yellow point stayed unchanged for long minutes, until finally the polished rails caught its glow, showing it closer. Then all at once, the platform vibrated beneath their feet and the train loomed over them, impossibly heavy and huge. The diesel locomotive was a blue-and-yellow giant, and it seemed like it would crush them. It rolled past, though, and up the track.

"I wish it was a steam engine," Chloe said. "I've never seen one, but I feel like I remember them."

"I do too," Nick said, surprised. "I always have."

The carriages followed slowly, large steel wheels hissing softly. The passengers watching from the windows were unimpressed by the huge spectacle they were a part of. As the train came to a stop, the air brakes hissed loudly, and then people were moving in the aisles. Metal steps rattled down, and conductors swung themselves onto the platform like acrobats, moving with the ease of long practice.

Nick was suddenly heart-stabbed with impending loss.

"What if they have to operate?" he asked. "You won't be back this summer."

She glanced to where her mother stood, her back to them, and kissed his mouth quickly.

"I'll be back," she said. "We're just beginning."

She wrapped herself around him, oblivious to her mother's glare.

"I'm starting to wake up in the morning and feel afraid," he said. "Afraid that you're not real."

"I'll always find you, no matter what," she said into his ear. "You can't go far enough that I won't find you."

"I love you," he said.

She didn't answer. There was a bang as a baggage car door slammed shut behind them.

"It's time, Chloe," her mother called.

He felt the piece of paper that she pressed into his hand.

77

"Remember this," she said softly, let him go, and turned away.

She joined her mother at the steps. The conductor touched her elbow as she went up. Inside the car, Nick saw the two women stow their small bags and find seats. Chloe came to the window and pressed her fingers to the glass. Nick raised his own hand, and kept it there as the train trembled, hesitated, and then began to roll. The noise of the locomotive faded, and the carriages followed it almost silently, like spirits.

"You're not real," he whispered.

When the red lights of the last car had nearly disappeared up the tracks, he looked at the piece of paper in his hand, and then unfolded it. A pink heart filled it, carefully drawn in marking pen. The handwriting was no-nonsense, nearly elegant, hers, a single word: 'IcanFly'.

He stood there for a long time. When he finally left, the platform was quiet and empty.

~ * ~

On my way into Ansett the next morning, I turned off the highway just before it reached town, into the gravel parking lot for the local Provincial Police barracks. It was still semi-dark, but the windows were brightly lit. At the counter inside, I asked the dispatcher if John Park was in the station. He was.

"I only have a minute, Nick," he said, when he came from somewhere in the back. "I'm headed out on patrol."

"Just a quick question."

I briefly went over what Esteban had told me, and John confirmed that he had heard the same story.

"So why don't your people pick this guy up?" I asked. "I mean, he says he's going to kill Esteban. He couldn't be clearer."

"No, he actually hasn't said any such thing." Park shook his head. "Esteban's been his own worst enemy. Instead of claiming that the guy's threatened to kill him, he's been very careful to keep track of what he actually did say, which is different."

Another officer approached, with a document in his hand. John spread it on the counter and scanned it. After ten seconds, he flipped to the last page, signed and handed it back. He crooked a finger at me.

"Come back to my office for a second."

Halfway up a linoleum hallway that smelled like pine disinfectant, he indicated a coffeemaker. I nodded, and we filled and carried our cups to his office. He occupied a compact space, with a small window set high into one wall. He kicked out a chair for me, sat down behind his steel desk, and opened a manila file folder.

"Check this," he said. "I looked this up, and printed it for Esteban."

I picked up the piece of paper he pushed across to me, and read the lines that were yellow-highlighted.

264.1 (1) Every one commits an offence who, in any manner, knowingly utters, conveys or causes any person to receive a threat (a) to cause death or bodily harm to any person.

"So—uttering death threats is a crime," I said, still reading. "Looks pretty black and white to me."

"*I am going to kill you* is a threat." He nodded. "*I wish you were dead* is not a death threat. Even, *I want you to die within ninety days* is a wish, not a threat—unless the person uttering is known to have the power to make something happen."

"Meaning? What's the power to make it happen?"

"If a seven-year-old boy says *I wish you were dead*, that's different than Don Corleone saying the same thing. A gangster has the means, and the history to make it happen. Even though he hasn't strictly broken the law, we'd be likely to take it seriously, and intervene if we could."

I spread my hands wide. "I don't see the difference, to be honest."

"There's an unspoken *or else* that comes with the ninety days. Die, *or else*. I get that. The Toronto police get that. They take it seriously. It isn't a joke, and I know for a fact they visited Mr. Risa and made their views plain to him. He needs to hope

79

nothing ever happens to Esteban Martin, including illnesses or accidents. He'd be locked in an interrogation room in a heartbeat, telling us why it couldn't be his fault."

I gave him back the paper, drained my coffee, and stood up.

"I feel the same way the Toronto cops do," he finished. "If the guy even makes a wrong-number call to Esteban, he's in jail, so there's no percentage in it. The guy's stupid, a little crude, but he wanted to scare him, and he did. Payback. Esteban is going to be looking over his shoulder for months. End of story—no one's getting killed."

"I don't think Risa is stupid," I said. "I don't think this is crude, either. He strikes me as intelligent. This smells crafty, even wicked. I think he's enjoying the anxiety attacks he's causing, and expects Esteban to snap and to kill himself before the deadline."

I turned around in the doorway. "If he doesn't, I think the account is going to be called overdue. I think he means it, and overdue always carries a penalty."

~ * ~

"I talked to John," I said. "I've been thinking. What if I went down to the city, and talked to this Risa guy? Esteban isn't my favorite, but if it clears up his situation and gets him back home, I don't mind."

"What could you possibly say to him?" Nora asked. "What good would that do?"

We sat across from each other at a table in Kate's coffee shop. The place was nearly full, but there was little noise other than the murmur of quiet conversation. The dark wood walls and the antique curios on wall shelves seemed to inspire a sort of restful hush, even during busy periods.

"Esteban shouldn't talk to him again," I said. "If he's still willing to throw this guy the money he thinks he lost, though, it might leave the emotion, the—macho crap, out of it if a neutral stranger brought the offer."

Nora was distracted, glancing repeatedly out the front window.

"At the very least, it drags the situation into the open," I persisted. "If the guy even insinuates a threat, I'll be able to go to the police and put some weight behind Esteban. What do you think?"

She didn't respond right away. I didn't know if she had heard anything I said. Her blue eyes were vacant, staring into mine.

"I don't know . . ." she said, vaguely. "Maybe."

Then she seemed to brace herself, and focus. She reached across the table and took my hand.

"The baby isn't yours, Nick. At least I don't think so."

The noises of china and silverware, cash register and conversation faded into a ghastly hush. The odors of cinnamon and coffee, the low lights, tables, chairs and antique ornaments moved away from my vision, leaving only Nora's face. I watched her mouth move, but I couldn't make out the words.

"In the summer, when you were away . . ."

"What? What?" I said, stupidly.

"I'm sorry," she said. "You have no idea how desperately sorry and sad I am. I wanted your baby, for a long time."

"Whose baby is it?" I asked, because my brain had stopped functioning, and I didn't know what to say.

There were no tears this morning. Nora looked resigned, composed. "I'm still married. Whose baby do you think it is?"

"You're not married," I protested. "He ditched you years ago."

"There were never any papers signed, and just because one person gives up, it doesn't mean the other has to. Not completely."

The restaurant came flooding in, as though someone had twisted knobs to bring back sight and sound. Kate appeared beside our table, and set down a cup of coffee and a small plate of pie in front of me. She filled Nora's water glass, wordlessly.

She glanced at me from the corner of her eye, I thought sympathetically, but the look didn't linger. She left us alone.

"That doesn't matter," I said. "A baby is a baby. I don't need a blood test to make it mine."

Nora's composure cracked. She visibly sagged. "I was afraid you'd say that."

"It doesn't matter, Nora. I don't need a DNA match to make us a family."

I babbled, scrambling to get off the trap door that had dropped open beneath me. It was unreal like a nightmare. It felt like I was losing everything, again, and I couldn't stop it this time, either.

"Nick, I love you for that, I really do. I love it—I knew you were going to say that. This can't change, though."

"So, you cheated on me."

"With my husband?" An edge of coldness crept into her voice.

"What are we doing here, Nora? You're telling me the baby isn't mine—that you made a mistake. I can live with it. I don't like it, but I can live with it. Just do me a favor, and get him out of the house."

"Nick . . ."

The anger left her, and her tears began in earnest, which scared me far, far more. When she spoke again, she didn't even try to dry her eyes. Her hand went slack in mine.

"All our plans—I was moving in with you. Then he shows up."

"It's over," she said, hardly able to speak. "Don't blame Esteban. He isn't leaving Hollow Lake. We both are. I'm going to Toronto—with him."

The rest of my world fell in. She nodded, as though I had asked a question.

"I'll bring your things out to the island."

We sat there, in silence.

"You don't have a boat in the water," I finally managed. "There isn't much. Leave it on your dock, and I'll pick it up when I pass by."

There was, all at once, nothing else to say. Just like that.

She nodded, took her hand back, and stood up. I started to stand, too, and she motioned me back. She seemed to brace herself against an unseen wind, my Nora. Small, dark and pretty, she appeared impossibly vulnerable and hurt. She collected herself, as best she could, looking at my face but not into my eyes.

"I'm going now," she whispered.

I nodded. It was all I could manage.

"Be okay, Nick," she said. "I'll always care about you—I'm more worried about you than you know. Kate and Bill, John...You have friends here. They'll take care you."

I didn't say anything, because I couldn't. She gave me a last, long look, and turned away. I watched her walk between the mismatched wooden tables to the door. The old men sitting at the tables she passed barely glanced at her. The bell over the door tinkled when she pulled it open. She crossed in front of the large front windows, headed for her truck.

"Wait," I whispered, but she didn't. Nora was gone.

I felt a hand on my shoulder. Kate stood next to me. She didn't say anything, and after a minute she went into the kitchen area at the back. I sat there for almost an hour. Then I got up and went out, without saying anything to anyone.

~ * ~

The sun was thinking about going down. Light left the forest, and the lake prepared itself for night. The small box of my things wasn't much of a remembrance for two years of my life. I carried it from the dock, under my arm.

"I'm not real."

The voice was soft, sweet, and right in my ear. I looked back. The clearing behind me was empty.

"Chloe?"

There was no answer. Across the lake, an unseen boat powered its way home, and its engine echoed against the trees and hills. It startled me. The lake was deserted, and everyone else was gone. Unbidden, I had an image of a red mahogany Chris-Craft. When the noise faded, nothing else disturbed the hush. I spoke a little bit louder.

"Chloe?"

After a minute, I gave up and went up the steps. A canopy of bare branches and late sun was mirrored in the cabin's front window, a curtain woven from light and shadow. I caught my breath. She stood in the reflection, her back to me. She stayed very still, watching something in front of her.

There were trees and hills, but they weren't my trees and hills. A strange breeze, colored by blossoms that I had never seen before, brought the faint sound of drums. I could taste the sweetness of far away.

I wanted to reach out and touch the glass, but I was desperately afraid of breaking the spell. The growing dusk brought wind that moved the trees behind me. She disappeared and reappeared, impossibly lovely, lace and light. Inside of me, something moved.

"Everything's different now," I whispered. "I'm not real anymore, either."

I stood watching her until it got dark. When the glass showed no more glimmer, I went up the steps and to bed.

-Eleven-

Hollow Lake, Canada
Saturday, August 2, 1980

"*That's absolutely foolish,*" *she said.*

Nick stood at the sink, finishing the dinner wash-up.

"*I know where to find the ski,*" *he said.* "*It's going to be floating over the Hole. There might be a storm tonight, though, and then it'll be gone.*"

"*I just don't see why it's so important that you'd go out so close to dark.*"

"*It's important to Chloe,*" *he said.*

She smiled at him, fondly. "*Are you going to bring it to her like a bouquet of flowers?*"

"*Maybe.*" *He smiled back.*

"*Just be careful. Wear a life jacket, okay?*"

He waved to her over his shoulder as he hurried out, and headed for the marina.

The old Hercules started immediately, as though it were eager and had been waiting for him. At the sound of the exhaust, a startled turtle slipped off a rock and hit the water with a splash. Afternoon had gone, but the summer evening lingered, a gold that would slide into blue before it fell into warm night. The marina was in a lull. All the boats had gone where they were going, and were now tied up.

Cottages that were nestled along the lake's edge, tucked into inlets, squeezed between trees, gathered themselves into themselves. Fathers started fires in barbeques, and mothers hung bathing suits on the lines. Beers were opened. Radios were tuned to ball games, beamed from cities where the less fortunate sweltered in the summer heat.

Nick piloted the red Chris Craft out past the marina buoys and the first of the channel markers. The surface was like glass, more like an extension of the sky than water. He wished even

85

more that Chloe was there. The smooth water would have extended her a perfect invitation.

It turned his mind to the task at hand. She believed that her lost water ski was gone for good, washed up on a wooded shore, or departed entirely from the lake, following the flow into a river or estuary. Nick knew the lake, and knew where it might be. He had an idea of how the currents in Hollow Lake worked, and the deep Hole between Echo and Long Duck Islands was reputed to have an outlet. It created a drain four hundred feet below the surface, and enough flow to keep the things that sank into the Hole from ever rising.

The bathtub drain effect was strong enough that floating debris tended to stay in the middle of the sound, over it, rather than washing to shore. It needed a strong breeze, or even a storm, to break the downward current's hold on what it collected.

As Nick piloted the ski boat across the sound, he saw what he had come for, bobbing in the water, exactly where he had hoped and expected it to be. When he saw the varnished ski, with its black rubber boot, it brought a smile to his face. He calculated the course that would take him closest to the floating ski without running over it, and cut the engine back to dead slow. He went back, close to the stern, and waited for the lazy propeller to bring him close enough.

His calculation was perfect.

"Got you," he said, reaching over the side.

At the very last moment, the boat's wash caught the ski and pushed it away. So close, Nick leaned out to his limit, and reached for it. He felt his balance go, went momentarily weightless, and then hit the water. He went under, in a cloud of bubbles, and was shocked by the cold. Breathless, he shot to the surface, and hit his head on the ski.

"You bastard," he gasped.

He thought himself an adequate swimmer, though certainly not as home in the water as Chloe. Still, he was shocked at how heavy his blue jeans were on his legs. The boat moved away, *barely at a crawl, and he put on a burst of speed. He swam choppily, and stopped several feet from the stern, feeling the current from the slow propeller.*

The swim ladder was stowed in the boat. So was his life vest. This antique had no step or swim transom, but the stern was low. Nick knew his way around boats, though, and he realized that he had no idea where the propeller was positioned on the old Chris. If it wasn't recessed under the hull, he might have his legs and feet severely lacerated if he tried to climb into the boat from the rear. Bleeding to death posed a bigger risk than drowning.

There were no boats on the lake, which made it unlikely anyone on shore could hear him shouting, but he tried anyway, with feeble results. He was already winded, and didn't try again.

Face underwater, he tried to see the prop, but there was no visibility in the swirl. In the time it took him to go under and check, the boat moved away, and he had to swim hard again to catch it. He hoisted himself up, and caught the top of the port gunwale with the flats of both hands. He tried to pull himself up, and over the side, but after two attempts he gave up. It was impossible. Tired, his clothes sodden, the slow-moving boat seemed to tear itself from his hands.

He began to understand the depth of his trouble, although he didn't quite believe it yet. He turned in a circle, treading water. Echo Island was the nearest land. Since no one stayed in the dilapidated cabin there, he would be stuck there for at least the night. There were no options, and he started to swim.

After fifteen or twenty minutes, the island came no closer. He turned onto his back. The red boat had continued on its crazy, looping course away from him, and he couldn't see it any more, although he could still hear the engine. The surface, which seemed so calm from the boat, was increasingly choppy. More than once, a wave slapped his face as he reached for a breath, making him cough.

He pushed on, but as twilight settled, Echo Island seemed to retreat further from him. His arms and legs started to cramp at the same time. The water got colder, and then he stopped feeling it at all. He thought for a fleeting second about his mother, and more, about the father he had never met and never known.

When the end came, he was surprised. He wasn't prepared for the fear, and he wasn't ready for the hurt. His limbs simply became too heavy to move. He told himself that he was resting, until he swallowed frigid water and woke from swimming through the middle of a strange, feverish dream. He began to drift.

His body came to the surface, in painful spasms, once, twice, three times. A last breath of air, and then mercifully, he breathed in the lake. He signaled his surrender with a paroxysm of arms and legs, and then the splashing stopped. He lay on the surface for a little while, as if asleep.

His last image was of the girl, Chloe. She was lovely. The sun caught at her dark eyes and her smile.

"I won't leave you," he thought. "I found you, and I won't leave you . . . no matter what."

Her hair was wet, and lay against the honey-tinted skin of neck and shoulder. She looked at him, said something he couldn't hear, and put out her hand.

"No matter what."

He reached for her, and then slowly began his long, long flight to the bottom.

~ * ~

Early in the morning, I worked with Bill to get the last boats under cover, onto the racks. He worked the forklift, while I managed the straps. The ground under my feet was reddish and sandy, rutted by old tire tracks and still soft and dimpled from the night's rain showers.

He shook his head sadly when I told him the news about Nora, but his face was an open book. I suspected that I was the last to know, the only one who hadn't seen the ending of our story.

"So, what are you going to do?" he asked.

"Don't know. Everything's upside down right now. Just keep doing what I've been doing—without Nora."

"First thing you have to do is find a place for winter. That can't change. You're probably already having ideas about waiting out the ice this year—staying out there all winter. Don't."

I had already made up my mind to do just that.

"There's a spare room we don't use," he said. "I talked to Diane. When we go away for the winter, you'd be doing us a favor to look after the marina. Don't need rent."

I smiled. "I do that anyway."

"Do me a favor." He planted his hands on his hips, and peered at me from under the brim of his hat. "Just don't be an asshole. Nora says you can use her house. Same deal—you'd be doing her a favor, watching the place until she decides what to do with it."

"Never."

He stumped off and climbed onto a forklift nearly as elderly as he was. I started to get the straps around the next boat going onto its cradle.

I turned at a noise behind me, and started when I saw the black bear standing about thirty feet away. She swayed upright, halfway between me and the edge of the woods. In the gloom behind her, I saw the shapes of her adolescent cubs moving in the trees before they turned and seemed to melt away, leaving her with me. Our eyes met, and neither of us moved.

I heard the forklift shut down, and then Bill, behind me.

"Easy, Nick," he said very softly. "Just stay still. She'll get a little sniff of you and leave. Just stand quiet."

It seemed to me I had read that one should shout and scream if confronted by a bear, but I didn't raise the point. I had no voice anyway.

"Just stay with it," Bill breathed. "She's not gonna do nothing."

As if on cue, the bear took two swaying steps forward and sat down, like a very large dog. Something was wrong with her head. The bottom half of her jaw was missing. Her tongue fell grotesquely toward her chest, and then furled back towards the black hole in her face. She tilted her head to peer at me myopically. She appeared as irritable as an old woman caught without her glasses. Her small black eyes held mine. The hair around her snout and eyes bristled, spiked with moisture. Her breath huffed, snorted, and gobbled from her nostrils and ruined mouth.

The noises she made came faster, and she pawed the dirt in front of her, hitching her hindquarters sideways. Her rump left a broad furrow in the wet sand as she slid, and I had a sense of how large and heavy she was. She pointed her black nose skywards and began to growl. Her voice rose into a high keening noise that sang on and on. Her upper body rocked, and her tongue swung and swayed, with a mind of its own. The black pelt on her chest was matted stiff with the uncontrolled and constant discharge from her mouth.

Lowering her head, she turned it from side to side, as if to find the eye that could see me best. She grunted like a pig, over and over, the wreckage of her tongue seeming to block what she tried to say. Finally, she sat perfectly still, her head cocked to the side, gazing at me as if to find reassurance that I had understood.

I fought the irrational impulse to walk over to her and gather her enormous, devastated head to my chest, to soothe her and to find some elusive comfort for myself.

At last she broke the contact, and gathered herself and rose. She slid away backwards as she did so, as if not to alarm me. She turned and headed for the trees in the fat, deceptive, rolling shamble that bears use to hide their grace and speed, and in a blink she had entered the trees. A single branch snapped, and she was gone completely.

Bill came up beside me, and took my elbow. "Holy cow. I don't think I ever saw a bear act like that. It was like it was trying to talk to you or something," he said, shaking his head and gazing after her.

"Or something, I guess. Let's get this done."

"Missing half its face. You see that?"

"It was just a bear, Bill."

I shook off his hand, and started to strap the boat. I knew my irritation came partly from fear and shock, but there was something more. I had seen the jawless bear somewhere before, but I didn't know where. It didn't make sense. I wouldn't forget a thing like that, would I?

~ * ~

I eased the boat into my dock just as the phone vibrated. I finished tying off, and helped Kuba out before I checked the display and saw Nora's number. I called her back.

"What about the dog?" she asked. "Are you keeping him?"

Her tone was flat. I glanced at Kuba, already trotting up the path to the cabin.

"Why would I not keep the dog, Nora? I don't understand."

I had felt almost numb since our conversation in the coffee shop. Hearing her voice ripped at me. A gale of grief swept in to blow me off my feet.

"I don't know. Getting him was my idea. I never knew if you really wanted him."

"You gave him to me," I said. I heard the unwanted emotions seeping into my voice, and struggled to check them. "Do you want to take him back, too? Like the baby?"

"Screw you," she said.

The words were so unlike Nora that I wondered, crazily, if I was actually talking to her. The silence overheated. I could feel the blood in my face.

"No, not screw me," I finally said. "You're taking away everything else. I'm not giving you my dog."

"I'm not taking your dog," she shouted. "It's our dog, and if you're going to sit on that island all winter, I don't want him with you. If you're planning to finally go crazy, Nick, don't take him, too."

"No one's crazy!" I shouted back.

I disconnected. I thought about throwing my phone into the water. Across the sound, I could make out Nora's small white house on the opposite shore. I wanted to call her back, or to jump into my boat and go to her. The reality crushed me. There was no reason to make up, not anymore.

Nora and I were neighbors, now, and not even that for much longer. Someday, perhaps, we'd be friends, in the vague way only former intimates can be. In a matter of days, her dock light would be dark. Even if future owners turned it on again someday, it would never again be lit for me.

That night, I dreamed I followed Nora to Toronto. I walked the sunrise streets, searching for her. I wanted to bring her home.

In the early morning dream, the city had barely stretched and yawned, and the air was warm and carried the smell of wet pavement. The sun tried to find its way over the tops of the buildings. It chased the night before, playing with the shadows that ran from it and hid in corners and under steps.

Across the street, a Korean grocery rolled down its awning with a rattle of chains. Red and white stripes caught the new light and pronounced the day begun. The owners called quietly to each other as fruit and greens were carried out to the racks on the sidewalk. I figured they might have coffee ready inside, so I stepped between bumpers at the curb and waited for a break in the trickle of cars.

She appeared from nowhere, not-there one moment, and there the next. She had her back to me, looking at some oranges. I could feel the warmth of her from where I stood.

I hadn't seen her in months. Until she turned her head to speak to the greengrocer stocking his display, I wasn't sure. The light caught hair and cheek, and made her real. I was bewildered. This wasn't her city, and she didn't belong here any more than I did.

She shook her head at something the old man said, smiled at him, and turned to go. She glanced back when he called out, laughed and caught the orange he tossed. She put it into her purse as she walked away.

I paid the man inside the store for my coffee, black in a white Styrofoam cup.

"Just a second," I said.

I went out, got myself an orange from the display and brought it back in to the counter.

"How far to the train station?" I asked.

"Three miles, four," he said. "Too far to walk. Buses running soon."

A few doors up, I stopped and set my coffee on a cement planter, beside a single pink flower that was struggling along bravely. She had been smiling, happy with things I couldn't see, and that had to be enough.

I looked up at the street she had vanished into, and shrugged. I wasn't the first one who had gotten wet in a river of tears.

I put the orange in my pocket and started walking the other way. A woman shared the sidewalk, approaching from the other direction. She wore dark glasses, but I recognized the dead girl, Chloe.

I woke up, and felt wetness on my cheeks. The clock said it would be hours yet until dawn. I picked up my phone from the bedside table and dialed Nora's number. The phone rang and rang on her end, but she didn't answer. The dark sky outside my window went gray before I fell back asleep.

-Twelve-

Hollow Lake, Canada
Thursday, November 27, 1980

Her headlights found the entrance, and she reached out and
snapped the car radio off. Turning down the drive, she felt the
tires slip on the frozen gravel. The marina property spread out
before her. The buildings and sheds ran down from the trees to
the covered slips and docks. Beyond them, the huge lake
sparkled darkly in the moonlight. Her heart moved in her chest,
just a little.

"No trouble finding a parking spot," Chloe Hunter said to
herself, and was startled by the sound of her own voice.

She put the gearshift in park and got out, not bothering to
lock the door. In the trunk, she found her bag, last summer's
gear. She hung her pink swimsuit from the rear bumper and
began to undress. The cold wind immediately found out all of
her warm secrets.

As she adjusted the nylon shoulder straps with her thumbs,
she turned around and gazed out at the water. She had never
been here when it wasn't summer, and she realized that she
hadn't seen the place denuded of leaves, and of boats. It was
beautiful in a different way than she was used to, and more
powerful.

Her bare feet were already starting to feel numb, and she
reminded herself that time was her enemy. She found a towel in
her bag, pulled it out, and then stood looking at it in her hand.
She smiled, a little bitterly, at her own reflex, and tossed it into
the trunk on top of her clothes. Around one ankle, she wore a
slender chain with a tiny bell on it, like a charm. It gave an
occasional faint jingle as she walked down to the water.

The dock felt smooth underfoot, worn wood, and the water
lapped a promise beneath her. She stood and looked out, and
wondered if any of it could be true, any of the stories that he was

still alive, her love, still extant and conscious and aware, somewhere here, out on this water.

As if in answer, she heard the first shout. Soft, more an echo than anything, it came from the lake, but also from the trees, the unseen clouds in the black sky, and everywhere else. It was a boy's voice, panicked. There were words, and more and more of them became clear as she listened.

Her own voice was soft, almost inaudible. "I love you," she said, "even if I never told you so."

She glanced up at the Moon, gathered herself, and dove.

The shock of the frigid water didn't bother her. She was an athlete and conditioned to physical discomfort. She broke the surface cleanly and started moving through a November temperature that would have seized the lungs of any casual swimmer. Her stroke was clean and beautiful, but as she moved out into the lake, no amount of athletic grace could stop the heat fleeing her body.

She knew instinctively that she had no destination, no spot in the lake that she needed to reach. The boy's voice would reach her when she had come far enough, and she felt it closer and closer. When it was near enough, she stopped in the water. She could see her breath. The trees on the nearest banks looked on, darkly. The Moon had nothing to say.

Her frown cleared as splashing began, all around her. At first it was gentle, hardly perceptible, but as she tread water in the middle, it crescendoed into frenzy, and she heard his voice calling. He sounded utterly desperate. She held her hands out, fingers spread. Her strong legs churned beneath her. They were long since numb, and beginning to feel heavy.

"Nick," she called. "Nicky! I've got you! I'm here!"

Her diaphragm was so tight that there was no volume. Her voice sounded hoarse and too soft, and she worried he wouldn't hear. The splashing lessened, and she was relieved.

"You're okay, baby," she gasped. "I'm here. I've got you."

All at once, the water around her was completely still. The lake lapped gently at her shoulders, though she didn't feel it.

"*Nicky?*" *she asked, confused.* "*Nick, talk to me. Where are you?*"

Alone, in the middle of a vast, midnight winter lake, she began to cry, without making a sound. Her last conscious thought was that she couldn't see her breath anymore. As legs and arms became too heavy to move, she simply went to sleep in the water.

On shore, the bare trees flared green, once, in salute, though she couldn't see them. The Moon closed his eyes.

She sank, very slowly. Her body was still slightly warmer than the icy water, and it lost buoyancy reluctantly. Occasional bubbles left her lips, soft kisses, and they rose back to the surface that she had left behind. Eventually she reached the bottom and curled up there, a stone for her pillow. Her open eyes stared at nothing, and saw everything. The water held her tight, and rocked her gently.

"*A stillness like no other . . .*" *the Moon whispered.*

Chloe slept, and the sky over the lake looked down on her slumber and called her the very, very best girl.

~ * ~

The warm spell continued. The afternoon bucketed rain, with no hint of the coming snows. I had always hated autumn rain, since it seemed wasteful somehow, the watering of dead vegetation. The torrential downpours of November mocked the droughts of August. I pretended to work around the cabin, but mostly I drank coffee and watched the storm.

I didn't hear the tiny boat's engine over the downpour, as it approached the island. I saw it from my kitchen window, though, trying to land. It bobbed in the heavy chop. The wooden screen door slammed shut behind me as I bounded down the front steps. I heard the dog bark once, as I bolted through the screen of trees to the dock.

Kate Bean balanced herself in a small aluminum skiff, which pitched and rocked about twenty feet from the end of the dock.

Her hand was on the tiller of the tiny outboard on the stern. I heard the buzz of its exhaust as she struggled to bring it in. I motioned for her to throw me her line, even as I realized it was impossible. I hesitated for just a moment, and then went into the water beside the dock.

"Go back!" she called above the rain. "I can do it!"

As the lake flowed first into my boots, and then splashed me to the waist, the cold was astonishing. I waded in and made my way along the dock. The bottom dropped quickly under my feet, and I was in up to my chest before I could grab the yellow line Kate had tossed into the water. The skiff with its woman cargo was surprisingly light, and I hauled it to the dock, looped the line, and stumbled back onto shore.

I clambered onto the rock, and stood bent, with my hands on my knees. I fought for breath. The rain on my face felt almost warm. From the corner of my eye, I watched Kate calmly finish the securing of her boat. She wore a yellow rain coat and hat.

"Let's get you inside," she said, putting a hand lightly on my shoulder. "That wasn't really necessary, but I appreciate it, Nick."

"Worried about you," I gasped. "Who put your boat in? Good way to get drowned."

"I've been on this lake since I was a little girl," she said, calmly. "And I'm very capable of launching my own boat. It doesn't get put away. It sleeps on its trailer behind my building."

Kuba greeted and nosed her at the door, happy for the company. I stood in a growing puddle by the woodstove in my living room until Kate shooed me off, toward the shower. She began to remove her rain gear as I headed for the bathroom.

When I came out, considerably warmer, she looked up from the tea she was making at the kitchen counter.

"What have you decided?"

"Decided about what?"

"You're planning to winter here," she said, sharply. "I'm not really asking."

"I'm thinking about it," I admitted. "I've never liked leaving the island for the winter. There's no real reason not to stay, this year."

I struggled to keep my voice even. Kate came to the table with two mugs of tea. She put a brass key down beside my cup.

"You already have one of these," she said. "Here's another key from Nora, so you get the message. She still wants you to winter in her house. It's going to be empty, and you're at home in it. There's no reason to risk being stranded out here with a problem. With her gone, this end of the lake will be entirely deserted. There's no reason to risk it."

The offer brought home the finality of my loss, and my throat ached.

"I'll think about it, Kate."

"You probably won't, but you should," she said. "The offer is sincere. She loves you, you know. That hasn't changed."

"Enough," my voice hitched and rose, "to leave me? Enough to move away and have someone else's baby?"

"Drink your tea," she said, looking at me evenly. "I'll try to give you my own insight, in the hope it comforts you, but I really came because I have something to talk to you about. Something that can't wait."

I nodded, and she stirred her own tea, thinking. "I've known Nora since she was five years old. Her mother died. Drugs, I think. Never knew who her father was. She was fostered in the area, and I became her school teacher."

"She's never talked to me about it," I said. "Not a word."

"Because she's put it away for good," Kate said. "She can have a strong will, when she decides something."

The truth of her last statement stabbed me. Nora didn't make decisions lightly, and she could rarely be swayed, once she had. Kate saw it on my face, and changed the subject.

"I never really wanted children," she said. "I sometimes think I started teaching too young for it to ever really appeal to me. I saw enough children all day. Nora was always one of the good ones, the ones that made me feel like I was spending my energy the right way."

She shook her head, remembering.

"She was a solemn little girl, and she never had much. She did well in school, never got into the usual trouble—but she never had a mom and dad growing up, and I know that hurt her, scarred her. She dreamed about growing up and finding it—a family of her own, forever love that wouldn't ever leave her. Safe and secure, even if she had to make it for herself."

"She would have had that with me," I said, and Kate shook her head.

"No, she wouldn't," she said. "You've never settled down, because you can't. You don't just see ghosts—you're haunted. You're a good man, but you're damaged. If Nora had grown up different, she might stay in love with you forever—but you're a huge risk, with your past. You may be gentle, but violence seems to find you."

"Violence? Why do you say that?"

"I've read some of your articles," she said, and smiled quietly. "You've made a good living going to the places nobody else wants to go, and writing about them."

"I'm retired now," I protested. "I fix boat engines, and daydream about writing a book."

"Nonetheless, whether Nora Martin realizes it herself or not, you were just too big a risk."

She sipped her tea, and it was a little while before she spoke again.

"Her husband has faults, but he isn't a wild card. Getting pregnant with Esteban wasn't an act of faithlessness toward you, though you might never accept that. It was the only way she could remove herself from being in love with a man she could never live with."

I felt the tears, and realized I was crying silently. Kate didn't remark on it.

"At the end of the day, you were too big a risk for that little girl. Never think she doesn't love you, in her way. Never imagine there won't be regrets."

"Do you think she'll ever come back?" I asked.

Kate gazed out at the lake for a little while before she answered.

"No," she said. "I don't think she's ever coming back. I'm sorry."

Outside the kitchen window, the rain lessened and the sky got lighter. Kate moved to go.

"You have friends here," she said. "There are people who care about you. You have a life on this lake, not just on this island."

We went slowly down the steps, and started across the clearing toward the dock. Behind us, the wet forest dripped softly. I heard the tiny chime of a bell from somewhere in the trees. It was hardly any louder than a thought, but Kate stopped in her tracks and gripped my forearm.

Her voice became different, almost fierce. "I told you I had the sight," she said.

"You told me," I agreed. "Your mother before you, and her mother."

She stared into the trees. Her expression unsettled me.

"She's here, isn't she?" she said softly. "I thought I could sense her. I was right."

"Who's here, Kate?"

"Don't treat me like a fool," she whispered sharply. "You know who I'm talking about. Chloe Hunter. She's hanging around here. What does she want?"

"I have no idea," I answered, truthfully.

"She's singing, or humming—I can hear her. I don't like this at all."

Her eyes continued to scan the woods, and then suddenly narrowed at me.

"You haven't seen her inside your cabin, have you?"

I admitted that I had, and told her about my nocturnal visits. She shook her head, looking worried.

"That implies invitation, Nick. It makes me afraid. She has no clear connection to this island in life."

"Maybe she does. Maybe she was here when she was alive, and there's some attachment. She had to have known her way around the lake."

"Spirits don't usually hang around places that meant nothing to them when they were alive—unless they've been invited. That's the basic premise behind a séance, after all."

I shrugged. I hadn't invited anyone here. I had a sudden thought. "You told me her parents might still be alive," I said. "Could you hunt me up a phone number, an address?"

"For what?" Kate asked. "What good is it going to you to disturb her parents in their old age? Are you going to tell them their daughter has become a—haunt? A specter? That she's dark and terrifying now, and comes in your dreams, walks barefoot in the snow—writes things on mirrors?"

"I'm not as convinced as you are that she's malicious."

"She frightens me," Kate repeated. "Whatever she wants from you isn't something you're up for right now. I'm very serious, Nick Horan. Get yourself away from here for the winter. If not Nora's house, then anywhere. This isn't safe."

"Can you get me the number, Kate?" I persisted.

"I can get the Hunters' telephone number for you, but I wish you'd leave the girl in peace."

"I'm not trying to stir things up. I just want some answers."

Her pale blue eyes searched the trees. She shook her head.

"She isn't at peace, and she isn't safe. Not for you. Not right now."

"I'm writing a book, Kate. You said it yourself. I'll chase a story where nobody else wants to go. That's what I'm doing now."

"Even if that's true, Nick, you shouldn't be doing it now." She trailed off and looked at the water. "You're emotional, and you're grieving right now. Some spirits feed off that. Every bone in my body tells me Chloe Hunter is one very dangerous girl, and you're not strong enough to deal with her. Not by half."

Her blue eyes searched mine.

"She wants something from you," she murmured. "Once you've realized what it is, you may be in a terrible situation, with no way to get back from it."

~ * ~

I walked along the path behind the cabin to the cliffs on the western shore of the island. The rain had stopped, and Kate had puttered away in her little boat, refusing my offers to see her safe to the marina. The lake lapped softly at the rocks below me. The shade was deep, and the woods had the strange stillness that comes just before twilight, when everything that lives in the forest finally believes night is really coming, and is hushed by that knowing. I could smell snow on the wind coming off the lake.

The dog ranged a few feet ahead of me. He stopped at a bend in the trail and barked once, softly.

The girl came into view, a few feet away. She hung upside down from a low branch, knees hooked over and ankles crossed. She gazed at me, trying not to laugh. Her pink bathing suit was wet, and her long braid dripped water onto the soft blanket of pine needles beneath her.

"Why do you do that?" I asked.

"Hang upside down?"

"Surprise me this way. I never expect you."

"Because I like it," she said. "Hanging upside down, and surprising you. Anyway, you should always expect me. I'm not real, after all. You said so yourself."

She pulled herself onto the branch, stretched out along its length, and looked at me hopefully. I looked back, until finally she spoke. "Are you lonely?"

"Who isn't?" I shrugged.

"It's because you miss me."

"I don't even know you," I said. "I can't explain you, even to myself. You aren't real."

"I came to tell you something."

"Imagine that," I said. I leaned against an oak, opposite her, and idly ran my fingers over its rough bark.

"Too bad, so sad," she sang. "You won't like it. You have to leave here if you're going to find what you're searching for. You'll have to take the Train, across time, love, and the deepest ocean ever. You'll have to remember who you are."

"Too bad, so sad," I agreed. "What happens if I don't go?"

"How should I know?" She laughed. "I'm not in charge of rules. I hate rules." She pulled herself into a sitting position, and swung her bare feet. "You already have a ticket."

"A real ticket?" I smiled. "For a real train?"

"This is real," she said.

She lifted a hand, fingers extended toward me. She blew into her palm, as though blowing me a kiss. A small shower of pink fluttered out and floated to the ground. I looked at my feet. Tiny flower blooms littered the forest floor.

"This is real," she said again, took a deep breath, and blew harder. "Take this with you."

A storm of petals gusted and blew past me. I was enveloped in color, brushed softly, everywhere, by sweetness. I turned away and stared out over the lake, disbelieving. The air was full of blossoms, and the breezes caught and lifted them up and up. Suddenly, the sky burst into sunset. Trees on the far shore exploded into a thousand shades of white and pink and gold that ran and dripped into the lake, tinting the water bright.

A bell tinkled as Chloe ran past. After a soft splash, she swam away from me, into open water, out toward the colored sparkles that were spreading across the entire surface.

"Wait!" I screamed. "What about the train?"

She stopped in the water and faced me. The rose light was swelling fast, and had nearly reached her.

"You have to say yes first!" she called back. "You have to decide yes, no matter what, and say it! No matter what!"

Chloe started to swim again, and didn't turn back, stroking her way gracefully out until she was lost in the shimmer, swallowed by the light.

Part Two

"A Perfectly-Perfect Fairy Tale"

-Thirteen-

Sanctuary Shore
Saturday, November 29, 1980

Chloe woke up, as if from a deep sleep, the kind that is full of good (and bad) stories you can't quite remember.

She stood on the beach, looking back at the Train that had brought her here. The light sea breeze blew clouds of steam away from the enormous locomotive. The whole thing, engine and handful of carriages, appeared battered and exhausted by

105

the ocean crossing it had just completed. Strands of kelp decorated it, and a starfish clung to one of the nearest windows.

The sea was turquoise, the palms were lovely, and the sand was fine and white. The air smelled wonderfully sweet, of promises kept, and of dreams not yet dreamed. The Conductor set her bags at her feet.

His name was Ginger, she knew. On the long trip west from New York City, through Chicago and St. Louis across the Mississippi River and the Rocky Mountains, the desert, the Port of Los Angeles and finally the ocean crossing to here, he had said very little. He brought her meals, made her berth with fresh, clean sheets and pillows, and had given her books to read. It had all come with a sympathetic smile, and without comment.

"What is this place?" she asked.

"This is Sanctuary," he said. "The entrance to it, anyway. The Shangri-La Hotel is just up the path over there. It looks out at the water. Most folks rest here a while before they go on to where they're going."

"It's beautiful here," she said. She was lovely, and she looked very, very brave. "I don't want you to think it isn't— but, I think I've made a mistake. I wasn't supposed to come here alone."

The old man regarded her gravely. He wore a splendid blue uniform with brass buttons, but he didn't seem to put on any airs about it. His face was very kind.

"Everyone is supposed to come here alone," he said, gently. "It's an 'alone' that only lasts a moment—but it's the Rule. You come here by yourself. No exceptions."

She nodded. "I understand that. Still, there was someone who left there—just before me. I expected to meet him on the Train, or at the very least find him waiting here for me."

"Had you agreed to meet here?"

"Not exactly. He left before me, though—and he was stuck. I unstuck him, so he should be here."

"He was stuck, and you unstuck him?" he wondered. "Why don't you tell me about that?"

So she did. When she finished, he nodded, excused himself, and walked up the beach to think a little. Chloe waded into the surf while she waited for him. The waves were warm and mild, and the water was clear as crystal. It all reminded her of something, though she couldn't right away think of what it was.

When the Conductor came back, his face was very serious.

"I have bad news," he said. "The boy you're looking for isn't here. He's back there, in the linear world. He woke up."

"He woke up?" Chloe asked, perplexed. "How could he wake up? The doctors said he would never wake up again. Over and over, everyone told me to forget him because he couldn't wake up."

The Conductor gave her an elaborate shrug. "What can you do?" he asked. "You unstuck him, but he didn't take the Train. He woke up instead."

Chloe began to cry just a little, despite herself. The Conductor took a white handkerchief from his pocket and gave it to her. It was very clean, and smelled faintly of lemons.

"He broke the Rules. I don't think he meant to. He stayed behind because he thought that's where you were, and now—he doesn't quite belong back there where he is, and he doesn't quite belong here, either."

He squinted at the bright water.

"So he's stuck?" she asked, excited. "That's easy. I'll unstick him, again."

"It won't be as easy as you think," he said.

"Of course it will," she said. "I know exactly what to do. I'll tell him a story—a perfectly perfect fairy tale. He'll remember me."

"The Rules aren't harsh or unreasonable, and it isn't strictly forbidden to break them, but you expose yourself to dangers, if you do. A person could be lost, or worse. There are dark things that prey on the lost."

The Conductor regarded her with enormous sympathy. His eyes were liquid. "He's going to die again," he said. "In eleven days. You have eleven days to get him here safely before he dies again, or the dark things will capture him, for certain."

"He's going to die?" Chloe exclaimed. "That's so sad. It's awful when people die. Do you know that for sure?"

The old man looked at her sharply, and relaxed when he saw she was joking.

"It should have been sure thirty years ago," he said, and cleared his throat with great delicacy. "Somebody we both know interfered."

"I did, didn't I?" she smiled.

She had a sudden thought. "Does he know that he's stuck? That he isn't supposed to be where he is?"

"Not quite, no. He doesn't remember. He's tried to be a good man, most of the time, but he's never really managed to be happy. How could he be, where he doesn't belong?"

She listened to him, so hopeful she could scarcely breathe.

"You're asking to go back where you came from," he said. "That isn't allowed."

"Not for long," she said, eagerly. "Only to look for him—to bring him back, if he'll come with me."

He held up his hand. "Do you like baseball?" he asked.

"I play baseball when I drive," she nodded. "When there's a bottleneck situation, I let one car into the line in front of me, and then I 'crowd the base'. It's a beautiful maneuver."

She drew her name in the sand with her toe, while she thought. "There's another one, too, but I can't remember it until I do it."

"To have any chance at all," he said. "You'll almost certainly have to call a Squeeze Play. That takes more courage and conviction than anything else I know. It requires a willingness to lose everything, if necessary. Sometimes, it wins the game, but other times no one survives."

"Courage and conviction," she said. "I have those. I think."

The old conductor looked at her for a long time. Finally, he nodded. "I think so, too," he agreed, and sighed. "Let's get started back, then."

They turned and waded out together. The Train waited for
them, beyond the small breakers.

"There are a few things that you need to know, before we go
back," Ginger said. "Listen carefully, my dear. Everything
depends on it."

Chloe stopped and faced him. The water came almost thigh
deep, and she had the hem of her dress lifted in one hand. She
noticed that the old Conductor was unconcerned with his wet
trousers, so she dropped her skirt and listened closely.

"The Train normally goes back without passengers," he
said. "You'll be allowed on board this once, as an honored
stowaway, and the trip should be uneventful, as much as they
ever are."

As he thought about his next words, he reached up absently
and took the starfish from the window glass, and put it into the
water.

"The boy you're looking for is different now. He's remained
behind, grown older, and forgotten his own when and why. You
have eleven days to convince him to return here with you. Time
doesn't matter so much here, but it does there. It isn't enough
time for him to remember who he is. You'll have to talk him into
getting on the Train, and hope he remembers and decides to stay
with you."

"Why can't he remember?" she asked. "How did he get
stuck again? Why is he still back there?"

"His state isn't natural. Love got him into the mess he's in.
Hopefully love will get him back out."

"It will," she said, somewhat shyly. "I do think he loves
me."

"He does love you," the Conductor said. "Even if he's
forgotten it. Sometimes love is enough, but not always. When you
find him, get to the Train as quickly as you can. Speaking of
which, we should get on board. Time is short, back there."

He took her elbow, and helped her onto the metal step. She
was a little bit embarrassed to lean on him, because of his age,
but he was surprisingly strong and steady. He followed her into

the dining car, and then disappeared. She gazed out the window at the line of palms on the beach. It looked like a seaside resort, except that there were no bathers in the water.

"This next part is very important," he said, reappearing at her elbow. "You must listen very carefully."

He had wheeled a silver tea service on a trolley to the table. He served them both, and then seated himself across from her.

"Do you love him very much?" he asked. "No matter what?"

She nodded. "No matter what."

"Good. This Train, and others like it, makes regularly scheduled trips according to carefully plotted timetables. The return trip we're making right now is scheduled, so there are no concerns, other than your presence, which should go unnoticed by everyone but me. Duties and tolls are paid in advance, tracks are maintained and rights-of-way are secured according to the Rules. It's always been so, and always will be so."

She tasted her tea, and reached for a slice of buttered bread. The tension lifted, and she was suddenly starving. She would sleep through most of the trip back, she was sure.

"If you persuade him to make another trip west with you, you'll have to understand some things. First, there are Gatekeepers along the way. They watch and protect the tracks. Each Gatekeeper will treat you variously, from sympathy to hostility."

"I have to talk to them?"

"Not all of them, no. Some will be satisfied, and remain invisible. Others will step forward and issue a challenge. Those that do will require a Treasure—and will allow his expired ticket to pass only when they receive it."

"A Treasure?" she asked. "Like what? What are they for?"

He carefully placed a cardboard cigar box on the table. It said 'Roi Tan' on the lid, in gold letters.

"Do you recognize this?" he asked.

"Those are my treasures!" she exclaimed. "My collection!"

"A Treasure is a memento, a memory, a basic element of your life. It shows the Gatekeeper that you are forthright, that you are who you say you are, and that you have business on the railroad. It proves that you aren't real."

"A memento, a memory, an element of my life," she repeated.

She reached into the cigar box, and pulled out some items. She spread them on the table. There was a small kaleidoscope, a metal button, a seashell, and a yellow baby pin. Then came a butterfly pinned to a square of cardboard, and one of her father's cigars, dried nearly to dust. She had been in a hurry when she asked him for the box, and the last cigar had been left behind, unsmoked. Now it was a reminder of him.

"Those are actually called 'diaper pins'," he said helpfully, *as though he could read her mind. "Not 'baby pins', which makes no sense, if you think about it."*

"I call then 'baby pins', because that's what they are," Chloe said, absently. *"What if I don't have the Treasure the Gatekeeper wants?"*

"You can't proceed. You'll have to leave him, and come back without him."

"Leave him behind? Alone, in a strange place?"

"He'll be lost," Ginger said, gravely. *"There's nothing you'll be able to do."*

"Except stay lost with him," she said. *"If that's what I choose."*

"You're talking about forever," he reminded her. *"It's a big chance you're taking."*

"I'll do what I have to," she murmured. *"No matter what."*

"There are those who will try to harm you."

The floor vibrated under their feet. The locomotive in front was building steam, getting ready to go. Chloe looked out at the shore of Sanctuary, suddenly apprehensive.

"Harm me?"

"There's a group of gangsters, called the Low Gang. They are led by a man who mocks everyone else—the Grinning Man.

They prey on those wandering outside of the Rules. They smell the vulnerable, and feed on them—literally feed on them. If you don't want to be eaten, stay ahead of them."

Chloe set her bread on the plate, suddenly unable to finish it. She picked up her cup of tea, trying not to show the tremble in her hand. Ginger slid a book across the table toward her. She read the title, without picking it up, The Giant Silver Book of Elves and Fairies. She opened the cover with her index finger. An atlas was printed on the flyleaf, with the legend:

Time is a Map

"If you read the beginning," Ginger said, "you'll see that you are starting in the cemetery where your body is buried."

"I don't have to visit myself, do I?" she asked. "Pay my respects? View any remains?"

"Of course not. You'll simply board the Train with your boy and travel west until you reach Sanctuary. Satisfy the Gatekeepers who you meet, and avoid the Low Gang. What could be easier? Or harder?"

"That sounds easy," Chloe said, doubtfully. "And hard."

"Of course it is. Refer to the book whenever you're not sure, and watch for things that are underlined . . ."

The Train shuddered and gave a small jerk. Cars bumped against each other, and the beach outside the window began to move. They were rolling, very slowly.

"Here's the final point, Chloe. You cannot tell him what you are to him. He has to remember you by himself, and he has to do it before he dies in eleven days. Remind him where he came from, or you will not reach the shores of Sanctuary."

"I have an idea," she said. "I'm going to tell him a fairy tale. Once upon a time, I promised him that I would. Also, I may use crumbs. I read about it in a book."

Ginger handed her a small velvet box, with a hinged lid. Chloe opened it. A Mickey Mouse watch nestled inside, and she *took it out and turned it over. The back of it had been removed, because it was broken.*

"Do you recognize this?"

"I do," she nodded. "It was mine, when I was little."

She gazed, without touching it.

"It's lovely," she said. "Is it for me?"

"Yes. It will tell you when and where you are."

She thought about it, and then nodded. "Time," she said, "is a Map."

"Time is a map," he nodded. "You have eleven days to get him back to the Shangri-La Hotel, or the boy will be gone for good."

The Train gained speed. They felt the tremors as it crashed through the larger combers that were rolling in, to the shore of Sanctuary. The windows were splashed with spray, and a another starfish clinging outside the glass got washed away.

"There's one last thing, Miss Chloe." The Conductor's expression became terribly serious. "It might be the most important thing of all. You took your own life, and that makes you an attractive prize for the Low Gang."

"I did no such thing!" she protested. "I just swam out to unstick..."

"Technically, you did." He held a hand up. "Technicalities are everything, where the Low is concerned. Since you took your own life, you belong to them, and they will claim you as their right. You are in far worse danger than the boy you're trying to save. If they catch you, they will eat him all up—but your fate will be even worse."

"Nobody belongs to them," she said. "Everyone goes to the Shangri-La, and decides from there. Absolutely everyone."

"You did go to Shangri-La," he reminded her. "You went, and now you're choosing to leave its protection. You're breaking the Rules, and you'll be subject to the rules that the Low make up."

Her voice was small. The Train ran at full speed now, and sheets of water hit the windows and ran down the glasses. "What will they do to me?"

"Everything you were afraid of when you were little," he said. "Every nightmare you've ever had. Everything in the dark that follows, and laughs, and bites. It isn't too late to turn back. This is your last chance—are you sure you love this boy enough to risk it?"

Chloe stared out the window a long time, and then she nodded.

~ * ~

Present Day:

I didn't see Nora go. I didn't say goodbye to her, or speak to her before she left Hollow Lake for good. She left her dock light on every night until the last night, and the sight of it, twinkling from across the dark reach each evening, gave me some slender thread of hope. One night, it was dark, and that was that.

I had come back to Hollow Lake after a lifetime away, without knowing what had drawn me back. I needed rest, I needed a new start, and I needed some sense of who I had become. Slowly, day-by-day and piece-by-piece, I had reinvented myself. Nora had been the architect of all of it, and now she had gone, and taken my fresh start with her.

There were only two things in my days that held any vestige of interest for me, two spots of brightness in the gloom of my days.

First, the ice was coming. Leaving my cabin each of the previous two winters to wait out the coldest part of the year in a rented trailer or apartment rankled me. I would have preferred to stay put. The ice presented a problem in early January and late March, when it got thin.

It skinned over the lake, usually after Christmas, and made boat travel impossible, but was unsafe to walk on until it had thickened to a depth of several inches. When spring approached, it became unreliable, with cracks and running overflows appearing unexpectedly. During those two periods, safe travel became impossible, and I would effectively be stranded on the island.

This year, I had decided to stay. The complete isolation was immensely appealing, and I had no intention of staying in Nora's house. I knew that I would hear her voice in every room. It would be intolerable.

The second diversion was the haunting of the island. I didn't know why the ghost of Chloe Hunter lingered, and I didn't know why she had chosen me to engage with, so many years after her death. Her family had summered on Long Duck Island, across the channel, but nothing I had discovered about her life explained her presence on Duck Island.

I was reluctant to leave for the winter with no answers. I sensed if I left, she might, too. I didn't understand her, but I didn't want her to leave. I clung to the idea that a novel might be what saved me, and the haunting was my best shot at writing it.

My life took on a familiar routine, as I prepared the cabin for winter-over. I scoured the seven or eight wooded acres of island for usable deadfall among the pines, aspens and oaks that covered it, since I was reluctant to cut trees. It meant hauling firewood over some distance, through areas with no paths. I used an old wheelbarrow, and welcomed the diversion. Eventually I had a couple of cords stacked by the back door, enough to feed the woodstove through the cold months.

I added insulation, ran my water feed deeper below the surface of the lake, farther down than the ice could possibly reach. Trips into town resulted in everything from over-the-counter medications to paperback books being added to my shelves. I walked the island from east to west, and back again, every morning. I told myself that it was part of getting ready, in some vague way. I didn't ever admit to myself that I searched the cold earth for the prints of bare feet.

Traffic on the lake stopped, as November moved into December. The last weekend fishermen, the autumn foliage watchers, the late cottage-closers finally left, and there were no more lights at all on the lake at night. The nights were colder and colder, and I filled the woodstove before I went to bed. I lay in the dark, and listened to the old cast iron pop and sing with heat.

My days felt busy with preparation, but a good deal of my time was spent staring across the sound, at the small white house where Nora had lived. I watched the lake, remembered her, and waited for the ice to come.

On my way home from errands in Ansett, I signaled a right turn onto the highway that headed toward the marina. The car behind me honked. Impulsively, I wheeled the Jeep left instead, and headed for Huntsville. I had twenty miles to realize I didn't know why I was going there.

Once inside the city limits, I passed the large shopping malls and turned into the old business district. When I saw a florist's sign, I pulled to the curb. The air in the tiny shop smelled green, and was humid enough took make my face wet. The glass doors on the display cases were crowded with foliage. The woman behind the counter wore red-and-white checks. She seemed comfortable.

I stopped in front of her, and looked at the show of blooms, unsure of myself.

"I want to buy one pink flower," I said. "Just one. I'll take a bouquet, if I have to."

"You won't have to do that," she said. "I'll sell you whatever you want. A pink rose?"

"No, not a rose." I was definite, without knowing why. My thoughts formed themselves as I went along. It was strange, almost like reaching for a memory.

"Something very small," I said. "Something a little bit— wild. Do you have something like that?"

"A flower you'd pick yourself, if it weren't so cold and miserable outside? A summer flower?"

"Exactly. That's exactly what I want."

She smiled, perhaps at my expression, and turned around to consider her displays. Then she pushed herself off her stool and went through a door, into the back of the store. When she returned, she showed me the small pink blossom cradled in her palm.

"This is a sweet pea," she said. "Seem right?"

"Perfect," I said.

"Should I wrap it?"

I shook my head and pulled out my wallet, but she waved me off.

"I don't want your money, not for one little flower. You're in love, and for you it's a charm, obviously."

"Not in love," I smiled. "Not exactly that."

She shook her head, definite. "Yes, you are. I can tell. Maybe some of the magic will rub off on me. I could use it."

The tiny bell over the door tinkled as I went out. Light rain spattered the sidewalk in front, but the cemetery was within easy walking distance. I set out to find Chloe's grave.

The cemetery lay near the heart of the downtown area. A wrought iron fence surrounded it. Chestnut trees curved bare branches over the sidewalk. I could see that the interior was liberally planted. It was probably pleasant in summer.

A black metal gate arched over the street entrance. I wandered along the brick path, unsure of where to start looking for her grave. The dates on the headstones seemed to get gradually more recent as I made my way further into the interior. The forest of granite and marble gave way to a newer section, where all the markers were brass, set flat into the grass.

I was searching for Chloe Hunter's name. It was starting to rain, but I wasn't in a hurry. I had been wet before.

A huge maple tree, off to my left, suddenly drew my eyes, and I walked to Chloe's grave as surely as if I were being led by the hand. The tree hung onto some of its leaves still. If the rain

117

got any harder, they'd be stripped from it. Her spot was under the great spread of branches. I looked down at her marker. It was no different than any of the others, but I'd gone straight to it.

Chloe Aanya Hunter
June 26, 1962 - November 25, 1980
I can fly

I set the tiny flower on the stamped bronze plate. I felt the heat of tears mixing with the rain on my face. I grieved her, this woman I had never known, but my weeping was also for Nora, and for the continual procession of goodbyes that life seemed to be.

Until now, I hadn't accepted the fact that the woman who visited me, the ghost I was beginning to think of as special, was in fact dead. She was a person whose body had been in a coffin for years. I wanted to speak to her, but I didn't know what to say. I stood and looked quietly at the splash of pink for a little while, and then I turned away and left the cemetery by the main gate.

It was warm and gray, raining steadily now. The city smelled wet. Tires hissed on the street in front of me.

"I feel like I'm not done with you yet," I said under my breath. "I feel like we haven't even started."

There was a noise, not quite music yet, but growing into it. I stopped and stood on the sidewalk, listening. Percussive, like a far-off parade or a concert heard from outside a lit theater, the sound rose into something noisy and sweet. A woman turned the corner and came into my view.

The downpour came to a sudden close, and she paused under the stop sign to shut her umbrella. It was Chloe.

The boulevard unfolded as she began to walk again, toward me. Her feet splashed the puddles on the sidewalk, into bright colors that overflowed into the gutters. She trailed light. Sparkles rose behind her and were caught in the tree branches overhead. The storefronts, restaurant patios, cars, and passers-by glowed,

118

electric and happy. Her steps were a dance that explained everything perfectly.

As she passed, she glanced sideways at me, the barest touch of eyes that marked me for good. She had light hair and dark eyes. Summer had brushed her skin with amber.

"It's all just starting," she said. "So there."

Her smile went by, and her dance with the city moved to the other end of the street. She looked over her shoulder at me, once, as she spun around the corner and out of sight.

"So there," I whispered back.

The song for Chloe faded slowly. The rain started up again, and it ran down my face. I stood there for a long time in the subsiding color, watching the place she had disappeared into.

~ * ~

The Bays Lake Community Arena had been a fixture in the town that neighbored Ansett for generations. Painted a flaking light blue, it sat in the middle of a large packed-dirt parking lot. It had a vaguely Quonset-like appearance from the outside. Inside, the lobby was invariably overheated, and smelled of ancient pine, and of the coffee and hot dogs that were sold at the snack bar in the lobby.

Beyond the double doors into the stands, the temperature plunged. The ice surface smelled clean and cold, and the air filled with scraping of skate blades, slaps of hockey pucks against the wooden boards, and shouts of players and spectators. The timekeeper's buzzer echoed against a high roof crisscrossed with metal girders. The place hadn't changed in at least fifty years.

I had a pair of ice skates that I had bought, second-hand and only used once, slung over my shoulder. My hands in my pockets, I went down the tunnel beneath the stands to a hallway lined with dressing room doors. The second one I tried was the right one.

"Nick!" John Park called. "About time you got here!"

119

He was sitting on one of the long benches bolted to the cinder block wall, strapping on hockey pads. Six or seven men in various states of undress were scattered around, fishing in equipment bags, or tightening skates. A couple of them looked over and nodded. The rooms smelled like mildew and old sweat.

I was a little bit embarrassed, and I made my way over to Park.

"Your equipment's here," he said. "This is all extra stuff. Take it home with you. None of it matches, but it's still in okay shape. If you have fun with this, you can buy better."

"It's great, thanks. I hope I don't make you sorry you invited me."

I unzipped the bag. I knew I had played hockey as a kid, but not after my drowning as a teenager. I didn't remember it. The coma had done some funny things. There were things I had done before the accident that I couldn't do afterward. I sat in a dressing room with a bunch of guys who had grown up on the frozen lakes and ponds around here, and strange as it seemed, I had no idea if I knew how to skate.

"Just get yourself on the ice, and get comfortable," John said, reading my mind. "This isn't even a game tonight. We're just shooting the puck around, getting some exercise. No one's watching you."

I pulled out a blue-and-red jersey, and green socks. The equipment was old and mismatched, and seeing it made me feel better.

"You feeling okay?"

John stared at me, concerned.

"Just nervous."

"I mean with what's going on with Nora," he said. "It's too small a place to be a secret, and she's my friend, too. You look tired. It's only been a little while, and you already look like you're losing weight, or getting sick. You didn't shave this morning."

With cop friends, there was never a shortage of blunt.

"I haven't been sleeping much," I said. "Comes with the territory."

"Not overdoing the booze?" he asked. "Not—using anything, to get you by?"

I gave him a long look.

"Okay then," he said. "No chemicals in play. Well, get out there. Some fun will do you a lot of good."

"Fun," I said.

"Exactly. Go for a skate, and we'll be pouring a beer before you know it."

After ten minutes on the ice, I wondered what I had been thinking. My stick felt awkward, and my skates threatened to go out from me every time I changed direction. The first time the puck came to me, I lost my balance reaching for it, and a man thirty years my senior knocked me sprawling. John skated over and gave me a hand up.

"Takes a bit to get the hang of it again." He laughed. "I can tell it's been a while for you."

"I've don't feel like I've ever really done this, even though I know I have."

"Just relax. No one's got an eye on you. A few times out here with us and you'll be turning pro. By the time we start playing games, you'll be having a blast. I guarantee it."

I was grateful for the kindness, and the inclusion.

"My ankles are killing me," I said. "Think I'll sit a few minutes."

I skated to the players' bench, unlatched the door, and sat watching. I dropped my stick and set the heavy hockey gloves down beside me. The arena air was cold on my sweaty hands.

The door at the far end of the ice swung open, and a solitary skater emerged. From where I sat, the slender figure appeared to be a woman, and she began to glide along the far boards. Her skating was slow and graceful. She wore a gray sweatshirt with the hood up, and dark glasses. The hockey players paid no attention to her, although it was unheard of, and dangerous, for a pleasure skater to venture onto the ice when hockey was being played.

Serene, she didn't even glance at the players buzzing around her. When she reached the spot where I was sitting, she stopped.

"Did you decide?" she asked. "Is there an answer?"

"Chloe?" I said, stunned.

"You're surprised I can skate so well, aren't you? Better than you, that's for sure."

"Why are you—what's with the sunglasses? You act like you're in disguise. Can other people see you?"

She looked over her shoulder at the hockey players.

"These people? They can't—or, don't believe it if they do. I'm invisible. I'm running a little bit of a risk here, coming to find you. There are others—who can see us. They might be after us, a little bit."

"After us? Why would anyone be after us?"

"We're taking the trip together," she said. "The Train is waiting for both of us."

"What do you want from me?" I asked softly. "We don't know each other. I don't have any connection to you."

A shot slapped the boards, inches from where she stood. I flinched, but she didn't seem to notice. Two players chased after it, sticks held high. She made a shooing motion with the fingers of one hand, and they wheeled away and skated up the ice. Her dark eyes looked deep into me.

"Have you ever felt like you didn't belong? Like it was all strange?"

"Everyone has," I nodded.

"No." She shook her head. "Really alone, really lost. A feeling things have never quite worked out for you, because they can't work out."

She leaned over the boards. I caught her faint scent, cinnamon and oranges.

"They can't work out because, even with the best intentions, you don't really belong here. Most of all, they can't work out because . . ."

She traced a finger down my cheek. I tried not to pull back. Her touch was ice cold.

"They can't work out because you're not—real. You're not real."

"You're the one who isn't real," I said.

She pushed off, started to skate away, but then looked back at me.

"I know who you are," she said. "I'll tell you, if you want me to, but you have to come with me."

"I know who I am."

"You don't act like it." She smiled. "Actually, I can't tell you. It's against the Rules, but I can show you, and that's the same thing. Meet me tonight, in Huntsville.

"Where in Huntsville?" I asked. "What time?"

"Across from the cemetery, of course. Time doesn't matter. Time takes care of itself."

She glided off, slipping easily through the scrum of hockey players. She let herself out of the gate, and then I didn't see her any more.

~ * ~

At the Echo Island Pie Company, Kate Bean brought my coffee to the table and slid in, across from me. We had the café to ourselves. I thought about stirring in my usual ration of cream and sugar, but it seemed like a lot of bother. I sipped it black.

"Jessica Ward at the real estate office mentioned she saw you yesterday," Kate said. "Were you thinking about selling, after all?"

"I didn't go to the real estate office yesterday." I thought about it. "I'm not selling. Why would I go there?"

"No, you didn't go into the real estate office," she said, keeping her voice carefully neutral. "You sat in your jeep in front of it for two hours. Jessica said as best she could tell, you were just staring out through the windshield at nothing. She started to worry. Were you waiting for someone?"

"I have no idea what you're talking about."

"I was afraid you'd say that," she said. "One trouble with worrying Jessica is that she feels obliged to let the whole town know, so they can worry with her. I normally dismiss gossip, but if you want to sit in your truck in a fugue state, you might want to do it someplace other than in front of Jessica Ward's office window."

"Must not have been me."

She reached across the table and touched my hand, a gesture very unlike her.

"Nick, I'm fond of you, but I would describe you as pleasant-looking and fairly ordinary. If it were only you, I would believe Jessica saw another man. Your yellow Jeep, however, is neither ordinary nor mistakable."

I didn't want my coffee. The beginnings of a headache were creeping in, and I tried to reach through it to change the subject. Kate did it for me.

"Have you seen your mother lately?" she asked.

"I had dinner a couple of weeks ago with her," I said. "She's fine."

"I also ran into her yesterday," she said. "It's been a lot longer than a couple of weeks."

"The baby and Nora kept me busy," I said. "Closing up the cabin for winter, helping out at the marina. Autumn's a busy time. I'll catch up with my mom when the snow flies."

"Actually, you might not be able to do that," she said. "Not if you're planning to hole up on that island, trapped by the ice. Better see her now, before it gets really cold."

"What's wrong with you, Kate?" I asked. "You don't usually talk to me like this."

She glared at me. Her eyes were too bright, and I wondered if Kate Bean ever let the tough exterior slip enough to cry. She looked like she was close to it. She pushed her chair back and picked up my coffee cup.

"I've warned you the best way I know how, Nick Horan," she said. "There's nothing else I can say to you."

She went to the kitchen without looking back. The girl behind the counter glanced at me, her expression slightly apprehensive. The bell over the door jingled as I went out.

-Fourteen-

I got to the public library in downtown Huntsville about midnight, and settled in to wait. I sat on a cement planter out front, and watched the night. The late flood of theater-goers and dinner-eaters gave way in the early morning hours to the trickle of drunks headed home from the bars and patios. They went by in groups, in pairs, or alone. Worst were the faces of strangers going home together in pairs, pretending for an hour or two that their loneliness wasn't desperate.

Finally, the last of the boisterous cars, with their squealing tires and blatting mufflers, had gone, and the giant machine that was the city groaned and sighed and settled itself into real darkness. Only the occasional lost ones rippled the quiet. They crept out, into the street's light here and there, then blended back into doorways and darkened recesses. Yellow police cars drove by slowly at intervals, their blank windshields staring at nothing.

It seemed like a night for cigarettes. I wished briefly that I still smoked, but I didn't, so I watched the city sleep instead. The concrete beneath me got cold, but I didn't move.

I saw her coming from a long way off, in the last hour before the eastern sky lightened. She came toward me, passing in and out of the illumination of half-lighted storefronts, walking like the whole night belonged to her. Finally, she got to me, reached out and touched my hair. I didn't say anything.

"How long were you going to wait?" she asked.

I had the absurd urge to kiss her, even though I still ached for Nora. It didn't make any sense, but this woman felt more and more familiar to me every time I saw her. A kiss seemed natural, and right.

"Longer than this," I said. "A lot longer."

We looked at each other some more. After a while, she broke the silence.

"I want to tell you a story, but I can't," she said. "I have to try to show you, with your eyes closed. Let's go. There's only a little night time left."

I stood up. The early hour felt damp, and I was cold from sitting. Chloe took my hand, and warmed it. We started walking, past the darkened, expensive shops, lit windows full of clothing and books, jewelry and art and furniture. Emptied of voices and movement, the stores seemed a little bit forlorn, as though they were making a brave attempt to stave off the bigger things in the universe with moneyed bravado.

The moon dangled above the city lights, forgotten. A church spire reached for it, lit softly blue.

"We're going to the cemetery, to get your train ticket."

A cloud passed overhead, spattering rain on the sidewalk, and then was as quickly gone. The spotted cement made it seem as though we walked over a spill of dark coins.

"They sell train tickets in the boneyard?" I asked. "Since when?"

"I have no idea," she answered shortly. "I make it a point not to hang around—boneyards."

The cemetery was dark as pitch until my eyes adjusted, and then everything seemed to have its own low blue light. Off to our right, a sprinkler turned on, a familiar tsk-tsk-tsk-tsk-tsk that came toward us, paused, and then swept back the other way. I saw headlights moving slowly on a street in the distance, and caught a glimpse of the main gates in their shine.

Even though I couldn't see the maple tree in the dark, I had a feeling that we were quite near to the grave marker I had visited earlier. Chloe's marker.

It was late autumn on the streets outside the cemetery gates, but inside it was warm, and I could smell fresh-cut grass. I heard the sound of crickets. They sang about mid-summer.

"Look," she said, and pointed into the darkness.

"Look at what? It's too dark to see anything."

She took my face in her warm hands and pointed me toward the sounds of water.

"Look with your ears," she said. "They're out there. There are lots of them tonight."

I heard the sprinkler ratcheting, the hiss and spray of cold water—and then farther off, the pound of surf, the sway of trees, and the moan of winds against volcanic hills. Finally, they emerged, swam into my hearing and my view, brown ones and black ones and white ones, leaping in the arcing spray.

"See them now?" she murmured.

"Bears?"

"Yes, of course. They come here to play on hot nights."

"I remember bears—something about bears. I don't even know if remember is the right word."

"Remember is exactly the right word," she said. "Remembering is what you're doing."

She kissed me, and I tasted ginger. She took my hand and pulled me deeper into the graveyard. Here and there among the markers I saw the glimmer of white clock faces, with black hands I couldn't read. Far ahead of us, I saw a tiny pinpoint of light.

She pointed. "That way."

As we came close, I recognized the small shape that sparked and glowed. It was a dragonfly. It had lit on a grave marker, and changed colors softly. Peach went to white, and then to yellow. A child's teddy bear, with a bow around its neck, sat on the inscription. Chloe picked it up, and tucked it into the canvas bag she carried.

"Not much farther," she said.

The grass was soft underneath my feet. I tried to avoid stepping on the metal markers. We came over a rise, and a pale building came into view. It glimmered in the blue light. It appeared to be a mausoleum, but it was entirely a false front. A lone figure stood before it, motionless, in a booth that came to his waist. He wore a striped coat and a straw hat. When we were close enough, he saw us and stirred.

"A million thrills," he called. "Step right up, only one bear each. What's a single small bear, folks, for the things you'll see?"

128

His features were terribly pale. His black moustache and eyebrows floated on a white face. It made me think of the clocks. The façade behind him was barren of the carnival hand-painted colors that I would have expected to see. There were just two doors, one word inscribed over each, which marred the blankness. One door was marked 'YES', the other, 'NO'.

"A million thrills," the man repeated. "Do you dare?"

I felt Chloe's fingers in my palm, and I looked at what she had slipped me. It was a coin, brown-gold, with a bear cast into its face. I glanced up at her.

"I already have my ticket," she said.

"I have to do this, right?"

She nodded, uncharacteristically solemn. "It's too late," she said. "It went too far, too fast. Unseen currents, what can you do?"

"Step right up, sir," the barker crowed. "Things you've never seen before, the farthest corners of the earth brought right here to you, a million thrills!"

I gave him my coin. Up close, his white face was frightening. He handed me a small square of printed paper, which I read in the odd light.

Pacific Railway
COACH CLASS ONE WAY
Good for One Passage, also in Sleeping Cars
Stopovers Allowed

I turned it over. The other side said 'Issued July 2, 1980-good for ONE YEAR'. I started back toward Chloe, and she shook her head.

"It's expired," she said. "It's better if you carry it, though. It might prove your intentions, if anyone asks. Remember I asked your intentions?"

"I have to say 'yes', no matter what?"

"No matter what," she nodded. "Before we get started, you have to choose a door. 'YES' or 'NO'. The choice has to be freely made."

I clutched my ticket, and didn't take my eyes from her face.

"It isn't bad on the 'NO' side," she said. "I have to be honest. There are birthdays and Christmases, and new cars, and grocery shopping, and even—love. It's a little grayer, but you hardly notice after a while. There are fewer unseen currents."

"And on the 'YES' side?" I asked.

"What you were born to do is there. Everything you love, and all the colors. It's where you belong, your heart's desire. You've walked a long way to get here, and here it is, finally, but . . ."

She was silent. I waited for her, and finally spoke.

"But . . .?"

"Your heart will be broken, and broken again, if you go through the 'YES' door. You'll have more to lose, and there's always loss. It's part of the deal, no matter what."

I looked at the small white building, and at the two doors set into its face. None of this was real. I knew I had to be dreaming all of it, but at that moment my life on the island seemed like the dream.

"'Happily ever after' hurts like hell, sometimes," she said.

I nodded to the barker, and walked up the couple of steps to the door marked 'YES'. I reached behind me for the knob.

"You have to do this, too?"

"Do you see me?" she asked.

"You're all that I do see."

She nodded. I turned, opened the YES door, and stepped through. I stood in a darkened theater. The house lights were up, but the ancient space was dim. The place was huge, but somehow warm and intimate. Rows and rows of padded seats watched for the heavy velvet curtain at the front to go up.

Chloe was waiting for me. We found our seats.

Lauren Bacall swept by, trailed by an abashed-looking Bogart. Scott Fitzgerald stopped when he saw me, and pumped my hand delightedly. Zelda put her hand on my arm and leaned across me to kiss Chloe's cheek.

"Garbo's a complete slut," she murmured to her. "Don't let anyone tell you different. She has the most fun of all of us."

I smiled and shook my head, smelling the gin on her breath. Natalie Wood, seated further down our row, leaned forward and gave me a small wave. Her dark eyes melted me a little bit. She tilted her head in Chloe's direction, raised her eyebrows and gave me thumbs-up, thumbs-down. I shrugged. 'Good luck', she mouthed, and leaned back again.

Edward R. Murrow stopped and stood with his arms crossed. He gave me a small nod, waiting for Zelda to leave. When she finally did, Chloe saw him and gave a glad cry. She plucked the cigarette from his mouth and kissed him. I was a little bit jealous.

"*Romeo and Juliet,*" he said, and smiled at her fondly. "How many times have you seen it?"

"It's my favorite." Chloe laughed. "I'm going to keep watching until there's a happy ending."

Fay Wray squeezed by me to join them, and I stepped back into the aisle. A hand clapped me on the shoulder.

"Enjoyed myself at your island," Chandler said. "I'd like to do it again."

"I didn't know you were there, Ray. You're quite welcome, any time."

"Here's Bob Parker," he said. "Someone you might like to know."

I shook hands with a burly man with a pug's face, wearing a leather jacket and a vintage Braves cap.

"I don't much go by Bob," he said. "Known Ray a long time, so I let it go."

They filed in and to their seats, the kings and queens of trances, fantastic phantoms, fives, sevens and eights. They were the masters of all things askew, silver ghosts who peeled up the corners of reality to play in magic, to dress in cobwebs, and to dance in breathless dreams.

Ethereally, impossibly lovely, Chloe paled them all to invisibility.

"Where do you know Murrow from?" I whispered.

"Hush," she smiled. "The curtain's about to go up."

~ * ~

I opened my eyes. The police car door latched open, and a shiny black shoe reached for the curb. The officer was paunchy, and moved slowly. The eyes that watched me were anything but slow.

"How you doing tonight, sir? Are you okay? You have to move. You can't sleep here."

The approach was typical for police contact anywhere in Canada. His greeting was superficially friendly, a little bit formal, and slightly wary. This officer had seen it all, and wanted to deal with me quickly and directly. He didn't wait for my answer.

"I'm sure you're going to tell me you haven't been drinking or drugging, here in the bar district," he said. "You haven't been celebrating, and you probably just happen to be waiting for someone, right?"

"I was waiting for someone, as a matter of fact," I said. "I must have dozed off. Sorry."

"In point of fact, you've been here for nearly five hours. This is the third time I've passed you. You haven't moved."

"I'm going to head home."

His voice got kinder.

"This may not be the big city, but you can still get robbed here. If you're coming down to party, it's good to have a plan, a friend who doesn't drink as much, maybe, to keep an eye on you and get you home safe when the bars close."

I decided not to debate it with him. I was tired. He watched me carefully as I stood up.

"You okay from here?" he asked.

"I'm okay," I said. "Thanks for checking on me."

He nodded, and I turned and started walking. It was breaking gray dawn. It seemed as though I had been in the cemetery with Chloe for hours, but the sky hadn't changed. I was cold to the bone.

The street was nearly empty of cars. A diner was opening up. Through the plate glass window, I saw a woman wiping tables. I smelled exhaust from the fryer in the chilly air, and thought about going inside for a cup of coffee. She sensed me looking, and stared at me with such a mixture of alarm and distrust that I kept walking.

I spotted my jeep at the curb a block up. I checked my pocket for my keys, and pulled out a small square of heavy paper and stared at it. It was printed card stock, badly worn, with lettering so faint as to be unintelligible, but I made out the words 'Coach Class', and 'stopovers allowed'.

Chloe seemed suddenly near, and I looked for her on the empty street. I didn't see her. I heard just a breath of her song, a whisper. I shook my head, and headed for the truck.

The marina parking lot was empty, when I pulled in at dawn. I checked the dark windows of the main building. Bill and Diane were gone, perhaps to town. The lake spread out beyond the docks, the same steel gray color as the sky, completely still. The pine and aspen forests were quiet, left to the animals who readied their holes for hibernation. The cottages were vacant along the shorelines. It was all a massive ghost town.

I untied the boat, and startled a flock of birds with the sound of the engine. I hurried a little, since I had left the dog alone on the island for most of the night. He could go in and out of a dog door set into the back kitchen wall, had enough food, and there was nothing on the island that would bother him. Still, I felt guilty for the abandonment.

The breeze was icy. I wouldn't be able to make the trip back and forth for much longer. At last, Duck Island appeared when I cleared the trees and rocks that bordered the channel. I expected to see a dog-shape waiting on my dock, but the dog wasn't there. I felt a stab of alarm.

133

Tied off, I whistled for him as I hurried up the path. An answering bark came, and my worry blew away.

Chloe sat on the cottage roof, her chin rested on one raised knee. She appeared to be painting her toenails. The dog sat beside her, panting happily.

"How did you get the dog up there?" I asked.

She raised an eyebrow at me. "Is that a real question, or just one of those things you blurt out?"

I took a breath. "You're going to say that you didn't put the dog up there. He's there because he loves you. He can fly."

"Of course, he can fly."

She glanced at me, completely contained, and then went back to what she was doing. Her concentration stayed absolute, and her pursed mouth advised no interruption. I stood there, in front of the cabin, watching her. After a few minutes had passed, she thumbed stray hair behind her ear and looked down at me. I took it as an invitation to speak.

"You could do that inside, you know," I said. "Might be more comfortable than sitting on the roof."

She straightened a tanned leg along the roof edge and examined her work. "Like real people?" She wiggled her toes. "Is that what you mean?"

She pointed the tiny brush at me. "I can see the whole lake from here. Where should I sit? The kitchen table? Or do ladies do this in the bathroom?"

I raised my hands in surrender. "I wouldn't change you for anything. I absolutely promise."

"I'll never let you change me. I absolutely promise."

I laughed. She spun the polish cap back on, the ghost of a smile at the corners of her mouth.

"I do always see you the same way when you're here," I said. "Always in pink. Always wet from the lake."

"Do you want to see me some other way?" she asked, her tone darkening. "We can do that, if you like."

I remembered a skeleton lying in the shallows, a cup full of dirt, a dark shape sitting across from me in the dark, and I hurried my answer. "No. I just wondered."

"Maybe this is the way I really am. I may not be real, but maybe I'm the one thing you really see. That makes me as real than anything else in your life, doesn't it? What does that tell you?"

I had no answer. She stood on the roof and gazed at the lake. "Everything's going to change for you, one way or the other," she said. "You're going to have to accept things as different."

She put an arm around Kuba. "He's a lovely dog. He's also her dog, and you know it. I don't know her name, but you do— the woman who you were with. You're keeping him here out of spite."

"That isn't true at all," I said. "She gave the dog to me, as a present, almost a year ago."

"Saying you own something doesn't make it yours."

I felt a bewildering wash of grief. The words felt stupid, but I said them anyway. "He's all I have left. If he goes, I don't have anyone. I'll be alone."

"Needing someone isn't enough reason to hold them in a place they shouldn't be. He belongs with her. Better to be alone than to keep him here."

I looked at the dog. She was right, but losing him would mean losing the last of Nora.

"What's her name?" Chloe asked, curious. "The woman who loves this dog."

"Nora," I answered. "Her name is Nora."

"You should call Nora, then. Tell her you're bringing the dog home to her."

I nodded.

"Even if your ticket is no good, you'll have a broken heart," she said. "Sometimes, finding your heart's desire means you have to break your own."

-Fifteen-

The next time I went to town, I stopped at the coffee shop to get Nora's Toronto telephone number from Kate. She surprised me with another piece of information.

"I talked to Charlotte Hunter yesterday," she said. "We had a nice talk. I'd forgotten how much I like her."

"I had the general impression she was snooty," I said.

"She may have been—I'm not sure. Except for Christmas cards, I think I avoided her after Chloe drowned. It's hard. Time changes perspective. I may have convinced myself she didn't want any contact with me, since I felt awkward around her."

I liked Kate's honesty, with others and with herself. Thinking about it, I felt another of the surprising, out-of-nowhere pangs of missing Nora. She favored honesty, too.

"She's well," Kate went on. "I didn't ask if the doctor was still alive. No reason why not, they're only in their seventies. They've moved from the city back to Long Island. She's willing to talk to you about her daughter."

"What reason did you give her?" I asked, surprised.

"The truth. I told her you're writing a book, but I also told her that you believed her daughter's ghost visited you. People have seen Chloe for years. I'm sure she's heard the rumors. If you've seen her daughter, or think you have, I'm sure she'll wring every detail from you. Any parent would."

"It may hurt her," I said. "More than it will give her any comfort."

"Of course, it will hurt her. Tell her what you know, though, and ask her what you don't. Personally, I don't think the shadow of Chloe Hunter is up to any good, but if it helps either of you to talk about her, do it."

"I think I'll fly to New York, and do it in person."

"Charlotte and I both expected you would. She'll put you up for the night, if you need it. Just call her before you go."

"I have another reason, Kate. I want to get away for a day or two."

I told her that the visitations from Chloe Hunter's ghost had taken a different quality. I seemed to be landing somewhere else when she came around. Kate's expression grew serious, almost grim. She listened intently

"I'm not sure what you'd call it," I said. "A fugue? A trance? I certainly seem to be in my own body. It's just that—she takes me somewhere else."

"You need to see a doctor," she said. Her voice went flat. "You need to get checked."

"I thought you of all people might not think I was crazy," I protested. "You've seen things, too."

"I'm not saying anything about crazy," she said. "I'm saying use common sense. What you're describing could be the onset of schizophrenia. That isn't what I'm thinking, though. What if it's small strokes, or seizures? A tumor? You need to know."

I thought for a moment, and nodded. "You're right. I'll make myself a doctor's appointment as soon as I get back from New York."

I knew I wouldn't.

She nodded. "Good. We can concentrate better on what's going on here if we know there aren't any underlying causes."

I accepted the small paper bag she handed me. It held a coffee for the road, and something sweet. I pulled open the door, and the bell jingled over my head.

"Oh, Nick," she called after me. "I'll be glad if you're off of the island for a few days. It'll do you good, but remember the ice is coming. You might want to get your boat out of the water before you leave, just in case."

I waved to her, and went out. When I got into the jeep, I tried to put the key in the ignition, but the switch was in the wrong place. The street through the windshield was different. I saw palm trees. Ansett had disappeared, and I was somewhere else.

I sat at a stoplight, wishing the little Corvair had been available with the air conditioning option. It was an ugly summer. The sun beat down on the streets; hot, indifferent, and somehow alien. The palm trees were dusty and didn't even pretend shade. The big truck sitting in the lane next to mine revved its engine impatiently.

Elvis was in town, filming something or other, a beach flick, and the radio was full of him. I spun the ivory knob and watched the dial move across the band. I finally snapped it off.

When I looked up, the light still glared at me, red. A woman came out of the five-and-dime and crossed in front of my car, right to left, a small boy in tow. I could only see the top of his head. When he came fully into view, I saw that he was very young, perhaps three or four years old. He wore a little blue Dodgers baseball cap. A yellow helium balloon bobbed crazily behind him, its string tethered uncertainly to one small fist.

I watched, afraid he would lose his grasp and the balloon would sail away from him, up and up, gone for good. On cue, as they reached the truck, he did.

Freed, it rose a few feet, and then, defeated by the lack of breeze and the day's blistering hot air, dropped. It bounced gently on my hood. I hoped it wouldn't pop on the hot metal. I glanced left, and watched the woman and boy reach the far curb. She seemed unaware of the situation, but he looked back, dragging on her. I started to open my door, and hesitated.

The balloon caught a puff of air, rose from my hood, and then dropped to the pavement between the truck and me. The little boy stood on the curb, perfectly still. His dark eyes found mine and held them, imploring. I reached again for the chrome door handle. Another tiny breeze picked up the yellow globe and seemed to play with it for a moment before spinning it under the front of the truck.

"Who's going to be the hero?" I wondered.

My heart broke a little.

"Not worth it, kid," I said under my breath. "There'll be other days, other balloons."

I settled back in my seat. The light turned green, and my foot moved to step on the gas. The little boy watched me. He waited all alone. His mother had vanished. I stared at him in disbelief, and felt the blood drain from my face. The car stalled. I stared at the boy, and I saw myself.

It was me. I stood there, and I was little.

The truck roared and lurched forward. When it had gone, a young woman wearing a green-and-white flowered sarong stood on the corner, with three-year-old me. She gave an exaggerated bow, presented his balloon to him, and bent to tie the string around his wrist. She was improbably lovely, her grace unmistakable. It was Chloe.

A horn honked behind me. She spoke to the boy, straightened, and pointed at me. Her smile was brilliant. The two of them waved to me as I moved off. I tried to find them in my rear-view mirror, but I only saw the impatient driver crowding my back bumper, and the streets of Ansett.

Back on the island, I called Toronto before I changed my mind. The dog sat beside me on the dock. I couldn't look at him. Nora answered on the fourth ring. She had been sleeping. I could hear it in her voice.

"I'm bringing Kuba down to you," I said. "He belongs with you. I was wrong to keep him."

"You're staying the winter on the island, aren't you?"

We sat there, in silence.

"I haven't decided," I finally said.

"You have decided. You're calling me from the dock, because there's almost no phone reception, right? A million things could happen, and you couldn't even call for help. You know that."

"Nothing's going to happen."

Behind me, in the woods, I heard a twig break, and then the tiny sound of a bell. Nora's voice was very, very soft.

"You're killing yourself. Whether you know it or not, you're killing yourself."

I had no answer. I gripped my cell phone, tightly.

"Bring me the dog, then," she said. "You're going to do what you want."

139

She disconnected without saying good-bye. I walked up the path to the cabin in the dark. In the kitchen, I checked the dog's water dish, and then went back to the bedroom. I undressed without turning on any lights. I was exhausted.

The dog settled himself on the end of the bed with a sigh. He didn't stir again. As my eyes adjusted to the dark, I stared up at the exposed wooden beams of the ceiling. The woodstove popped once, in the next room. Warm and drowsy, I had nearly drifted off when I heard Chloe's voice, floating somewhere above me.

"Close your eyes and kiss me," she said. "Kiss me the way you used to."

Unbidden, I remembered Nora's face, and felt a flash of guilt, a stab of faithlessness.

"You aren't unfaithful," Chloe whispered. "The opposite— you're faithful again."

I shut my eyes and breathed in her fragrance. I heard running water and saw floating orchids. I found her mouth, tasted ginger and lime, and was lost.

I slept, and while I slept, the snow came to stay.

The flakes spun out of the black sky, huge and soft. Twirling and dancing, they clutched at pine branches on their way down, a silent invasion that covered and changed everything. They were nearly invisible in the dark, but on the lake there was enough refracted light to catch them as they fell. Tumbling through the air, falling, they were a legion of white ghosts who relived their own deaths when they hit the water.

Inside the cabin, the wood stove creaked and pinged with heat. I stirred restlessly, but I didn't wake up. I pushed my pillow onto the floor, and dreamed in black-and-white about a Train that hissed and steamed, standing in an empty station. A girl in a long coat stood on the platform, waiting for me. Her eyes were so dark they were nearly black. She wanted me to hurry, hurry, hurry, because the ice was coming.

The Train was leaving and we had to get aboard. A Conductor stood on the step of a carriage. He waved to me urgently, and I knew something terrible was chasing me. It was too late, but it didn't much matter. It had been too late for years, so I ran for the Train.

"Cumin, Turmeric, Cayenne, Blueberry . . ." I murmured, in my sleep. "A dash of each, and all together."

The dog padded from room to room, uneasily. His nails clicked differently as he crossed from one floor surface to the next. He wandered through the kitchen, up the hall, and back again. Then he was still. He sat for a long time at the front door, listening.

Outside, the sound of a tiny bell came up the steps, onto the veranda, and stopped. The knob turned slowly to the right, and then to the left, but the door didn't open. There was no need, because I was already gone.

My journey with Chloe had begun.

-Sixteen-

"Ever tried this stuff?"

The man wore a snap-brim fedora, yellow plaid with a gold band. He stood in front of me and held up a shallow paper cup, filled with something raspberry-colored. I leaned back against the tiled tunnel wall, propped on one heel, staring at him.

"Frozen yoga," he said. "You should try it sometime, pally."

"Who are you?" I asked.

He took a scoop with a tiny wooden paddle and popped the whole thing in his mouth. He chewed up the little spoon and spit it out. It landed at my feet. He gave me a huge smile.

"Some people call me the Grinning Man," he said. "You should call me your worst nightmare. I've been waiting a while for you—and now that the splat wants to be a hero, I'm her worst nightmare, too. Two for the price of one, and she's a tastier prize than you are, bub. Much tastier, and I'm sorry if hearing that hurts your feelings. She's a suicide, and that makes her prime."

"You shouldn't eat that," I said. "It turns your lips all purple. Doesn't go with the hat, at all."

The smile drained from his face, and he stared at me, his jaw slack. "You're a wise guy, and I don't like you, pally." His breath whistled in and out. "Guys like you have no respect, and that's why there's guys like me—to get you in line. I'll make you a deal, though—give her up, and I might let you go."

"No deals," I said.

"You have no idea what you're getting into, bub. No idea at all."

I didn't answer, and he turned suddenly and hurled his dessert up the tunnel. It hit the floor, rolled up against the wall and stopped. He faced me, cheeks reddening.

"Where's the splat?" he hissed. "You better wise up, but fast, pally. But fast."

"You sound like a tea kettle, screaming that way," I said. "Do me a kindness and scram, would you? You make me nervous."

"Give her up, wise guy," he snarled. "I'll take her, and let you go—but I'm losing patience with you."

"Go ahead and lose it," I said. "She's my heart's desire, and I'm not giving her up."

"You're going to get eaten, pally," he said. "I'm getting good and hungry. Wait and see."

He tightened the belt of his trench coat, glared once more at me and stormed up the hall. As he passed the fallen yogurt cup, he lashed out, launching a kick at it. He missed, and his polished shoe smacked the wall, spider-webbing cracks in the heavy tile. I felt the vibration in my back, even from where I stood.

The bathroom door behind me opened, and Chloe came out.

"Everything okay?" she asked.

I glanced up the empty tunnel. The paper cup started to bleed, a small violet pool spreading beneath it.

I shrugged. "We're good."

We walked down the steps from the main concourse into Union Station. I stopped halfway down, and stared. My gaze moved upwards to the glass-paned roof, high over our heads. Arch after arch, intricate, delicate and beautiful, supported by rows of tall, slender iron columns. A huge clock hung suspended, white-faced and Roman-numeraled. Chloe checked her wristwatch against it.

"This is . . .?"

"I don't know when," she said. "Sometimes, when we're about to move, it's hard to say for sure. We're a little in between. We'll get to New York for 1951, if we're on time."

"Do we have to buy a ticket?" I asked. "I don't even have a wallet. Just this expired ticket stub, and I think it's a different railway, anyway. The Pacific Railroad."

"No, no wallet, no career, no credentials. Someone else is living in your house, and your car is already sold. Check your pockets, though. You have the sound of someone's laugh that always made you laugh, too, and a spoonful of frosting from a birthday cake. You have a bird's nest you found once with tiny, perfect eggs in it. That's enough for your ticket, except you don't need one. You bought yours a long time ago."

Below us, the tracks and empty platforms ran in parallel lines, with not a soul in sight. A single Train waited on platform number eleven, the massive black locomotive and tender tethered to seven passenger carriages. The rearmost one had a gondola roof. The cars were dark blue, painted with figures of the moon, stars, and the sun.

"Oh, and you have the taste of your first kiss. Remember how surprised you were?"

I looked at her, curious, but her dark eyes held the faraway, so I didn't say anything.

"Coming here is a kiss," she said. "At first, you think, is that all? Is this what all the fuss was about? And then, it opens for you, and you know that you can fly."

We reached the bottom of the steps, and made our way down the line of railway cars. Blue steel skins, rivets, glass, and silver wheels rested on the oily tracks. The huge engine seemed to acknowledge our approach with an exhalation of steam. Everything gleamed in the diffuse light.

"No one brings a wallet here." She smiled. "Everyone has to buy a ticket, sooner or later. Absolutely everyone."

She paused for a moment, and counted the cars. "Eight," she breathed. "Including the engine. What a relief."

"Do we have luggage?" I asked.

"It's already on board," she said, smiling. "We've been here before, you and I."

About halfway up, a door slid open, and an old man swung himself down. He wore a blue cap, and a Conductor's suit with gold-colored buttons.

"Ginger!" Chloe called, and ran to meet him.

His face split in a smile, and he allowed her to lead him by the hand over to where I waited. He looked me up and down. I put my ticket into his outstretched hand.

"I've been thinking about things," he said, gazing down at it. "This is expired, and expired is expired. I can't let you do this, Miss Chloe."

"You said just bring his ticket, expired or not!" Chloe exclaimed, close to tears. "We did everything you said!"

"I can't let you do this to yourself," he repeated. "I've grown to love you, Miss Chloe, so the answer is 'no'. He can't board."

"Then I'll stay here," she said. "I won't go back without him."

"You can't stay here. You'll perish. You'll be caught, eaten—or you'll go insane. You'll end up hanging around the basement of some old house, banging the pipes. You'll make pictures fall off walls, and rattle silverware in drawers, scaring people. You'll never have a chance to reach your heart's desire."

"What if he's my heart's desire?"

She crossed her arms, and they stared at each other. Neither of them paid me any attention. Chloe stood a little bit taller than he did.

"He was supposed to be on this Train, Ginger," she said. "You know that as well as I do. He has a ticket that he never used."

"He was supposed to be on this train about thirty years ago, and never showed up," he said. "Supposed to be, was, and will be, are all different things. He has no business with Sanctuary now. It isn't natural, and it's against the Rules."

Chloe grew increasingly frustrated. It wasn't a thing I had seen before.

"He has no business where he *is*, either, Ginger! He isn't natural in the first place! How can he choose, if he doesn't ride the Train? How can he be where he's supposed to be, if he doesn't ride, and remember? Answer me!"

Ginger thought about it silently, for a long time. Finally, he looked at me. "All right," he sighed. "Once in a while, the Rules don't mind being broken. Cross your fingers and cross your heart this is one of those times. All aboard. First stop is here—but 1949."

145

I found myself feeling more angry than grateful.

"I have a question," I said. "Seeing as you're in charge."

"I'm a Train Conductor. I take tickets. I'm here to help you with your bags, and turn down your berth at night. If you need a pair of pants pressed, I'll take care of it. I'm not in charge of anything."

He glanced at Chloe. She nodded for him to go ahead.

"If you have a question, I'll do my best with it."

"Why isn't the Low Gang against the Rules?" I asked. "The Grinning Man—we're being chased by a group of psychopaths who want to eat us. Why isn't that against the Rules?"

"They aren't really called psychopaths anymore," Chloe offered, helpfully. "They call them sociopaths, now. They're just souls who have trouble getting along with others, mostly."

She put the back of a white-gloved hand to her mouth, and coughed daintily to cover her laughter. I glared at her, fiercely, and struggled not to laugh, too. I turned back to the porter.

"Why are horrors like that allowed? If there are Rules, then why don't they protect people from monsters?"

He swung onto the metal steps, looked up the length of the Train, and blew a single note on a small silver whistle.

"People allow monsters," he said. "They allow horror every day. They don't want protection. People never forget to feed their monsters, keep them safe and sound, and tuck them in at night."

He regarded at me bleakly. Up the platform, the locomotive released a huge cloud of steam, and the air began to vibrate.

"Get on board, then." He put a hand out to help Chloe. "All aboard."

~ * ~

I slept late. The sun through the bedroom window caught my eyes and woke me up. I heard the dog barking outside. Behind his noise, I heard the sound of a marine engine. I cast my eyes around the room. I saw raw pine paneling, a throw rug, my

146

mismatched furniture. There was no curtain on the window. One of these days I would hang one, so I could sleep late more often.

The boat on the lake sounded close. It already sounded strange. In the summer, the boat traffic passing the island was unceasing, but not at this time of year. I hadn't heard an outboard in two weeks. I figured it might be Bill, checking on one of the summer cottages at this end of the lake.

Then it occurred to me that if there had been a fire or break-in reported, it might be the police launch on its way to check. The cabins on the south shore were accessible by the road, but those on the north shore could only be reached by water.

If it were John Park, or Bill, they would likely stop by on the way back to the marina. Either of them would expect coffee. I still had time to sleep for a few minutes before they landed. I was usually an early riser, and didn't know why I felt so exhausted this morning. I closed my eyes again.

~*~

Lavender light turned purple. The beach was deserted. Soft waves moved in, washed the wet sand, and then left foam behind. There were drums, far off, and clapping hands. I didn't know where the sounds were coming from.

"Why are you hurting so badly?" she asked. "You believe in 'happily ever after', don't you?"

She sat, cross-legged, on a wall, braiding pastel night flowers into her hair. Her hands were strong and sure. I couldn't answer, and she didn't speak again until she was done.

"I do," she said. "I believe."

I could barely see her in the dusk. Down the beach, the first of the burning torches appeared and began to make their way toward us, a parade.

"I spent my last 'happily ever after' a while ago," I said. "I'm all out, none left. Not in this lifetime."

"You spent it on something, right? You just have to remember what you bought—and lost." She handed me the last flower.

I lifted it to my face. Its perfume was as pale and sweet as the coming night.

"We'll find it," she said.

"I believe in you," I said.

"Good, because I believe in you." She smiled. "Come with me. It's almost time to stop being sad."

~ * ~

"Gosh, you scared me," Bill said, peering in the door of my room. "You're still in bed? You sick?"

"No. Didn't sleep last night. Go make coffee, and I'll be out in a minute."

"You always sleep with your jacket and shoes on? Muddy blankets? You haven't been drinking, have you?"

I gaped at my feet, still clad in white running shoes. They were covered with dirt. Dead grass. "No. No drinking," I said.

No grass grew on the island. The loamy ground was mostly covered in pine needles. The few parts not forest-shaded were carpeted in low bushes and blueberry plants, but no grass. There had been grass in my dreams, though.

"I'll get the coffee," he said, and turned away.

I dragged myself awake and through a fast shower. When I came out, Bill was sitting at the kitchen table, both hands wrapped around a mug of coffee. He stood up, went to the counter and poured a cup for me.

"What are you doing at this end of the lake?" I asked.

"Usual. Hansens—the log place down by the falls, talked themselves into believing they left the propane connected. Asked me to check."

"Did they?"

"No. Everything was buttoned up nice. They do this every year. They'll call me a month from now, worried about

148

something else. There won't be a way to get here in a month except by snowmobile across the ice, and I'm not an idiot. I'll just tell them it's all fine, when the time comes."

"Better you than me," I said, and sipped my coffee. "Didn't think you had a boat in the water."

"I don't. I keep the aluminum skiff on the trailer, for just in case. I won't risk it much longer. Can't launch it without getting a little bit wet, and the water's getting too cold to stand, at my age."

I nodded. "At anyone's age. The spray numbs me every time I cross."

"Heard from Nora last night," he said, sitting down. "She phoned Diane. I talked to her for a minute, too. Good to hear her."

"How is she?"

He handed me the cup, eyebrows raised. "How is she? She said you talked to her right before she called us. You're the reason she called. You're taking the dog down to Toronto to live?"

"She gave me this dog, Bill, but there was always more of a bond between the two of them. They miss each other. I want to give him back, that's all."

I had a sudden thought. "It's not a problem, with the baby coming, is it?"

The baby. It hurt, saying it.

"She would have said so." He smiled. "She has a big heart, Nora does. Room for more than one thing. She's fine with the dog."

"That's good. I didn't even think of that."

"You're not thinking of a lot of things, right now. No matter what, there are people who love you, and want you safe."

"I appreciate that. I think Nora's overreacting. Every year I think about staying over. This is my house, my home. You wouldn't want to leave your place for three months every year, either."

"I wouldn't live on an island. This was never intended as anything but a summer place—and a darned inconvenient one."

"Worst case, I'm just stuck here during the freeze and the thaw. When the ice is in, I can walk across. I'll leave the jeep at the boat launch down from Nora's house. It's a mile, not much more. It'll be good exercise. I can come to town every day if I want to."

He looked troubled. "I want you to listen to me, but good," he said. "The sound right off this island is the worst place on the lake for ice. You'll never see ice fishermen out there, or snowmobiles crossing. Not if they're from around here. You can't trust the ice."

"Why not?"

"The channel between Duck and Long Duck empties into the sound, and the currents are still strong for a half-mile or so. Also, you've got the Hole off the western end of your island. Some people say it's like a giant drain, and it makes weird flows that come and go."

"What should I do? I'm going to have to cross, at some point."

"Go east off your dock, then turn south to shore. Even a quarter-mile should be enough. You just have to get past the reach of the channel current. Remember that. I don't want to get back from Florida and hear you fell through the ice while I was gone."

I thought of the water, dark, black and freezing, and shuddered. "I'm a little afraid of deep water at the best of times," I said. "I won't forget."

I walked him to the dock. I saw him off with a promise to come and check a troublesome outboard, later that day. I headed back to my kitchen for more coffee.

I was still exhausted. I went out onto the long covered front veranda, and crunched through the drift of dead leaves that covered it. I sat in one of the canvas chairs, sipped at my cup and set it down beside me. The dog looked at me incuriously, and then lowered himself to the boards with a sigh.

The breeze from the lake gusted chilly, but not cold. The snow in front of the cabin made me think of Christmas. I supposed I would be spending this Christmas alone. I had done it, often, so it wasn't something new, but I missed Nora and the unseen baby, all the same. I closed my eyes.

-Seventeen-

Chloe sat cross-legged. *She* had a large book opened in her lap, and she consulted it carefully. She held a yellow pencil in her front teeth.

"*The Giant Silver Book of Elves and Fairies?*" I asked.

She nodded, without losing her place. "This is Toronto." She ran a finger down the page. "We have to get to New York City. I'm hunting for the Treasure that lets the Train pass, so we can go to New York."

"We have to go to 1949?"

She looked up at me. "Time is a map," she said. "The when and the where go together."

"I hope we don't get lost."

She circled something on the page, and nodded to herself. "This is going to be easy," she said. "The Treasure is a bear. We already have the teddy bear. We just have to find Santa."

"It feels kind of warm for Christmas, doesn't it? It snows here in the winter."

"This thing is tricky." She checked her watch. "It seems to be 1980, or thereabouts, and we need 1949. It reads 1968 when I point it south, and 1952 east. The years go up, into the 1990s northwest, so we're heading south or east."

She got to her feet, and began to move off.

"It works like a compass?" I asked. "For time?"

She shrugged. "I suppose so. I've never used a compass. We'll have to split up. I'll go south. If you see any sign of Santa, send up a flare."

Before I could think of any questions to ask, she had turned the next corner and disappeared. I started walking by myself. It was funny. She'd been gone for less than a minute, and I missed her already.

I was hungry, in a vague sort of way, but there wasn't much I could do about it. The city slept, everyone but me. The all-night diners were closed, the theaters were let out, dark, and any would-be rebels were trapped in taxis or police cars. Bulbs still flashed on a discount emporium called "Honest Ed's". It pretended to be open, but it wasn't.

The garbage trucks were biding their time, headlights off, waiting for the last of us to leave so they could crawl out and begin to feed.

I headed away from the colored light still reflected in the wet pavement, and walked through an underpass. A drip-drip of water came from somewhere over my head, and I listened to my footsteps and wished that I was anywhere else. A '49 Imperial idled by the curb, wheezing like it was infected. I didn't look at it as I walked by.

A man stepped from the shadows ahead, blocking the sidewalk. I knew he would be trouble.

"Whereya going, pal? Lose a button or something?"

I stopped a few feet from him. He pulled the brim of his hat down, got out a package of Camels, and offered me a cigarette. I shook my head.

"Suit yourself," he said.

A bunch of the Low Gang materialized from the gloom, identical in dark fedoras and dusters. They emerged from under parked cars, the shadows between buildings, and from sewer grates and manholes. They formed a rough circle around us, but kept their distance and said nothing.

The Grinning Man lit a smoke, popped it into his mouth, and chewed thoughtfully before he spoke again, a question. "Who are you?"

"I'll ask you first," I said. "Who are you?"

"A friend," he said, and smirked. "Here to give you some advice, for free."

"I don't need it," I said.

"Oh—you need it, all right."

He finished chewing the cigarette, swallowed it, and then blew a perfect smoke ring.

"First of all, 'happily ever after' is a lie. Second, the Turtle is dead. He's been an empty shell at the bottom of the universe for years. He doesn't care about you. Third, give up the dame."

"I have to be somewhere. Scram, would you?"

"You're fishing for something, I can tell . . . but you're the kind of chump what hopes the fish just swims up on shore and dies. If wishes was fishes—fish in one hand and wish in the other—and see which hand fills up first, I always say."

His grin widened. His teeth were yellow and very, very strong-looking. A small dark fleck marked one of his incisors. He took a deep, shuddering breath, opened his mouth huge, and screamed. "DO . . . YOU . . . HEAR . . . ME?"

"I hear you. Anything else?"

He collected himself, with difficulty, and slanted a sidelong look my way.

"Yes, matter of fact. Lose the company you're keeping. She's a splat, whether she knows it yet, or not." He turned up the collar of his trench coat, and adjusted his hat brim lower. His eyes glittered, and his voice dropped. "Save yourself, bub," he hissed. "She belongs to me, forever and always. When she killed herself, we got engaged, so to speak." He burst out laughing. The smell of cigarette smoke washed over me, with a nasty odor underneath it, something viral and meaty and rotten.

"She's never belonged to you," I said. "Oh, and I don't mind trouble. I've never really known better, or different. I was born for this, so to speak."

He shook his head, regarding me sadly. "We'll see. Catchya later, pally. Keep in tune."

With a swirl of his coat, he vanished.

He left me standing alone in the cold. A late, last streetcar paused, but it wasn't going anywhere that I was, so I let it go. I listened to the metal moan of its wheels, all the way down the empty boulevard. I knew where I was, but I didn't know when. I had no idea what to do.

An old Volkswagen approached the intersection, hunting, and darted toward me. One headlight blinked out over a bump, like a wink. It stopped in front of me with a long squeal of brakes. Under the streetlights, its paint appeared light blue or gray, with one mismatched fender. The driver's window lowered as it came abreast.

"Get in," Chloe said. "I found him."

I did. The little car was moving again before I could close the door. The engine rattled and roared as she shifted gears. It smelled good inside, like clean water and oranges.

"I still have things to do, but it's too cold for you to stand outside. I'll drop you at the subway."

"Why can't I go with you?" I asked.

She shook her head, once, brushing off my question. "I like this car," she said. "I'd hang around here a while, if I could drive this."

The wheels suddenly caught in the streetcar ruts, and we slid on the rails for what seemed like a hundred feet before she jerked us back onto pavement again. Unperturbed, she took the next right, fast. We rocketed through empty streets. Lights flashed by, and then we plunged into darkness again.

"I met the bad guy in this story," I said.

"How'd it go?"

"Do you know about him?"

"I was warned," she said. "We're operating a little bit outside of what's usual, and that makes us vulnerable. Me, anyway. His name is the Grinning Man, and he has a bunch of henchmen who do a lot of his dirty work for him."

"What can we do about him?"

"I'm not sure. Stay out of his way, mostly. He's a coward, and would rather sneak than confront. Once we reach the Port of Los Angeles, and put out to sea, we'll lose him. He won't try an ocean crossing. He hates water."

"We're going clear across the country?" I asked.

She nodded, and wheeled the little car hard onto a wide boulevard. When leaned into the turn, her shoulder pressed warm against mine. She glanced over at me.

"And further. You're still in?"

I shrugged. "After the 'once upon a time' part, there aren't options, are there?"

Brief, passing neon caught her smile, but she didn't look away from the road.

"If you think there's a shot at happily ever after," she said, "then no, there are no options."

"So, I'm in until you tell me not to be. Deal?"

She laughed a little, thinking about it, and wheeled the car hard into another left turn.

"Deal," she said.

-Eighteen-

I made sure everything was turned off in the cabin, and loaded the boat long before sunrise. The air snapped with cold, and turned the crossing to the marina into a dozen miles of misery. The water was dead calm, however, and I got there quickly. In the parking lot, I tossed my luggage in the back of my jeep, loaded the dog, and started the engine.

Three hours later, the sun came up. By then, the empty single-lane gravel road had turned into a major freeway flowing south into the city of Toronto. The flood of cars and trucks carried me into the heart of the city. I got off at Yonge Street and headed south. I turned right, onto Castlefield. It was a residential street crowded with door fronts, a mix of single homes and apartments.

I found a space, and squeezed the jeep against the curb. Kuba had never worn a collar and leash during his time with me, and we were awkward in the routine. I felt a strong sense of regret. I was taking my only companion away from the freedom of the island, and into the restrictions of the city. I wanted to change my mind, but it was too late for it. At last, I got him out, and gazed around me. The neighborhood didn't appear expensive, but I knew that it was.

Nora answered the door of the sand-colored townhouse. It looked nearly new. There had been pre-war row housing on this block the last time I had driven along the street. She stood in the door, regarding me silently. After a long moment, she turned her attention to the dog.

Even after only a couple of weeks away, she looked different. Her hair was pulled back, and she wore exercise clothes that were deliberate and coordinated. Her visible pregnancy was somehow fashionable. Her eyes were the same, though, when she glanced up from the dog.

"You've been feeding him, anyway," she said. "He seems okay."

I felt a flash of irritation. "Of course, I've been feeding him."

"Bob Bickford"

"Have you been feeding yourself? You've lost weight, and you don't look like you've been sleeping much. You look like crap."

She led me inside. The interior was light and airy, larger than I would have expected. The furnishing was quiet, and displayed Nora's taste. A small fenced area with a deck lay beyond glass doors at the rear. I saw brown grass and a birdbath. I sat down, and after she had given me a cup of coffee, Nora sat in the chair across from me. It appeared she had gotten used to sitting in that chair, and it gave me a small ache in my chest.

"I have something to say," she said. "I loved you for a long time, and I still love you, even if it isn't enough. Will you listen and do something for me, with no questions asked?"

I thought for a moment before I answered. With Nora, there was only 'yes' or 'no'.

"Yes," I said.

"A while back, when Esteban and I were having problems, we went to see someone," she said. "I still go to see her now, once in a while, by myself. She's very wonderful."

I felt myself shrinking inside. Things were in the open.

"Her name is Mary Ellen," she said, as though it explained everything. "She can help you. I made you an appointment."

"When?" I asked. My voice sounded invisible. "I just came to drop off the dog. I have to get back."

She glanced at her watch. "In just a little more than an hour. I told her it was an emergency. She isn't far from here. It will be faster if you take the subway."

I stood up, without protesting. I usually pushed back at Nora's bossy streak, but right now it was a relief to have someone else take charge.

"Come back when you're done," she said. "I'll drive you to the airport."

~ * ~

158

Mary Ellen Katz kept her office in part of an old house, a short walk from the Davisville subway station. I got there a few minutes before the time, and sat in her waiting room. There were magazines on the table, perfectly arranged in rows, with their margins lined up. I started to pick one up, and thought better of it.

The door opened, and she stuck her head in. "You're allowed to read them," she said, smiling as though she knew my thoughts. "One of my regulars does the arranging. They're even in alphabetical order, but not many people notice that."

She was different than what I expected. I didn't know what I had imagined, but she looked as if she ought to be doing something more elegant than this. She had a good smile.

Her office was very clean, with shelves of books and a couple of deep armchairs. She motioned me to a chair. She went and poured water into a Styrofoam cup from a cooler in the corner, and handed it to me. I set it carefully on the table in front of me. I wasn't thirsty, but it seemed good to have it there, just in case.

"I'm not even sure why I'm here," I said. "I didn't make the appointment."

"I'm not sure if it matters who made the appointment," she said. "It might matter that you kept it. Should we talk about why you came?"

It got easy once I started, and I talked for a long time. I told her about seeing a ghost on my island, and about my idea that I should do research, that it was a chance for a book. I told her about Nora and me, even though I figured she already knew about it since she saw Nora in this office, too. I told her that I had vivid dreams about the ghost of Chloe Hunter.

"At least, I thought they were dreams," I said. "I'm not so sure, any more. It's like I just go away, and I'm not sure how long I'm gone. Sometimes I come out of it, and just a few seconds have passed. Other times, I wake up somewhere else, hours later, with no idea how I got there. Hours are missing."

She didn't interrupt, and she didn't take notes. She just sat very quietly and listened. Her eyes didn't leave my face. I thought she must be very good at what she does.

"It's a good thing to rule out physical cause," she said. "Have you seen your doctor recently?"

"I'm perfectly healthy. I haven't needed to."

"Tell me about growing up. Were there any medical problems, any significant traumas?"

She stayed very contained, watching me.

"I had an accident when I was a teenager," I said. "I drowned, and then I was in a coma for three months. When I woke up, things were strange for a while. I lost a lot of my memory, mainly of the whole year before it happened."

"The memories never came back?"

"No, but other ones did." I struggled to explain. "I can remember the cake at my birthday party, the year I turned two. I remember my grandfather's voice, and the smell of his aftershave. He died when I was a baby. You aren't supposed to be able to remember such an early age, but I do. The memories are so real I can touch them."

"The visits might also be a manifestation of something else," she said. "Something in your own mind."

"A psychiatric condition?"

She steepled her fingers under her chin, and gave a tiny nod. "If you like," she said. "Yes."

"Schizophrenia," I said.

"I think we should avoid putting words to things right now," she said. "A consult would be a good next step, and I can arrange that if you'd like."

I felt a huge sense of relief, having the word out of my head and into the room.

"I drank a little too much when I was younger," I said. "It caused me some problems. I haven't had a drink in years, and I'm not drinking now."

She nodded. "The third possibility," she said, "is that these are genuine psychic manifestations."

I was surprised. "You people believe in that kind of thing?"

"Why not?" she asked. "It isn't a matter of believing or disbelieving anything, at least to start with. It's a matter of helping you to find the truth, and since we don't know what the root cause is, it would be foolish to dismiss anything at this point, wouldn't it?"

"There's a lot we don't know," I said. "After almost an hour of talking, we don't know anything at all."

Her smile was unoffended, and nearly serene. "That's how it works, more often than not. Would you like to start with a referral?"

"I have to fly to New York in a few hours," I said. "Can I think about it while I'm there and call you? I'll be back here in a day or two."

"Of course."

The session ended. I drank my water, surprised at how thirsty I was.

"If we could take these visits away," she said. "If there was a prescription you could take that would make the visits from this girl stop, would you take it?"

She didn't seem to be in a hurry, and didn't look anywhere but at me.

"A pill, you mean?"

"A pill, therapy, a magic wand . . ." She waved the details away. "Were it possible, would you want this girl Chloe to go away and leave you alone?"

I thought about it. There was no point in coming here and being dishonest. Even so, my own words shocked me.

"No," I said. "I'm in love with her."

She spread her hands, in a graceful *imagine that!* gesture.

"You see?" she asked. "We do know something, after all."

~ * ~

The subway train rushed into Davisville station, a silver snake preceded by a blast of warm air that smelled of electrical transformers. I got on for the short ride north to Nora's. I was exhausted by the session, and I still had to get to the airport to fly to New York. The train was only half full, and I had no trouble finding a hard vinyl bench to myself. In the dark tunnel, lights flashed past in rhythm, and I leaned my head back on the steel seat frame and closed my eyes. When I opened them again, the car was empty and Chloe sat beside me.

"This is nice," I said.

I looked around at the accommodations on the antique Pullman car. The carriage was far larger than I would have guessed. The dark paneling on the walls appeared to be real wood, and rich drapes hung on the windows. Vases were filled with sprays of fresh flowers; peach carnations and yellow roses were arranged with some sort of white blossoms I couldn't identify.

"Hibiscus," Chloe said, reading my mind.

She was sitting on a berth, focused intently on the book in her lap. She turned a page, and then another.

"I thought hibiscus were red."

She glanced up at the flower arrangement. "No," she said absently. "Those are white."

"I see that," I said. "So they are."

She went back to her reading, and I went to the window. It was dark outside, and I watched the illuminations of buildings pass, more and more infrequently as we moved south out of the city. From time to time, the lights at a crossing flashed back and forth and bathed the ceiling in red glow. After a while, she closed her book.

"Do you think you're crazy?" she asked. "Is that what you think this is? Is that why you went to see the therapist?"

"I'm a little worried," I said. "Wouldn't you be?"

"I don't worry. I just quit."

I looked at her, surprised. "You quit?"

"Quit—as in 'surrender', not as in 'give up'," she said. "There's a big difference."

The Train rumbled deeply, over a series of switches. It sounded like thunder. Chloe held my eye, and I caught the fragrance of hibiscus, and then more. I smelled an approaching storm, the scents of oranges and clean salt water, the perfume of island air. It all washed over my face, and I closed my eyes.

"The sooner you learn to surrender," she said, "The sooner you'll be able to sleep. Trust me."

"I do trust you. More and more."

"Good. You'll need it. I think we have a lot of trouble waiting for us in New York . . . and some fun, too."

She stood up, stepped out of her sandals, and pulled the white shift over her head. She draped it over the back of a chair and turned to face me. I couldn't breathe.

"Surrender," she said.

~ * ~

Esteban came into the living room, took my hand, and shook it.

"Good to see you, Nick," he said. "Really good. You look great."

Nora tried, and failed, to avoid my eye. She stood up, and led the dog toward the glass doors at the back of the living room.

"Let's go out to your yard, big guy." She stopped, and inclined her head toward me. "Are you staying for dinner?"

"I can't, thanks. I ordered an airport cab. No need for you to get in a car at rush hour."

"I wouldn't have minded."

She still didn't ask me where I was going.

"You got time for a short walk before you go?" Esteban asked. "I want your opinion about something."

I glanced at Nora. Her eyes were expressionless. After a moment she gave me a small goodbye wave, and took the dog out into the yard. Esteban got his jacket, and locked the front door behind us. I followed him to the sidewalk.

"They're talking about a white Christmas," he said. "Not likely. We always had them when I was a kid, but it's getting warmer now. You have snow on the lake?"

"Some, yes."

At the corner, he stopped, unfolded his wallet and pulled out a slender joint. He looked at me, warily. I kept walking. He lit it, and hurried to catch up to me. I waved off his offer to share.

"You won't mention it to Nora, will you?" he asked, visibly embarrassed. "There's been so much stress, lately. This is all I do, and just once in a while."

"You're none of my business," I answered shortly. "Nora's none of my business, either."

He seemed surprised. "I hoped you saw us as—friends," he said. "We've..."

"Skip it," I said. I regretted the harshness of my tone, but not much. "What do you need? Just say it."

"I want you to take the money to Sonny Risa. I want you to make him take it, before his stupid deadline. I want you to make him see some sense."

I had offered to do exactly that, but I had made the offer to Nora, not him. He took a hit from his smoke, as if bracing himself, and threw the end of it into the gutter. I didn't feel like helping him.

"I don't have anything to do with this guy," I said. "Why would he talk to me?"

At the bottom of the hill, we turned into Eglinton Park. Barren playing fields were bordered by lightly treed hills. It was a nice park to find in the middle of a big city. Two big dogs romped with a small one, while the owners stood together and chatted, in the slightly awkward way people thrown together by circumstance show.

"You've dealt with rough stuff like this before," he said. "I haven't. He'll listen to you."

"More to the point, Esteban, why would I want to get involved in your mess?"

"I figured you'd help, because of Nora and the baby."

"What do they have to do with your problem?"

We turned onto a running track bordering the perimeter of the park. He didn't answer right away, and I glanced over at him. His expression became closed, almost sly.

"It could be your baby, you know," he said. "She won't say for sure."

I had a wild impulse to hit him. The entire time I had been with Nora, he had been hovering in the background, a specter I could never compete with. In the end, he had swept in, smug and undeserving, and taken everything I hoped for. I forced my hands into my pockets and kept walking.

"Get to the point," I said.

"He may try to get to them if he can't get to me," he said. "He sent me a Christmas card. It scared the hell out of me, if you want to know the truth."

Our feet crunched the red gravel. The afternoon turned colder, and I tried not to shiver inside my light jacket. The nearly empty park, with its echo of barking dogs, brown grass and bare trees, began to feel ominous.

"Why? Was there something in it?"

"No. It was addressed to 'the worst daddy in the whole world'. It was like a kid's Christmas card, a cartoon." He paused, seeming to have trouble with the words, and then plunged ahead. "The printed message in the card was all scribbled out so hard that the pen made holes in it. He wrote, 'Next Christmas you'll be all alone'. Then he signed it. It was perfectly legible, his signature. He didn't give a rat's ass."

"Give it to me when we get back. I'll take it to a cop I know, when I get back from New York."

I thought that maybe John Park could do something with evidence in writing.

"I don't have it," he said. "Nora put it in the garbage can on the curb. She got really upset when she saw it. She didn't even want it in the house."

"You're idiots." I shook my head. "You and her, both. Idiots."

165

I was suddenly exhausted. My whole body ached.

"She stood at the sink and washed her hands for ten minutes when she came back inside," he said. "I started to worry she had gone crazy."

The group on the grass was leaving more or less together, headed for the exit on the far side. The dogs followed, still playing. Esteban and I walked in silence, watching them. When he finally spoke, his voice sounded forlorn, childlike.

"I'm surprised you'd call her an idiot," he said. "She talks about you like you walk on water. Says you're the best man she's ever known."

I felt indescribably sad, all at once. I knew, at that moment, Nora was gone for good.

"So, will you help us? Please?"

"I'll help you," I said. "I'm only going for a day. I'll call you tomorrow, when I get back."

-Nineteen-

I loved New York City, and La Guardia had always seemed to me the perfect entry to the place. While other major airports continually reinvented themselves, always trying to shine the gloss, ever seeking to awe and enchant, La Guardia didn't. Its dingy, dim hallways, low-ceilinged waiting areas, yellowed fluorescents, and general sense of grime, all said one thing to me. This is New York. You've arrived. This is the center of everything, and we don't give a damn about impressing you.

The man at the rental desk tossed the car keys onto the counter in my general direction. He gave me the idea that he didn't much care if I never brought the car back, and halfway expected I wouldn't. I took the nearly new, but battered sedan gingerly onto the Grand Central Parkway, and headed for Long Island.

Two hours later, Huntington surprised me. There was a small-town feel to it, and its old Yankee ghosts ran close to the surface. It was late, so I found a chain hotel at the edge of town and fell into bed. If Chloe came around, I slept right through it.

The next morning, the Hunter home was surprisingly easy to find, at the end of a street that branched off the main drag. I got out of the car, and zipped my jacket against the chilly day. It felt cold enough to snow.

The old house had been built well back from the street. The windows were shaded with canvas awnings. A brick walk was set into a lawn that had gone colorless with the season. It flowed from curb to veranda, between terra cotta planters and two matching trees that I couldn't identify. The red front door opened before I reached the steps.

~*~

The summer day hummed with insects and heat. A sprinkler moved a rainbow of water across the green grass. In the middle of the lawn, a brick walk flowed around terracotta planters to the

167

steps. The awnings that shaded upstairs windows that were different than those on the ground floor. Chloe took my hand as we went up the steps.

A dragonfly sat on the honeysuckle bush by the porch, stretching its wings in the sun. The woman who opened the red front door was the kind that stayed cool as ice cream, even on these really hot days. I knew her from somewhere. She ignored Chloe, and stared at me. "Are you all right?" she asked. "You don't look well. You've come about Horace, I expect. You'd better come in."

"Horace?" I asked, feeling stupid.

"Yes, Horace," she said. "He's around here somewhere. She lets him out, you know. He does as he pleases."

We followed her into the house. I cupped a hand to Chloe's ear. "Who's Horace?"

"He's the shinny pig, of course," the woman answered from in front of me. "There's no need to whisper." I felt my face go red. Chloe hugged herself, nearly bursting with silent glee.

~.*.~

The woman who stood in the doorway was in her seventies, and quite beautiful. She waited for me, cool and composed.

"Are you all right?" she asked. "You don't look well."

"I'm sorry," I said. "I'm Nick Horan. Long flight. I was gathering cobwebs, I guess."

She reminded me of someone I had known, though I had no idea who it could be. From out of nowhere, I thought about ice cream, and the day became unreal.

"Charlotte Hunter," she said, and put out her hand.

I took it. It was warm and delicate, but gave no sense of age or frailty.

"You don't seem at all like I remember you," she said. "You appear quite—determined."

"Remember me?"

"From when you were in your teens," she said. "I recall you as less intense, perhaps."

I realized that when my path had crossed Chloe Hunter's so many years ago, it must have crossed hers, too. I didn't see how she could possibly pick me out from a large group of Chloe's summertime friends. Kate had no doubt mentioned that I lived on the lake during Chloe's last summer, and she was being polite. I instinctively shied away from conversations involving my own memory loss, and I searched for a way to change the subject. A small white dog beside her looked up at me solemnly. His eyes were quiet and dark.

"Nice dog," I said. "Looks like a pug."

"French bulldog," she responded shortly, and stood aside to let me enter. "My husband is asleep. If he wakes up, he'll meet you, but he isn't likely to. He sleeps most of the time, now."

I didn't know how to answer, and I followed her into the dim interior. The walls were filled with paintings, hung both in naturally lit spaces and softly illuminated alcoves. There were vases filled with fresh flowers on several tables.

"Lilies," she said, as if I'd asked. "Orchids."

The dog followed us into the living room, and sat beside my chair, gazing up at me.

"I like orchids the best," she continued. "Orchids remind me of ice cream, somehow. You've come to tell me about my daughter? You have news?"

I masked my surprise as best I could.

"You've seen my daughter's spirit," she said. "There's no need to tiptoe around it. Katherine told me what this was about, or I certainly wouldn't have let you in, a stranger. I'm not going to report you to the American Psychical Society. I think I've misplaced their telephone number, anyway."

She took off her glasses, set them on the small table beside her, and joined the dog in watching me expectantly.

"I've seen someone, or something," I said. "I live on Duck Island, west of Long Duck, where you . . ."

"That isn't anything I don't already know. Tell me what you've seen."

"I've seen a woman. I can't tell her age, really. I saw her come out of the lake, the first time. I hear her in the woods, and I've seen footprints in the snow. Bare feet. Something written on a mirror, in the steam on the glass."

"What did it say?"

"I can fly."

I knew now that her daughter's grave marker had the same words inscribed on it, and I worried a little bit about her reaction. She sat quite still for a moment, looking at nothing, and then nodded.

"I also dream about her," I said. "At least, I think it's dreaming."

"You'll have tea," she said. She stood up and went out.

The dog stayed with me. We glanced at each other, but he didn't seem to be inviting pats, so I left him alone. A painting on the wall across from me drew my eyes, and I got up to have a look at it. It was a single flower, pale pink, all alone in failing light. Something about it arrested me.

"What does she look like, now?" Charlotte asked.

I took the cup she offered, and collected my thoughts.

"Now? I'll try to describe her," I said. "When I see her, it's as clearly as I see you now, but it's hard to translate, somehow. It's almost like I see her with—different eyes."

She nodded over the rim of her own cup.

"When I first saw her, she was always in a pink bathing suit, and always wet from the lake," I said. "Her hair is light, and very long. Mostly she wears a braid, sometimes with a flower in it."

I closed my eyes, and tried to picture her.

"There's something exotic about her face. I can't really put my finger on it, I'm sorry. Something about her cheekbones, her eyes—she's very beautiful, anyway."

"Is this her?"

I took the small photograph she held out to me. I put it up to the light from the window. A young Chloe looked back at me, her head thrown back in laughter. She was sitting on the deck of a boat. Water sparkled in the background. The boat was red, and I realized it was Bill's boat, *The Letter*, currently in a shed at the marina.

Seeing her this way made it hard to breathe. I felt an ache, a deep grief that made no sense. I handed the picture back.

"This is my daughter, Chloe. Is this the woman you see?"

"Yes," I nodded.

"You can keep it, if you'd like to," she said.

"I don't think so. It belongs to you. It should stay with you."

She regarded the photograph for a long time, and then set it on the table beside her glasses. I sensed that she cried inside, but her tears had gone dry years before. I sipped my tea, to give her time. It was some sort of herbal blend I didn't recognize. The mug was fine china, nice but heavy and deliberately without pretension, like most of what I saw in this house.

"Does she seem happy?" she asked.

"I talk to her, when I'm dreaming, or whatever it is," I said gently. "It seems real when I do. She seems like a happy person."

"She always was, in her way. She saw past things, saw things the rest of us don't. Even when she was a little girl, she was—wise. Sometimes with her I felt like the child, in the presence of a very old soul."

"You lived in New York, in the city, when she was little?"

"We lived here," she answered. "We've always lived here. When Chloe's schooling and her father's work made it sensible, we stayed in an apartment in Manhattan, but this was always home. We always came back here, at least on the weekends."

It surprised me. "Was she living here when . . .?"

"She died? Yes, of course. Would you like to see her room? I always called it her parallel universe."

I followed her up pale-carpeted stairs, and then along a hallway. She rapped once on a door at the end, and glanced at me apologetically.

"I always do that," she said, and opened it. "I don't know why."

The wood floor gleamed, reflecting light from the bare window. The walls were the color of the orchids downstairs. There was nothing at all in the room. The closet door stood open, empty, without as much as a single wire hanger on the rod.

"I'm not one of those parents you read about, that keeps a shrine," she said. "I know she's gone. I've had over thirty years to ponder that, and to be sure of it. Still, there won't be anything or anyone else in this room while I'm alive. When I'm gone, then this house and this room can have a different story."

"Another little girl will get lucky someday and sleep in this room." I smiled. "It's sacred space, a place for good dreams."

She looked at me, gratefully. "It is, yes," she said. "So why did you come here?"

"I'm not sure," I admitted. "I'm interested, of course, in why I see her on Duck Island. Did you have any connection to my place when you summered on the lake?"

"No. We could see it from our kitchen window, of course. It's a pretty island. The marina's the other direction, of course. I don't remember ever even going toward that end of the lake. It was pretty much abandoned all the years we summered on the lake. The owners never went there."

"Chloe wouldn't have had any attachment to my island that you know of?"

"I wouldn't necessarily know if she did. My daughter kept her own counsel on a lot of things. She spent a lot of time wandering on little Echo Island, across the reach. Nothing stood on it but a tumbledown shack."

"It hasn't changed," I said. "It's still empty. Somehow the cabin is still standing. You can see it through the trees."

I walked into the empty room, and looked out the window at my rental car on the street. I could feel the little girl, and the teenager, who had lived here. I wondered if she was close right now.

"This is hard for me to ask, Mrs. Hunter, but I'm trying to understand your daughter. Can you tell me about how she died?

What you think happened? I don't mean to make you uncomfortable."

She shook her head. I didn't think at first that she would answer, but she was only collecting her thoughts.

"It wasn't what people thought," she said. "It wasn't what it seemed."

She took a deep breath. The air in the room seemed to thicken and swirl. Charlotte Hunter watched me, concerned.

"Are you all right?" she asked. "You don't look well, again. Perhaps you don't have enough time to hear this, anyway."

"I'm fine," I said, and glanced at my watch. "We have enough time."

~ * ~

My wristwatch, on a metal band, was completely unfamiliar to me, and said it was five minutes past three in the morning. The whole night shone dirty yellow. Warm fog brushed at my cheeks and against the back of my neck, whispering, insinuating. I touched letters on the brass plaque.

City of New York
Robert F. Wagner, Mayor

It felt haunted, infected, and I pulled my hand back and stuck it in my coat pocket. The gun tucked inside was heavy and brutal. It wouldn't help me, and I thought about throwing it over the side. I wanted to be anywhere else. This wasn't my place, and I didn't belong here. I started walking.

The fog swallowed the sound of my steps. Bare light bulbs buzzed over my head, louder and then fading as they passed by, one by one. I thought about the people who had stood at this railing before they went into the East River below, and I wished there was more traffic to keep me company.

I looked down from the walkway. A car waited ahead, in the far left lane. The smoke from its tail pipe curled around cat-eye taillights. It was a '59 Bel Air, just a few years old, but hard-used and exhausted. The passenger front window squealed as it rolled down. The Grinning Man peered up at me. He was eating Chinese food from a white paper carton.

"Looking for your splat, buster?"

I ignored him, kept walking.

"So are we!" he called. "We're looking for her, too! Check the television programs. She might be on 'Lost in Space', maybe."

He laughed at his own joke. Behind me, I heard the window squeak again as it went back up.

"Out of context," I muttered. My throat hurt. "It's 1964. 'Lost in Space' won't be air until next year."

A member of the Low Gang stood against the rail, huddled into a trenchcoat. When I got close enough, he stepped out into my way. His hat brim was pulled down low. I knew that he didn't want me to look at his eyes, so I made it a point to do it.

"Have you seen her, pal?"

He pulled a black-and-white photograph out, and thrust it at me.

"Have you seen her?" he asked again. "You don't have choices here, if you know what's good for you."

I didn't much like his tone.

It was too dark on the bridge, and I had to tilt the picture toward the city lights below us. A young Chloe looked back at me, her head thrown back in laughter. She was sitting on the deck of a boat. She was dangerously beautiful, and seeing her again made it hard to breathe. I put the photo into my pocket, very carefully, and started walking. I ignored the shouts behind me.

~ * ~

"Are you sure you're all right?" Charlotte Hunter asked, again. "You really don't appear well."

"I'm fine," I said. "I'm just tired. My throat hurts a bit. I might be coming down with something."

174

She took her hand away from my arm, looking doubtful. "Chloe was never the same. She never got over it, not that it was very long..." She looked at me, sharply. "You don't know what I'm talking about, do you?" she asked. "Kate said you lost all of your memory after your accident."

When I shrugged, ever so slightly, she plunged ahead. "You drowned, and right away people started saying that they heard you out on the water at night, crying for help. Ridiculous. You were in the hospital."

I stared at her, aghast. She was either crazy, or suffering from some form of early dementia. Her memories were scrambled.

"What are you talking about?" I blurted. "Nobody said they heard me out on the lake."

"It was just a summer time fling. Teenagers. She thought she was in love, though. Chloe thought it would be forever."

"You're confusing me with someone else, Mrs. Hunter. I might have met your daughter once or twice, but we didn't know each other."

She glared, instantly furious. "I don't have you confused with anyone else," she said. "Not when you cost my daughter her life, I don't."

I made my voice gentle. I had no idea what she was talking about, but I didn't feel well, and wasn't ready for her anger. I tried to steer her back on subject.

"So, what happened to her?"

"People were talking, saying they heard you at night, screaming." She struggled to collect herself. "All over the lake, people were saying it. Hysteria. I think they even went out in boats, searching, a few times."

"Nobody heard me out there," I said, humoring her. "I was in a coma. If a lot of people heard it, though, maybe there was something to it. Maybe somebody was in trouble out there."

"Nonsense," she spat. "I lived there the entire time, right on Long Duck Island, and I never heard a thing."

175

Her eyes glistened. She had a few tears left, and I wondered if, in her desperation to preserve her daughter, she could be entirely truthful with herself.

"Chloe thought she heard it?" I asked, very softly.

"Chloe did," she said. "She told herself that she did. She sat on our dock, sometimes all night, and listened for it. We tried to take her back home to New York, we *insisted*, but she wouldn't leave."

Outside the room, up the hall, a tiny bell chimed once.

"Did you hear that?" I asked.

She didn't hear my question, or ignored it.

"We finally got her back here, and I thought things would be better. I thought time would heal. I shouldn't have believed it. I should have watched her. She went back to school. She never had perfect marks, but that's because she was so bright, so independent, she just didn't believe everything she was being taught."

Her eyes and her voice had changed. I knew she had gone back to 1980.

"That fall, she didn't care anymore. Not about school, not about herself, not about anything. She was—haunted. One afternoon, she didn't come home from school. She kept her little car here. We came out and it was gone. Her father knew, somehow, that she had driven up to Canada, by herself. He called the police up there, right away. He didn't wait."

She stopped. Her body tensed, and her face went wretched. I felt bad for stirring this up, but I needed to know. I didn't say anything.

"They found her car in the marina parking lot. We were already driving up there. We didn't know anything until we got there, but I knew. God, I knew."

"I'm sorry," I said.

"There was a letter on the seat. It was addressed to me, a final cruelty. Her father was always hurt that he wasn't included, but he never knew what it contained. Not all of it."

"Do you still have it?"

"Yes, but I won't show it to you. I read it once, and resealed the envelope. I've never looked at it again. I'll tell you what it said, though."

She walked across the room, heels tapping the wood floor. She touched a spot on the wall near the window, as if she were remembering a picture that had once hung there.

"Chloe explained to me about you. You were in a hospital bed, comatose, but she said your spirit was trapped on the lake. You were drowning again and again, over and over, because you refused to leave her. You lingered here because you wouldn't give her up, and you were imprisoned in the moment of your death. You suffered endlessly, because you wouldn't leave her. You needed permission to die."

I was nearly overwhelmed. The truth of her story was like a punch in the stomach, and I didn't know why. She had me confused with another boy.

"She had to set you free. She had to find a way to let you go."

"That's beautiful," I said. "It's—sad. Really sweet."

"It isn't sweet at all," she spat. "It cost her life. She felt the only way you would budge is if she went out to you. She tried to release you, by swimming out to the sound of your voice."

She started to cry.

"She knew with water that cold, she couldn't make it back to shore. She had to have known it."

"Maybe," I said, "she hoped that love would protect her. Maybe she believed in happily-ever-after, enough to risk it. Maybe she thought she had a chance."

"My daughter died for a fairy tale. She died for nothing—for a fucking fairy tale."

I was shocked by her vulgarity. I wondered if she had ever used the word before. I turned her shoulders, and gathered her to me. Her face was hot against my chest. Her whole body shook, racked by her sobbing.

"The most beautiful girl—the most beautiful thing I ever saw. Gone for no reason. Gone for—nothing."

We stood there together for a long time, in that lovely, empty room. It was then, for me, that everything changed.

-Twenty-

I had breakfast when I got off the Train. The waitress looked utterly worn out, as though she hadn't left the counter in years. Every item on the menu included eggs. I didn't like them, so I settled for dry cereal. The heavy china clattered when she set the bowl in front of me.

When I came up the stairs from the train station, I realized that the milk had been slightly turned. I could still taste it in my mouth. On the sidewalk, no one looked at me. The traffic was louder than I was used to, but the morning noise did nothing to dispel the night before. I checked the watch again. Breakfast had taken too long, and I needed to hurry a bit.

I found the apartment numbered 1115, and I knocked on the door.

"Who is it?" a woman's voice called.

"Room service," I said.

She opened the door and contemplated me. She had a beautiful, tired face, and a no-nonsense, regal quality in her comportment, tired or not. I knew her from somewhere, something to do with ice cream, but it really didn't matter.

"What are you talking about?" she asked. "You make no sense."

I nodded agreement, and brushed by her.

"Are you here for Chloe?" the woman called after me. "Don't wake her up if she's sleeping."

A television flickered in a corner, the sound turned low. Walter Cronkite looked at me, in black-and-white.

"General Maxwell Taylor, chairman of the Joint Chiefs of Staff, has been appointed by President Johnson as the new U.S. ambassador to South Vietnam. Don't look behind you, there are dragons."

He seemed happy about it.

The bedroom door was open, so I went in. A little girl, solemn, light haired, and pretty, was tucked into the middle of the bed. Sun from the window lay on the covers. She held a book

179

in her lap, and her dark eyes looked as though they knew everything. Her voice was beautiful.

"I know who you are, and you aren't really a grown-up."

"No," I said. "You're right, I'm not."

"There's a newspaper outside, moving. I think there's a cat under it, or an elf. Maybe a Low Man. Do you know about them?"

I was startled.

"How long has he been there?"

"I know about elves," she said, indicating her book.

"How long has the newspaper been out there moving, Chloe?"

She shrugged, handed me the book, and indicated the woman in the other room.

"She was reading it to me. It's my favorite."

I checked out the cover. "*The Giant Silver Book of Elves and Fairies*," I read. I turned pages, looking.

"Ghosts aren't white," she said. "When you were little, you knew that."

"I knew a lot of things that I've forgotten. I'm trying to remember them."

I closed the big book, and gave it back to her.

"Do you remember me?" she asked.

"Not yet," I said. "I will."

"Hurry up. Forever is coming, soon."

~ * ~

Charlotte Hunter walked me to my car.

"You were a nice enough young man, Nick," she said. "I always thought you were intimidated by me. In hindsight, I'm sorry about that, but at the time I must have been glad you were."

"Glad?"

"I had plans for my daughter. What parent doesn't? Chloe was bright and beautiful. She could have gone anywhere she wanted. Being tied up with a small-town boy from Canada wasn't the way to get to those places, obviously."

I had no reply. I had almost given up arguing with her delusion. Maybe because I had drowned the same summer, she had somehow connected my story to her daughter's.

"My mother would have said something." I tried.

"When you woke up weak, and sick, and confused?" she asked. "When she had given you up for dead, and you were back? She should have told you that the girl you loved died while you were asleep? I wouldn't have said a thing. Ever. No mother would."

"My friends—someone would have mentioned something," I floundered.

"You were a poor local kid, sneaking around with a rich summer girl. The groups didn't mix socially. They despised each other. You know how young people are. Who would you have told? When a New Yorker died in a suicide, who would connect her to a local boy who had been unconscious in bed for months? The doctors had said you were likely to die. People had already started to forget you, I'm sure."

I shook my head, knowing that part of her crazy story was true. My old friends were polite, but they stayed away from me for a long time after I came back, like I had something they didn't want to catch.

"You disapprove of me for being so mean-spirited, but my daughter scared me. She had a streak of rebellion. Not in the classical, sullen, teenage way, maybe, but it was there. It started when she was tiny—that old soul thing. She viewed all the trappings of success with some amusement, like she knew they didn't really mean anything."

I had no idea about traffic here, and didn't really know how much time I had before my flight. Instinctively, I glanced at my watch. Charlotte misunderstood, and hurried her story.

"Your mother reached out to me, and I acted terribly ungracious. I'm ashamed of that, now. They found Chloe's body the day after she died. We weren't tortured by uncertainty, at least."

She shook her head. I could see the self-loathing on her face. "I didn't even go to her funeral," she said. "I could have, should have, but I didn't. Her letter said she wanted to be buried close to you, and I honored that, but I didn't go. I've never seen her grave."

I forgive you, I wanted to tell her, but that made no sense.

"She's beneath a big tree," I said. "It's a lovely place."

"I said for a long time that you killed my daughter, but you didn't. You were only guilty of loving her. Poor boy."

She shook her head, remembering. Her voice went hoarse. "You poor, poor boy."

I didn't know what to say. I looked across the street at the neighborhood park, barren now, but probably lovely in the summer. A woman walked a dog across an empty baseball diamond in the corner. Chloe had gone there to play when she was a small girl, and maybe to sneak her first kiss or her first cigarette when she was older.

"She loved baseball," Charlotte said, following my gaze. "She dragged her father to that diamond to throw a balll every chance she got."

~ * ~

"I'm not really allowed to be doing this," Chloe said. "It's against the Rules. The first thing you should know about me is that I hate rules."

We moved along with the crowd, headed for the stadium entrance. The sky gleamed the hard, brilliant blue that means autumn on the east coast. Along the parapet over our heads, huge, orange-and-black letters spelled out HOME OF THE NY GIANTS.

Chloe took my arm. "The Polo Grounds," she said. "I love it here. The Giants are my favorite team, of course, but I can be fickle."

182

The crowd overflowed the sidewalks and filled the street, ties and hats and dresses. Groups of wide-eyed boys raced around. An occasional shout or laugh rose above the huge, constant noise that surrounded us. Those with tickets moved purposefully, heads up, toward the gate.

"They're playing Brooklyn today." She laughed. "Aren't we lucky?"

"They tore the Polo Grounds down before I was born," I said. "This is impossible."

"It doesn't look torn down to me," Chloe said. She checked her watch. "It's 1951, and there it is, big as can be. See?"

She pulled me to a stop, and faced me. She took off the dark glasses and put them in her purse. Her voice wasn't much more than a whisper, but I could hear her fine.

"Do you know the best time to see the Moon? It's when everyone else is watching the sun."

The crowd flowed around us, smelling of perfume and cigars. Her eyes were luminous.

"You need to stop worrying about what isn't," she said. "You need to love what is."

She pulled me by the hand. A woman with a pillbox cap and bright red lipstick took the pair of tickets Chloe produced and with a quick sleight-of-hand movement turned them into stubs, which she handed back. The small turnstile ratcheted loudly, adding its noise to an orchestra of identical turnstiles arrayed to either side of it. We went through, and into a steel-and-concrete cavern that echoed with cries of those hawking programs, and a million footsteps.

Chloe's fingers tightened on my arm. "Look," she said into my ear. "That guy—over there."

She indicated a man leaning against a pillar, attempting to be inconspicuous by reading a scrap of newspaper. He wore a large fedora with a snap-brim, and a belted coat that came nearly to his ankles. He was clean-shaven, and his eyes glittered. Even in the dim light, he appeared to be standing in deeper shade than what surrounded him.

"He's one of the Low Gang," she said. "I'm not supposed to be here. Until I get back to Sanctuary, they'll be after me. That one's not dangerous, by himself. The Low Men don't have much will of their own. It's when they're directed, in a group, that they become terribly dangerous."

She shrugged, apologetically. "They're after—us, actually," she amended. "Both of us, but they can see me better. You're still alive, so they'll concentrate on me. They might find a way to reach you in the real world, though, so you have to be careful when you're there, too."

"What are they? A kind of police?"

She laughed, a little bit sadly. "Not at all. They don't care about the Rules, either. On the contrary, they just smell people who are vulnerable. They catch anyone who's running loose, outside of Sanctuary."

"And—they arrest them?" I asked.

She moved off, and looked back at me over her shoulder.

"They eat them," she said. "They eat the people they catch. All up."

I glanced at the Low Man as I passed by him. He looked away, and studied his newspaper. I followed Chloe to the brick passageway that led to our seats. When we emerged into daylight, I was stunned, as I always was, by the green, green grass and the brilliant white lines on the diamond. It had always been so, baseball had, and I supposed it would be after I had gone.

The Dodgers were taking batting practice, in road grays with blue script. There was the periodic hollow crack of a bat, and the outfielders got themselves under the fly balls, cranked their bodies and whipped the balls back. They were easy, relaxed in their movements, but deceptively fast. In the infield, loose groups played catch, wrists flicking, balls snapping loudly in gloves.

"We're sitting right behind the Giants' dugout," Chloe said. "I thought you might like that. We have a Train to catch. It won't wait, but we should be able to see most of the game."

I settled back in the wooden seat and watched the stadium fill. I let the sun warm my face and watched Chloe beside me. Vendors filed up and down the aisles, selling peanuts and pretzels. Chloe flagged down a man selling red-and-white paper bags of popcorn.

"Not buttered, please," she requested. "It will get my tote bag greasy."

I watched her tuck the popcorn into the canvas bag she always carried over one shoulder. I didn't comment, and she didn't offer an explanation.

Finally, the Giants took the field, white uniforms brilliant against the grass, and the crowd roared. Sal Maglie threw the first pitch for a strike, and the place nearly exploded.

It got quiet, though, when Robinson singled. The ball bounced lazily out to right field and rolled as Pee Wee Reese crossed home plate with the game's first run. The stadium groaned, a soft, massive sigh that filled the place. Chloe jumped to her feet, clapped, then glanced down at me. Her expression was a little bit embarrassed. "I can't help it," she said. "Jackie Robinson might be a Dodger, but I like him."

I smiled. "Fickle."

The game turned into a pitching duel, inning after inning. The tension in the ballpark mounted. Chloe produced a roll of cinnamon candy from her bag, and shared it with me.

"Where are we going on the Train, anyway?" I asked.

"Somewhere warm," she said. "A place where beasts are mild."

I could see it, the faraway, in her dark eyes.

"The tracks mostly run through woods," she said, "at least this far east. It will be desert later, and then the ocean. When the Train stops at stations, we'll be able to get off and search for the things we have to find—bears and turtles and whatnot."

"Why are we looking for things?"

She leaned over, and kissed me on the ear. "Some of them will help you to remember, and others will keep us safe. I'll worry about that, you worry about baseball."

185

"Baseball?"

"Yes," she said, all at once sad. "If it comes down to a Squeeze Play, you'll have to be the one to call for it. Understand?"

Batting second in the eighth inning, Duke Snider smacked the first pitch he saw, straight back at the mound for a single up the middle. The man sitting on the other side of me groaned.

"The roof is going to fall in now," he said. "See if it don't."

We watched glumly as the Dodgers scored three fast runs, blowing the game open and taking a 4-1 lead to the ninth inning.

Chloe stood up. "Ladies' room," she said. "I might wander down to the dugout for a bit, to see if I can stir things up. You'll find me at field level if I don't come back."

She fished in her purse, came out with a single brass-colored coin, and handed it to me. It had a bear stamped on it. I had seen one just like it somewhere.

"Get yourself some more popcorn, if you want, but I'd steer clear of anything else they want to sell you here."

She kissed me briefly, slipped on her hat and dark glasses, and moved off, down the cement steps. A vendor passed her, on his way up, balancing a steam box made of stainless steel. He wore all-white; short sleeves, trousers, and paper hat.

"Hot dogs! Get, get, GET-cha HOT DOGS!" he screamed. "Fresh red-hots HERE!"

He paused in the aisle beside my seat, and looked down at me. It was the Grinning Man. "So fresh they're still screaming. Gonna take me up on it, bub? One skinny dime is all."

He opened his chest, and pulled out a long bun, wrapped in a white paper napkin. Something inside of it squirmed. He squeezed, and the napkin was immediately stained red. He offered it to me, and I shook my head.

"Suit yourself." He leaned down close, and lowered his voice. "You came in with someone, pally," he said, confidentially. "Nice looking splat, matter of fact. You got good taste. Don't let anyone tell you different."

186

He straightened up, and scanned the crowd. "There's a problem, though. Trouble is, the splat belongs to me, and I need to talk to her."

"Beat it," I said. "Not interested."

"You're a reasonable guy," he said. "I got her best interests at heart. She's making things worse for herself. I got no beef with you. I said I'd take her, and let you go. Help me out."

"Not interested," I repeated. "Scram, Grinning Man."

His face went furious. He took an exaggerated bite from the hot dog in his hand, and chewed deliberately, glaring at the field. He glanced at me again, and his grin came back. His lips and teeth were bright red.

"I could tell you things about her you wouldn't like so much, pally."

A bat cracked, and Alvin Dark laced a ball into left. It hit, bounced, and rolled on the grass as he raced to first. The crowd came to its feet, roaring. The Giants were still alive. I stood up from my seat, and pushed past the Grinning Man. Chloe had been gone too long.

"I figure you can tell me things about myself that I wouldn't like, either," I called over my shoulder. "Makes no difference."

His voice followed me down the cement steps. "See you around, pally. Keep in tune."

To my left and right, I could see men in hats and long coats moving down parallel stairways and angling toward the Giants' dugout below me. I felt a pang of alarm, and looked back. The Grinning Man stood on the steps where I had left him. He had his eyes closed, and his arms outstretched. He directed the Low Men like they were an orchestra.

I started to hurry. A policeman was stationed at the field entrance. He looked at me closely, and then pulled the gate open. Down here, the crowd noise was oppressive, overwhelming. I hurried along the infield wall, to the dugout entrance. The New York team had gathered outside the steps, willing the rally along.

Mueller singled through the gap into left, and Alvin Dark took third base standing up. The noise in the stadium became nearly unbearable. I went past a knot of white uniforms, and into the dugout. No one paid me the slightest attention.

The area was dim, lit only by the chest-high opening onto the field, and by a couple of bulbs in wire cages. In a corner, between a water cooler and the bat rack, a bunch of the Low Gang, identical in dark fedoras and long coats, had Chloe cornered. One of them turned to face me.

"She's coming with us," he snarled. "The boss says so. Go and see him if you don't like it."

"The boss says so," the other Low Men muttered. "The boss says so."

"I just saw your boss," I said.

". . . And no, we don't like it," a voice finished, from behind me.

A Giants' player loomed behind me, holding a baseball bat in each hand. Tall and husky, he seemed to awkwardly balance himself on his cleats, but there was no mistaking the power in his arms. His eyes were dark, piercing.

"Don't you have somewhere you should be, Bobby?" Chloe asked, calmly. "I seem to remember that you do. I can manage this."

"Won't take long," he said. "I'm still on deck, anyway. Good to see you."

"It's nice to see you, too," she said.

He tossed me a bat, one-handed, and I caught it the same way. He took a practice cut, and I heard the whistle as his swing sliced the air. Side by side, we advanced on the group that surrounded Chloe. The Low Men squealed and flapped backwards, in a swirl of dark coats.

"We're done for, boys," one of them growled. "Every man for himself!"

Thomson caught my eye. "Done for?" He smiled. "Isn't that already a cliché?"

"We'll never take them alive," I said, and we both laughed.

Chloe caught the diversion, and ran. She vaulted the railing in a flash of pink, and was gone. The Low Men took off too, the other direction, flapping away like bat wings, evaporating like smoke. Bobby Thomson and I were left alone in the dugout.

"She'll be okay, now, you think?" he asked. "I like her. We all do."

"I hope so. I'll do my best to make sure she is."

I started to say, 'I like her, too,' but the truth mattered more than that. I was already deeply in love with her. Leo Durocher stuck his head down the stairs. He glanced over, and decided to ignore me.

"Thomson, what the hell are you doing down here?" he yelled. "On deck! You're up!"

He disappeared again, and Bobby Thomson watched my face and smiled gravely. "Good luck," he said.

"You too," I answered, and went up the steps first, back into the bedlam on the field. The PA horn announced Thomson as the next batter, and I turned to him as he went by.

"Second pitch is going to be a fastball, high," I said. "I probably shouldn't tell you that."

"I already know. Chloe let it slip. One for the good guys, I guess." He tipped his cap, and winked.

I sketched a wave, without looking back, and went to find Chloe. I went through the tunnel, and into the concourse, and I heard the crack of bat. The ground beneath my feet started to vibrate, and then the sound washed over me, a tidal wave of noise. The red-coated usher standing at the gate clapped my shoulder as I passed him, screaming to make himself heard in the rising pandemonium.

"Bet they heard that one around the whole world, mister," he yelled.

I smiled back at him.

"Count on it," I said.

~ * ~

It was time to get going, and I worried about Charlotte Hunter.

"Thank you for having me," I said. "Are you going to be okay?"

Her expression was arch, but also hollow. "I've been all right with something that can never be all right, for quite a long time now. I imagine I can go on with it for a while longer."

I pulled open the door of the rental car.

She touched my sleeve. "Will you be talking to your mother?"

"Of course," I said. "Not about this, though. I'm not sure I have the stomach for stirring up more pain. I wanted to understand what's been happening on my island. I'll admit I thought there might be a novel in it, but I seem to be making other people pay a price for my curiosity."

"Is it just curiosity?" she asked. "When you talk to your mother, will you tell her I'm sorry? Will you give her my telephone number, ask her to call me?"

"Of course, I will."

"And—I feel strange asking, but if you see my daughter, please tell her that her father and I love her. That we've never stopped loving her."

The moon hung pale, almost invisible, in the late autumn sunshine. I started to say that Chloe already knew that, I started to say a lot of things, but in the end I nodded, and didn't say anything.

"When she was very small, once, we were going inside the house. She touched the doorframe and asked me what it was. 'It's the doorway', I said, and she shook her little head. 'But what is it? What's inside it?' I thought for a minute and said, 'It's wood. The house is wood.' 'What's inside it?' We went through trees, and so on, and after a while we got to an atom, which is an impossible subject for a four-year-old. Do you see where I'm going with this?"

"Not yet," I answered.

"She wanted to know what was inside the atoms, what lies behind them, at the heart of everything. She could barely articulate it, but I understood her question. I'm her mother. I didn't have an answer. Atoms are where I ran out of track, so to speak."

I got into the car, and put the key into the ignition. I looked up at her. "I understand."

"My daughter always had a sense of what was inside. She understood that something lay—*behind things*. That's what made her Chloe."

I started the engine.

"Good luck," she said. "I hope you find what you're looking for."

I watched her in my rear-view mirror. She stepped into the street and watched me back. Then, a lonely woman in front of an empty house, she was gone.

-Twenty One-

Chloe was sitting on a bench in one of the pocket-sized parks that were tucked into the city's shadows. She stood up when she saw me coming, and I pulled the car to the curb, and got out to meet her. I had never been so glad to see anyone in my life. I kissed the place where her neck met shoulder, smelled warm skin and green Bermuda grass, saw bright sun and heard surf.

She pulled me back, and leaned away, her eyes searching my face. "Did you see it all?" she asked.

I considered. "Probably not all," I said. "Enough that whatever I missed, I'll remember later."

She thumbed the hair away from her face, and looked at her watch. "We need to get back on the Train," she said. "We have a long way to go."

"Can I ask you something?"

She regarded me steadily. Her skin was lovely, flushed with sun, and her eyes were warm.

"You made me think that I would dream," I said. "I wouldn't feel so crazy about all of it, if it was a dream, right? This isn't a dream, though. I don't know what it is, but it isn't a dream."

I found her hand with mine, and waited for her answer. She spoke slowly, when she finally did.

"We live in such modern times," she said. "Imagine you take a jet plane from Los Angeles to London. There's a kind of seat you can reserve that turns into a bed. You can have dinner, before you sleep. You can listen to music, or plug in your computer and do some work. If you're in the mood, you can go upstairs and have a drink. All in all, a busy day. Still, there's a fundamental fact that doesn't change. Do you understand?"

"Go on."

"You're flying. You're thirty thousand feet in the air, crossing the earth below at unimaginable speeds, on your way to London, England. No matter what else you do during those hours, what normal things—you're flying through the air, hurtling through space. Even if it seems impossible, even if the chicken you're eating seems more real—it's true."

"I understand," I said. "At least I'm starting to."

"You can go on with your life. You can tell yourself that I'm a dream, but whatever you do, you're on a Train with me. We're on our way to the Port of Los Angeles, crossing a map of Time, pursued by the Low Gang. Nothing changes that, no matter what."

"No matter what," I echoed. "No matter what."

She smiled. "Let's go find ourselves a Train."

She stood up, smoothed her skirt, and took my hand again. We started walking.

"That was a good game," I said. "Thanks for taking me."

"It was, wasn't it? I'm sorry you missed the ending."

"I pretty much knew how it turned out, anyway. Where are we?"

She looked around us. "Between here and there," she said. "Still somewhere in New York. We have to get to Penn Station—not the new one, the old one. Our train leaves from there."

"How do you know the way, if you don't know where we are?"

She indicated the moon, which floated over the street. "We follow Moon, but I also cheated a little, just in case. I used an old, old trick on the way here."

She bent, picked something up from the sidewalk, and held it out in her palm. "Crumbs," she said. "Crumbs are the best way to find your way back to anywhere. Remember the old story?"

"That looks like popcorn," I said. "And I don't think crumbs worked out so well in the old story. I think the birds ate them, and they got lost."

"Of course, it's popcorn—and we don't have to worry about birds. Just bears. Anyway, we have each other. We won't get lost."

We walked for blocks, but nothing seemed to move in this part of town. Buildings rose on either side of the street. The windows were empty of glass, lights, or anything else. Graffiti covered every surface within reach, with new tags painted on top of old. It seemed like desperate work, and I wondered how they didn't get tired of it.

"I miss it here," she said. "I lived in this city, once. It's the funny little things you miss the most. I had a Mickey Mouse watch when I was small. I loved it, but it died. My father helped me take the back off it. The innards fascinated me—watches, clocks—I knew about Time, even then."

Her face became inconsolable, and I unconsciously moved closer to her.

"I kept it in my box of treasures. Broken, totally open, and beautiful. I'm feeling sad, seeing it gone so clearly."

An occasional snatch of music wafted by. I couldn't tell where it came from, since the cars parked at the curbs were as vacant as the buildings. Still, I felt watched. Chloe walked beside me, lovely and sad, but unafraid. I reached for her hand.

"Aren't you afraid of anything at all?" I asked.

"Don't be silly," she said. "I'm afraid of nearly everything."

We heard a bell ringing from a long way off. After a block, we came upon a pay telephone jingling insistently in front of a boarded-up convenience store. Chloe picked her way through the broken glass on the sidewalk to answer it. The cord for the handset was missing, but she picked up the receiver anyway.

I couldn't hear what she said, so I turned away to watch the street. I could smell the dirty ozone from a storm, but I didn't think we'd get wet any time soon. I had a feeling it didn't rain much around here. Chloe hung up and joined me at the curb.

"That was the Queen," she said. "Calling from St. Louis. We'll be there in a few days, and she's invited us for a picnic. She wants to give us something. A presentation."

"The queen?" I asked. "The queen of what?"

"What do you mean, 'the queen of what?'"

"The Queen of—England? What is she the queen of?"

She looked at me, puzzled. "I really don't see why she should be the queen of anything at all," she said. "Although,

since she called from St. Louis, I suppose she's the queen of—
there."

"There is no Queen of St. Louis," I said, patiently. "It's
America. There are no queens in America."

"Well, there's one in St. Louis. I just spoke to her. Maybe
you should discuss your theories with her, when you see her."

I shook my head. She pulled my hand, and we started
walking again. Chloe skipped, just a little.

"A picnic with the Queen," she said, happily. "Think of it. I
can't wait."

~ * ~

The traffic in downtown Toronto seemed nearly bucolic
after the madness of Long Island and Brooklyn. I left the jeep in
a parking garage and made my way on foot. I wanted to finish
with Esteban's business here and get back to the island as fast as
I could. The Diamond Investment offices were on the fourteenth
floor of an ice cube on Bay Street, with a lobby of cold blonde
granite. I thought about taking the stairs while I waited for the
elevator, and decided against it.

Sitting all by herself, the receptionist had been marooned on
a mahogany island. She ignored me for just long enough to send
me a message, and then looked up brightly.

"I'm here to see Esteban Martin," I said.

She appeared baffled.

"He works here," I clarified. "I have an appointment to see
him."

She started to thumb through a company directory on her
desk, and then her expression cleared. She seemed to stifle a
smirk.

"Of course," she said. "Mr. Martin."

She spoke into her headset, and I wandered over to look at a
loud, and undoubtedly expensive, oil painting on the wall over
the waiting area. I heard Esteban approaching before I saw him.
He bounded over to me to shake my hand, well dressed, artfully

195

tousled, and smelling of an aftershave cologne that would be wasted on me.

His eyes were nervous, though, and I wondered if he was in over his head, here in this high stakes poker game. There was something wistful about him, like a boy playing at grown-up. His suit and tie appeared pasted on. Esteban's movements were naturally elegant at home, in a restaurant or a bar, but not here. I followed him back to his office. The receptionist eyed us speculatively as we passed by her.

His office wasn't much more than a desk and telephone. One wall was glass. "Man, am I glad to see you," he said. "We're running out of time, you know."

I ignored the plea in his voice, and wandered over to stare out the wall-window. Far below, streetcars ran along Bay Street like toys along their tracks, and tiny people hurried to wherever they were going. The slices of sky between tall buildings were gray, and I saw that it was beginning to sleet. I wondered how bad the drive north to the lake would be.

"Twenty thousand," he said, from behind me. "I'm making it so much that he can't say no. It's about five grand more than I owe him."

I looked back at him. He had a desk drawer open, and held an envelope. "Not that I really owe him anything," he amended. "You know what I mean."

"What am I walking into, Esteban?"

"Nothing, man," he said. The color rose in his face. "You're just the voice of reason, here. Drop the money off, and maybe talk a little common sense to this idiot. I wouldn't ask you to do anything that would get you hurt."

"You wouldn't get me hurt?" I was incredulous. "You'd take away the woman I loved, and turn my life upside down. You'd hound her, and keep coming around when she was with me. You'd badger her for money and a place to stay every time you got into trouble. Not get me hurt? You're the worst thing that ever happened to her, and to me."

"You're talking about my wife, man." He took a step toward me. "You slept with my wife for a year, and you have the balls to complain to me that I took her away from you?"

He clenched his fists. His fury surprised me, and I almost admired him for it. My own anger left me as suddenly as it had come. I felt tired, and I sat down on a bench by the window and looked out.

"Forget it," I said. "I wouldn't trade places with you."

"You never had a chance once she found out she was pregnant. It doesn't matter whose baby it is. She didn't plan to stay with you."

"You're saying you'll make a better father?" I asked.

"You can say I've done some crazy stuff," he said. "Maybe I still do, but it's not weird-crazy, know what I mean? There's something about you that just isn't all—*there*. You don't care about what happens to you."

I shook my head, and waited for him to finish.

"The day Nora told you she was coming back here with me, and the baby wasn't yours, I worried you were going to beat the hell out of me. Nora said you wouldn't. She was positive."

There was no good reason to dredge this up. I became more and more uneasy.

"It wasn't like you didn't care—it seemed more like you expected it, and were sad. You felt bad, but you knew it was coming."

"Leave it alone, Esteban." I kept my voice low. "This is pointless. Tell me where to take the money."

"The thing is, Nora never had anything predictable in her life, except me."

"You're saying that she can depend on you?" I asked.

He shook his head emphatically, no. "It isn't that, at all. She doesn't want to depend on anyone. She wants to know what they'll do, is all. She wants to wake up in the morning, and know that things today are the same as they were yesterday. She wants to count on things being the same."

"That's a kind of dependence, isn't it?"

"I think whatever bothers you happened a long time ago, and you know you can't ever fix it, or get over it. Things are never going to be quite okay again for you. It makes you look at things different."

"Thanks for the analysis," I said. "I better go."

I held out my hand for the envelope. It was heavier than I expected. It felt dirty in my hand, so I shoved it into the pocket of my jacket. He stuck out his hand. I hesitated, just for a second, and then felt bad about the waver. I shook his hand, briefly.

"I feel better," he said. "This is the first time since this started that I think it'll be okay."

"I don't know what it is I'm going to do. You needed a postage stamp, not me. Where do I find this guy?"

"His dealership is on Yonge Street, the BMW place. You can get on the subway downstairs and walk there. It's just south of York Mills station."

"I'm driving. What's his name, again?"

"Risa," he said. "Sonny Risa. He's usually in his office, over the showroom. I went there a few times, before all this started to get bad."

He snorted, bitterly. "I thought he was my friend. I thought he would give me a great deal on a new car."

I moved to go. Esteban stuck out his hand again. This time, I pretended I didn't see it. Later, I felt bad about that. I went to the elevator, without looking back. Out on the street, I started walking. People hurried by, intent on their business. Nobody even glanced at me, and nobody guessed what a strange mess I was in.

~ * ~

The streets turned green as we walked to old Penn Station. Brownstones crowded the sidewalks. Sunlight shifted under a canopy of leaves. The afternoon was hot, and the breeze carried a scent of watermelon. The city moved slowly, mellowed by the heat and by memories.

"This is 1953," Chloe said, checking her watch. "Give or take."

A glossy red fire engine stopped at the curb opposite us, with a long squeal of brakes. Firefighters in dark blue dungarees and t-shirts jumped down, and used a long tool to open the valve on a hydrant. The baking pavement flooded with coolness, and the effect was astonishing. Water mixed with sun to produce children.

They came from everywhere. They flew down apartment steps, jumped off scooters, and left bicycles where they fell. More than a hundred of them were wet in moments, laughing and leaping in the spray.

I heard a song that I knew, although I had forgotten the words. It was being played with bells, and an ice cream truck followed the sound of it around the corner and pulled over. Chloe reached into her canvas bag and pulled out a double handful of bills, as much money as I had ever seen in one place.

"Did you rob a bank?" I smiled. "I had no idea you were so rich."

"I don't have a penny," she said. "Do you not understand what this is?"

The ice cream man appeared in the small window on the side of his truck. He was dressed in white, with a small black bow tie at his neck. She left me, crossed to the truck, and laid the cash on the counter in front of him. On cue, the boys and girls left the hydrant's spray and began to line up. The man beamed, and passed out popsicles, shakes and bars as fast as he could.

Chloe came back, holding three cones. She gave me two of them, both vanilla, and kept chocolate for herself.

"You got me two?' I asked.

She tasted hers, and shook her head. "No. I got you one. The other is for—her."

She pointed across the street, through a rainbow arcing across the hydrant's mist. A tiny park took up the corner, shaded deeply by the old trees bordering it. A woman in a pale dress stood beside a fountain. She appeared cool and elegant, and had a small white dog on a leash with her. I knew her from somewhere, something to do with ice cream.

"I think I'm starting to understand," I said. The bright-colored memory floated just out of reach, like a butterfly. "This is about ice cream?"

Chloe laughed, slipped an arm around my waist, and hugged me to her. "Everything's about ice cream," she said. "Absolutely everything. Especially love."

She led me to where the woman and her little bulldog waited. When we reached them, the woman watched my eyes as she accepted the cone I offered her. Chloe produced the paper bag of popcorn from the baseball game. She bent and gave a handful to the dog. He finished it and then looked up at her, hopefully.

"I wouldn't give him any more than that," the woman offered, helpfully. "He'll eat too much of it, and be sick if you let him."

"Wait, wait," Chloe said to the dog, and kissed his wrinkled face. "There will be more. Things are just getting started."

"Sometimes I'm sad," the woman said. "It all feels like Beethoven, slowly going deaf, writing all the music in the world as fast as he can."

She turned to me. "Are you remembering what you've forgotten? Do you remember her?"

Chloe sat on the rim of the fountain, and swirled the water gently with her hand. A large orange fish came and nibbled at her fingers. She didn't look at us, but I knew she was listening to every word.

"Not yet," I answered, truthfully. "I hope that I will."

"I hope you will, too. She's risked everything for you."

She addressed Chloe. "There's a psychopath after you. I hope you aren't blind to that."

"You're supposed to call them sociopaths now," Chloe said.

"I call them monsters. Say I'm old-fashioned . . ."

Even in the day's breathless heat, the ice cream didn't show any signs of melting, and I had an idea the woman could hold the cone all day without a single drip.

"He's going to see the head of the Low Gang," Chloe said. "Put his head right into the monster's mouth, so to speak. He's either a hero, or completely crazy. He doesn't even know himself."

"Sometimes crazy is what it takes," the woman said, and nodded solemnly. "Remember—the Grinning Man is completely preoccupied with Rules. It's what allows him to eat lost souls—but his slavish adoration of the Rules might be what you can use to defeat him."

"Are you the Gatekeeper of New York City?" I asked her.

"No." She shook her head, decisively. "He is."

She indicated the dog. He shifted his gaze between Chloe and me.

"He can't speak—but he talks, all the same. He says you'll need grace. Do you have that?"

"I have no idea," I said. "I never thought about it."

The little dog flopped himself down, onto his belly. He sighed loudly, and put his head on his front paws. A butterfly landed on his head. It sat, content, moving its wings very slightly in the warm breeze.

"Grace," the elegant woman said, "is very simple, but nearly impossible to catch. It's the curious result of courage and humility. You can't have one without the other, yet they are almost never, ever seen together."

"How do you find it?" I asked. "Grace?"

"You can't," she answered, shortly.

The dog got up and wandered over to Chloe. He put his paws up on the fountain's edge and watched her as she fed popcorn to the fish. His eyes were very dark. He looked as though he knew a great deal about many things, and kept most of it to himself.

"Humility is the knowing that you can't find it," the woman said. "Sometimes, though, it finds you." She tried her ice cream, delicately, and lingered over the taste for a little while. Then she

201

nodded at me, ever so slightly. "I might have misjudged you," she murmured. "The butterfly is for you, for later. Be good, and be in love—no matter what."

"No matter what," Chloe agreed.

The woman regarded the small white dog. "He says you may pass," she told us.

Chloe glanced over at me and smiled. The day drowsed on around us, warm and green. I understood that it was for always, and didn't wish for anything else.

-Twenty Two-

The green spaces in the middle of the city make Toronto unique. There are surprising pockets of forest, and unspoiled valleys with rivers and streams pop up in unlikely places among the asphalt and brick. One of the stretches I remembered as wild had been bulldozed and paved. Sonny Risa's glass showroom sat in the middle of it. I figured the real estate had probably cost less than the political pull necessary to get the place built. He was probably doing well.

I parked in an area marked for employees, and walked around the back of the building. I didn't know what I wanted to see. Perhaps I felt some atavistic warning, and instinctively wanted to scout. There was nothing in the space behind the dealership but hoods-up parked cars and garbage dumpsters.

A knot of mechanics stood in the cold, talking and smoking cigarettes. One of them, an older man with long blond hair and a drooping moustache, stared at me as I walked by. A garage door rattled up, and a low-slung black saloon chirped its tires on the way out. I heard air ratchets and impact guns at work inside the shop. One member of the gang behind me cleared his throat and spit loudly. From the general silence in the group, I had a feeling that it was a gesture, and that it had been meant for me. I didn't turn around.

These workers weren't a team of Black Forest elves. Another illusion went down in flames.

I made a complete loop of the building. The pressed steel walls at the back gave way to sandstone and granite on the front façade. I went up a sweeping, curved walkway to the front door of the showroom. The glass door was heavy, bronze-tinted, and it opened onto a fluorescent field of polished automobiles.

They were set apart from one another, deliberately staged as artwork, sculptures of speed and money. I stopped at the one nearest to the door. I could smell the leather through the open window, an impossibly rich and brand new scent. I reached in and touched the headrest, matte black and soft. I wasn't much

203

interested in cars, or in money, but I reacted to the seduction in play here.

Three salespeople, a man and two women, stood off to the side and eyed me hungrily. They each had a turn at the next stranger who walked in without an appointment, and I was an 'up'. In my jeans and boots, I represented a remote possibility, but they couldn't dismiss me out of hand. I smiled to myself at their dilemma, and walked over to them.

"I need to see Sonny Risa," I said. "Can one of you point me in the right direction?"

Their eyes immediately catalogued and dismissed me. Here to see the owner, I must be a contractor, or a service provider. I hadn't come here to buy a new convertible, and so had no further meaning. One of them waved vaguely at a reception desk, and the three of them turned away.

"There's a Nick Horan here to see you," the receptionist said into her phone doubtfully, and looked up at me for confirmation. She appeared relieved at the response.

"He'll be down in a few minutes," she said. "Have a seat. Would you like a coffee while you wait?"

I nodded, and she went off to get it.

~ * ~

The street was cold and damp, lit here and there with neon. The metal signs on the corner were illuminated only by the stoplight above them. I didn't see Chloe, anywhere.

The young woman behind the cash register of the all-night restaurant greeted me by name. I knew her from somewhere. She handed me a coffee to go, in a Styrofoam cup.

"Wait a second," she said. "It's hot."

She took it back and slid it into a small brown paper bag. It seemed more awkward that way, but I didn't want to be rude, so I thanked her.

"He already paid," she said, waving off my coins. "He's waiting for you in back."

I walked back, past red vinyl booths, tired faces, through the smells of eggs and vinegar and old cooking grease. The man waited for me in the last booth. I felt the first stirrings of real fear, but slid onto the seat opposite his. He was leaning forward, his hat brim hiding his face.

He contemplated the table while he fixed his coffee. He poured sugar from a glass dispenser, shaking the chrome top gently every time the flow slowed. He poured and poured, until the dark coffee overflowed into the saucer. He laughed.

"I'm the same as you," he growled. "I like sweet things, and sweet things like me back."

The Grinning Man peered up at me. "Surprise," he said, "Me again."

"You again," I agreed.

"I want to scare you and the splat very badly. To death, and more."

He laughed again, a deep rolling sound that rose into something like barking. I had a sudden urge to look under the table, to see what might be crouched there, at my feet.

"Some people, like you, don't know enough to be frightened," he said. "I'm a generous man, though, and I believe in warnings."

I forced a smile. I felt sick. "I do too," I said. "So, consider yourself warned."

"Are you some kind of wise guy?" he wondered.

I stood up and walked, leaving my untouched coffee on the table. His laughter followed me out.

"Keep in tune!" he called after me.

~ * ~

Five minutes later, a man came down the curving staircase from an upper mezzanine to the showroom floor. There was no mistaking him. He was brisk, but not in a hurry, a king surveying his court. He wore a better suit than I would have expected, even

205

in this setting. His tie was knotted perfectly, and his shoes gleamed.

He approached me without hesitation, not even glancing at the young woman behind the desk.

"Sonny Risa," he said, hand out.

His blue eyes measured me. I watched him warily. I didn't want to take his hand, but I did. His palm and fingers were warm, and he grasped my hand firmly.

When he touched me, the showroom darkened, and the temperature dropped. The smoky air smelled damp, of raw earth and spoiled fish. I heard a hissing noise behind me, and glanced over my shoulder. Chloe sat in the back seat of a silver four-door saloon, gazing at me through the open window. Her face was in deep shadow.

"Be careful," she mouthed, silently.

I turned back to Risa. He let go of my hand. The lights seemed to waver, and then the showroom went bright again. His smile was unchanged. My voice sounded hollow.

"Good of you to see me without an appointment."

I looked back at the silver car. The back seat was empty.

"Always make yourself accessible to your customers," he said. "The first rule of good business."

His hand gestures were expansive, giving me a lesson. "A lot of guys don't understand that. If the customer sees you personally, they can trust you. Don't depend on the people you hire to speak for you. I keep my eye on every single employee, all the time. I'm always front and center. I make it my business to know everything. Those are my rules, and I believe in following rules."

"I'm here to give you some money," I said.

"Absolutely," he said. I had his full attention. "You wanna buy a car, pay a lease off? Say the word, and I'll get someone on it right away."

"I'm here to give you some money," I repeated, shaking my head. "You might want to do this in your office."

The smile flickered, faltered for just a moment, and then returned. "Whatever you say, friend."

His tone became slightly less jovial. I was relieved to have the pleasantries out of the way. He glanced at the receptionist, and put a hand on my back to guide me to the stairs. I tensed the muscles of my shoulders, almost imperceptibly, and his hand dropped away.

On the mezzanine, I leaned over the railing to check the tops of the cars below us while Risa unlocked his office door. The knot of salespeople looked up at me curiously.

"Come in," he said from behind me. "Tell me what this is about."

I thought it passably strange that he had locked his office door before he came downstairs to meet me. I followed him inside. The brightly lit space surprised me. Instead of the plush, baroque quarters I would have expected from such a self-important person, it was almost antiseptic. There was no dark wood, and no leather. Pale ceramic tile patterned the floor and the walls to chest height. The cabinets on the walls were white, and his desk was stainless steel.

He sat down and waved me to a metal chair in front of him. "What's this about?" he repeated.

I resisted the impulse to check under the desk for a drain in the floor at his feet. The office reminded me of an autopsy theater. I pulled the envelope of money from my pocket and held it up.

"This is the money Esteban Martin owes you," I said. "In reality, he doesn't owe you a cent, but he's going to give it to you anyway. More than you figured on, in fact. There's twenty thousand here."

"I don't want it," he said promptly. "It's too late for that."

"You'll take it. This is over, as of now."

He leaned forward and put his elbows on the desk. His face creased into a smile, but I could see the color flooding up from his immaculate white collar into his neck, and I could sense the building rage. The insanity in the room became palpable.

"You and I are going to tread very carefully right about now, friend, you got it?"

I tossed the envelope onto the desk in front of him. He backhanded it onto the floor on my side of the desk.

"This isn't about your scary act," I said. "You say Esteban Martin cost you money. There it is, and then some. As far as I'm concerned, you should be in jail. I would have handled you a whole lot different than he has, right from the start."

"You would have—handled me?"

His breath whistled in and out. It appeared his blood pressure had spiked high enough to explode his heart, but his smile widened.

"You think I don't know who you are?" he asked. "You think I didn't know the minute you walked in here? I make it my business to know everything. You visited moron Esteban day before yesterday. You think I'm not watching him? You think I wouldn't run your license plates, check you out?"

"Big deal," I muttered.

"Nick Horan. You're a two-bit, underemployed loser. You left your lousy writing career and ran off to hide in the woods. You can't stick with anything. You have a mother lives alone, you never see her. Totally inexcusable. Everyone in your town thinks you're weird and arrogant. They say you have been, your whole life."

I felt the shock seep into me, almost like paralysis. He ticked off points on one hand. Suddenly he stopped, and stabbed his index finger at me.

"Worst of all, you're a reformed drunk. I have a dried-out drunk sitting in my office—reprimanding me. Telling me what's what. Sticking up for an irresponsible prick who disrespected me."

"I haven't had a drink in ten years," I managed. "I don't drink."

"You're a no-good tosspot. You think you can walk in here, into my place, and disrespect me, too? I'll eat you alive." His voice dropped, and his eyes got sly. "They say you had some kind of scandal when you were young—got a girl in trouble and she ended up dead. You a ladies' man, Nicky? That what you are? A lady killer?"

He snorted laughter at his own joke.

"Are you going to take the money?"

"Sure, I'll take it." He smirked. "Leave it right there on the desk. My deal with the weakling doesn't change, though. He better find a way to be dead before the ninety days are up."

"No deal."

I pulled my cell phone out and called Esteban. He answered quickly enough that I knew he had been waiting for the call. Sonny leaned back in his chair and stared at my face while I spoke.

"This Risa guy's a loser," I said into the phone. "I don't think he's going to talk sense. You'll have to deal with this a different way."

"What are you saying?" Esteban asked. "He won't take the money?"

"He'll probably take the money, but he isn't going to let you off the hook. No point in wasting the twenty thousand."

"He has to. If I pay him back, he has to leave me alone." Esteban sounded close to tears. He had reached his breaking point.

"I'm going to bring the money back to you."

"This is against the rules," he said. "He's breaking the rules."

I looked at Sonny Risa.

"Esteban says you're breaking the rules," I said.

The effect on him was astonishing. The color drained from his face, and he came to his feet. He picked up a model car that was displayed on his desk and hurled it against the wall, hard enough to shatter a tile. The display of strength made me doubt my own eyes.

"Call you back," I told Esteban, and disconnected.

"What do you know about the rules?' Risa screamed. "What does a dead guy know?"

"You tell me," I shrugged.

"You don't belong here," he said. "You have no business here. You're out-of-bounds, and you don't even know you are. You're dead. This isn't dead people business."

"As the saying goes, I'm making it my business."

"You don't have a clue what I'm talking about, do you? You're a fish out of water. You don't belong here. I'm telling you that, and you're so busy running your big mouth, you don't hear me."

I picked up the envelope full of money from the floor beside me and underhanded it across the desk, toward him. It hit him on the arm and fell onto the floor beside him. He ignored it.

"Esteban's out," I said. "That's the rules. He paid you, and now it's done."

"I'll tell you one thing," he snarled. "You're not out, meddler."

"No, you're out," I said. "Out at first. Inning over."

"You know what the penalty is for being as out of place as you are?" he asked. "Care to guess, wise guy? I'll tell you."

"Please do."

"You get eaten alive, friend, that's what. You get eaten right up, that's what. Now get out of my office, and off my property."

I stood and left, leaving the money behind. I sensed him stand up and follow me as far as his office door. From the mezzanine rail, his voice trailed after me, all the way across the showroom to the big glass door.

"You know what you just did?" he yelled. "You know what you just did? You bought your way into this, that's what! You don't belong here, but now you're in. I'll eat you alive, you son of a bitch. I'll eat you alive!"

I fought the impulse to run.

~*~

The air was heavy with unseen currents. A skinny moon rode over the warehouses and tenements, but it kept ducking behind the clouds and peeking out. Shy. I didn't blame it a bit. I didn't want to be here either.

"They have guns. You know that," I said. "Sooner or later, they'll pull them out."

Chloe sat on a bench, and rummaged through her bag. The nearest streetlight was broken, and she had only the red illumination from the bar signs across the street to work with. I scanned the street, searching for Low Men in the shadows. I didn't see any.

"We knew what we were getting into," she said simply. "This is Chicago—and 1939, no less. Bound to get rough, and now it has."

"Doesn't mean I have to like it."

"You think you always get to choose," she said, troubled. "Sometimes the bad things have already chosen you—and no matter how dark it gets, that's a fight you shouldn't run from."

She seemed to be satisfied with what she found in her purse, and she snapped it closed, slung it over her shoulder, and stood up.

"Cumin, cayenne, turmeric—and blueberry. We're as ready as we're going to be."

I had no idea what she was talking about, but I decided to keep it to myself.

We walked, until she put her hand on my arm at the entrance to a flea-bitten hotel. Behind glass doors, the lobby was darkened. The front desk made an island of yellow light in a sea of dusty potted plants, standing ashtrays and threadbare carpet.

"I'll wait for you here," she said. "Third floor. Find what we need, quickly, and get back here."

"How will I know what I'm looking for?"

She regarded me, eyes bright. Her head was uncovered, and the rain beaded in her hair. She looked like a million bucks.

"You won't have to," she said. "It's going to be looking for you."

She pulled open the door, went in, and crossed the lobby to the elevator without glancing back at me. The doors slid open as she approached, and then closed behind her. She was gone, and I missed her instantly.

When I turned around, I saw a black Dodge coupe stopped on the opposite curb. It seemed like a giant insect, a dung beetle, and I almost expected to see antennae twitching on its hood. The headlights went out as the driver's window cranked down.

"C'mere, pally."

The Grinning Man stuck an elbow out the window and gestured me over. I stepped off the curb and into the empty street, keeping some careful distance between him and me. He stuck a cigarette in the corner of his mouth and hitched sideways behind the steering wheel, fishing for something in his pocket.

It spun and glinted under the streetlight. I caught it, and looked at the brass button in my palm. He stared at me and tipped back the brim of his hat.

"We're getting close, pal," he said. "Starting to understand where your best interests lie?"

"Anything else?"

He stared at me, furious, and then his grin widened. "Sure, why not?" he asked. "Give us a kiss."

He palmed the lit cigarette into his face. He chewed for a moment, and then opened his smoking mouth and spat the mess at my feet. It hissed on the wet macadam.

"Best get with the program, pally," he said. "Your road is getting short. Very, very short. Keep in tune."

He laughed as the window went up. The starter ground and the headlights came back on. He pulled off, and I heard the tortured strip of gears as the taillight went around the next corner. I stood in the middle of the street and considered the button in my hand.

On impulse, I kissed it before I put it away and started walking.

-Twenty Three-

I got lonely on the island without the dog. I hadn't counted on how much I'd miss him. The mornings were especially hard. He always woke up as if the day would be amazing, and losing his early enthusiasms hurt me.

I missed Nora, too. She had been my best friend, and her absence would heal slowly, if it ever did. In the early winter evenings, I stood on my dock and stared across the water, to where her light used to burn. It was dark now, but I didn't forget the spot where it had been.

December rolled in, and the last of late autumn rolled out. The snow had come to stay, although the lake remained unfrozen. I was still able to take the boat to and from the marina, though slowly. The freezing spray off the water made the trips almost unbearable. I brought more and more supplies back with me every time I made the trip into town. I tried to envision every scenario, everything I might need when the ice locked me in.

I never knew when Chloe would show up, and I would be thrust back into a world of trains and conductors and a long trip to somewhere in the west. Sometimes, she came in the morning, and I found myself back in my kitchen at dusk, missing a whole day. Mostly, though, no matter how long I spent in that other place, time here seemed to stand still while I was gone. I picked up exactly where I had left off, as if I hadn't gone anywhere.

I played hockey again, with John Park and his friends. I helped Bill with what tasks he made up for me at the deserted marina. I shopped, and found new ways to get the island, and myself, ready for the isolation of winter. I had coffee, and sometimes a piece of pie, at the coffee shop with Kate. I needed her common sense, and her affection. I went to see her every chance I got. She was the only local person who knew about my visitations with the spirit of Chloe Hunter.

No matter what I did, I waited for Chloe. Her visits were the center of things for me, and time without her became an ache. I stared blankly at trees and water and snow, and only saw her face.

The night I returned from Toronto, I stood at the end of my dock, talking on the phone. The cloud cover was complete, and my boat made a white shape in the dark, hardly visible next to me. Freezing wind blew across the water, steady and unrelenting. It moaned, a low noise like thousands of voices in a stadium when a big play is called back.

"So, he took the money?" Esteban asked.

"I didn't really ask him. I left it there. Tell me, what exactly did you mean when you started talking about the rules? It made him mad, and it—scared him, too, I think. What rules?"

There was such a long enough silence that I thought we were disconnected. I had started to check the small screen on the front of the phone, when he spoke.

"I don't know why I said that. It just came out."

He was lying, but I couldn't make him tell me. "Well, it was the right thing to say."

"You think he'll leave me alone, now?"

"I don't know," I said. "He has his money, but I think he's more angry with me than you, now. I think it might be the last you hear of him, if you're lucky. Be careful, anyway."

"Good," he said. "That's awesome. Amazing."

His relief seemed palpable. I don't think it occurred to him that his problem had potentially been transferred onto me. He didn't think to thank me. I didn't much care, on either count. I said good-bye, disconnected, and went up the dark trail to my cabin. It looked strange and dark. I wished I had left more lights on.

~ * ~

I rapped on the door of Room 333, three times. Chloe opened it at once, and pulled me inside. The room was unlit, and went dark when she closed the door and lost the light from the hallway. I heard the rattle as she put the chain on behind me. Her shadow crossed the room, toward a dim red glow.

I followed her to the window. She parted the venetian blinds with two fingers, and looked out at the street. The neon hotel sign shone directly beside the window, and it illuminated the room in red flashes.

"They're coming," she said. "This isn't a good place for us, this city. It's a good place for them, and they'll try to end it here."

"Will they find us?"

"They sense fear, and I'm always afraid. Nothing I can do about that."

A siren warbled below us. Somewhere on the night streets, somebody was hurt, or in trouble. It gave me an idea.

"Why don't we call the police?"

"It's 1939," she said. "The people here are ghosts—or else we are. I'm not really sure. Some of them can hear us and see us, but most of them can't. It doesn't matter, anyway. We have things to do here. We can't waste time in a police station."

One siren turned into several, and they sang to each other off-key, getting louder. I put my arm around Chloe, and watched the city street. She trembled a little bit.

"We'll wait until they get here, and then go out the window." She nodded. "I'd rather start running when I know where they are, than turn a dark corner and run right into them."

"We're on the third floor, don't forget. Out the window might be a problem."

I glanced at the dark shape of the bed in the corner.

"When I was little," I said, "maybe five years old, I found out about parachutes. I had never been so excited—I figured that I understood how they worked. It was simple. One afternoon, my babysitter walked into an upstairs room and found me standing on the windowsill, ready to jump. I had a bed sheet in both hands. I held the afternoon hostage, but she talked me out of it and I never made my jump. Maybe we could try out my design now."

"When I was little," she countered, "I glued eagle feathers to my arms, and jumped off a stool."

Despite the closing-in danger, I felt a smile tugging at my face.

"Then we have a plan."

"I knew we would."

"Remember when you were little?" she mused. "Remember when your parents went away and left you with friends they trusted, or relatives?"

The hotel sign outside the window flashed its 'vacancy' message to people on the street. Chloe came and went with it, alternating red and dark. The parted venetian blinds made neon stripes on her face.

"You had fun all day, but night came and you found yourself in a strange bed, not yours. The sheets felt a little damp, and smelled like other people. In fact, the whole house smelled different than your house. The light in the hallway was cold, and the bathroom was strange and echoey and too-bright."

I sat quietly, and listened to her.

"They told you goodnight but they didn't say they loved you. You wouldn't have believed it, anyway."

Somewhere on the streets below us, the siren we had heard earlier started up again. It sounded closer now.

"You understood, even though you were small, how alone you really were. The world was huge, and it was almost always nighttime. Strangers didn't know your name, and they didn't want to. Home was a dream, and you didn't know if it was even real, or if you'd ever see it again."

Her voice sounded desolate. I stood up, and crossed the dark room to her. The skin on her face felt hot, but her hands were ice-cold.

"It's what you have to be to me," she finished. "It's what I need. It's all that counts for anything. Even in this strange place, this awful city—you're my home."

I thumbed the tears off her cheeks, and didn't say a word.

216

"It's what you have to be," she repeated. "You have to promise with your eyes, and your voice. You have to make me believe that home is real, and no matter what, I'll always wake up in my own bed."

"I promise," I said. "No matter what."

"You did a long time ago. That's why we're here."

The sirens were loud as they turned onto the block we were on. I peered out at the street below. Two dark saloons nosed into the curb. They both had red lights mounted on their radiator grilles. The doors opened, and men piled out. Some were cradling long guns in their arms. They ran to the front door of the hotel, directly beneath us.

"Cops," I said.

Chloe shook her head, eyes wide. "No," she murmured. "It's the Low Gang. Not that it makes any difference."

A noise in the hallway, and then a pounding started on the door, hard enough to shake the frame. I looked at the crack of light surrounding it, and hoped the lock would hold.

"Come quickly."

Chloe had already gone out the open window and onto the iron fire escape. I followed her awkwardly, scraping my knee painfully on the sill. The neon sign buzzed loudly beside me as I started down. Beneath me, she dropped lightly onto the sidewalk. I landed on the cement with less grace.

"Check their cars for ignition keys," Chloe called. "It'll slow them down."

She headed for the first police car, and I put my head into the window of the second. It smelled unpleasant inside, of dirty laundry left in a basket for weeks, a sandwich forgotten in a desk drawer. I scanned the spare dashboard, with its oversized gauges and large spoked steering wheel. I didn't see any keys, and pulled my head back out.

"No keys," I called, looking around for Chloe.

"I forgot, these old cars started with a button, not keys," she called back, from across the street. "Everything starts with a button, remember?"

217

She was already getting into a '36 Chrysler coupe. She threw herself behind the wheel, and the starter ground. Yellow headlights came on. She turned it into the street, engine racing, and as she passed me I jumped onto the running board and hung on for dear life. Gears howled, and the car rocked on its wheels as we careened around the next corner.

"Slow down!" I screamed into the open window. "I'm going to fall off!"

The first bullets hit the back of the car, a cascade of metallic pop-pop-pops. It sounded as if someone was throwing rocks at us. I turned to look back, and the wind took my hat, spinning it back toward the police car's headlights behind us. There were bright flowers of light as the Tommy gun opened up again. Bullets whispered and sang all around my head, and I heard a window shatter somewhere behind us.

The second pursuing sedan was silhouetted as it slid around the corner behind the first. Parked cars whizzed by me in the dark, close enough to catch my tail, if I'd had one. I looked forward again. We swung left and drifted, toward bricks and plate glass, with terrifying acceleration. The tires screamed like they were alive as Chloe wrestled the car through the intersection.

The coupe slowly won the battle with gravity, and straightened itself. I managed to wrench the door open and pull myself in. I collapsed against the seat back, barely able to breathe. In between gear changes, Chloe reached across me to latch the door shut. Her face glowed in the passing lights.

"You see?" she smiled. "All of it proof that I'm not paranoid. The child psychiatrists were wrong."

I didn't have time to wonder what she was talking about. We ran straight along the lakefront, and the buildings changed to warehouses and darkened shipping offices. There were no lights in any of the windows. I checked behind us. The Low Men were gaining. Our little six-cylinder coupe was no match for the larger saloons. As if it sensed me looking, the Tommy gun opened up again. It grew blossoms of hot yellow and blue in the dark.

My shoulder pressed against Chloe's as she spun the wheel. I grabbed at the edge of the small bench seat to keep myself from sliding into her. She accelerated along a dock, and our tires rumbled as we left cement and rolled onto wooden planks. The high metal side of a tanker ship flashed by my window, and then we left lights behind.

"The Low Gang can't deal with water, did you know that?" she asked. "They're like cats in that way. They won't follow us."

I watched her. She appeared serene in the dim glow of dash lights, but I felt a growing alarm.

"What are you doing?" I asked.

"It'll be cold when we go under, but it makes the tears feel warm on your face. Don't forget—you can breathe under the water."

"I can't!" I shouted. "I'll drown!"

Her smile was a riddle. "You won't drown. You're done with all of that."

The tires went suddenly silent as the car left the dock and sailed into space. I braced myself, and waited for the splash.

~ * ~

Kate stirred her coffee. Nearly lunchtime, and the place was empty. The young waitress wiped some tabletops, and went back to the kitchen.

"Do you blame me for being worried?" she asked.

I had no answer. We both stared out the front window at the falling snow.

"The nights are getting seriously cold. You're going to wake up one morning, probably in the coming week, and the ice will be in. I think we'll see it by Christmas—early this year. I can feel it in my bones."

I nodded. "I think so, too."

"And the boat?"

"I have a block and tackle rigged in the trees," I said. "When there's ice, I'll pull it onto shore and tarp it until spring. We'll

219

use Bill's barge to yank it back into the water next year, after the melt."

"So, what's your plan? You're going to spend a long time stranded with only your own company."

"Not that long. A week after the ice comes in, it'll be thick enough to cross on foot. This is the first place I'm coming. I'm still counting on Christmas dinner with you."

She reached across and touched my hand, a rare gesture for her.

"You'd better be at Christmas dinner," she said. "Safe and sound. If you've had enough of your own company by that time, there's a spare room upstairs, and you're welcome to it for the winter. I'll put you to work here to earn your keep."

"Tempting." I smiled. "You never know. I just might take you up on that."

"Why are you doing this to yourself, Nick?" she asked softly. "Why the exile?"

"It isn't exile, Kate." I answered. "This is my third winter on the island, and every year the ice chases me out of my own home. I just want to stay, and see how it works out. I don't want to find a place on shore, like a refugee. I've had enough of that in my lifetime."

She stood up, and went behind the counter. The phone rang, and she stayed to answer it. I closed my eyes, and breathed in the aromas of the place, apples and cinnamon with an underlay of old wood. I heard Kate's chair scrape back, across the table from me, and I opened my eyes again. She had brought the coffee pot back with her.

"So, it's an adventure——staying the winter."

"Something like that," I said. "A chance to finally get this novel written, or at least started. Think things over. In hindsight, I wish I had the dog with me."

"I bet. I want to ask you something—a bit personal, maybe. Is the spirit of Chloe Hunter still appearing to you?"

I nodded.

"And you talk to her?"

220

"Mostly she talks to me," I said. "But yes, I talk to her."

"More than most people," she said. "I have an ability to see the other side, the spiritual side of things, including ghosts. Everyone can, to some degree, but most suppress it."

She poured herself more coffee, and offered the pot. I shook my head. Outside, the snow came down harder.

"Point is," she continued, "I've been able to see ghosts, but never to communicate with them. The women in my family have generally had the ability to hear them, and sometimes to speak to them—but rarely the sense of sight. Most of the time, the ability to touch, to sense what's—beyond, is a gift that's limited to one or two senses. For you with Chloe, it's much more, am I right?"

"Much more," I confirmed. "When she's with me, it's no different than any other time. I can see, smell, and hear. Everything. Real as real."

"I don't want you to take this wrong," she said slowly. "That's extraordinary. A fugue state—a trance. Mystics go to great length to experience it, even for a few seconds. Indigenous people used peyote, for example, to try to get there. It isn't every day, for anyone."

Her blue eyes were steady.

"What are you saying, Kate?"

"You're in a transcendent state. Far too often. It doesn't add up. I wouldn't be any kind of friend to you if I didn't point it out. Something's very wrong."

I drained my cold coffee, and waited.

"A lot of people find the idea of ghosts crazy," she went on. "I certainly don't, but you're seeing Chloe Hunter in a way that disturbs me. It's too often, too clear, and you're too—engaged. Something's terribly wrong. I think you need to think about addressing this."

My voice went dry. "You think I've lost my mind."

"I think you need to see your doctor, yes. We talked about this, you said you would, and I know you haven't. The cause could be physical. If you're ill, it's all the more reason you shouldn't be isolated for weeks at a time on that island."

"I'm starting to realize that she's..."

I stopped and thought. I had been dwelling on it, without admitting it, even to myself.

"She's the love of my life, Kate. It's as simple as that. I love her to the bottom of me."

She put her hand over mine. Her face showed tears, even if she kept her eyes dry.

"I know you think so, Nick, and that's why I'm so worried. I hate to say it like this, but . . ."

She shook her head, took a breath. "She isn't real. You have to face it. She died a long time ago. What you're seeing isn't real."

"Are you my friend, Kate?" I asked.

She pressed my hand, and nodded.

"Then leave me alone."

"You're more fragile than you think, Nick," she said. "You're teetering at the edge of your own senses, and it will take less of a fall than you think to shatter what's left of you."

I stood up, kissed her cheek, and went out into the snow.

~ * ~

"Remember him?" Chloe asked. "From when you were little?"

She pointed at a figure sitting balanced on the parapet of the building across from us. It took my eyes a moment to adjust, and then I saw it was a giant egg. It shone, huge and pale, in the moonlight, and I made out a tiny hat and bow tie.

He puffed at a cigar, and he flicked the ash again and again. He swung his legs back and forth. A constant low babble came from his mouth, but I couldn't make out the words. His enormous eyes rolled madly.

"Shhhh." She looked at me and held a finger to her lips.

222

"He's a little bit dangerous," she whispered. "Most children know that. Don't attract his attention, whatever you do."

"That's Hum—"

She put her hand across my mouth. "Don't say his name out loud," she said. "It's the same as calling him. He's the gatekeeper of Chicago, and that's all that matters. He's smoking my father's cigar. I left it where he'd find it."

"What's he holding? A telescope?"

"No. It's a kaleidoscope."

"Why?" I wondered. "What's he going to use it for?"

"To see forever, I imagine," she said. "That's what they're generally used for."

The low tumble of words grew into near shouting. The giant egg spat the cigar from his mouth. It lay there, smoking at the base of the wall. He held the kaleidoscope to one eye. His garbled words came faster and faster.

"Get ready," Chloe whispered. "He's going to say it soon. We have to answer together."

She held my hand tight, and we stood up from our crouch. The egg's gibbering rose into an incomprehensible question, and Chloe pulled me into the street.

"Let us pass!" she shouted up at him.

I followed her lead. "Let us pass!"

Humpty Dumpty roared, and dropped the kaleidoscope. Chloe darted into the street, bent and picked it up, as over her head the great egg hoisted himself off the wall. He fell toward the street in slow motion, like something from a nightmare.

We turned and ran. She led me through a maze of unlit alleys and deserted streets, until at last she turned and collapsed into me. We held each other and laughed. After a few minutes, she looked up at me.

"He let us pass?" I asked.

"Yes, he did," she nodded. "He said it. 'You may pass.' Not happily, and he'll take it back if he can get his hands on us, but we're on our way."

I smelled a fire burning, somewhere in the distance.

"I've had enough of this place," she said. "Let's find the train station."

"St. Louis?"

"St. Louis," she nodded, "and a queen."

-Twenty Four-

My mother's house was easy to find on the outskirts of Ansett, nestled in a small depression where the road to Hollow Lake left the highway. It was the house I had grown up in, and I passed it every time I went into town. A century old, it had been sided in gray asphalt shingles that were supposed to look like bricks. The window frames were painted white. It was neatly kept, and I helped when she needed it, which was seldom. Old trees were scattered around the property.

I decided not to phone ahead. I drove there and parked behind her old blue Dart. It had a white vinyl roof and a faded decal on the trunk lid that said 'Swinger'. I got out and stood in the driveway. The sunlight was weak, with no warmth. Above me, on the highway, a big black car pulled onto the shoulder and stopped.

The windows were tinted, and I couldn't see the driver. The car sat quietly. Nobody got out.

~ * ~

A pale station wagon, a '56 Nomad, idled at the curb. *St. Louis Finest Taxicab Company* had been lettered on the door. I checked my wallet, but at this time of night, the taxis could be more dangerous than the streets, so I started walking. The rain had stopped, for at least a little while.

I stopped at a lit telephone booth and checked the chrome coin return, just for luck. The phone rang when I touched it, as if it was offended. I picked up the heavy receiver.

"What are you doing?" Chloe asked.

"Wandering around," I answered. "Lost, I think. My feet hurt."

"I had no idea that you really walked. I always thought you were a part of my imagination, and probably floated. Where are you?"

"I have no idea," I said. "Downtown St. Louis, somewhere. I'm looking for you."

"I'm looking for you, too."

Over the telephone wire, I felt the burst of her smile. The wet city was all at once clean, and the shiny pavements reflected pinks, greens, and soft blues. Warm night air carried the fragrance of music and ginger, the scents of faraway.

"You're not lost," she murmured. "It's 1957, if that helps. Follow the crumbs, and you'll find me."

The connection broke, and I put the phone back on the hook.

A manhole cover in the middle of the block exhaled steam. The cloud hung motionless over the dark street. It looked like a ghost, waiting for me and shifting ever so slightly to keep warm. When I got close enough, it spoke.

"I hate camels. That's why I smoke one, every chance I get."

The Grinning Man stepped out of the fog, laughing at his own joke. His fedora was pulled low, and his long coat was belted tight. He aimed carefully, and threw his lit cigarette at me like a dart. It landed at my feet and writhed sluggishly on the wet cement for a few moments before it died.

"Thought you lost me?" he asked.

"I hoped so."

"Open water does it, but only for a little while."

I nodded. He seemed to be thinking, and I waited.

"I have questions for the splat," he finally said. "So far, I'm not getting answers."

"Too bad."

"You know what every kid is most afraid of?" he asked. "You know what's really at the bottom of every bad dream?"

I shook my head, and started walking. My footsteps echoed against the empty buildings.

"Being eaten," he called after me. "Being eaten all up."

I stopped and looked back. The mist behind him glowed and began to slowly swirl. He lit another cigarette before he spoke.

"Stop following the crumbs, or I'm going to eat you. You and her both. You don't belong here, and I'm going to eat you . . . all up."

His laughter followed close behind me as I walked away. I turned the next corner, and started to run. I needed to get to somewhere safe.

~ * ~

I shrugged, and went up the steps to the front door. My mother opened it before I knocked. She was small and neat, and she didn't look like she agreed much with being an old lady. The eyes of a quiet young woman contemplated me from her almost eighty-year-old face.

"I haven't seen you in a while," she said. "Kate Bean told me you'd be coming by. Are you staying for dinner?"

The house smelled clean and dry. She led me through to the kitchen in back, and sat with me at the linoleum-topped table.

"Something's been going on at your island," she prompted. "Kate said that's been bothering you more than losing your wife and baby."

"Nora isn't my wife, Mom," I said. "For that matter, it isn't my baby, either."

She appeared startled, but just for a moment. "Then you should know there's always new pain, and no point in stirring up old pain."

I thought about that, and nodded. Charlotte Hunter had said much the same thing.

I told her what had been happening to me, since Kate had probably told her most of it. I described the girl in the pink swimsuit who had walked out of the lake, the writing on the mirror in Nora's bathroom, and the footprints in the snow outside my cabin. I left out the details of Chloe's visitations, since they seemed to take a haunting and push it into the realm of mental delusion.

"I started out researching an old story to maybe write a novel," I said. "It's more, now. I seem to be at the center of whatever happened to this girl at the end of her life."

"Her suicide, you mean?" She looked away.

It was time to confront her. "Why didn't you ever tell me about her?" I asked. "Why keep a secret from me?"

"Do you think you were all right when you woke up in that hospital bed?" she asked. Her voice rose. "Do you think you just came out of it, like you were? You were nearly a zombie. You were in therapy for months. You didn't remember her. You had enough trouble remembering how to walk. Should I have tried to remind you, to tell you that while you slept a girl you loved had killed herself?"

She put her face in her hands. I tried to feel bad for upsetting her, but I felt betrayed instead.

"You should have told me," I said. "I lived my whole life not knowing something that mattered."

"You were fragile," she said. "It would have set you back, and we were fighting for your life."

She looked around the room for a way to change the subject. "I never quite believed she was a suicide, evidence to the contrary."

"Why not?" I asked. "No one else doubts it."

She didn't answer right away. After a moment's thought, she stood up and went to the cupboards. She turned back toward me, with a teacup held up as a question. I nodded.

"You two had only been dating for a few weeks," she said, over the sound of the faucet. "I didn't like her. In hindsight, I think I felt just normally protective of my son. She was, in many ways, much—older than you."

She filled a kettle from the faucet while she thought things over.

"She was one of those people who comes across as— haughty. I'm not sure that's the right word, but they seem like they know and see things other people don't. Things we couldn't possibly understand, and it makes them seem smug. I was a dowdy school secretary just past my fortieth birthday, and she was a young, beautiful sophisticate from New York. A private school girl, who had captured the son I had borne and loved, and might just throw him away when she was done with him."

She opened and then closed a cabinet and a drawer, firmly. I wondered if she was angry. She crossed the kitchen rapidly, and got a container of milk from the refrigerator.

"So, you didn't like her?" I ventured.

"Like her?" She looked at me, surprised. "I didn't, at first. I did later, and I do now. I think of her as the daughter-in-law I didn't quite have, these days. Family, almost."

"What changed your mind?"

"We spent time together, in tea and talk after you drowned. Like this. We were the two who loved you best. In a way, we were all each other had left of you."

She poured hot water, and leaned on the counter to face me while the tea steeped. Her face got inexpressibly sad.

"I think Chloe did know and see things," she said. "I think it separated her from the rest of us. I think it was a terrible, terrible burden for her. If she seemed aloof, it was because she was a deeply lonely young woman, one who had been lonely since she was a little girl."

She came back to the table, served tea, and then sat across from me. "Chloe came to see me one afternoon in the fall. I was surprised when she knocked on the door, because she had gone back to school in New York by then. She told me that you were still out on the lake, stuck. That was the word she used—stuck. You've heard the rumors by now? You've been asking?"

She regarded me directly, and I could see the pain in her eyes. I decided to be direct. "People heard something out on the water at night," I said gently. "When I was in the hospital."

"They heard—screaming. Screaming for help. Can you imagine how that made me feel?"

I shook my head, neither a yes nor a no.

"Chloe said she had to unstick you. She had heard you on the water, from her dock. She didn't know what she could do, but she had to help you. She said you couldn't move from where you were, and you kept drowning and drowning."

I shuddered inwardly. Drowning was the death I would choose last. Cold, dark water made the loneliest, most horrifying end that I could imagine.

"The poor girl had lost weight since I had last seen her," my mother continued. "She was hollow—haunted. A few weeks later, she was dead. I wish I could have saved her, but I never saw it coming."

She reached across the table and touched my hand. I turned mine to take hers, but she withdrew it and picked up her cup.

"Her mother thought Chloe swam out in that cold lake because she knew how to—free you. I know she hated me for it."

"I saw her," I said. "She doesn't blame you for any of it."

She stared out the window, and visibly went somewhere else. I listened to the old house tick and creak around us while I waited for her to speak again.

"I think we live in winter," she finally said. "We tramp around in the ice and the snow. It isn't all bad. We have the warmth of our houses, fires in fireplaces, and headlights on dark roads that pick out swirls and flurries. There's hot food and television and sleep."

"Stars at night," I nodded. "Black skies."

"Yes. Stars at night. We have our comforts, and our routines. When it's suggested to us that there are fish swimming beneath the ice, and that the bare trees have sap running in their veins ready to burst leaves, it makes us afraid, because we've never seen such a thing."

I saw where she was going. I nodded.

"We're snowmen," she said. "Rumors of green grass, talk of flowers and running water are threatening. We're terrified and angry that we're going to lose everything we love, all of the things we know. We bury our dead in the slush, with icicles folded into their hands, say freezing words over them, to guard them against the coming warmth."

I drained my tea. The cat jumped onto the table, and she shooed it back onto the floor.

"We can't take the piles of snow that we've collected with us," she murmured, "but we secretly don't believe it. We'll always be cold, we hope, because it's all we know. It's why spring makes us ache. We remember, almost, where we're going, and where we've come from. We can't quite put a finger on it..."

"We're snowmen," I said. "Afraid to melt."

"Exactly. We believe that when we aren't snowmen any more, when we've melted into waterfalls and rivers and run out to the ocean, we won't exist at all. So, some spirits cling to winter. They won't leave, no matter what. They remake themselves in ice and promise that they'll be frozen solid forever."

"They miss out on everything," I smiled. "They're stuck."

"Some people see the summer, even when it's snowing," she said. "They play by different rules. You're very lucky."

She stared into the window, perhaps looking for her own refection in the glass, and perhaps something even more. She spoke very slowly.

"She died for you," she said. "Even if she was tragically deluded, she loved you enough to dive into freezing water to save you. She died for you, and not many of us ever get to experience that kind of love."

The day had clouded over. She didn't seem to notice the first drops of rain that spattered against the glass.

~ * ~

The rain made a noisy downpour, beating at the forest canopy over our heads. We followed a dark path through the trees. The greens and browns of the woods were scribbled into blacks and grays by the unseen clouds above us. Here and there, streams of water drained from a hundred feet up, through holes in the leafy roof, and spattered on the loam below.

231

Chloe stood still, expression intent, looking down at her watch.

"When is this?" I asked. "Where?"

"I don't know. 1950s, I think. I don't think time much matters, here. Somewhere outside the city of St. Louis, I suppose."

We started walking, again. It grew lighter, and the path curved around a particularly large tree and then ended all at once in a meadow. The gray sky fell into the open space like a waterfall. Outside the cover of trees, the rain grew into a torrent. It became almost impossible to hear the crashes of thunder over the constant roar of the deluge.

The clearing made a nearly perfect circle, covered with long grass. At the far end, a solitary figure sat alone, slumped on a huge chair. It shimmered in and out of my vision in the wet afternoon, wavering as though underwater. The person appeared dead, or asleep. Even so, I felt eyes watching me.

"It's the Queen," Chloe said. "Finally, after all this time."

"The Queen of St. Louis?" I asked.

Chloe's hair was plastered to her cheeks and neck, and water ran unheeded down her face. She gazed raptly across the clearing at the figure slouched on the throne, motionless in the rain.

"The cupcake queen," she nodded. "She's wearing magenta. I knew she would be."

I wiped the rain from my eyes. The robe made a small splash of color in the gray day.

"That was always my favorite crayon in preschool," Chloe said. "I'd search for it in the big shoe box, find it, feel happy— and then not know what to do." She glanced over at me. "It's only lately that I've started to understand."

She took my hand, and led me into the clearing, through the knee-deep grass.

The queen sprawled sideways, arms and legs askew. She didn't move. Her face was painted white under a startling corona of pink hair. Lipstick made her mouth into a wide smile. Mascara tears ran down her cheeks and turned her eyes into black holes.

As we got closer, the rain lessened, and by the time we stood in front of her, it tapered to nothing. The silence after the downpour was complete. The forest that surrounded us waited, stunned and dripping.

"Should we bow?" I whispered.

"I never know what to do in cases like this," Chloe said. "Generally, I stay invisible."

The queen's eyes were slitted, and her mouth gaped behind the garish smile. The magenta robe hung open. Her crown lay in the wet grass at our feet.

"She's dead," I muttered. "I really do think she's dead."

Chloe bent to pick up the tiara. As she touched it, the woman's eyes snapped open, yellowish white orbs in the pools of black.

"Boo," she said.

"Boo, yourself," Chloe replied, cheerfully. "You dropped your crown."

She helped the Queen of St. Louis to sit up, and then she carefully replaced the headdress, arranging her wet pink curls as becomingly as possible.

"Let me see how I look," the queen said. "Let me borrow a telescope."

Chloe rummaged in her bag and produced the kaleidoscope. The queen awkwardly placed it to her eye and pointed it up toward the clouds. After a moment, she grunted in a satisfied way and returned the looking-device to Chloe.

"See for yourself. I look very nice, despite the wet. You, however, do not. You look like a drowned rat."

At the word 'rat', an enormous spotted cat emerged from beneath the throne, where he had been keeping dry beneath the folds of the royal gown. He looked us over, and not seeing any rats, sat down and began to lick one of his paws.

"This isn't a telescope at all," Chloe said. "It's a kaleidoscope, but you still look very nice."

"You can't see yourself in a kaleidoscope," I told the queen. "You're confusing it with a mirror."

She straightened up in her seat and bared her teeth at me. Her gums were gray. The cat looked up from his paw, interested.

"Do I seem," she hissed, and took a deep breath.

I was already shaking my head.

"Do I seem," and her voice rose to a gaspy scream, ". . . quite—stupid, to you? Is that how I seem? Stupid?"

I took several steps backward, quickly, and found myself stopped by Chloe's hand at my waist. She interrupted, gently. "We've come a very long way," she told the queen softly, "to have a picnic with you."

The woman stopped in mid-scream. Her chest heaved, and her eyes rolled, from Chloe to me and then back again. It took several minutes before she found her breath.

"A picnic?" she finally asked. "Will there be presents?"

"Of course, there will," Chloe said. "Whoever heard of a picnic without presents?

"I have cupcakes."

"I counted on that."

The queen was mollified. She stood up stiffly, and hobbled out of sight behind her throne. She came back with a huge tray of cupcakes, frosted pink and peach and yellow.

"These are for everyone to share," she said, glaring at me. "Not just for you."

"He'll share," Chloe said. "And we'll take a few of them west with us, if you don't mind. They have meaning."

The queen sat and thought about it for a little while, and nodded. Then she turned her attention back to me. "You've invoked the dead," she said solemnly. "I hope you know what you're doing. It's very dangerous."

"It's also a terrible sweetness," Chloe said. "It's turquoise tears—warmth, and protection. When you call love, it almost always comes."

The cat stood up, arched himself, and went to Chloe to be petted. His back came easily as high as her waist.

"I haven't called the dead," I protested. "Or invoked them."

"Is he serious?" the cupcake queen asked Chloe.

"I never really know," she answered, smiling. "It's one of the things I like best about him."

The clouds rolled ever faster over our heads. They faded from dark to silver, and began to shred. The thunder went with them, sounding more and more distant. I thought we might see the sun, before long.

"I haven't called anyone," I insisted. I felt lost. "Not the dead, or anyone else."

"Of course, you did," the queen scolded me. "You're quite mad. The sooner you get used to it, the happier you'll be."

Chloe broke a cupcake in two, and handed a half to me.

"You might have waited until the Tyger left," the Queen said. "You'll hurt his feelings, not offering him any."

"That isn't a tiger," I said. "It has spots. Tigers have stripes."

"Of course, it is," the Queen snapped. "It's a real Tyger. What else would it be?"

She glared at me for a full minute, and then leaned over to speak privately to Chloe, in a very loud voice. "Where did you find him?" she demanded. "I think he has Oldstimers."

"He might," Chloe said, and smiled serenely. "I often have to pick him up and point him in the right direction. 'Yes, that's where you were going', I tell him."

I took a deep breath, and counted to fourteen while I gazed at the willows across the river. I wanted to weep, too. "It isn't called Oldstimers," I said. "It's called . . . "

The Queen's face turned purple, and she stood up, spilling the cupcakes she had been holding on her lap onto the ground. They rolled away in every direction, glad to be making their escape.

"Silence!" she screamed. "Guards!"

"You don't have any guards," Chloe remarked, unperturbed. "You never did."

The Queen looked wildly around her, and then subsided. She sat back down. "Well, I shall certainly get some," she said, petulantly. She pointed imperiously at me. "You! Place an advertisement, at once!"

She turned to Chloe. "And you? Will you go on to the end? Will you get past the Low Gang?"

"I'm going to try. There are a lot of them, and only two of us. It's going to take all the courage I have."

Above us, the sun struggled with the clouds. The dripping woods looked on, hopefully.

"You seem brave enough."

"Actually, I'm always quite frightened," Chloe said. "Of everything, mainly."

She lifted her chin, and I saw she was trying not to cry. I wanted to go to her, but I stayed put. She had to say this, by herself.

"There's nothing wrong with tears, you know," the queen said gently. "If there are enough of them, they drown the very low, the things that hunt in the middle of the night. The things that follow and laugh—and bite."

"It's a good thing I can see with my eyes closed," Chloe confessed. "They're so often swollen shut from crying."

The Queen of St. Louis leaned forward on her throne. Her voice was kind. Despite her pink hair, the magenta robe, and the enormous lipstick smile, I saw what made her a queen. Behind the running mascara, her eyes were alive with wisdom, the kind that survives fashion.

"You see everything. It's why there are kaleidoscopes—to see it all. The good and the bad. The trick is to see through the black and the wicked, to know that another turn brings enough magic and beauty and color to break your heart."

"It does break my heart," Chloe said. "My heart—is broken, in the best way. It's just that sometimes it all seems—so much. I feel as though the unseen currents are going to sweep me away. No one else seems to be as afraid as I am."

"It's because they don't have your gift. They can't see what you do. They run around in the dark, bumping into things."

"Sometimes, I wish was like that. I wouldn't be so terrified."

"Don't confuse courage and blindness," the queen said. "They aren't the same thing. You're the bravest of them all."

The clouds broke, all at once, and the world turned from gray to pale green. The faded flowers that were scattered around the throne brightened. Chloe opened her hand to the queen. Something glinted and glimmered on her palm, reflecting the new sun. I watched the light play across the queen's face. Her lipsticked mouth spread into a real smile, and I was startled to see that she was beautiful.

"It's lovely," she murmured. "You remembered—there are no coincidences."

"Numbers and colors—birth and death," Chloe answered, very softly. "There are letters waiting to be read, but there are no coincidences. It's synchronicity, no matter what."

"Numbers and colors," the queen echoed. "Synchronicity, no matter what. You may pass.

Her eyes shone as the butterfly moved slowly, delicately, from Chloe's hand to hers.

"You may pass," the Queen of St. Louis told us.

-Twenty Five-

I couldn't remember the last time I had been in my old room. I hadn't slept in there since I had left for college. It seemed unchanged. My mother wasn't the type to keep a shrine, and I supposed she simply hadn't needed the space. The house was too big for her, anyway.

Sports Illustrated covers were taped to one wall. I walked across the bare wood floor to look at them. I saw dry, faded images of Pete Rose, Roberto Duran, and the Steelers. They were forgotten heroes, the toasts of a ghost town that had blown away.

A green plaid spread covered the single bed. There were no pillows. A small wooden desk stood under the one window. I could imagine myself sitting there, staring out at the street, forgotten homework in front of me.

A single sheet of paper lay on the desk. I picked it up. It was a sketch on notebook paper, a little bit finer than a mere doodle. I had been a fair artist. A girl water-skied. She was captured leaning into a turn, spray flying behind her. There were three words written beneath her image, underlined twice.

"Best day ever," I murmured. "Chloe?"

"You may have been out of your league with her," my mother mused. "You were so happy, though. I keep that paper out, and look at it when I come in here. I hope someday you're as happy as you were when you drew that."

"I think none of this was supposed to turn out the way it did," I said.

Outside the window, I saw the black car pulled over on the shoulder again, at the top of the driveway. As if he sensed me watching, the driver put it into gear and sped away. I knew it wasn't coincidence. The black car had come for me, and it certainly belonged to Sonny Risa. The fun was about to begin.

~ * ~

238

It's the kind of summer night that starts out warm and sticky, until the heat mostly leaches away, leaving the humidity behind. The small hours are damp and clammy, and that's the best time for ghosts, the time they like to walk around and do what they do. We sat on a bench and watched to see if we could catch one in the act.

The city skyline sparkled against a warm black sky, a jewelry box spill on velvet. The inlet shimmered with the reflected colors, and over all of it the moon swung whitely, so bright that I couldn't make out its face.

Down by the water, someone played a saxophone. The notes floated by in the dark, a song about barely remembered summers. I was so tired that my eyes hurt, but I wouldn't be sleeping any time soon.

"Where are we?" I asked.

Chloe put a finger to her lips. "Memphis," she whispered. "The train stopped to take on water."

A freighter moved by, prowling the late night harbor. A few holiday bulbs were strung out across its superstructure, but it was mostly unlit, and it cast a huge dark shadow on the water. A pelican roosting on a piece of wood near where we sat got disturbed. It stretched its neck at the ship's passing, then ruffled its wings and went back to sleep.

"Hush," she murmured. "Can you feel it? The show's about to start."

~ * ~

I opened my eyes. The cabin was dark. I didn't remember coming home. I had piloted the boat across the lake in whatever absent state I had been in, and that worried me. I hoped I had said a coherent goodbye to my mother. Maybe I had stayed for dinner with her, and talked about boats and baseball. Nonetheless, I had been somewhere else.

Outside the window, early winter dusk had settled across the lake. I waited for a moment, to see if Chloe would back, and then decided I was stuck here for the moment. I rubbed my face, and got up to turn on a light.

I went through the dark cabin into the bathroom, and flicked on the light. The face that looked back at me from the mirror was gaunt and dark. The rasp of stubble on my face startled me. I had always stayed clean-shaven, but the shadow on my face was dangerously close to becoming a beard. I turned on the shower tap, and while I waited for the water to run hot, got out my razor.

I showered until the water was cold, and found clean jeans. In the kitchen, I ate standing up at the sink, staring out the window at nothing. The forest behind the cabin was pitch black. The wind outside caught at the eaves and corners. I thought I heard the sound of a tiny bell, but I wasn't sure.

I took my tea into the main room, and put on a lamp. The room had gotten cold, so I stocked the wood stove. I sat down with a book that I wasn't going to read. The fire hissed and popped as the heat rose, and I leaned back and closed my eyes.

~ * ~

"Stop," Chloe said.

I parked in the middle of a long bridge.

No traffic rolled in either direction, so we left the car where it was and walked to the side. The superstructure over our heads gleamed pale, nearly white. The sun had come up while we drove, and it glinted off the bridge's cables and the turquoise water that flowed slowly beneath us.

We stood, side-by-side, elbows on the rail. Her shoulder touched mine. I caught a waft of lavender, from her, or from the water. I suspected it was the same thing.

A small island floated beneath us, moving almost imperceptibly in the current. It left the shelter of the bridge by degrees, until it was totally revealed. I looked down at the canopy of trees covering it and saw birds, flitting from one branch to the next, appearing and then vanishing into the leaves.

A canoe was tied to a post on the bank, and it trailed behind the island on a tether, tracking back and forth in the stream.

I leaned over the railing, and peered to my left. From behind one of the bridge's piers, a rowboat appeared. The oars were shipped. A man in a crushed bowler hat sat in the stern, reading aloud from an open book. A woman with a flowered parasol lolled in the bow, listening idly.

A gold-colored periscope rose from the surface about twenty yards from them and held steady against the current. It pointed in their direction until they were past, and then submerged again.

We heard excited shouting, and saw two small boys smiling and waving to us from a large raft, a striped bed sheet draped from a broomstick fixed in the middle of the craft. The wind filled the makeshift sail, and they were making terrific time. Shirtless and tanned, they ran around the platform excitedly and pointed us out to each other. A large brown dog leapt and spun between them.

"Look," Chloe pointed. "This is Time—or at least a tiny bit of it. It's the part I know."

On the nearest bank, buildings formed, seeming to materialize from nothing. Churches and barns, office and apartment buildings, houses and storefronts sprang up and then as quickly melted away, eroded like sand castles by the river's current. They were replaced by other structures, which then disappeared in their turn.

"Everything washes away," I said sadly.

She kissed me. "That's what you think you see because you've forgotten how to fly. Everything washes downstream, but it's all still there, and always will be."

She kissed me again with real heat, and I suddenly didn't care much about rivers. She tasted and smelled like flowers and warm earth. She broke off and looked at me, eyes dark.

"Time isn't unkind, like you think it is, but you and I have to do something if we're going to do this. We have to swim."

She trailed off, gazing at the turquoise water. "We have to learn to swim," she repeated. "Both of us."

241

~ * ~

Sometime during the night, I opened my eyes. The room was warm. My book had fallen off my lap onto the floor. I looked around for the dog, and had a moment of alarm before I remembered he was in Toronto with Nora. I hauled myself to my feet, and slipped on my boots at the door.

The screen door squeaked shut behind me. The night air was seriously cold, well below freezing. The forest stayed utterly silent, and my steps crunched through the dead leaves in the clearing. The usually spongy loam surrounding the cabin was rock-hard and felt unfamiliar under my feet. I had never been here after it had frozen.

The night was clear. I figured it must be about three in the morning. Out on the dock, I stood and listened to the lap of water beneath me. No illumination at all showed on the opposite shore. The entire area was black and deserted. The porch lights, the campfires, barbeques, fireflies and sparklers were all gone until spring.

I missed the light on Nora's dock. I missed Nora, for that matter. I wondered again if I was making a mistake, staying here for the winter. The ice would be here any day now. I watched the lake, square miles of it spread out at my feet. The waves on its surface glimmered in the winter light.

"Stay away, ice," I murmured, and didn't like the sound of my own voice. "Stay away, bitch. Just for a little while longer."

I looked behind me, at the cabin sitting in the trees. I knew I couldn't risk leaving. I was utterly immersed in the train trip, and captivated by Chloe. I needed to know what secret I was being propelled toward. I didn't know what role the island played in my memories and reveries, but I couldn't take the chance they would follow me elsewhere.

From the other side of the lake, I heard a car engine a long time before lights appeared across the reach, following the south shore road. The vehicle moved slowly, driven by someone cautious about the dark, or unfamiliar with the area.

I had been looking across the water for two years now, and I didn't need the lights on shore to mark the car's progress. I knew exactly where the headlights were, as they passed cottage after cottage. They stopped at the spot on the shoreline in front of Nora's house, and I instinctively moved a step toward the boat tied up beside me. Then they started moving again.

The car disappeared for a short while behind a screen of trees, and finally emerged at the public boat launch, the cement ramp which sloped into the water. The lights turned and faced me, shining across almost a mile of open water. There was no human possibility that the driver could see me at this distance, standing in the dark on my dock, but I knew he watched me, just the same.

As if to confirm it, the car horn sounded, three long bleats. There was no wind, and the sound was startling across the silent reach. The horn sounded another group of three, then one more. After nine blasts, the lights backed and turned, and started back the way they had come, faster now, moving back along the shore road until they vanished.

I stood at the end of the dock, waiting. I watched the nighttime water, until I started to shiver. When I headed back inside, my feet crunched through a carpet of dead leaves.

~ * ~

We came into a clearing. Chloe motioned me to be quiet. She carried a wicker basket in her left hand. She set it down, and tied the arms of her sweater around her waist.

The gray birches were surrendering to autumn, and the ground was scattered with their leaves, as bright against the dark earth as a treasure chest spill of gold medallions. A young girl knelt at the far side of the clearing, partially turned away from us. Her blue skirt and white pinafore were arranged demurely over her knees.

A fat bear cub sat beside her. She brushed its light brown fur glossy with a pearl-handled brush. It kept its face turned up, gazing at her as she spoke. She was telling a story. The cub's parents sat on either side, enormous as giants at a children's tea party. The larger bears were listening, and stirred impatiently whenever the girl paused to work out a knot in the baby's fur.

As we watched, the father bear reached out with a long black claw to touch the ribbon in the girl's blonde hair. Without turning around, she gently swatted his enormous paw away.

"Who's she?" I whispered, looking at Chloe. "She seems familiar to me."

She shook her head, not taking her eyes from the group in front of us. "Goldilocks seems *familiar* to you?" she murmured. "Sometimes you talk like you were just born yesterday."

I was cold, and I put my arm around her. "Does this have to with the other bears we've seen?"

"Is it relevant, do you mean?" she asked. "Too much relevance is boring."

Goldilocks mouthed the words 'The End', and beamed at the three bears sitting with her. The baby cub at once began to cry, and the mother rose from her sitting position. I could hear the faint beginning of her growl, like a far-off chain saw. The girl sighed deeply, theatrically, and again mimed opening the invisible book in her lap. She began another story, and the bears settled happily.

"It's like those dreams where you keep finding money," she went on, "and after a while you say, 'okay, so what now?' As for horoscopes, I never read them. They're consistent, much too relevant. Boring."

She took my hand and pulled me across the clearing, toward the little group seated there. Goldilocks set her book aside, motioned to the bears to stay where they were, and got up to meet us.

"Horoscopes," Chloe sniffed. "There's far too much magic in real life to spend time there."

244

Chloe pulled me by the hand, toward the bears. A wind kicked up and sent an eddy of leaves down from the sky, into the center of the clearing. It spun for a moment, red and yellow and orange, and then sank to the ground. When we were close enough, she held the basket out, and Goldilocks took it. The bears shifted their attention away from us, and raised their black noses, sniffing the air.

"Are these the bears who follow me, and eat my crumbs?" Chloe smiled. "If I get lost, they'll have themselves to blame."

"I don't think so," Goldilocks replied. "I keep them pretty busy. Perhaps when I'm asleep they get into mischief. They wouldn't tell me if they did."

She opened the lid of the basket, and gave each of the bears a pink cupcake. She took one out for herself and considered it for a moment. Then, with a small moue, she put it back.

"Maybe later," she said. "They give me funny dreams."

"Oh, me too," Chloe agreed.

The first cold drop of rain hit me at the top of my brow, and I started. A cartoon wind whistled music through the trees. It was a song that I knew from somewhere, but I couldn't remember what it was called.

"Not that I have anything against dreams, mind you," Chloe said. "My very favorite thing, when I'm asleep. They just never seem to turn out quite the way we hope."

Her waist was warm against my arm. I wanted to gather her to me, but I knew she wouldn't allow it. Clouds rolled across the sky above the clearing, black and angry. The three bears gazed up at them, the cupcake in their paws forgotten. At the first rumble of thunder, the baby cub yowled, terrified. Goldilocks patted and shushed him, wiping pink frosting from his snout.

"We have to go," she apologized. "Thank you for the cupcakes, and I hope you like it in Kansas City."

"Even if we don't, we have to carry on—no matter what."

"You may pass."

Goldilocks rose and smoothed her pinafore. She took a dollar from one starched white pocket, and gave it to Chloe.

245

"This is for you. I'm sorry, it's the only thing I have to give you."

"It will be perfect. Perfectly perfect."

Goldilocks gathered her things and put them in the basket, saving the invisible storybook for last. When she was ready, she turned away and led her companions up the path and into the woods. She held the baby by its paw. The mother and father bear trailed behind, looking worriedly at the sky.

My voice felt tight. "The worst thing about dreaming," I murmured, "is that you always have to wake up, every single time. Dreams can't last."

Chloe glanced at me and raised an eyebrow.

"But we dream anyway—even though we know we're going to wake up," I finished. "That's what makes us foolish."

"Hopeless dreams don't make us foolish," Chloe said. "They make us beautiful."

~ * ~

I sat in Kate's, finishing a cup of coffee and a piece of cornbread. The little bell over the door jangled, and Sonny Risa came in, by himself. He stood in the opening for a moment, framed against the day outside, letting in the cold.

He walked over to me, sat down, and tossed his fedora onto the table next to my plate. He looked and smelled like the city.

"Found you," he said.

I stared at him, and didn't answer.

"Wasn't hard," he said, and leaned back. "I looked you up. You've made the papers once or twice."

"Big deal."

"You're a loser," he said. "About what I expected—a nothing, holed up on an island in the middle of nowhere. Doesn't seem to me like you've managed to do well at much of anything. You pretty much screw up anyone who cares about you. I checked in on your girlfriend, not so long ago. She was with a mutual friend of ours."

246

My hands were balling into fists. I opened them, and spread my fingers on my knees under the table.

"Which explains your interference, your little visit to my place of business," he said. "It defines 'loser' about as well as it can be done, don't you think? Coming to the rescue of the pathetic slob who's screwing your girlfriend."

His shoulders shook with laughter. His face crinkled until his eyes nearly disappeared. He laughed until he was out of breath. "Am I right?" he wheezed. "C'mon, admit it. Am I right? You're a mess."

His merriment was so infectious I almost smiled, and then as quickly as it had come, his laughter left. His face stayed flushed, but his eyes were cold and dead. "Speaking of screwing—now you've screwed with me," he went on. "So, your sad, forgettable life is about to get memorable. How about that?"

"How about that?" I agreed.

"You don't belong here. You never have, never will."

The teenaged girl who helped Kate in the mornings set a cup of coffee in front of him, and tried a smile. He ignored her, and she went away. His eyes were fixed on mine, more than a little bit crazy. I waited, and when he finally spoke, his voice was soft.

"What do you say we play a little game, you and me?" he asked. "I'll let you lose."

We sat and stared at each other for a while.

"We're closed."

Kate Bean had materialized beside us. She held a white dishtowel, and twisted it in both hands.

"We're closed," she repeated. "You can go play your games, somewhere else."

"You giving me the bum's rush?" Risa smiled. "Kicking me out? Who are you?"

She was definite. "This is my place, and I'm telling you to go."

Risa tipped his chair back, and bared his teeth. Kate turned to me.

247

"Is this the man who's been bothering you and Nora?" she asked. "It's him, isn't it?"

Her expression became savage.

"I got this, Kate," I said quietly.

"You might want to dial this down before I start to get seriously annoyed with you, old woman," Risa said, smiling.

His face was bright red. He stood up and faced her across the table. I stood up, too. Kate bristled beside me, and I got ready to jump between them.

"You're a coward," she said. "A small man. Wipe the stupid grin off your face."

"Go back in your kitchen, old woman," he said. His voice was deeper, and somehow dreadful. "Go back to your pies, before I remember your mother's face. I'll find her, and we'll have fun until she curses your birth."

The normal quiet clatter of the coffee shop fell away to nothing. Two men at the nearest table appeared as though they were going to get up to defend Kate, but then they looked at Risa and stayed where they were.

"You've embarrassed me," he said to me. "You should have minded your own business. People who mess with me get eaten alive." He was breathing hard, nearly hyperventilating. "You have eleven days. Are you clear? Eleven days. Same deal as your friend. I want your ass, meddler."

"Eleven days—or else?" I asked. "Aren't you supposed to say, 'or else'? Sounds better when you do."

"Eleven days, and the game's up. Do it your way, or we'll do it mine. Nice island you have, by the way. A little busy, but I bet you hardly notice."

He picked up his hat from the table, and put it on. He got suddenly calm, and his smile came back.

"You should come for a visit," I said. "Come straight out to see me, instead of sneaking around the shoreline at night."

He cocked an eyebrow at me. "I don't much like the water," he said. "Especially open water, as I think you know."

He gave Kate an odd little bow. "As for you, I'll be seeing you. One of these days. I'll keep an eye out."

"Get out of here," she snapped.

He walked to the door, his good humor restored. "Eleven days," he called back over his shoulder. "Keep in tune."

The bell over the door stayed strangely silent as the door closed behind him.

-Twenty Six-

The platform vibrated under our feet, and the crowd stirred around us as a single headlight brightened and waned, searching the murk. The tired locomotive pulled in, slowly, breathing hard. It was immense, heavy, wreathed in fog and clouds of steam.

Chloe turned me to her, and spoke over the ringing bells. "Memories," she said, "are just what you use to set things on fire."

Vapor rose behind her and caught the light, like the dreams ghosts walk in. She wore a wide-brimmed gray hat with a green ostrich feather, a calf-length coat, and pumps with heels. Her hair was pulled back, and she wore more makeup than I remembered. She was utterly elegant.

The Train rolled to a stop, clanging and hissing, alive. The wheels were nearly as tall as me. Steps dropped noisily, and the Conductor put his head out, looking up and down the platform.

"This is . . .?" I asked.

"Kansas City."

I scanned the crowd around us, searching for familiar faces.

"I know you're expecting Dorothy," she said, "but this is Kansas City, Missouri."

"I'm glad you're here, with me again."

"Are you?"

"I miss you more and more now, when you're not around," I said. "I know I'm not supposed to, but I do."

"Why aren't you supposed to miss me?"

"I'm not sure," I said, suddenly at odds. "I pretend like it doesn't matter to me, but you're an ache. When I'm missing you, I miss——everything. It's dangerous."

She regarded me severely. "You aren't worried about dangerous. You were born for this. We both were."

The people around us began to scramble with luggage and tickets and goodbyes. The night was cold, and colored steam floated, damp and lonely. I wanted to get aboard.

"Excuse me," a voice said. "None of my business, but do you folks know you're being followed?"

"Thanks," I said. "What makes you say so?"

The owner of the voice was a young man, a slender number in an eight-button coat with a fresh carnation in the lapel. He was a marcel-haired dandy, but his eyes were tough as nails. He jerked a thumb over his shoulder. I saw at least six furtive men, identical in dark dusters and snap-brim fedoras, melting into the crowd.

"Uh oh," I said. "I wasn't expecting that."

"Best to always expect your friends from low places right when you don't expect them," he replied. "Cunning is what they are."

He stuck out his hand. "Charlie Parker."

He kissed the air over Chloe's hand.

"I saw you at Monroe's, Mister Parker," she said. "A couple of years ago. You were with Miles Davis."

"Miles is here with us now," he said, surprised. "You can call me Bird. You like jazz?"

"I like music," she said simply. "I like infinite travel."

He nodded approvingly. "You get it, all right. You sure do."

He looked over his shoulder. The crowd was beginning to thin as people boarded the train. The men from low places had fewer places to hide, and were darting into and out of the clouds of smoke and steam that drifted across the platform. Parker's companions stood in a small group, surrounded by luggage. I recognized the horn cases. They watched us, faces emotionless, and made no move to join us.

"You want help?" Parker asked. "Miles is fixed most of the time now. He might not be much good for something like this, but that's Coleman Hawkins and Freddie Webster over there. We're headed for the West Coast. We ought to be able to keep you out of jams that far, anyway."

Chloe rummaged through her clutch, and came up with the single bill Goldilocks had given her. She folded it lengthways and proffered it to Parker. "I only have a dollar."

251

"We don't need your money," he said. "Keep it."

"I only have a dollar," she repeated, and smiled at him, keeping her hand out. "You're the Gatekeeper of Kansas City, if I'm not mistaken."

He stared at her for a moment, and then took the money. "Now that you say so, a dollar's just about what a job like this cost."

"May we pass?"

"Yes'm. You may pass. You have things to do here in Kansas City, before the train leaves?"

She smiled at him. She was gorgeous. "We do, indeed."

"Music's good here," he said, "If you get to it, I can tell you where to find the scene, if you like."

"Music is good everywhere, Mister Bird Parker," she said. "Wandering around and searching for it is the whole point."

"Since you like music, I have a dance card for you," he said. "Think you can use it?"

She looked at what he had put in her hand. "A dance card?" She laughed. "I imagine I'd put it to good use."

"So, we'll share the train as far as the Port of Los Angeles, if you don't mind."

"It will be a pleasure," she said. "Perfectly perfect."

When he had gone, Chloe took my elbow and we headed for the metal steps of the Pullman car. I looked over my shoulder, and didn't see any of the Low Gang among the milling people.

"Parker, Davis, Hawkins and Webster," I remarked. "That's a pretty rough crowd. Are you sure you want to be mixed up with people like them?"

"Sometimes," she said sweetly, "You need fire to fight fire."

~ * ~

The repair shed was absolutely quiet, except for the hum of fluorescent lights over us, and the gentle hiss of the oil heater in the corner. Bill was finishing adjustments on a carburetor, and his concentration was absolute. The tip of his tongue was visible at the corner of his mouth.

I leaned against a bench and watched him work. Boats were stored in rack upon rack in the open sheds outside the door. Some were wrapped in plastic or tarpaulins, but most were in the open and had to content themselves with what shelter the roof over them provided. The fuel pumps at the dock were locked up, tanks drained for the winter. The office and store had been closed for more than a month.

There was a sense of sleep. The whole marina was wrapped in it. Sleeping boats, sleeping buildings, and soon the lake would sleep too, under a blanket of snow and ice. Only I would be awake here, through the cold season.

"I wish you weren't staying," Bill said. "There's room in the truck. Why not help me with the driving? We'll catch some ball games, and hit this place running in the spring, when it's warm enough for people again."

Bill and Diane were headed to Florida to sit out the worst of the winter. They were both busy here most of the year. The marina was like the lake, and it didn't really ever stop; if it flowed, it was busy. When the ice came, they both relished their annual rest. Diane spent most of her time shopping and going to movie theaters. Bill sat in the sun, reading newspapers and waiting for spring training to start.

Bill had attended the Blue Jays' spring exhibition games in Florida for years, rarely missing one from mid-February until the beginning of April. Opening Day of the regular season in Toronto was usually opening day here at the marina, too. Bill and Diane returned north when the team did.

"You like baseball," he insisted. "We'd have fun. You could do your own things, too. Walk on the beach, whatever."

"Tempting," I said.

"Sure it is. There's nothing like spring training. Some of these kids trying out are pretty good, but they won't make it. It'll be their only taste of the majors. Some of the old guys are facing the end. Everyone plays their heart out. I love it. I love every minute of it."

"I'm thinking about it—but, no. I can't."

He finished what he was doing, straightened his tools on the bench, and picked up his coffee cup.

"It makes for good memories, Nick. You could use some of those."

I couldn't leave the island, and more than that, I couldn't leave Chloe. I didn't know if the train trip depended on a proximity to the island, but when I had gone away to New York and Toronto Chloe hadn't felt as close.

"I just can't leave, Bill. Not now, not this year."

"I really thought with Nora gone for a while, you'd rethink things."

"I just can't. It's complicated. The island has started to feel like home. I'm realizing at this point in my life that no place ever really has, and I like the sense of it."

"Good. You are home. You're part of things around here. I don't see why you put up a fuss over coming on shore while the ice is in. You're at home, and needed, here at the marina. Stay at our place while we're gone. You wouldn't be leaving."

"Maybe next year," I said. "If I stay over one winter, maybe I won't feel like the ice is chasing me off."

We went up the steps to the marina main building. He called up the stairs to Diane, and then I followed him through the small store to the office. Bill checked his messages, and returned a call. I wandered through the store while I waited. The shelves in the shop were mostly bare. The snack bar echoed, clean and empty.

"Kate Bean says she had a ruckus in her store," he said when he came out. "She's worried about you."

"It's that idiot Esteban was having trouble with," I said. "You know I took him some money, tried to pay him off to go away. I guess I got him off Esteban's back, and onto mine. He found out where I'm from and followed me up here. I'm not too worried about it."

"So, what happened in Toronto?" Bill asked. "Why would the creep come up here?"

"I guess I offended him." I shrugged. "Pride seems to be all that matters. He's been after Esteban over a lousy fifteen grand—and he owns a BMW dealership."

"Maybe he doesn't have as much money as it seems. Fifteen thousand might mean more than you think."

I shook my head. "You know what I think, Bill? I don't think he even needs a good reason. Some people are just nuts. He's a psychopath."

"Now he's floating around Ansett. Kate said it was a nasty scene in her place. He scared her, and Kate doesn't usually scare."

"I think maybe she scared him," I said, and we both laughed.

"So that's all—he's just crazy, and it's all the reason he needs. What's he planning to do with you, or to you?"

"Scare me, I guess."

He peered at me. His bright blue eyes had none of their usual humor. "You better talk to the cops about this. If he's crazy enough to find you, there's no telling what he'll do. Don't try to guess what crazy people will do. They don't play by any rules."

"I already did. I called John Park last night. Nora went to him at the very beginning, when this guy started up with Esteban. I think John is frustrated he didn't help more. He'd love to take a piece out of this guy."

"Good," he said, and drained his coffee. "I hope he catches up with him before you do. You have enough trouble in your life."

He stood still, contemplating the darkened shop. "Let's go on upstairs," he said. "Diane'll have dinner on the table, soon enough. God help us."

He looked upward, as if to check that she hadn't heard him. We smiled at each other.

"You still ought to think about spring training," he said. "Best baseball all year, as far as I'm concerned."

"Squeeze play?" I asked. "Would I see any of those?"

"I suppose so," he said. "Here and there. Why do you ask?"

"Don't know. Someone mentioned it to me recently. The idea's kind of stuck with me—deliberately giving yourself up to advance your runner."

"Sometimes it's the right thing to do," he said. "Sometimes it's the only play that works."

~ * ~

The grandstand was painted dark green, peeling in most places, but nice just the same. The simple wooden benches were hot from the sun when we first sat on them. The air was full of tobacco smoke and excitement. It all felt like real baseball—green grass, white uniforms, and the blue-and-yellow day.

I smiled at Chloe. "You promised to take me to the best baseball game of all time. Is this it?"

"Yes," she smiled. "Bobby Thomson's shot heard 'round the world was the second best. This game is the best of all time."

"How could this be better?"

"It's 1946," she said. "It's a Monday in July, and Satchel Paige is pitching for the Kansas City Monarchs. Boojum Wilson is going to have the most important at-bat that ever was. It's the Negro League, so only about three hundred people are here to see it. It never got written up on a single sports page."

"That's sad."

Her eyes lit up, and she shifted on the wooden bench so she could look at my face.

"It isn't, though! We're here, aren't we? Time is a map, and nothing ever goes away."

"A bike ride when I was ten?" I asked. "That's on the map?"

"Yes, except for the falling off part, when you tried to bump over a curb, to see if you could. You can skip that, if you want to."

"Outside at night? Fireflies and the Man in the Moon?"

256

"Swimming in a river for the first time, and being scared by all the warm and cold currents playing with your legs," she said. "Money in your pocket for chocolate, and a bad report card."

"Seeing fireworks at the park, and being allowed to walk home with your friends—"

"And suddenly being a tiny bit afraid," she finished. "Of the dark, and of growing up."

"Soup for lunch, and ant farms."

"Really, really cold watermelon, spitting the seeds at each other, and clean sheets on your own bed when you're too tired to stay awake another minute."

"You were too old to be kissed good night," I said, "but your mother thought you were asleep, so you kept your eyes closed and let her think so."

Chloe nodded and kissed my cheek.

"A hopeless crush—"

I caught her fragrance, citrus and clean perspiration.

"—who danced with someone else."

The Washington Grays ran onto the field, red caps and numbers, calling to each other. The crowd collected itself and got ready.

"Mostly, it's the knowing that time is a map, and that it's only just beginning," she said. "It's all just starting."

The game went seven scoreless innings. Satchel Paige seemed unhittable, but Frank Thompson pitched heroically for the Grays, doing his best to match him. While Paige unlimbered his long body in the strange corkscrew motion that blew ball after ball past batters like smoke, Thompson gave up walks, and allowed a spray of balls across the infield. Still, no Monarch made it as far as home plate.

"Sooner or later, Satchel put 'em away," said a fat man sitting nearby. "He got Long Tom going today."

"Long Tom?" I asked.

His smile got so wide that his eyes were squeezed shut. I found myself smiling back, and I heard Chloe giggle delightedly beside me.

"Long Tom a fastball so hard the ball ain't real again 'til the catcher has it in his glove," he explained. "Most of the time he go with Little Tom, his regular fastball, and that one dang near impossible to hit, but when Satchel feeling real good he bring out Long Tom. Satchel feeling good today."

Top of the ninth, and with one out, Cool Papa Bell finally got a good look at Long Tom and pounded the ball off the wooden fence in right field. He held up at third, the potential winning run. Jud 'Boojum' Wilson came to the plate. He had struck out twice already, and his face was grim.

"Big man," I commented.

"He's called Boojum because of the sound the ball makes when he rattles it off the fences," Chloe said. "Some people say he does it on purpose. He'd rather dent the fence than hit a home run. He hits it wherever he wants, but he's got his hands full with Long Tom."

"Is this the important at-bat you were talking about?"

Chloe nodded, took the roll of cinnamon candy from her bag and popped one into her mouth, and another into mine. She spotted the fat man eyeing her, and squeezed by me to go up the aisle to share with him. He watched her come back to me, his face lit warm.

"It's important because Bell is on third, and he's fast," she said. "If Boojum lays down a bunt, the catcher won't have any choice but to pick up the ball and go to first. It's a perfect Squeeze, and the Grays will score."

Her face was suddenly sad.

"He won't, though. He's afraid. He's already been sat down twice by Satchel. He's been slumping, and he's wondering lately if he's losing it. His stomach has been bothering him, and he's lost weight. He thinks a home run will make everything right, even though it won't."

Wilson took a huge cut at the first pitch, and missed.

"Bunt, Boojum!" Chloe shouted.

On the mound, Paige unwound from his strange corkscrew motion, and the second pitch snapped into the catcher's mitt.

Wilson hadn't moved. His eyes were wide, stunned and nearly terrified.

"Bunt!" Chloe screamed. "Squeeze Play, Boojum! It's okay—bunt!"

The pitch came. It wasn't Long Tom. Little Tom streaked in, perceptibly slower, and down the middle. Wilson hadn't expected it, and swung a mile ahead of its arrival. The force of his swing spun him around in the batter's box. Strike three, and he was out. Chloe had tears in her eyes as she watched him trudge back to the dugout. The next batter popped up, and Bell was left at third.

In the bottom of the inning, Willard Brown parked a Frank Thompson curveball in the empty right field bleachers, a walk-off home run. 1-0 Monarchs, and game over. The jubilant crowd lingered in the grandstand after the players were gone. The dark gold sun said the afternoon was going, too.

"He couldn't not be a slugger," I mused. "He couldn't bunt—do something he never tried, even if it was the right thing to do."

"If he had bunted—if he had committed himself to a Squeeze Play, then everything would have been okay for the Grays. He would have been out, sure, but the runner would have come home safely from third. They would have had the lead."

"He didn't though," I said. "He went down swinging".

"It was pride, and even more than that—fear."

"Fear? What was he afraid of?"

"Failing—being out of the game. It was the best pitcher against the best hitter. He was afraid that if he bunted, people would have said he was a coward, so he took the easy way out."

"His team would have won! He would have been put out at first, because it was the only play, but Cool Papa Bell would have come home safe."

"I know." She shook her head. "It's hard to do what you really have to, sometimes. Pride and fear."

She stopped us with a hand on my arm, and turned me to face her.

"Do you understand that when I left the real world—I bunted?" she asked. "That it was a Squeeze Play?"

I didn't know how to answer. Chloe had drowned herself, swimming in a lake so cold it was about to freeze, late at night. It was suicide, even if she had a reason.

"What do you think happened to me?" she persisted.

I became uncomfortable almost to the point that it was physical. I had to press forward, regardless.

"I think you—hurt yourself," I said. "That's the story I've heard, anyway."

She looked directly at me. Her eyes were overflowing. "I would never, ever do that."

"It was a long time ago," I said. "It wasn't a wrong thing. It's just what happened."

"No." She sounded emphatic. "No, it wasn't like that. It was a Squeeze Play."

She turned herself away, and gazed at the field. The players were all gone, and the seats were empty. The shadow of the grandstand fell across the first base line. This wasn't a place I wanted to sit in after dark. It echoed too much.

"The winning run never came home," she said. "The bunt was perfect. The catcher threw to first, and I was out. There was no play at the plate. It was a perfect, perfect squeeze play, but the runner at third just—disappeared."

She stood up and put her bag over her shoulder. It was time to go, and I stood up, too. Her voice got very soft. She sounded almost defeated, and my heart broke a little.

"The runner never came home. I'm still waiting, and hoping that he will. The game is still going on."

~ * ~

"Be careful of the bears," Diane said. "They can be really bold in the winter."

She ladled out a huge portion of something that was probably chicken onto my plate. Diane was a famously bad

260

cook, and even worse, a completely enthusiastic one. Bill looked across the table at her, and his face crinkled in a smile.

"Bears are all asleep, Diane," he said. "They won't bother anyone 'til spring."

"Wolves, then," she said, unperturbed. "Whatever they are. I want Nick to be careful."

We sat at the dining room table in the MacMillans' apartment, upstairs over the marina store. The entire building had started its life as a large house a century before. Upstairs, little had changed. It had been home for families who wrestled a living from the forests and the water, people who were tough and competent enough to outlast the long Canadian winters. The Tiffany lamp that Diane hung over the table, the prints on the walls, and the floral fabrics in the living room didn't dispel their ghosts. I liked the place.

I tasted my chicken. It was awful. I smiled at Diane, and she beamed back at me.

"I'll be careful," I said. "I promise."

"We'll be back the beginning of April, or whenever it is that Bill gets tired of his baseball."

"There's no such thing as tired of baseball," he said.

"Baseball is like life," I agreed. "Can't get tired of it."

She shook her head, and offered me more chicken. "Stay in the guest room tonight," she said. "That way you don't have to hurry up and leave, like you usually do."

We lingered at the table and said our goodbyes, without ever saying goodbye. They were my friends, and the closest thing to family that I had left. We raised our coffee cups, and toasted the bears. Just in case the bears were all asleep, we toasted the wolves. Bill and Diane had an early start to look forward to in the morning, and so they headed off to bed, and I went into the guest room.

On my back, I stared up at the dark ceiling. I thought about ice and snow and wolves as I dropped off to sleep. Mostly, though, I thought about bears and crumbs, and Chloe. Soon enough, she came.

-Twenty Seven-

I woke up the next morning at ten. I hadn't slept so late, or so soundly, in months. There had been no dreams, only darkness and silence. I had needed it pretty badly. The apartment was utterly silent. I swung my feet off the bed and onto the floor.

The place was empty. Bill and Diane were gone. They had probably wanted an early start on the first leg of the long drive to Florida. I pictured them right now, excited and happy. Diane was probably chattering at Bill, while he watched the road with a half-smile on his face. I missed them terribly, already.

I looked out the window, at the lake. The water reflected a deep gray that matched the silvery winter sky. It appeared that snow was on the way. It struck me as odd, that a couple of years ago I had come here, unsure of boats and myself. I was like a stranger, the newcomer among the lake denizens. Now Nora had gone, the cottagers were far away, and Bill and Diane had left. I was alone on the lake, and I was the one who knew her all year round, and knew her best.

I didn't feel as though I had ever been anywhere else.

There were a couple of keys on the table, with labelled plastic tags. One read "Front Door," and the other "N's House." The first was lettered in Diane's hand, but the second one was Nora's. I smiled. She stayed persistent, my Nora.

There was no note. I thought about making coffee, but decided to have it at my house. I wanted to get out of this empty place. Still tired and groggy from sleep, I sat down in a chair near the window and looked out at the lake. I'd rest just for a minute, I thought, and then get going.

My eyes closed.

~ * ~

The dining car was elegant, bursting with soft light, china, linen, crystal, and silver. A small jewel, like a single drop of water on a fine silver chain, rested on Chloe's chest. It caught the muted lamps and glowed blue. The carriage swayed gently, and the noise of the rails sounded faint beneath us. Lights passed by the windows periodically, and then gave way to the gathering darkness again.

"You're allowed to miss me, you know," she said.

I shook my head and didn't answer. Ginger collected our menus.

"Mister Charlie Parker sends his apologies," he said. "He and his party are tired. They had a very early supper, and have gone to bed. They'll have dinner with you tomorrow night, before we reach Los Angeles."

"Is that the end of the line?" I asked. "Los Angeles?"

"Oh, we're going farther west," Chloe said. "Much farther west than that."

The Conductor caught my expression of surprise. "Mister Parker and company will be leaving us at Union Station in California, but some things are better underwater, as you know." He turned back to Chloe. "If you're going to have trouble, I should think you'll have had it by then."

"Absolutely," she beamed. "I'm starving, but I think I'll have champagne first."

"I thought so," he said. "I have a 1915 Bollinger, and a 1901 Veuve Cherlin, both cold. Whichever you prefer."

"I think a half-glass of each might be right." She glanced at me. "Do you think so?"

"Absolutely yes." I smiled. "I always hoped you'd say that."

Outside the train's windows, afternoon was gone. Early winter evening lingered, a dark gold that would slide into blue before it fell into cold night. I struggled for the right words.

"I miss things," I said. "I miss what I've lost—but it's more than that."

Chloe didn't say anything. She took the kaleidoscope from me, and looked through it.

"Sometimes," I went on, "I miss places I've never been, people I've never known, things I haven't seen. I almost ache, I want to cry, and I can't even figure out why."

She put the looking-device down, and turned to me. "It's because your heart remembers," she said. "It remembers what you won't, what you can't, what you've been taught to forget."

Her dark eyes were very solemn. "Time is a map. When we were children we knew that. You just have to remember how to go where you need to."

"Is that why you've been taking me to all these places—these times?" I asked.

She offered me the kaleidoscope again. I was afraid to use it.

"The good things never, ever go away," she said. "They're always there, not lost at all. You just have to know how to get to them."

~ * ~

It was close to lunchtime before I locked the marina door behind me and headed to the dock for the long, cold ride back to the island. I left Nora's house key where it was, on the kitchen table.

The spray off the water stung like sleet, and I went numb by the time I had tied the boat off and headed up the path to my cabin.

I loaded the stove with wood, and spent the afternoon with a book in my lap. From time to time, I ventured out to check the lake. The water gurgled in the rocks under the dock. It looked like black gelatin. The day slipped away into a gloomy twilight by four o'clock.

The abandoned landscape seemed to promise disaster. The waves were hostile, and the trees were bare and silent. There is a deep feeling in us when we see the end of autumn, some tribal memory that tells us we should have migrated south while there was time. We are going to be trapped soon, this ancient voice says, by the coming winter. Winter, winter, winter is coming like a locomotive, and we won't survive the cold and lack of food. We should have gone. It's too late, too late now.

The smell of nearly frozen earth and water reminds us of our own deaths.

When dinnertime came, I stood at the kitchen counter, piccking at food I didn't want. I was glad when the clock said it was late enough that I could go to bed, and to sleep. I checked the wood stove, undressed, and pulled a pillow over my head. I fell asleep, wishing Chloe would come and take me away from this.

Some time later, I woke up. The clock on the bedside table said just past three in the morning. I had been awakened because the Train's horn had changed. There was something disturbing about the way it sounded. I stared at the ceiling of my bedroom until I heard it again. It wasn't a train horn; it was a car horn.

I rolled out of bed, pulled on my boots and grabbed my coat as I went out the kitchen door. The night shone clear and cold, but the moon was thin, and I had trouble negotiating my way through the clearing in front of the cabin. I cursed myself for not taking a flashlight. Even before I made my way onto the dock, I could see the headlights shining across almost a mile of water.

The horn blared clear on this quiet night, the sound carrying on the freezing air. Two long blasts, a short one, and then another long, repeated over and over. It was the pattern a railway locomotive made, in warning, at crossings and bridges. I didn't doubt that it was Risa making the noise.

All at once, blue and red lights bloomed and spun, reflecting off the hills and trees that ran down to the lake. A second set of headlights came on, behind the first. John Park had arrived.

"I smiled. Got you, you son of a bitch."

I watched the lights across the water for a few minutes. When I got too cold, I went inside, and back to bed.

~ * ~

I stood outside, on the tiny balcony at the back of the very last car. The night air was frosty, damp, and a little too cold for snow. I watched the rails roll by underneath me, slush and ice piled on either side of them. Lights shone here and there from the houses and towns we passed, crystalline in the winter air. I thought about smoking a cigar, and decided against it.

It was warmer where we were going, and that was good.

I turned and looked up at the roof of the carriage. I knew that a half dozen of the Low Gang hid up there in the dark, clinging to whatever handholds they could find. I pictured them, grabbing their hats, long coats flapping in the wind, crouching silently and waiting.

"I hope you're cold," I said. "I hope you bastards freeze to death."

I slid the door open and went inside. The sleeper passage was hushed and dim, lit only by the night-lights set into the wood paneling. I passed door after door, glancing at the numbers. When I reached the right one, I raised my hand, but Chloe opened it and pulled me in before I could knock. I kicked the door closed behind us, gently. I could taste the champagne on her, and I smelled limes and clean water.

"Do you miss me?" she asked. "Does it get too dark?"

The door banged behind me. The knocking was hard enough to shake it in the frame. I turned and pulled it open. A Low Man stood there. His hat brim shadowed the top half of his face; the bottom half smiled. There was a stirring behind him, and the narrow passageway filled with his colleagues, rustling and black.

"You know who sent us, I imagine," he said. "He's waiting at the next station, and you're getting off. You and the splat, both."

"Like hell," Chloe spat, from behind me.

"End of the line. Easy or hard, and we'd like hard a whole lot better. Tell you what . . ."

He gripped my shoulder and tried to move me aside. The shadows behind him stirred excitedly. "Make me an offer," he sneered at Chloe. "Make it worth my while, and I might just let you take your coat with you."

The Low Men all shook with laughter.

The train whistled a crossing, high and mournful. The sound trailed off and became Coleman Hawkins' tenor sax. Miles Davis' trumpet chased it into the opening bars of 'Body and Soul', faint and clear, from somewhere on the train, filling it from front to back and hanging in the air behind it. The men in hats shrank back, visibly shaken. A couple of them squealed and growled, softly.

Bird Parker and Freddie Webster dove into the melody, and then with only a sound of rustling coats, like wings, the corridor was empty again.

Chloe pulled me close. I felt her smile against my mouth.

"Don't open the door again until Amarillo," she said. "I don't care who it is."

~ * ~

When I woke up in the morning, I smelled coffee. I went to the kitchen, and found John Park sitting at my table. He was still wearing his provincial police uniform; a light blue shirt, dark trousers, and a gun belt that creaked when he shifted in his chair. Dark almond-shaped eyes regarded me over the rim of his cup.

"Find everything you need?" I asked.

"I did, thank you. I feel right at home. Your coffee's fresh, and the milk in the fridge hasn't spoiled. It's better than being at my own house."

I tried not to smile. "Glad I passed inspection. You still on duty?"

"My shift ended a couple of hours ago," he said. "I came straight out here. Launching a freaking boat wasn't on my list of things to do today. I have to pull it back out when I leave. Gonna get wet doing it, too."

"You could have called. It's why they have phones—so you don't have to get wet."

He tipped his cup toward me. "Would have missed out on free coffee," he said.

I went to the counter and poured myself a cup. I held the pot toward him, and he nodded. I brought it to the table with me, and sat down across from him.

"I had a talk with our friend Mr. Risa last night," he said. "He wasn't too happy to see me."

"I saw your cherry top on the shore road last night. You were tailing him?"

"Can't tell you. It's official police business. If I told you, you'd know how we operate. It's a secret."

"A secret—okay. And he was unhappy when you pounced on him?"

He shook his head and laughed, just a little. "Pounced," he mused. "I like that. Yes, he was uncooperative. There wasn't much I could do. It isn't against the law, really, to honk your horn like a lunatic in the middle of the night. I still ticketed him for creating a disturbance out here in the middle of nowhere, and since he has no local address I took him into the station and kept him sitting in a hard chair for an hour or two."

"He disturbed me," I said. "He still does."

"Me, too. I sat him down in the barracks, while I took my time writing him up, and checking him out. I didn't talk much to him, and he sat there and cursed me the whole time."

"Worse language than you're used to?"

"That isn't what I mean." He shook his head. "Not bad language. He *cursed* me. It's hard to describe. He wished things for me, like a hex."

"Like what?" I asked. "Wished things like what?"

"Let's see. Cancer, and to die alone in an old age home. To be cheated on, to get fired. Homelessness. Hunger. Guilt. To do the wrong thing and be haunted by guilt. Oh, and sex stuff, lots and lots of twisted sex."

He shook his head, remembering. "He knew me, somehow. It was the creepiest thing I've ever listened to. It was like he knew about everything bad I've ever done. I planned to keep his ass in that chair all night, but I kicked him out just to get rid of him."

"You've done bad sex things?"

"Not as many as I'd like, tell the truth."

"You think he's gone?" I asked. "Back to Toronto?"

"I think so. I made it clear I would trail him around if he stayed up here. I don't think he listens much to anyone though, except maybe the voices in his own head. He's a psychopath."

He leaned back in his chair, and rubbed his eyes. "The worst thing about him is that smile," he finished. "He just sits there and—grins at you. Grins and snickers, while he curses your unborn children."

The white-faced railway clock on my kitchen wall chimed gently, eight times. Park's voice sounded suddenly exhausted. "I gotta get going. And anyway, I think you have other things to worry about."

He stood up, and went to look out the kitchen door at the lake. "Ice is coming," he said, without turning around. "Probably tonight."

"Tonight? You think so?"

"I know so. Lived here a long time. You'll be iced in by tomorrow night. Get off now."

I felt a pang of fear in my stomach, even though I had been getting ready for weeks. The ice was coming. Park shrugged on his heavy uniform coat.

"Walk me down," he said.

Outside, the morning was bitterly cold. I stood at the top of the cabin steps and felt the air deep in my lungs. A loud crack came from the forest, as a branch snapped in the cold.

"You hear that?" Park asked.

~ * ~

I stood up and gazed into the trees, hunting for a glimpse, a trace, anything at all, but saw no flash of pink, no gleam of dark eyes. The woods were black and still, and I heard no laughter or quick footsteps in the soft, steady wind.

269

After a time, I became aware that she had appeared, and was standing quietly beside me.

"What are you looking for?" she asked.

I thought before I answered. "You."

My voice sounded hoarse, rusty. I glanced over at her. She looked back at me, serene.

"Where have you been?" I asked.

"Deep in the forest," she said. "You know."

She held out her hand, and I took it. "I used to love the cold," she said sadly. "You're warming me up, and I'm starting to worry—that it's going to be a problem for me."

~ * ~

"You okay?" Park asked. "Probably just a branch snapped in the cold."

I nodded.

"You've been under some stress, Nick. You don't seem altogether okay lately to me. Other people are worried about you, too. Including Nora."

"What are you saying, John?"

We walked onto the boards over the water. An inflatable launch was tethered behind my boat, with police markers on its sides. He stopped, hands on hips, and looked at me. I was conscious of him as a law officer, as well as my friend. I saw him as others must. He was intimidating.

"I'm saying that staying out here is going to be dangerous over the next month or two. Lots of people have done it, because they had to. You don't have to. You have enough money, and plenty of opportunity to move on shore."

He held up a hand to silence my response.

"I've said that all along. I'm saying more than that, now. There's something wrong with you lately. Your eyes are vacant. If I didn't know you better, I'd think you were doing drugs—something heavy." His eyes searched my face. "You aren't doing that, are you? Drugs?"

270

I shook my head no, and felt a sudden well of emotion. I wanted to give this up. I wanted to catch a ride back to the marina with him, and spend the winter somewhere warm. I wondered if I could drive my old jeep fast enough to catch Bill and Diane. Maybe I'd spot them eating breakfast in a diner somewhere in Tennessee or Georgia, and walk in and surprise them. I couldn't, though. I rode on a Train, and I didn't want to get off even if I was able to.

"Most of all," John said, "my concern is that you aren't fit right now to stand two or three months alone out here. I have a feeling that I'm going to be out here in an official capacity before spring. I consider you a friend, and it will bother me that I didn't stop you. You're a grown man, though."

He finished untying the launch, got in and started the engine. He spoke louder, over its idling engine. "If you wake up tomorrow and the ice is coming in, what are you going to do about your boat?"

I pointed to the block and tackle apparatus I had rigged, hanging from the trees opposite the dock. "I'm going to drag it onto shore," I said. "I may scrape up the bottom a bit, but it won't be serious."

"Here's a better suggestion. You'll have twelve hours or so after the first ice when it'll still be thin enough not to be a problem for a decent-sized boat. Get in yours and get the hell out of here. Call me tomorrow and tell me you were smart enough to do that. Where's your jeep? At the marina?"

I pointed across the sound. "I parked it at the boat launch. If I need to, I can walk a mile across the ice and drive to town."

He stared at the opposite shore. "Better than crossing over and walking fifteen miles of shore road to the marina." He nodded. "Good thinking for someone stupid enough to do this in the first place. By the way, don't ever walk straight across the sound. Even when the lake's frozen hard, there's always enough current from the channel that you'll usually run into an open lead between here and Nora's house. Walk east from here at least a half mile, and then cut across."

271

"Bill told me exactly the same thing," I said. "I'll remember."

"I hope you will. Good luck."

He waved, and clunked the police boat into reverse. It swept away from Echo Island in a curving arc, and then headed for the passage between the neighboring islands. It was the last boat that would run the waters of Hollow Lake that year. I didn't know that it was also the last flight out.

~ * ~

The Gypsy Moth banked hard enough to shudder its frame. I didn't know if we were going to lose a wing or fall into the treetops flashing below us, but I knew this would end badly. The Train snaked along the track below us, stopped at the small depot in Amarillo.

"Who's flying this thing anyway?" I muttered.

"You worry about absolutely everything," Chloe said. "I can fly, remember? So can you."

We straightened out, and the ancient engine settled again into a choppy, smoky roar. A green river passed below us, and I gazed down at it longingly and wondered about jumping.

"Are you afraid of anything at all?" I asked.

"Of course, I am. I'm afraid of the things that have no name."

"The unknown, you mean?"

"Stop trying to think so much," she said impatiently. "There are things that walk around wearing disguises, looking for trouble. The worst of them have no names. Why do you think they are called nameless anxieties?"

"I never thought about it that way," I said.

"That's what's so terrible. They creep around causing mischief and don't even care enough to call themselves anything."

-Twenty Eight-

The freeze came that night, exactly as John Park had predicted. Even before I went outside, I was struck by the hush. The lake's ceaseless motion was hidden, silenced under a skin of ice. I had listened for so long to the sound of moving water beyond the cabin, waves and currents and lapping, that I felt as though I had gone deaf when it stopped.

The cold hurt my lungs when I went onto the veranda. I went back inside to find a pair of gloves. I walked through the clearing, and slipped and nearly lost my footing on the rocks leading down to the dock.

"Shit," I breathed, looking at the lake.

I had seen the frozen lake from shore many times, and had anticipated this. I had waited for it and imagined it, but nothing could have had me ready for what I saw. What had been uneasy black water the previous afternoon, a huge expanse of waves, was now still, quiet and white. Across the reach, I could still see a dark strip of open water, but I knew the lead was closing, even as I watched.

The early sun turned the ice into a blinding orange sherbet. I needed to get my boat out, right away. It would be a day or two before the freeze went deep enough to lock it into the lake, and for expansion to damage the hull, but pulling it out by myself was going to be difficult. I made my way up to the edge of the trees, where I had rigged the block and tackle.

Over the next hour, my boat got freed from the lake and made its way slowly onto the frozen shore, like a strange turtle come to lay eggs on the beach. I winced as the hull ground its way onto the rock. The craft looked much bigger out of the water. I had planned to pull it back into the water with Bill's boat after the spring melt. Seeing it beached, I wondered how hard it was going to be, and how much damage we were going to do to the hull.

That would be a problem for spring, though, and I covered the boat with a tarp and went to stand on the dock. The wooden platform sticking out onto the water, was the island's front porch; a place of coming and going, it was strange to see it stripped of boats. It made my situation seem more final, and I felt a stirring of fear.

I tried to reassure myself. The kitchen held enough canned, frozen, and dried food to last me for months. I had ample fresh water. The intake pipe, which fed the cabin from the lake, went deep enough that the ice wouldn't come close to reaching it. I had plenty of fuel for the stove. I didn't like cutting trees on the island, but if I ran out of deadfall, I had indefinite firewood.

Cell phone service reception was limited to the end of the dock, a year-round problem. The underwater cable that brought electricity from land was vulnerable, but power was more a luxury than a necessity. All in all, I seemed to be in good shape. If need be, I could walk out, across the ice, probably less than a week from now.

I could go to town in just a matter of days. There was nothing to be afraid of. I could buy groceries, go to Kate's for pie and coffee, or drive to Huntsville to see a movie. Being alone bothered me, but I wasn't alone, not really. I headed for the cabin to rest and get warm.

I wasn't alone. As long as I had Chloe, I wasn't alone at all, and the more I thought about it, the better that seemed. On the lake, the forming ice cracked, as though it heard my rationales and mocked me. I turned my back on the rising cold and went up to the cabin. Inside, I made tea, fed the stove, and sat in the warmth. The old cabin creaked comfortably around me, the stovepipe ticked and clanked, and I closed my eyes.

~ * ~

We stood on a darkened, abandoned midway. A cartoon wind whistled and moaned through the rigging of a broken pirate ship, and the single bulb on a pole got reflected here and there in puddles. Pieces of trash blew and tumbled aimlessly. A blackened, burned-out roller coaster snaked over our heads, and the skeleton of an unlit Ferris wheel loomed over everything. I smelled standing water and scorched wood.

Chloe took my arm and pulled me forward. "Come with me," she said. "I want to ride the rides, and play the games. I want cotton candy, but I only want it if you buy it for me. Mostly, I want to go on the Ferris wheel with you, and feel how nervous you are—about me."

Her smile, even in the dark, dazzled me. "When it stops at the top, I want to see the terrified 'now or never' expression on your face before you try to kiss me."

We stopped, and she leaned into me. She wore a white wrap, and I was aware of the warmth and the weight of her, slender beneath the thin cotton.

"I'm going to hesitate, pull away just a little," she went on. "I'm going to let you feel every bit of the awkward that you are. I want you to wonder, just for a second, if you're going to crash and fall, and then, and then . . ."

She touched my face. Her fingertips were warm, almost hot. "Then," she finished, "I'm going to kiss you back. I'm going to kiss you so perfectly you'll always remember it. I won't stop until I'm perfectly sure you'll never forget me, that I've ruined you for anyone else."

Then she did it—just like that.

She tasted like everything good. When she let me take a breath, the lights were on; strings and strings of bulbs sparked and crackled and sparkled. Neon glowed and colored lights flashed. I smelled hot dogs and popcorn. Fireworks shook the black sky to its foundations. Green and blue and orange fire spread across the night, faded, then exploded all over again. The rides rattled and shook, and the crowds shouted. Laughing horses galloped at the edges of a merry-go-round, and a calliope played "Pink Flowers and Pink Hearts," madly.

I pulled Chloe in, kissed her again, and wished that it would never, ever end.

~ * ~

A week passed. Each day, another tick mark got entered against Esteban's ninety-day deadline. My own eleven-day ultimatum was also nearly done, although I wasn't frightened enough of Risa that it really mattered to me.

My mind went elsewhere, mainly riding on the Train with Chloe. I felt closer to what she wanted me to remember. Sometimes I looked out at the lake and the key to all of it seemed just barely out of reach. I wondered where we were going to end up with all of this.

"Somewhere warm," Chloe had said. "A place where beasts are mild."

More and more, I didn't doubt the reality of what was happening to me. Hour after hour, the ice spread inexorably across Hollow Lake, joining one shore to the other. My mind was increasingly occupied by the winds and the music of Faraway. The cabin, the weather, the changing light and dark of the sky over Echo Island became the dream for me.

I kept the woodstove burning, and made sure I ate something whenever I thought about it. I took long hot showers, kept the cabin tidy and my clothes clean. I stayed busy. I drank tea and stared unseeing at the pages of one book after another. Mostly I waited for Chloe to summon me.

"Do you miss me?" she asked. "Does it get too dark?"

"Yes," I always whispered, and she always came. One minute I was in the cabin, and the next, I was gone again.

~ * ~

I sat on the cement wall, waiting. The desert behind me hissed and whispered, huge and black. I felt the presence of birds, though I couldn't see them. The moon flooded the road at my feet with gray light.

The building across from me showed no illumination at all. Doors and windows hid in the shadows of a long series of white stucco arches. The whole thing looked like it had been crumbling in the salt air for decades. Chloe materialized from behind a pillar, and stood there, barely visible, motionless under the dark canopy. After a moment, she crossed over to me. She was impossibly slender, too graceful to be real.

"Where have you been?" I asked.

She stared at me. Her eyes were lit from within. "The forest," she said, gesturing vaguely. "You know."

"The road's getting short," I said. "Something's going to happen, soon."

She came closer, and put a hand to my cheek. She smelled like the sun, oranges and sand.

"We'll be here when it does."

"We can't run forever," I said.

I heard the smile in her voice. "Oh, yes we can."

She took my hand and pulled me off the wall. From across the street, the first strains of music floated by, something sweet and sad. A sea bird circled over us in the dark, close and silent, nearly invisible, a white ghost. I heard the sound of its wings ruffling the night air.

Chloe reached up toward it, standing on her toes. "I have a shrimp," she breathed. "Come closer, take it from me, touch me . . ."

I flinched as the bird banked into us, a burst from the dark, warm wind in my face, and then was gone. She looked out at the ocean, past her own outstretched, empty hand.

"Stay," she whispered.

A lamp, hung from a chain, flared over one of the doors, turning the row of arches a guttering, warm gold. Chloe turned from the sea reluctantly and led me to it. The street had been made of crushed shells, and crunched softly under our feet. The floor of the long mezzanine was black and white and very old. The door we went to was tall, slabs of heavy wood, painted white, with a cast iron pull handle.

"You have to do it," Chloe said, gesturing.

I pulled it open, and we went in. We stood at the top of cement steps leading down into a large courtyard, planted here and there with trees. The branches were silhouetted against the light from small shuttered balconies that dotted the walls. The stars overhead were bright. Torches, scattered here and there, flamed and guttered orange, yellow, and blue.

A small orchestra played in one corner of the garden. "La Cumparasita" wafted over the dancers, inexpressibly sad. A crowd sat and watched a handful of couples. Dressed in red silk and black lace, their heels and toes went to war with each other on the tiled dance floor. The smell of sex was overlaid with cigar smoke and lipstick.

"Cumparasita," Chloe murmured. "The little parade." Her eyes shone, taking it in.

"You can actually see the music," I said.

I pointed up, to where a bluish mist, visible against the yellow light from the balconies, twisted upwards in time to the tango below.

"This is one of the lost *milongas*," she said. "I never thought I'd find one. Even if you know about the secret doors behind things, these are closed salons. They don't let strangers in, normally."

Waiters circulated, balancing trays heavy with ranks of crystal. Chloe took a champagne glass, and held it up against the torchlight, counting and reading the rising bubbles. Satisfied, she nodded, set it on a potted palm, and turned her attention back to the dancers.

Spanish guitars grieved over unfaithful cellos; the violins watched and whispered to one another about it. One by the one, the pairs of dancers shrank from the violence on the floor, retreating to the sides, the safety of chairs and amber liquids and lovers' laps, until a single couple remained.

"That's Valentino," Chloe said. "Rudolph Valentino. He's gorgeous. He's a lot like you, romantic, no crying, and pink flowers. He's our Gatekeeper."

"What do we give him?"

She reached into her bag, and showed me a dance card. It was as fresh as if it had just been printed.

"Where did you get that?"

"Charlie Parker gave it to me—remember?"

Dressed in caballero trousers and flat hat, Valentino tangoed our way, discarding his partner into the crowd just before he reached us. He stood, liquid-eyed, bent slightly at the waist. Chloe introduced us.

"Hello," I said, nodding politely. "No matter what."

"He doesn't talk," Chloe said. "Not out loud, anyway. No one's ever heard him say a word."

"That's only because his movies were silent," I said. "I'm sure he can talk."

"Only because his . . ." she trailed off, looking perplexed. "His what?"

"His movies were silent," I explained. "He wasn't."

She stared at me and shook her head. "You have the strangest ideas sometimes." She smiled. "I like that about you."

She took Valentino's arm, and moved onto the floor. The last of the high heels, crimson satin, and the promise of lace underthings or no underthings, fled in the path of her simple white shift and plain sandals. She took his measure, met him as equal, and they began to move, taking the orchestra with them.

I felt the soft press of a breast on my arm, and smelled jasmine and a hint of perspiration. I glanced around, into huge dark eyes.

"Do you know who I am?" the woman asked.

Her face was heart-shaped and pretty. Her lips were slightly parted. I had never seen her before, and told her so. She looked delighted.

"I knew you were someone new!" she exclaimed. "How absolutely—well, I don't know. I'm Lila. Lila Lee." She leaned close, and put her mouth against my ear. "I'm fried to the hat," she confided. "You can't tell anyone, but you can take me home if you like."

"I'd like that very much," I said gently, "but I'm here with someone."

I indicated the dance floor, where Chloe was locked in combat with Valentino. Lila Lee peered at her, and then looked over at me, reconsidering.

"She's quite beautiful—the bee's knees. Are you very much in love with her?"

"That's an odd question, from a stranger."

I smiled to take the offense from my remark. She sipped champagne, and smiled back at me over the rim of her glass. Her lipstick was red as red, and her teeth were very white.

"And her in the arms of the great Valentino," she said. "Poor baby. You don't stand a chance."

"He doesn't talk, though. Not out loud."

"Well, there's that," she agreed. "And you talk very nicely. She can look you up when she wants to—talk."

I nodded, and searched for a place to escape.

"Pola's around tonight, and she's drunker than I am." Lila laughed. "She might not take to your Sheba over there. Not at all. You might want to cut in."

"Pola Negri? Really?"

She nodded and looked at me speculatively. "I figure if anyone's crazy enough to cut in on Valentino, it's you, baby doll."

Chloe and her partner had moved to the far side of the courtyard. The shades and shadows applauded, raising glasses and swaying, urging them on. I picked up Lila's hand and kissed it.

"Thanks," I said, and moved after them. "Here goes nothing."

"By the way, Valentino's a Gatekeeper. I'm sure he'll treasure the dance card she gave him. He already told your Sheba that you may pass. You might as well pass while the passing is good, doll."

I was already headed into the crowd.

"This is all ochoa!" she called after me, over the smoke and the music. "Eight! The more you look back, the closer you'll be!"

~ * ~

I went out on the dock to make a call, and I had just pulled the phone from my pocket when it rang. *Unknown Caller*, the screen read, with a number displayed below. It had a Toronto area code.

"Thought I was gone, pally?"

I knew the voice. It was Sonny Risa.

"Aren't you?" I asked. "Let me ask you something. Do you do anything with yourself, other than harass people that you imagine have done you wrong?"

He stayed quiet on the other end, as if he was thinking about it. "Not really, no. I bring people to justice. I hate people who break the rules. Your pet policeman doesn't see it, but he and I are a lot alike. Someday, maybe I'll cross his path and make him see that."

"You wouldn't much like it," I said. "Crossing his path. Better stay where you are."

"I'll eat him alive. Count on it. When his time comes."

There was silence on the line for a half-minute, and then Risa spoke again. His tone was almost jovial. "I like being crazy, if you're wondering," he said. "I like the adventure. Being rational doesn't work with me, and you should know all about it, right? Holed up on an island with imaginary friends for company. And you wouldn't trade it for the world. Am I right?"

I had no response. His breathing got heavy.

"It's nearly day ninety for the guy who screwed me, and is currently screwing your girlfriend. He hasn't done a thing to make things right for either of us. Just think, if he were out of the picture, you'd have her all to yourself. I'm surprised you haven't been cheering me on."

The wind was frigid. The late afternoon was gray, but the sun broke through across the sound, a deep, bloody orange. It colored the white that now covered the entire lake. The freeze was complete, and there was no more open water. The landscape looked like a desert of snow, with an oasis of pine forest and cottages on the far banks.

"Maybe you are rooting for me," Risa said. "Maybe that's exactly what you're wishing for, that I'll do your dirty work for you, and take the boyfriend out of the picture. If wishes was fishes—fish in one hand and wish in the other—and see which hand fills up first, I always say."

"You're an idiot," I said. I was tired. "You might be a psychopath, but you aren't even interesting."

"It's nothing personal, buddy. With him it's personal, but not with you. You broke the rules, and rule-breakers have to be brought into line. You should thank me, really."

I heard him breathing on the other end, but the gusts were making me strain, and I didn't figure he was worth the effort. I got ready to disconnect.

"You're forgetting something else," he said. "It's just about the eleventh day for you. Down to your last strike, so you better get the bat off your shoulder, buddy."

"Whatever you say, pally."

He grew enraged. His voice cracked and gargled, and I held the phone away from my ear.

"Don't you 'whatever' me!" he screamed. "This isn't a joke. DO YOU HEAR ME?"

I hung up on him. I stood out there, contemplating the winter day for a while. I was glad I couldn't see the future.

~ * ~

I looked up. The land we stood on was utterly black, but the night was full of stars. They were scattered from one horizon to the other, tiny white dots of cold light. The train had pulled into the tiny station on the outskirts of Albuquerque an hour before. It wasn't much more than a siding to take on water, with a dilapidated adobe building for decoration.

Chloe wanted to stretch her legs, and we walked up the steep hill behind the depot, feeling our way in the dark. We rested at the top. A handful of long-abandoned buildings huddled together below us. Nothing moved.

"Look," she said, standing behind me. "I want to show you something." She reached around me, took my hands and held them up against the sky. "Lean back a little bit."

She touched one part of the night sky, and then another, turning our bodies slowly from east to west, and back again. Cold sparks lit pinpoints in the blackness. She smoothed, shaped, and arranged them. They flashed like diamonds, leaving streaks of glimmer.

"Open your eyes," she breathed. "Open them wide."

She paused, long enough to shake my wrists and loosen them, and then twined her fingers into mine and began to move again, painting delicate dabs and long brush strokes. Planets dangled and spun, like glowing fruit. Constellations and galaxies sparkled purple and apricot and pale green, until the sky became more light than dark.

In the middle of all of the color, the Moon hung quietly.

"Is this where dreams come from?" I asked.

I felt her nod. "Yes, the Moon," she said. "The Moon, no matter what. All of your dreams, and all of your nightmares, too."

Finally, we were done. We stood quietly looking, her arms around me. The Train was a necklace of yellow lights below us. I wondered what year it was.

"It's 1950," Chloe said, as if she could read my mind.

"Do you like the desert?" I asked.

"I belong to the water," she said. "I'm never far from the seas, and lakes and rivers."

"Even here?"

She turned me to face her and held up the crystal she wore around her neck. It shone aquamarine in the strange light. Her skin was warm against the back of my hand. She smelled different tonight, like rain.

"It isn't a stone. It's a drop of water."

"It's beautiful," I said.

283

Chloe pointed at the distance. A mountain range lay on the horizon, old and smooth. "Those are the Coyote Islands," she said. "All the good dogs wait there."

She pronounced it properly: Kai-oh-tay.

"Islands? Those are mountains."

She looked at me archly. "The sea is coming back, Nick. This dead place will be ocean again. Those are islands."

"And the good dogs—wait there."

"Of course. Dead doesn't stay dead, except in story books."

A door opened in one of the tumbled buildings, and light flooded out. A man was framed in the opening. He paused for a moment, staring out, and then took off his hat and slapped the dust from it. We stood very still, and watched from the darkness as he lowered himself into a chair on the front porch.

It was the Grinning Man.

"He's here," I said under my breath. "Did you know he would be?"

Chloe didn't answer. Her gaze was fixed on the ringleader of the Low Gang. She was rapt, almost feral.

Partially illuminated by the lighted room behind him, he fished in a pocket, lit a cigarette, and spat on the sand.

"Can he hear us?' I asked.

She shook her head.

"When I was very, very small," I said, "maybe two years old, I was in the dark, put to bed for the night. Noises woke me. My parents were having a terrible fight. Someone was throwing things, breaking them."

Chloe watched the man on the porch, but I knew I had her complete attention. Her profile was severe. She was utterly, finally, beautiful.

"The police came," I went on. "I heard them talking downstairs. I looked out the window, and they were pulling her along the front walk and then they put my mother in a car and took her away. She cried and begged, but they took her anyway."

"They would." She shook her head.

"In the morning, she was home, and they told me I had a dream. It wasn't a dream, though."

"We know what dreams are, don't we?" she smiled. "We always have, you and I."

"The Grinning Man was one of the policemen. I remember him, now. He looked up at my window from the sidewalk and smiled at me. Then he hurt my mother's arm when he pulled her to the street. When he opened the car door, he said something to her so terrible that she stopped crying."

I felt my own tears start, and the stirring of a terrible anger. "You know what, Chloe? I understood him perfectly then. I still do now."

She took my hand and placed it against the glistening drop of jeweled water on her chest.

"Make a wish with me." She smiled. "Then hold on. It's going to get crazy around here."

She held my face with both her hands and her dark eyes. The ground began to shake under our feet, as though an enormous train was leaving its tracks nearby. On the distant mountains, there was movement. Starlight was caught and thrown back at the sky in strange patterns. The shaking grew and gained a voice, a dull roar that grew louder and louder.

"Head for the islands, Nicky. Stay with me—I'm so happy. I can't wait."

I wrapped my arms tightly around her. I felt her laughter against me, and just before the noise hit and swallowed us, I felt her lips move softly against my ear.

"Surf's up."

-Twenty Nine-

I spooned sugar into my cup of tea, and stirred it. "A dash of each, and all together," I murmured, and wondered vaguely why I had said it.

Outside the kitchen window, a sliver of lake showed through the trees. Now that the ice was forming, the opposite shore seemed to be retreating further and futher away.

It was incredible that the lake, bare months before, had been a summer playground. The fishermen, swimmers, and water skiers now seemed like the figments of a madman's imagination, something from a fairy tale.

The idea of walking across the ice to the far side seemed like absolute madness. Faced with the reality of more than a mile of treacherous ice, I came to a deadful realization. The risk was not one I was going to ever take. I had drowned in this lake once, and I wouldn't give it a second chance to claim me. I was going to be stuck on the island until Spring.

~*~

"Would you walk with me, please, and not behind me?" she asked.

I walked a little bit faster. Chloe was slightly put out, and waited for me at the base of an old-fashioned post with four wooden signs affixed to it. They were white arrows. The black lettering on them was peeling and faded, but legible.

"Coyote Islands," I read out loud. "Sunbathing, Seaside, Boardwalk, Beach."

They all pointed the same way, to a flight of stone steps that only led down. Chloe led me, so light on her feet that she left me behind, scrambling to keep up. We descended one empty flight of steps after another, darker and darker, until we reached the bottom. We went through a door into the muted daylight of a very long hallway.

It was made of old cement. The wall on the left side was arched, the openings mostly blocked by sand dunes covered in sea grass. The sky, where I could glimpse it, was a peculiar pale color. There were patterned tiles on the floor, covered with a dusting of fine sand that gritted beneath my feet. Although our steps echoed, sounds were hushed.

When we had walked for a time in silence, the hallway brightened ahead of us. It ended in a doorway that opened to the outside. Another sign was posted on a small pedestal. It said, "Warning, Unseen Currents."

Chloe gave me a sidelong look. "That's not necessarily a bad thing," she said. "Not by any means."

We were at the edge of a natural cove, formed by three cliffs that were rubbed and washed by an opaque sea. We stood on a small sand beach. The aquamarine water, green cliffs, and lavender sky all had an odd uniformity. I realized there were no shadows. Birds circled far overhead, near the tops of the cliffs, never straying from their circular path. There was virtually no sound, except for the curiously muted wash of the waves.

A large boat with a single mast was pulled onto the beach, with its striped sail furled. A carved dog snarled on the prow, above ornate letters that spelled out 'A-S-K-E-W'.

"I've dreamed about the *Askew* my whole life," Chloe murmured. Her voice was wondering. "Now I'm finally seeing it. It's a legend, you know."

Her face brightened, and I followed her eyes to a small dark figure that stood on the beach path.

"Look!" she cried, delighted. "It's Cynthia!"

She ran ahead. As I came closer, the figure resolved itself into a small gorilla. Chloe knelt, holding both her hands and speaking quickly and earnestly. They were still too far away for me to make out the words.

Chloe put her head together with Cynthia's. She showed her how to use the kaleidoscope that she had taken from her bag.

"No matter what," I whispered, to myself.

When I reached them, Chloe kissed the gorilla and stood up. She guided me past with one hand on my elbow. I felt Cynthia's dark eyes on me, but she didn't speak. Safely out of her earshot, I whispered a question. "Is she a young gorilla, or a child in a gorilla costume?"

Chloe stared at me, perplexed. "What possible difference could that make? Cynthia keeps the bad things out, keeps this place safe."

"Safe? A little girl in a monkey costume is a guardian here?"

"She's the Gatekeeper for Albuquerque, and the Coyote Islands. She keeps the bad things out," she repeated, and bent to take off her sandals. "The good things too, most of them, but I gave her the kaleidoscope, and she says we may pass."

I followed her down to the water, which was calm and still at the beach, but appeared to be turbulent further out. The sand was soft and fine under my feet.

"Remember the currents," Chloe warned.

"Is there anything dangerous in the water?"

"No," she said. "Whatever swims down there is sleeping." She pointed at the birds, wheeling and circling high overhead. "They're asleep, too. Except for Cynthia, everything here sleeps, and there are no dreams. It's perfect safety, you know—without dreams."

Chloe went to the boat, and I followed. Although ancient, its wood gleamed, varnished and pristine, and the seats were pillowed and embroidered. We sat across from each other.

"No love, but no loss. No dreams. Do you understand? Everyone that comes here is in-between, and needs to be safe for a while."

"Cynthia, too?"

She poured sand from one cupped palm into the other, and then back again. Her voice was soft, but I had no trouble hearing her in the hush.

288

"She has her reasons, I'm sure."

"Why are you so sad, Chloe?"

Just a woman, sitting braced against some private hurt, clutching a fistful of sand, but I watched her profile and understood the ancient ache Cleopatra had caused, the power of Helen, Nefertiti's spells.

"I'm sad," she finally sighed, "because someday you'll have to come here by yourself. You'll have to find a way to launch this stupid boat if you're going to get to me." She looked at the water, and shook her head, determined not to allow her own tears. "And I worry there's at least a chance that I'll be somewhere else, and you'll be sitting on this beach, fast asleep. It's coming fast, Nick—be ready for it. You're going to need to launch the boat . . . you're going to need to launch the boat . . . you're going to need to launch the boat . . ."

~ * ~

I went for an early morning walk, a circuit of the island, ostensibly to check things, but really because of boredom and needing the exercise. I walked the southern edge, through the pine forest. It was dark under the trees, despite the pale, bright winter sun that lit up the snow, orange and gold and blue.

I stood at the shore and looked across the bay at Echo Island. It slept in the distance, snow-covered. The pine forests on its back made it appear like a sleeping porcupine. The huge stretch of open water between Duck and Echo had frozen and been covered over with new snow, although the ice was still thin. The landscape was perfectly still, a white desert.

Between my island and Long Duck I saw the rush of dark water in the channel. The rapid flow only froze in the very coldest winters, and the ice anywhere in the vicinity of that massive, slow moving current would be suspect, with leads of open water appearing and disappearing all through the winter. The distant flow had the potential to cause dangers as far away as the bay between the island and Nora's house, which is why I would have to do a wide circuit to the east if I walked across to shore in a week or two. I had mostly changed my mind about attempting it, but I wouldn't forget Bill's advice.

I had a sudden image of an object out there in the middle of the sound. There was no ice in sight, and it floated small in the endless black water. It was varnished wood. *A paddle?* I thought to myself. *No. A water ski.*

A single water ski floated by itself, and I reached for it. Far beneath me, the Hole gaped, unseen on the bottom of the lake, a vast underwater canyon that was going to swallow me. My body would be held in the grip of the flow draining into it for months. I was going down, down, down . . . like falling down a well.

I fell to my knees in the snow. I was drowning, and I flailed forward. I gasped for air, my cheek against a frozen blueberry bush. I vomited ice-cold water. I was choking, my breath gone, dying. As I began to lose consciousness, the hallucination lessened, and gradually, my vision cleared. I was able to gasp down the winter air. Even after my breathing returned to normal, I could taste the mineral sourness of lake water in my mouth.

It was a long time before I had the strength to get to my feet and stumble back to the cabin. I was beginning to remember things that I didn't want to. I understood why I was so afraid of drowning, and why the mention of the Hole had always made my skin crawl.

Most of all, I was beginning to remember how I had broken the rules.

~ * ~

Black clouds skidded across the dark sky, shreds of ribbons and flowers, forming and reforming, faster than I could make sense of them. The surf crashed into the seawall far below us, sending up violent spray. I could feel the pounding assault of water, right through the cement we stood on. It scared me, being so close to so much force, and I stepped back. Chloe walked, heel to toe, along the edge.

Beyond the breakers, the Train waited for us. Each time a wave hit the locomotive's boiler, steam rose into the air.

"I'm sorry," I said. "I'm sorry I ended you. It breaks my heart."

She didn't look at me. She was concentrating on her balance.

"I'll say this once, and never again," she said. "I had my own ticket, and you didn't end me, because there are no endings. Do you understand that? I had my own ticket, and the ticket was mine, not yours to change."

"I understand," I said, relieved.

"The other thing is—I'm yours, and you're mine, but we don't belong to each other. I'm glad I broke your heart, so we know it was done perfectly."

"Do you ever miss me?" I asked. "Do you ever miss this?"

"I want my pictures back, mostly because I want to touch them, like when I was there."

A particularly large wave hit the wall, and ocean spray blew and drenched us both.

"I sleep a little deeper, now. Sweet tastes sweeter, and I see all the things that aren't there. Everything I ever wanted and couldn't have—doesn't matter, anymore." She took a deep breath. "Still, I knew when I met you that my life wasn't going to be long enough, and it wasn't."

The Moon, listening quietly, smiled and nodded. He brushed the clouds away from his face, and flooded us with silver and green.

"You're real," she said. "I'm not. I still see you, though, everywhere I look. I see you, so I don't miss you. Missing you is one thing I won't do."

"Will we ever come back here?"

"I don't think so. The Coyote Islands are a good place to wait, but I hope our waiting is over."

She hopped down from the wall, landing lightly. She came to me and put a hand on my chest.

"We're going to drive west from here. We'll follow the Train and get back on in the Port of Los Angeles."

"Drive? Why?"

"Detours are easier when you go a little slower," she said. "You're remembering, but not fast enough. It's time to meander."

~ * ~

I sat bolt upright in my chair. I didn't know what had startled me awake, and it took a moment of staring around the cabin's main room to get my bearings. The wood stove had burned low, and the place had gotten cold. I hauled myself to my feet and went outside to the stacked pile firewood at the end of the veranda. The kitchen clock ticked and told me it was just after three in the morning. Beyond the door, the clearing was strangely lit.

I looked up, expecting the full moon, but the sky was overcast. The luminescence came from the clouds. It was warmer than I would have thought, given the chill inside. I hoped that whatever front was moving through wouldn't stay long. Now the ice was here, I needed cold temperatures to settle in and stay. I already felt the first stirrings of being trapped. I didn't think I could force myself to walk across the ice and go to town. I just wanted to be free to do so.

I collected an armload of dry, splintery wood, and started back inside.

A sound like cannon fire echoed over the lake, and I realized what had woken me up. Thunder in the winter months was a rarity, but not impossible. It came again, rolling across the water and echoing off the hills. A massive warm front was moving in to battle the cold that gripped the region. It would lose, no matter how much of a fight it gave.

The sky flashed white over my head, and then flickered and began to spit down sleet. After a few minutes, my arms began to ache from the load of wood I still carried. I turned to go back inside, just as the entire sky ripped in half. A strobe lit the clearing, the cabin, and me in pulsing white light. It lasted several seconds, and was so bright that when it disappeared, I felt blind.

The ground shook with a rip of thunder. Through the spots in my vision, I saw the top of a tall jack pine close to the dock erupt in flame. The upper half of the tree seemed to teeter in mid-air, and then a second blast of thunder knocked it down. It fell, in a shower of sparks. I dropped the wood I was carrying, spun around and dashed for the cabin door.

I ripped the fire extinguisher from the plastic bracket that held it on the kitchen wall. My hands shook. A fire could spread across the entire island in minutes. It was my worst nightmare, and this was worse than I had imagined. My boat was on shore, grounded, and the ice remained far too fragile to attempt a crossing. I was trapped.

The air outside reeked of ozone and scorched wood. I flew off the steps and ran across the clearing for the dock, my boots slipping on the snow-covered pine needles under my feet.

The burning tree had fallen across the bow of my boat. Beneath a huge cloud of smoke, I couldn't pinpoint where the flames were. I pulled the pin on the bright red canister, pulled the trigger and sprayed blindly. I emptied the extinguisher, and the smoke got thicker. I threw it away and ran to the cabin for another one.

When I got back, the smoke had dissipated into the weirdly opaque night sky. I emptied the second canister into the fiberglass hull, and satisfied myself the fire was out.

My boat was only a couple of seasons old, but with the top part of a ruined tree laying on it, it seemed beyond salvage. I felt stirrings of deep unease. I wanted to get off the island, very badly. I headed for the cabin, slowly. I had picked up a limp, though I didn't remember from what.

"You're going to need to launch the boat . . . you're going to need to launch the boat . . ."

I sat in my chair and listened to the storm move off across to the far shore. Hours later, the victorious cold front settled in, and the sky outside the window cleared to black. On the lake, the thickening ice boomed and cracked. At some point, without realizing I was doing it, I got to my feet and went to bed.

~ * ~

I pulled the car as close to the water as I could get it, and shut the big engine down. The exhaust burbled for a moment, disappointed, and then was quiet. I rested my hands on the steering wheel, big enough for a sailing ship, and glanced at Chloe beside me.

"What kind of car is this?" she asked.

"Packard, I think. 'Ask the man who owns one'. Where, and when, are we?"

She looked down at the phosphorescent glow of her watch and considered. Her profile was timeless, exactly right. The depth of what was in her face troubled me, what took over my waking dream. It wasn't her beauty that bothered me, but rather a sense of rarity that made everything around her somehow breathless.

"I'm not sure where we are, but it's 1922," she said. "We're a little bit off the beaten track, here. How fun." She reached for the chromed pull handle on the door. "Let's get out. I want to smell the air."

She walked ahead of me, down to the water's edge. A simple white shift dress hung from her shoulders. Her feet were bare, and she had flowers braided into her hair.

"I gave up on feeling like this a long time ago," I said, to her back.

She looked over her shoulder at me. "It's because you forgot me," she said. "Take your shoes off."

The water was cold. I smelled the salt, but there were no waves. We were at the edge of some kind of inlet. Only a few scattered lights shone along the curve of shoreline. Her hand was warm.

"All these people here," she mused. "Finishing dinner, getting ready for parties, gone to bed early. Some of them are excited about tonight, while some are already planning tomorrow. Some are happy people and some are giving up. Bullies and saints, teachers and drunks. All of them—so busy."

She bent to cup a handful of water. She raised it to her face and tasted it, and then offered the hand to me.

"How often do you get to come here?"

She smiled. "Don't you want to just try—all of it?"

I smelled her skin. The clean water tasted alive, light and dark, salty as birth.

"All of these people, busy with 1922," I said. "None of them knows we're here. We're ghosts."

"Remember when ghosts were white?" She laughed.

I smiled at her. It wasn't just love; I thought that I liked her more than anyone I had ever known.

"When we were little," I said, "we knew better."

She smiled back. "We did, didn't we?"

The moon hung over the water, and the ripples sparkled with it. Across the reach, a single green light burned.

"It's funny," I said. "We're almost a hundred years from home, and it's the same moon."

"The same moon?" she asked. "Why do you think so?"

The car waited for us. Ivory and red, tinted by the night, it crouched top-down, wire-wheeled, ready for anything.

"Can you drive fast?" she asked. "Or should I drive?"

"I can drive," I said. "How fast?"

"As fast as you can. Fast enough to catch everything we've ever lost—all those things that have left us behind, by ourselves."

A wind came up and played with her hair. "Do you know where we're going?" she asked.

I reached out, across the bay, and pointed to the green light twinkling on the opposite shore. She nodded, smiling.

"I want to touch it," she whispered. "I've always wanted that."

We got in, and I pressed the starter. The engine roared, choppy at first and then smoothing out. The needles on the gauges jumped and danced. Chloe indicated a silver button set into the wooden dashboard, by itself. She touched it lightly with her index finger.

"Tell me when you're ready."

It had a tiny plate riveted beneath it, inscribed with a single word. I squinted to make it out in the low light. "Eight," I read.

-Thirty-

I was picking at an early dinner when the cell phone on the table vibrated. Even with lousy call reception on most of the island, I usually got text messages without any problem. I picked up the phone and checked the screen.

It was from Nora.

'BAD BAD BAD TROUBLE HERE. CALL PLEASE NOW.'

My heart in my throat, I hurried outside and onto the dock. The dock was a floater, a wood platform resting on a thick bed of synthetic foam, designed to be pulled onto shore in the winter. The constriction of ice could crush or damage it. I had decided to risk leaving mine in the water, because it represented my only reliable contact with the outside world until the ice was thick enough to walk on.

I needed it now. Nora answered right away.

"That man called me a few minutes ago."

She sounded breathless. I wasn't concerned. The deadlines he had imposed on Esteban and me were close, if they hadn't already passed. Some bluster and bullshit was bound to be coming.

"Risa? Don't let him upset you, Nora. What did he want?"

"He has Esteban, and he's going to hurt him!"

"What do you mean, he has him? Has him where?"

"I don't know. He put him on the phone. He sounded terrified. It's real, Nick. He said we have to meet him tonight at Union Station. The last train arriving from Montreal, at midnight."

"Wait a second, Nora. Go slow."

This was coming too fast. I needed to think.

"There's nothing else. He said he wants to talk to you, and that you have to be there with me. He can't cross water, and he said to tell you to stop hiding in the middle of a lake where he can't get to you. If you aren't there to meet the train, he'll hurt

Esteban. He'll hurt him, and then me, until you give yourself up."

"He's not going to hurt anyone, Nora. I won't let him."

"What does he mean— give yourself up?"

She was crying. My hand had frozen, so I shifted the phone to my other ear and turned my back to the wind.

"Esteban isn't like you," she cried. "He's sensitive. This has all just about killed him already. You have to come, please. You have to."

"This is kidnapping, Nora. If this is true, you can have the train met by about a thousand cops. I guarantee he won't bother you again."

"He thought of that. He said for me to write this down to tell you, 'The splat is next. The splat gets eaten before anyone else.' I don't know what that means—the splat."

I shivered, from the cold or nerves. "I know what it means," I said. "I'll be there. It's only six o'clock. I'll be there long before midnight. I'll see you at your place."

"Hurry up," she said, and we disconnected.

The lake stretched before me, uniformly white. There were no lights on the opposite shore to reassure me, but my head knew it was less than a mile across. I looked at my damaged boat. Even if the ice was thin enough to break through, it was out of the question. It was too heavy to move until spring, assuming that the burning pine tree hadn't totaled it.

He can't cross water, I thought. *I'm safe here.*

I shook off the temptation.

I needed to talk to someone who knew the lake, and I punched in Bill's number from memory. He answered, in the wary way of someone who gets few calls to his cell phone that aren't wrong numbers. He sounded closer in Florida than Nora had from Toronto. He seemed delighted when he recognized my voice.

"Diane's making dinner," he said. "Drive slow and you'll get here too late for it. Did you come to your senses? Coming down for spring training?"

"I need your help, Bill." I cut him off. "I have to walk out tonight. I have no choice. How can I tell if the ice is safe?"

His tone became serious. "How long has it been in?"

I had been spending so much of my time on the Train with Chloe that it was hard for me to reconcile real time. "I don't have any idea," I answered, honestly. "My best guess is that it came in three or four nights ago."

"That isn't long enough. How cold has it been?"

"Up and down. Mostly cold. A warm front came through last night, warm enough for thunder and lightning."

"It isn't safe," he said. "Simple as that. Not even close to safe. Trust it in a week if it stays cold. Really cold."

"I have to go tonight. I don't have any choice."

"Say goodbye then, because if you try to cross tonight, I'll never see you again. You won't make it."

"Listen to me, Bill."

I told him, as quickly as I could, about the situation. My jeep was parked a mile away at the boat launch, so close I could practically see it.

"Fifteen, twenty minutes of walking, and I'm driving away," I said. "I just have to do it and get it over with."

"Do not go out on the ice," he said. "Don't do it."

He sounded angry and sounded close to tears. I didn't answer, and he gave up.

"If you do something so darned stupid, remember one thing. Do *not* walk directly across the sound. The current from the island channel dumps out there, and the Hole does all kinds of funny things to the water. Walk east from the island, and then loop back toward Nora's house. You'll stay in calmer water."

"Got it. I already knew that. You told me."

"Can you remember? No matter how much of a hurry you're in?"

"I'll remember, Bill. I'll call you when this is over."

"There are baseball tickets waiting for you when you change your mind," he said. "Get on a plane. You can fall asleep in the cold and snow, and wake up where it's warm and sunny. Catch a home run ball."

"I'll keep it in mind."

I disconnected. There was nothing else to say. I went up to the cabin to get myself ready to walk across the ice.

~ * ~

The sky was low, dirty, and a smoky gray that didn't carry the slightest threat of rain.

"It's practically brand new, buddy," the guy sitting next to me said. "Peach, ain't she?"

I considered him. He wore a chocolate straw hat with a yellow band, and a white shirt with short sleeves. I had never seen him before in my life.

"What's brand new?" I asked.

"This place, dope—Dodger Stadium. Beats the Coliseum hands down, don't it?"

He waved a hand expansively at the rows of pale blue seats and the green field. The crowd filled and nearly overflowed the pale blue decking. I knew the structure, even without reading the sign in the outfield. The players ran out, tiny in their clean white uniforms. The man had to nearly shout over the swelling crowd noise.

"The '64 World Series is going to be right here, pal—City of Angels. Come back in October and tell me I didn't say so. Dare you."

"Whatever you say."

I stood up, and moved into the aisle. I felt a tug at my arm, and looked down. He had my sleeve.

"One more thing, buddy. The splat's brand new this year, too. Time to get off, all that's getting off."

"I'm not going anywhere unless it's on her say-so," I countered, and shrugged him off.

"Suit yourself, buddy."

I glared at him, but he had already lost interest in me and was staring at the field. I started up the concrete steps, heading away from the field. I paused to get my bearings and got jostled by a vendor in a white hat, selling hot peanuts from a steel tray. He gave me a dirty look.

"Peeeeea-nuts!!" he bawled at me, rolling his eyes. "Getcha peeea-nuts!!!"

I followed him up, knowing nothing, but hoping for an exit. The crowd was intense, feral, decorated with horn-rimmed glasses, fedoras, and sleeveless blouses. It smelled of body odor and cigars.

"Good of you to stop by. Keeping in tune, pally?"

The Grinning Man gazed up at me from an aisle seat. He was eating a hot dog from a paper napkin. It bled ketchup onto his hand, and he paused to lick his fingers.

"Who's going to be better this year, Drysdale or Koufax?" he asked. "You probably know, and you're not saying."

"I'm not saying," I agreed.

"As for you, it's the ninth inning. You're moving past the point where anyone can help you, even the splat. Did you enjoy the game?"

"Anything else?"

His face changed, just for a moment, and I had a glimpse of what lay underneath.

"You have a way of getting annoying," he said. "You're decompensating, pal, you understand that? Seeing things that aren't there. Nice work if you can get it, but it might not last long."

"Anything else?" I repeated.

"Yeah, matter of fact. Someone wants to see you. Men's room, top of the stairs. Say your goodbyes."

He jerked his chin in that direction, and then went back to his hot dog. I nodded.

"See you around," I said.

"Keep in tune, pally. You better believe we will."

I walked into the echoing concrete tunnel. The crowd was still filing in, latecomers hurrying to find their seats, and I dodged elbows and shoulders, fighting the current. Male voices shouted over the general hubbub, selling programs and souvenirs. At last, I ducked into the men's restroom.

It was empty and silent. Ranks of sinks marched down the ceramic gray wall, opposed by a long row of urinals. At the far end, a bank of about twenty stalls lined the wall. One gray metal door stood open. As I watched, it slammed shut with a sound like a gunshot.

Irresistibly drawn, my footsteps echoed on the tile.

I reached out and pushed on the door with two fingers. It swung open. The toilet stared back at me, white with a black seat. I went in and turned the chrome knob, latching the door behind me. When I turned back, I stood on a city street. It was dusk, and lights were just coming on, soft colors against warm air. I spotted Chloe a half-block away, walking toward me.

-Thirty One-

"Do you still think this is a dream?" she asked, and took my hand.

"Not anymore," I said. "Back there is starting to feel like the dream.

She nodded. "Exactly. That's what all this is—waking up from a black-and-white dream you were having, and finding that you're in your own bed.

The sign said "Chinese Food" in red neon, over and over, blinking at us from halfway up the block. The night wind picked up. A piece of newspaper blew out of the dark, down the middle of the street and past, on its way to somewhere else.

"Hungry?" Chloe asked.

"Not right now," I said. "I think we have company."

"All the more reason to get out of sight. They've been behind us for six blocks. Nine of them. Glad you finally noticed."

I glanced back as we turned into the restaurant doorway. Two of the Low Men scurried between parked cars and into the shadows of an alley, long coats flapping, holding onto their fedoras. I shook my head, and followed Chloe inside.

We were enveloped in warm and steamy air. A woman in red-and-gold brocade held menus in front of her bosom and watched us anxiously as we found a booth. We sat beneath a painted dragon with tiny wings. When we were settled, she came over and put a single fortune cookie onto the table between us. Chloe smiled at her, and she left. I broke the cookie open and pulled out the tiny ribbon of paper.

It was blank.

Chloe took it from my fingers and studied it intently. Her lips moved soundlessly as she read. I watched her dark eyes. She finished reading, and her expression became startled.

"They eat people here," she said suddenly, and stood up. "Hurry. We can go out the back."

We pushed through a swinging door into the kitchen. It smelled like cigarette smoke and spoiled fruit. The cook stood at a long counter, his back to us, wearing stained whites and a paper hat. Poised with a cleaver, he held an orange-colored duck carcass by the neck. He leered over his shoulder.

"Did you come to see the dead body?" he asked. "Pay your respects?"

It was the Grinning Man, large as life.

Neither Chloe nor I answered him. He took the lit cigarette from his mouth and crumpled it in his fist, before turning around to show us his teeth.

"Cry some crocodile tears?" he persisted. "Third time is always the charm, you know, and bad things come in threes. Sooner or later, I'm going to catch you and eat you."

His face suffused with blood, and he slammed the cleaver on the counter.

"ALL UP!" he screamed. "DO YOU HEAR ME? I'M GOING TO EAT YOU ALL UP!"

"We hear you," Chloe said, softly, apologetically, and glanced at me. "But we really have to fly."

She pulled me sideways, into a short, dim hallway paved in green linoleum.

"Run," she said. "Run like hell."

We ran to a narrow set of wooden stairs at the other end. They shook beneath our feet as we took them two at a time, around and around, seven or eight flights ending with a door at the top. It had a piece of yellowed paper taped to it, lettered in ballpoint pen.

"No Exit," she read out loud. "Danger. Unseen Currents." She looked at me. "That isn't always a bad thing," she said, and we both smiled a little.

I twisted the loose brass knob and shouldered the door open. Outside, on the rooftop, ventilators spun like pinwheels in the dark. We picked our way to the parapet. Los Angeles glittered below us, as far as I could see, and I sensed the black ocean spread out beyond the lights. The air rushed, strong and steady. Chloe cupped a hand against my ear.

"Don't fight the wind," she said. "It's time to fly."

"You can…?"

She nodded. Her hand was warm in mine. I looked into her eyes.

"You're all I see," I said.

We went over the edge, together.

I fell toward the pavement, like a bad dream, and then Chloe caught me, tugged at my hand, and we were soaring. The streets of Los Angeles rushed along underneath us, and cars and trucks followed their own headlights in every direction. The air cooled as we gained height. The wind on my face was exhilarating.

Chloe pointed at the horizon. There was a vast darkness beyond the lights of the city. I knew it was the ocean, and that the Train waited there for us. If it was true the Low Men wouldn't cross open water, then the dark water was our safe place. It was also the beginning of the last leg of our journey.

"Watch out!"

Her voice was right in my ear. She hugged me to her with her free arm, just as the air was filled with a wild flapping. The sky around us was nothing but black coats. Low Men dived at us, holding onto their fedoras, faces grim.

"They're forcing us down!" Chloe yelled. "Help me find a place to land!"

We angled toward an island of blue-and-pink neon on the street below, a nightclub sign. When we touched ground, I dug in my heels and skidded under the outline of palm trees and camels. The lettering on the sign flashed; it said 'Oasis', over and over. I fought for balance, and came to a stop, still on my feet. Chloe had me by the elbow. The neon buzzed and made everything glow.

The Low Men had also landed, and they formed a loose circle around us. One of them tipped back the brim of his hat. It was the Grinning Man.

"Imagine that," he said. His teeth gleamed pink and then blue. "Caught the two of you together. Knew if I followed you long enough, pally, sooner or later you'd turn up with the splat."

He inhaled deeply, an exaggerated sniff. He raised his eyebrows at Chloe. "Nothing I love as much as the smell of splat." He grinned. "Nothing quite like it."

The Low Men shook with laughter behind him.

"Cumin, Turmeric, Cayenne, Blueberry," Chloe said, very softly. "A dash of each, and all together."

"What did you say?" the Grinning Man hissed, taking a step back. "What did you say?"

Chloe's voice dropped to a whisper. "Cumin, Turmeric, Cayenne, Blueberry."

The Low Men moved back a step, in unconscious unison. One of them whimpered. The buzz from the glowing sign seemed to get louder. Chloe reached into her bag.

"A dash of each—"

The first of the bears moved into the neon pool we stood in, black and bulky, sniffing at the air.

"—and all together."

A second and third bear followed. All of them swayed to music that only they could hear. The Low Men noticed them, and began to stir and nudge each other nervously. The three animals approached. A low steady growl started up. The volume of it wound higher as the bears came closer.

The men broke their circle and backed up. Hands came out of pockets, and fedoras were clamped down firmly. The first and largest bear stood on his hind legs, and the Low Men broke ranks entirely and prepared to flee. Only the Grinning Man stood his ground. He glared at his troops, and they stood still.

"Parlor tricks don't scare me, splat," he said. "In fact, I can't think of anything that does—scare me."

"Cobwebs, hats and moths," Chloe murmured. "Rooftops and city lights, toes, a hundred years—water."

"Alice woke up in a Banyan tree, and she doesn't know why," I said, without the slightest idea what I was saying.

306

The Grinning Man shifted his attention to me. His smile was gone. Chloe looked at me approvingly.

"Alice?" he asked. "Who's Alice?"

"I just made that up," I said, confused. "I meant Nora. I think what I'm trying to say is—"

"Shhhhh," Chloe hushed me. "Don't think. You let him in, when you do."

The three bears closed in.

"Don't just stand there," the Grinning Man snarled at his men. "Blast them!"

The Low Man in front stepped forward, pulled his Tommy gun out and fired. The muzzle blossomed yellow-white, with a sound like fabric tearing. Fur puffed and blew from the smallest bear's coat. There was a yelp and crying, and all at once the cub sat down in the street. His parents hurried to him. Goldilocks flew out from the shadows, her white pinafore colored blue by the glowing sign. She wept as she knelt by the wounded bear.

"Stop it!" Chloe screamed, and everyone did.

She knelt down beside Goldilocks, and murmured something, holding the cub's front paws in both of her hands. After a moment, she and Goldilocks got up and helped the creature to his feet. He whimpered a little while they dusted him off.

"You'll be all right in the morning," Chloe assured him. "Go home and sleep. You were all very brave. Thank you."

The defeated bears shambled off into the darkness, followed by Goldilocks, who was still angrily wiping at her cheeks. She didn't look at us.

"The good guys lose—again," the Grinning Man laughed. "Got any more stupid magic up your sleeves?"

He tilted his hat back so the light from the sign shone on his face. His eyes were empty holes. He blew smoke my way, a long jet that swirled into a blue cloud in the neon light. He spoke to me, and only to me.

"I told you once, and I'll tell you again, 'Happily ever after' is a lie, and the Turtle is dead. He's just an empty shell at the bottom of the universe, and he doesn't care."

He turned up his collar and parked the cigarette in a corner of his mouth. Without his customary smirk, he was handsome, a Dick Tracy profile come to life. He jerked his chin at Chloe. "Last, but not least, she doesn't love you. You fell for a ghost, a phantom, a smoke-and-mirrors sideshow splat. You're a fool, pally. She isn't even real."

Beside me, Chloe began to whisper. She had her eyes shut tight, and was kneading her hands together. The light washed her in rose. "Pink flowers and pink hearts—elevens, sevens and eights—romance and no crying. Buttons and baby pins, buttons and nines—air and lace."

Her eyes opened. They were impossibly dark, endlessly deep in the strange illumination. "No matter what."

She held her closed fist out toward him, palm up. She stared, lips moving, and slowly opened her fingers. "A dash of each," she murmured, and blew a long breath softly and steadily into her open palm. "And all together."

A puff of dust blew up from her hand and grew. It began first to swirl, and then to fly. A cloud of butterflies filled the night sky and enveloped the Grinning Man. He began to scream. Chloe blew on her hand again.

"A dash of each, and all together—you son of a bitch," she finished.

He stumbled backward, clawing at the butterflies. His mouth gaped open, huge and dark. His empty eyes ran black, down his cheeks, and he blindly looked around for us, still screaming incoherently. The Low Men fled, taking to the air clumsily, a flapping and fluttering of coats.

"Run," Chloe said, and we did.

A long time later we stopped to catch our breaths, under a streetlight. We were in an area lined with warehouses. There was no traffic at all on the street.

"Can't we fly?' I asked.

She glanced over her shoulder, distracted, and shook her head. "We're almost free of him. It's safer to stay on the ground, and out of sight."

"Where are we going?"

"Can you smell the ocean? We're close to where the Train is waiting. Once we're on board, we'll be on open water. He can't follow—or won't. We'll be safe."

I followed her when she started moving again, down dark streets and through a maze of industrial buildings, until we turned a corner and saw the lights of the Port of Los Angeles. The place was lit as bright as midday. Cranes swung across the sky, and trucks hurried around the docks, busy. A huge red freighter with a red hull moved slowly away from the lights, out to sea.

Chloe pointed to a pier, away from all the activity. It was unlit, except for the soft illumination from the windows of the train that rested alongside it. I saw a tiny figure. Ginger, the old conductor, stood on the cement jetty. He waved frantically.

We started to run.

-Thirty Two-

I pulled the cabin door shut behind me, and locked it. It had been months since I had bothered with the key, and the lock was so stiff that I almost gave up on it. It finally turned and the bolt snapped home in the old wood frame. I fought the urge to unlock it again, and go back inside. I stood on the porch, and made a mental inventory of everything I had remembered to disconnect and turn off.

Finally, there was nothing left to do, and I went down the front steps and headed across the clearing to the edge of the lake. The moon shone full and bright, the air so cold it squeaked. I made my way past the beached hull of my boat and down to the shore a dozen feet away from the dock. The wind blew strong, and the lake was a reassuring expanse of white reflecting back the bright night sky. I saw blowing snow, and none of the black streaks that indicated open water. It looked like a farmer's field in winter.

I carried a large flashlight, and I flicked it on at the water's edge. After a moment, I turned it back out, and waited for my eyes to adjust. My vision was better with just the light from the night sky.

I put a boot tentatively onto the ice, and felt a stab of fear so strong it hurt my chest. The snow didn't feel a bit different, though, and after a moment I followed with the other foot. The ice was solid. I took a last look over my shoulder at the bulk of my dark cabin through the screen of bare trees, and then I started walking.

Directly ahead of me, a mile away on the opposite shore stood Nora's house, and a few hundred yards from it, the public boat launch where my jeep was parked. The current from the sister islands ran between me and there, so I turned to the left, as Bill had suggested. I would walk a half-mile or so east, toward the end of the lake and away from the moving flow, and then turn south to the boat launch.

310

I scuffed away the snow with the toe of my boot, to reveal the ice beneath. It was smooth, but it didn't feel slippery. It looked uncomfortably dark, and I didn't want to think about the water beneath it, so I didn't do it again.

I left the southern flank of the island behind me. It was strange to see the pines I knew so well from behind the wheel of a boat slowly disappear into the dark as my feet moved across the ice. As I left the shelter of land, the wind picked up, howling across the flat expanse. I turned my face away from the blowing ice crystals, but they found everything exposed and left my skin raw and wet.

Walking backward into the wind helped, but it slowed my progress. I concentrated on a mechanical rhythm, one step after another, and tried to ignore both the physical discomfort and my awareness of the seventy or so feet of black water inches below me. I was glad that I travelled away from the Hole. Facing its abyss would have been enough to send me scurrying back to the cabin.

After a few minutes, I stopped and got my bearings. The island had disappeared from view. I figured I was probably far enough to the east, and clear enough of any open water, that I could turn for the shore. I found myself suddenly unsure. No land showed in any direction. The lake made a white expanse all around me. The snow was ridged into tiny waves and crests by the wind. I felt another stirring of fear, deep in my guts.

The wind gave me a solution. I turned my face into it and knew I was headed east, just as when I started. I turned again, until I felt it on my left cheek. I headed for shore, doing my best to ignore the fact that I walked through the middle of featureless space three or four miles wide, and twenty long. If I started going in circles I would freeze to death.

I stopped again, and felt drained by shock. In front of me, twenty yards away and clear in the low ambient light, footprints trailed through the snow. Someone was out here on the lake with me. When I got closer, I saw they were small. The wind had done remarkably little to obliterate the outline of heel and toes. Bare feet had made the prints.

"Chloe?" I whispered, but no answer came.

The footsteps were pointed roughly north. Did she want me to follow her? The north shore was lined with cottages only accessible by water. There was no road. It didn't make sense. I turned south instead.

After ten minutes of walking, I saw pine trees looming from the gloom on the horizon, only a couple of hundred yards away. I stopped and scanned the shoreline, and didn't understand what I saw. I should have been the better part of a mile from the south shore. I was lost. I figured I had gone further east than I thought, and somehow reached the eastern shore of Hollow Lake, near Bear Falls.

I spotted the unmistakable outline of Nora's house and dock, and suddenly I realized what I'd done. I had lost my sense of direction and gone south instead of east. I had walked right across the most dangerous stretch of ice in the whole lake. Chloe's footprints had been an attempt to turn me in the right direction. I felt lucky to have made it to the far side.

I hadn't, though.

I took one more step toward shore, and the ice gave way. Soaked to the knees, I had time to be vaguely concerned that my feet would be wet for the drive to Toronto, and then the whole thing collapsed and I went underwater. Everything turned black, rushing and gurgling. There was nothing beneath me, and as I sank, I felt the currents tug and pull me violently.

The cold went beyond painful, and I reached up in the dark water for the surface. I felt as though I was upside down. I didn't know where the surface lay. Panic came, screaming in my ears. I was going to be swept from under the open lead, and come up under the ice. I would die trapped—again.

Again?

I was dying, breathing in the cold black water. My lungs were so heavy they ached, and I tried to scream, but I couldn't. I would never see Chloe Hunter again, I was just getting started,

I was only eighteen years old, and Oh God it wasn't right. My mother would wake me up in a minute and call 'Nicky you're going to be late for school' and why hadn't I listened to her and not come out here alone and Chloe didn't even know I was here and I wasn't going to see her again, and God I loved her . . .

"I've got you, Nicky." It was Chloe's voice. "It's okay—I've got you, baby."

My hands found a shelf of solid ice, and I pulled my head and shoulders from the water. Air had never tasted so good. I spread my fingers on the ice, and struggled to find my breath in the frigid air. I knew I had bare minutes to get myself out of the water and warm up before hypothermia had its way, but I needed to rest for just a moment.

I had to close my eyes, for just a minute.

~ * ~

I opened my eyes. Water sparkled in the sun, too dark a blue-grey to be anything but the Pacific. The breeze blew, cool and soft. We stood under a sign that read 'Playland'. I gazed around me, and had a revelation.

"This is Santa Monica Pier," I said. "Sort of."

"Isn't it beautiful? It's 1964!"

Chloe beamed, as though she had made it all just for me.

A roller coaster rattled in the distance, and I heard screams as the tiny cars paused and then plummeted. A large Ferris wheel turned slowly, decorously, next to it. The crowd on the pier wore lots of hats—baseball caps, fedoras, and kerchiefs. There were thick lenses in cat-eye glasses, canvas basketball shoes, lipstick, plaids and stripes. Everyone seemed to be smoking.

"Too bad," Chloe said. "They tore down the roller rink last year. We could have gone skating. Of course, they killed Jack Kennedy last year, too, and that's worse. Much worse."

She stared at the ocean, lost in thought, and I looked at her. After a minute, she shook the mood off and regarded me brightly. "The ice cream's amazing. Wait 'til you try it."

313

We set off to find it, walking the boardwalk slowly, soaking up the day. Suddenly, Chloe's hand tightened in mine, and she dropped it. I followed her eyes, to a man sitting on a bench that ran alongside a building. Unshaven, he took the cigarette from his mouth and spat on the oiled wood at his feet. Foot. One trouser leg was pinned up, and a crutch rested against the bench next to where he sat.

"I'm afraid he can see me," she whispered. Her face went pale under her tan.

"What's wrong, Chloe? What is it?"

"Oh, no," she moaned almost inaudibly. "Here I come. I can't stop it."

A young woman approached us. Even in summer wear, her bearing was elegant, nearly regal. A tiny girl led her.

"That's you?" I asked.

The little girl broke away and toddled toward the man, pointing. Her mother swooped in and picked her up, giving the one-legged man an apologetic look. As the woman passed us, she quietly scolded the child on her hip.

"Don't be rude," I heard her whisper.

Chloe looked sick. I put an arm around her and led her away. I glanced back at the man over my shoulder. He touched the brim of his hat and winked at me. I was flooded with a shock of memory. We went to a railing, out of his sight. The mother and daughter had disappeared.

"I know," I said. "I saw him, too."

She didn't answer, huddled against the rail.

"You don't understand," I persisted. "I saw him, too, when I was little. The same guy."

I took a deep breath. "When I was small, no more than three years old, we lived in Hollywood. I had a dream, if it was a dream. I came up the front sidewalk, walking by myself. Santa Claus sat in a chair on our veranda. He had no head. Just Santa in his red fur, sitting there with no head and no hat."

Chloe turned her head to watch my face.

"He started laughing," I went on. "A long, long laugh, coming from the neck of his suit. I can still hear it. And you know what the horrible thing was, Chloe? It wasn't the no-head, or the laugh. It was the fact that he knew me."

I saw the recognition on her face. I felt hot, and my stomach began to churn. "He knew me. He knew every bad thing about me, even if I wasn't old enough to have done anything bad, and it made him laugh and laugh."

"You know," she whispered. "You know the Grinning Man. We see the same things."

"One day," I said, "not long after, we were in the grocery store and I saw the same guy we just saw back there. Somehow, I knew he was the Santa, even though my dream-Santa had no head and I never saw his face. I told my mom, 'that's the man who was on the porch', and when she asked me what I was talking about—"

"—and I pointed at the man with one leg," she interrupted. "My mother was angry because I was so rude. Don't point at people who are different than us, right?"

She pushed herself off the rail and took my arm. We started to walk the other way, out to the ocean end of the pier.

"You were never pointing at the guy's leg," I said. "You were pointing him out because you knew who he really was."

"Who he really is," she corrected. "He's the Grinning Man. He disguises himself when he needs to."

"You saw him, and so did I, and they cover us in shame until we can't see anymore. We saw him then, and we see him now."

She brought us to a stop. We stood quietly in the sun for a long time, listening to the gulls squabble.

"You might not be as hopelessly dumb as you like to seem," she finally said.

"Maybe not, no."

"Let's get you off the ice," she said. "You were supposed to drown, not freeze to death."

"Get me off the ice?"

She smiled, healing the day a little bit. "I meant, let's get ice cream," she said. "We have to hurry. You need to wake up."

~ * ~

My upper body lay on the ice. The water below my waist was so cold that I couldn't feel myself. The Moon looked down at me and didn't say a word.

I felt myself begin to drift. I wasn't afraid anymore. My hands slipped a little on the ice, and I watched them hopefully. When they slid all the way off, I could sink beneath the surface and sleep, down where the lake was deepest and coldest.

Suddenly I felt myself lifted, just a little.

Warm arms slipped around me, and a body pressed against mine from behind. Soft breath in my ear, and a flood of luscious yellows and oranges, the colors of melons on a breakfast table in the sun. I smelled cut grass, and felt warm water. I bathed in gentle heat.

"I love you," Chloe whispered in my ear, "even if I never told you so."

I rose, lifted upward, all at once. My gloved hands left the ice, and I heard the water pouring and spattering as I came out of the lake and spilled forward. I landed hard on the snow, a dozen feet from the edge of the open lead. I turned over quickly, but I couldn't see her.

"It's a Squeeze Play," she said from the wind. "The runner's too far down the line to go back. The ball's still in play—do the right thing, no matter what."

There was a cold sucking sound in the air, and she was gone. Above me, the sky hung black and frozen, filled with stars from one horizon to the other, but I couldn't see the moon any more. On shore, I saw something that shocked me. A quarter-mile away, Nora's house blazed light. Every ceiling light, floor lamp, nightlight and fluorescent tube in the whole place had been turned on, to direct me to safety. Absurdly, I knew somehow that even the refrigerator door would be open, to add to the glow.

It was all for me, this beacon of warmth a few minutes away across the ice, and I started toward it.

Chloe's touch had warmed me just enough that the feeling crept back into my limbs, and the flow of blood began to hurt me. I moved, at first slowly and stiffly, but gradually faster. The skin of ice broke and then instantly began to reform on my wet clothes, and I heard my own cracking as I got closer to shore. I walked stiffly, leaning forward, a little off-balance to maintain momentum. I fell down twice.

At last, I pulled myself up the bank near Nora's dock, using the long dry grass poking up through the snow. The powder coated my wet, freezing clothing like icing sugar. I stumbled up the empty driveway to the back door.

It was unlocked, which didn't make sense. The key was at the marina, on the MacMillan's kitchen table. I pushed it open, and went into the kitchen. The room was warm and dry, completely odorless except for a very faint tang of bleach. No one had been here in weeks. Every light was indeed on, and the appliances and the sink looked back at me brightly. I closed the door behind me, to keep the warmth inside.

Down in the basement, I heard the furnace click and whirr, and then the rush of air through the floor vents. Chloe had opened the house for me, and turned up the heat.

I began to strip my sodden clothing. I felt the weight of my freezing, there in the comfortable kitchen, as my body struggled not to shut down. My movements became increasingly stiff, and I tried to hurry.

I took the pile of clothes from the linoleum into the small laundry room that opened off the back entrance. The fluorescent tubes were already lit, buzzing very gently. I stuffed everything into the drier and turned it on. After a moment, I went back to the door, retrieved my boots and put them in, too. The clunked as they tumbled around in the metal drum.

In the bathroom, I started the taps running in the bathtub, and checked the medicine cabinet for aspirin. The shelves were clean and empty, since Nora hadn't intended to come back. I put a foot into the tub to test the water, and couldn't really feel it. I could see the steam rising from it, though, so I turned the cold tap a little wider. I didn't want to scald myself.

I slid in, up to my chin, and tried not to remember that just minutes earlier I had been equally submerged in the cold, black nearly bottomless lake. I thought about Chloe instead.

~ * ~

We sat upstairs in the unlit, empty observation car. She finished the last of her champagne, set the glass aside, and looked pensively out of the clear dome at the night outside. The seats were plush, and I was exhausted and ready to drift off, but as the train struggled through the surf, it got hard not to worry, at least a little.

I thought about the cigars in my pocket, but I glanced at her and left them where they were.

Far behind, the lights of the Port of Los Angeles still hung over the horizon. The ocean ahead of us yawned bottomless, cold and black. Waves rolled suddenly out of the darkness and broke, whitely phosphorescent, over the locomotive and cars in front of us. The train shuddered deeply every time it got hit.

"Did we beat him?" I asked.

She turned her attention from the window, and smiled quietly at me. "He can't be beaten," she said. "Not in the sense you mean. You can move past the pain and loss he causes, though, so they don't matter anymore. You can win when you accept his hurt and move past it."

"I see," I said.

"No, you don't—not yet."

The Conductor appeared at the top of the steps, nearly invisible in the gloom. "I hate to bother you folks," he said. "We're off shore, so it's really just a formality."

Chloe tore her gaze from the window, and looked at him. Then she rummaged in her bag.

"He's not just the Conductor," she said. "He's also the Gatekeeper of Los Angeles."

"It's not much more than an honorarium," he explained to me. "Since the Low Gang stays off open water, not much happens west of Los Angeles. The trouble out here comes from rogue waves and hurricanes and such. Those things don't care much about Gatekeepers and Rules."

Chloe produced a scrap of yellow from her bag and put it in his hand. He held it to the dim light from outside the window. It was a deflated balloon.

"I'm sorry it's in such poor shape," she said. "It's had to come a long way."

I remembered it, lost by a little boy and bouncing under a truck in 1964. It all seemed like a long time ago, even if it had only been a few days.

"The balloon got old," the Conductor said. "Like all of us do. It's still as beautiful as it's supposed to be, and the magic is as good as new."

He put it away in his pocket.

"There's just one Gatekeeper left after this?' Chloe asked. "The Gatekeeper at Shangri-La?"

"Just one," he agreed. "You might not even see the last one. Not likely to bother you, if there's no reason to."

He turned and went back up the aisle, bracing with his hands on the seat backs, against the swaying. He turned at the top of the stairs, when Chloe spoke. "Aren't you forgetting something?" she asked.

"You may pass," he said. He nodded, smiled, and disappeared.

~ * ~

I found a jar of instant coffee. There were cups in the cupboard. I hunted for a kettle, but had no luck. I didn't have any time, so I ran the water from the tap as hot as it would get and added two spoonfuls of brown crystals. I hesitated, added a third, and gulped down the result.

I had no open water to protect me anymore, and I was frightened. I didn't know how the Low Gang moved in this world, but I had to hope that Risa wanted me for himself. Best to keep moving toward him. I got my clothes from the drier and dressed.

I would have liked to lock Nora's front door behind me, but I didn't have a key. I settled for turning off what lights were at hand and went outside. The bitter cold burned my skin immediately, and I wondered what damage I'd done to myself with the icy submersion.

The public boat launch was a five-minute walk up the shore road. My feet crunched the gravel, making the only sound other than the wind, until a couple of wolves started to cry from somewhere across the lake. I peered across the icy expanse and tried to spot my island a mile out, but it was invisible in the darkness. I tried to see the lead I had fallen into, but I couldn't see that either.

The yellow jeep huddled all by itself in the small parking lot which had been scraped out of the dirt. The trees had protected it from most of the snow. The engine started right up, and I turned on the headlights and waited for the heater to start working. I pulled out my phone and called Kate.

"I'm mad at you," she said. "You couldn't stop by at Christmas? If you're wishing me a good New Year, better keep the wishes for yourself."

"Christmas?"

"Are you that out of touch? Are you spending your time on a different planet?"

I hadn't even thought about Christmas. Had it gone by? I pondered it for a moment, and decided to move on. I told her briefly what had happened, and was happening now. I thought she deserved to know.

"My call display shows your cell number, Nick."

"I'm calling you from the truck. I'm about to pull out."

"How are you calling on your phone, if you went into the water? Don't they get ruined?"

"I spend half my time on boats," I smiled. "I ruined three or four phones before I learned to always put mine in a plastic bag before I put it in my pocket. The kind with the zipper things. It's a habit that paid off tonight."

"What set this man off? Is he serious?"

"This is pretty bad, Kate. I guess he's lost it."

"Call this off, Nick," Kate said. "I know you think you should take care of this, but call the police in Toronto. Please. You're almost certainly hypothermic. You need to get to a hospital. Don't try to be a hero."

I heard the echo of Chloe's voice. *I always wonder, "Who's going to be the hero?"*

"I have to take care of this," I said. "I'll be there in less than three hours. The last train gets in close to midnight. I have plenty of time."

"Tell Nora to call me tonight, no matter how late. Don't let her forget. And, Nick, if you're going to be reckless, at least don't be careless. There's a difference."

I had no good answer for that. I said goodbye to Kate, put the clutch in and headed for the highway.

It was late, and the Train was far out to sea. The lights had been turned off so we could watch the moon move across the expanse of waves. The carriage rocked gently, and after a little while Chloe tucked her head into my shoulder and fell asleep. I still felt too unsettled by the strange trip over water to relax. A storm moved across the ocean toward us. It blackened the night sky as it came, and rain began to pelt the glass dome over our heads.

We suddenly slowed in the water. The Train's cars bumped perceptibly, one against the next, as the great steam engine vented its pressure and brought us to rest. As soon as we were completely stopped, the force of the waves slamming against us increased, and I felt the Train rocking on its tracks.

"I'm back," Chloe said, awake now. She touched my sleeve and pointed out the window. "Look. What's that?"

Through the gondola windows, I saw lights shining through the darkness. They floated in the water, above and below the surface. Pale blue and green, there were perhaps seven or eight of them in all. I couldn't tell what they were doing, but they moved with purpose.

"So sorry about the delay," the Conductor said, from the aisle. "They should clear the track pretty quick. No ways to predict things like this. Coincidental damage."

"Oh, no," Chloe breathed. "Not the baby?"

He nodded. I could hardly see him in the dark. "It's too bad," he said. "Not every Train that sets out across the ocean makes it to Sanctuary. Some are sunk. There are no rules for these crossings, and the unseen currents can be treacherous."

I looked past him, at the busy lights. A huge locomotive lay on its side in the water; the cab and part of the boiler were sticking above the surface. An enormous wheel still turned slowly in the air. The number '102' was painted on the curve of one iron flank.

I watched as a wave swept in and over it, sending spray high into the air.

"Where's the rest of the Train?" I asked.

"Already on the bottom. They'll send the engine to join it. There's nothing else anyone can do."

I glanced at Chloe's profile. She gazed out at the wreck, tears glistening on her cheeks. The drops were lit softly blue by the lights moving outside the window.

"I won't let anything happen to Nora or the baby," I said. "I'm calling the play, and I won't let anything happen to either one of them."

"I hate this sometimes," she said softly. "I try to remember that there's beauty and magic. I try to remember my lucky stars, but the unseen currents can be too much. I get so tired."

She sensed me watching her, and wiped angrily at her cheek. "Don't look at me," she said. "I cry at absolutely everything, and I'm not even real. I'm just a ghost."

I stared into the night and watched the lights move around, working away at the dead Train. I reached and found her hand before I spoke.

"You're real," I said. "You're the only real thing I know."

-Thirty Three-

I was still on the secondary highway headed south when the snow hit. The road immediately became treacherous. I slowed down and reached to the lever on the floor and pulled it into four-wheel drive. The Jeep felt better at once, and I sped up again. A long grade descended into a valley, with a flashing yellow light at the bottom.

A blue-and-white sign indicated a town, but only a Shell gas station backed by a long white wood building sat at the intersection. Just past it, a concrete bridge ran over a small river, before the highway swept into the woods on the other side of the valley.

"Fill it, please," I told the young man who came to the driver's window.

I went up the steps into the diner and ordered a cup of take-out coffee at the register. The people at the tables inside paused in their eating to check me out. The waitress behind the counter had a heavily made up face and acted nearly hostile. The fluorescent lights over my head buzzed. I paid for the coffee and my gas and went back outside.

I pulled away from the pumps and to the end of the parking lot overlooking the bridge. The coffee was barely warm, but I drank it anyway, staring through the windshield at the river.

The dark water rushed over the rocks and I remembered the reality of my own drowning, so many years before. I didn't know the details. I only knew the inhalation of cold water, the feel of it my mouth and then my lungs. There was a refusal to surrender, even as the current swept my remains away from me. There had been the guilty knowledge that I broke the rules by staying, but the absolute, stronger fear of losing Chloe.

~ * ~

Chloe gazed out the window, her chin propped on an elbow.

324

"We made it," she said. "The shores of Sanctuary, and on the eleventh day. Imagine that."

As if on cue, I felt the cars bump each other as the Train slowed. We had been close to land for the last half-hour, and were now running in the surf, parallel to the sand. The turquoise water sparkled, and the gentle waves beneath our wheels ran away toward the sun-washed palms and acacias lining the beach.

She glanced at me, sitting beside her. "You don't have to get off, you know," she said. "They'll take you back across. They talk about Rules, but the more I think about it, maybe your expired ticket is really a blank ticket. Maybe losing me cost you a normal life, even if you didn't remember why. You can get Nora back, and have the baby. You deserve a life, and I won't hold it against you."

I picked up her free hand and kissed her wrist.

"I printed my own ticket a long time ago," I said. "It was never going to be a round trip."

The Train shuddered, and seemed to sink a little as it came to rest. It had been a long night. I stood up stiffly, and helped Chloe into the aisle. She smiled a little. She needed the help less than I did. The door at the end of the car opened, letting in the sea air. We left mahogany paneling and plush seats behind, and went to the small metal stairs leading down to the water.

The Conductor stood at the bottom of the steps, calf-deep, looking up at us. His uniform trousers were rolled up to his knees.

"Can I help you folks with your bags?" he asked.

"We don't need them," Chloe said. "Not anymore."

She stepped down, into the ocean. I followed her, and was surprised at the warmth of the water. The tide played at my legs, pulling and pushing, urging me forward.

"I didn't think so," the Conductor said. "You folks enjoy your stay at the Shangri-la, and have a good trip wherever you go from there."

I nodded my thanks, and gave him the last of the bear coins from my pocket. We waded toward the shoreline. The swells followed, splashing the backs of our legs. I looked over my shoulder at the Train that had carried us here. The massive locomotive sighed and snorted steam, and the breeze wafted the smoke away, toward the blue horizon. I felt both glad to be off the Train, and sad to see it go.

I caught Chloe's hand again as we waded onto the beach.

"You don't seem like yourself," I said.

"I'm thinking about Time," she said. "You know that there are changes, after this."

"Changes?"

She stopped, and turned to face me. She caught my face gently in both hands and turned me to look. It went suddenly dark. The bright, sunny beach was gone, and we stood on the rocks at the edge of Echo Island. Through the trees, I saw the old cabin where we had danced and slept together for the first time, and the clearing that had once been carpeted with butterflies. Across the reach, Duck Island floated serenely.

"You have to say goodbye sometimes," she murmured. "Everything perfect begins with an ending, but nothing perfect ever ends, not really."

In the dark, I heard the rustle of a million butterfly wings.

"What is Sanctuary?" I asked. "What is heart's desire?"

She got quiet for a minute. We lost the Moon. I couldn't see her in the dark, but I didn't need to. If I closed my eyes, I could see her just fine.

"Sanctuary," she said at last, "is walking across the desert, hot and dry. The sun is awful. You pray that you have enough warm spit left in your canteen to keep you alive until the sun goes down. Your last kindness is to hope your camel lives a little bit longer than you do."

From somewhere in the forest, a branch cracked.

"It's so much sand for so long, that you've forgotten everything but your footprints behind you. They fill in and blow away a minute after you make them, like you were never there at all. You're rubbed raw by grit and dust—your ears, your eyelids, everything. The insides of your thighs feel like they're bleeding."

She reached out through the dark and touched my face. All at once, I understood.

"It's climbing one more dune, because there's nothing left to do, and suddenly realizing that you can smell—"

"Water," we said, together.

"Yes, water," she said. "You can't see it yet, but you know it's close, and everything gets clean and blue. You hear a waterfall, and the camel starts to run in the ridiculous way that camels do. You laugh, and start to run, too."

She traced my face with a fingertip, and we stood on the sunny beach, the shore of Sanctuary, again. I saw leaves and palm fronds, smelled the green-and-blue, felt flowing coolness. I heard the roar of a waterfall, and tasted sweetness.

"All of the horror fades away, and all of the loss. You know Sanctuary is where you're from, and it's where you're going back to. You don't find your heart's desire—you remember it."

~ * ~

Sitting in my jeep, I watched the snow. I remembered Chloe, and I remembered loving her. I remembered Echo Island covered in butterflies, and the cabin on the night she had undressed, lit by a single candle. I remembered the bears in the dump, and the glory of her on water skis.

"I'll always love you," I whispered, "and I don't know what to do."

I hit the dashboard once with the heel of my hand, because it was all so big, so much bigger than me. I saw the water, and I felt more desperately scared than ever in my life, afraid of going forward, and afraid of going back.

I put my forehead on the steering wheel and cried. After a few minutes, I pulled my phone out. I scrolled down the screen. I found Sonny Risa's phone number, and dialed it.

~ * ~

A small plane buzzed lazily overhead.

This far out, the swells rocked us very gently. Chloe was lying on her back, looking at her toes. I floated beside her and looked at her toes, too. The nails were colored dark on her left foot, light on the right.

"Why are they different?" I wondered. "You've never told me."

"Stop changing the subject."

"I'm not. I really want to know."

"You can't be afraid," she said. "You've been afraid for long enough."

"I'm not afraid."

She smiled and spit water at me.

"Is it time?" I asked.

"Do you still think I'm not real?"

I thought about it. "I'm starting to wonder if I was real, before you."

"It's all a storybook," she said. "Everyone gets a page, and—you believe in your own story, or you don't. There's nothing in between."

I nodded, and she pulled me under. We sank, slowly, through clouds of bubbles. When they cleared, I looked up, through crystalline water. The sun-dappled surface was already far above our heads. Below my feet, I saw the sandy bottom coming up to meet us.

The ocean pinged and clicked and echoed, busy with being alive. A school of brilliant orange fish flashed by, in a hurry and late for something important. A couple of stragglers stopped to goggle at us for a minute before dashing off again. When our feet touched, she caught my hand and pulled me toward a meadow of turtle grass.

As we reached the edge of the green, Chloe somersaulted gracefully in the water. A slipstream of delicate froth followed her and then wafted upward. Her body was striped with the undulating sunlight from above us. She smiled at me, and I smiled back, infected by her happiness.

She sculled herself to the sea floor and parted the plants with both hands. Something glimmered. I swam to her and picked it up. A cloud of sand drifted down, leaving a tiny, perfect shell in my palm. Pale pink, impossibly delicate, it seemed to be lit from within.

Chloe touched my shoulder and pointed. I saw an amber point of light in the waving turtle grass. I felt the first stirrings in my diaphragm, and knew I would need air soon. I collected a second shell, as lovely as the first, and closed my hand tightly around both, terrified of losing them. I watched her as she swept a hand across the meadow. It rapidly got dark, bright day disappearing, and then hundreds of lights began to sparkle softly. It was perfect, enchanted, but the need for air became urgent.

I pointed upwards, and got ready to push off the sand and head for the top. She smiled and came to me. I felt her lips against my ear. Although underwater, her voice was perfectly clear.

"Breathe. You can breathe."

Over her shoulder, I saw that hundreds of lights had turned to thousands, millions, twinkling every color that ever was, a fairy tale come alive. My chest started to heave, and I knew I was out of air, out of time. I shook my head violently, and pointed up.

"This is our story," she said. "It always was, and if you remember it, then you know you can breathe. Look at me."

Behind her, the lights were a city, moving and alive, a place I had never been, but one that I knew perfectly. Chloe saw the recognition, and smiled. Her voice was warm.

"We won't drown, ever again."

"Never again," I echoed.

"Heartbeats are only where it begins," she said.

I looked into her eyes, and I remembered her. I spoke my heart.

"You're all I see."

329

I took a breath.

-Thirty Four-

The last traces of mango sunset streaked the deep blue in the west. The old hotel stood floodlit against the warm evening sky, its walls and towers like colored sugar. Stands of king palms glowed in reflected light. Shells crunched under the tires as I steered the Packard up the sweeping drive, and tucked it in between a pair of wire-wheeled Hispano-Suizas.

I went around the car, opened the passenger door, and gave Chloe my hand. She swung her bare legs out, and the rest of her followed. She was splendid, in something short and sweet, covered in gold beads.

Atop the porte-cochère, two women leaned on the railing and gossiped about us.

She kept my hand as we started toward the entrance. Below us, across an acre or so of smooth lawn, the ocean spread itself, dark and nearly infinite. Past the surf line, I could just make out the long string of dim lights that marked the Train. Something sparked, down on the beach.

"Is this where the green light is?" I asked.

"Sometimes, yes," she said. "It moves."

A man in a white suit and saddle shoes stood beside the path, smoking a cigarette. He touched his hat and nodded as we passed. I heard the first strains of music and laughter, coming from inside.

"What do they call this place?"

"This is the Shangri-La Hotel," Chloe said. "You're going to love it here."

Our feet crunched on the shells. I put my arm around her waist. Under the thin material of her dress, she felt like everything good.

"That was Al Bowlly back there on the path, by the way."

I searched my memory. "The singer?" I asked. "From the '40s? 'Midnight, the Stars and You'?"

"Yes, and I'm going to ask him to sing, later. It always makes him feel better. He's very sad, and doesn't talk much.

He's waiting for someone to come on the Train. He's waited a long, long time, and she still isn't here." The entry blazed with light.

A uniformed doorman smiled at us and spoke to Chloe. "So happy you made it," he said. "We were a bit worried."

"Of course, we made it," she answered, and kissed his cheek. "I'm not blocked very easily. It takes more than the Low Gang to do it. Anyway, I had help." She winked at me, and pulled me inside by the hand. Under vaulted ceilings, enormous potted ferns and palms marched along a black and white tiled floor. At the far end, the blue light from a swimming pool flickered. The music came from that direction. "He chose love badly, you know, Al Bowlly," she went on. "More than once. A lot of romantic men do. I don't know why. He finally met the right one, and didn't trust it. He was looking out the window of his London apartment, thinking about her, when a German bomb dropped into the street outside. Now he waits."

"Is she coming?"

"Who knows? She might still be alive, and very, very old by now, or maybe she decided to go somewhere else. His heart is broken, but in the best way. There's nothing wrong with waiting if your heart has been broken properly." I stopped in front of a painting on the wall. It was full of soft colors. When I looked at it, I could smell the flowers and hear a trickle of water.

"It's a Monet," she said. "A new one. Do you like it?"

I glanced at her, surprised. "A new Monet? How could there be a new Monet?"

She shook her head. "He stays here, and paints on the back lawn, every afternoon. You don't think people stop doing what they love, just because they're dead, do you?"

The back of the hotel opened onto an expanse of white swimming pool, clear blue water illuminated from below. On the lawn around it, torchlight turned colors lush, even in the dark. To one side, a striped awning sheltered an orchestra. Everyone in the crowd moved in time to the music; tuxedos and dresses, swimmers and strollers and storytellers. Even the waiters, circulating with their trays, seemed somehow to be dancing.

"There's Amelia," Chloe said, excited. "I haven't seen her in ages."

She took my arm and pointed to a group of people standing beside a fountain. A woman with a long yellow silk scarf draped over one shoulder waved to us. She wore knee-high leather boots, and a pair of flying goggles hung around her neck.

"She's fallen in love with a Sopwith Camel. You hardly ever saw her on the ground in the first place, and now she's never out of the cockpit of the silly thing. You have to meet her."

She pulled me by the hand, over to the group. The woman's lanky frame and tousled auburn hair seemed vaguely familiar to me.

"Amelia?" I said. "Is that . . ."?

The women embraced, and began to chatter. "It's been too long. You have to come up in the Camel. She's an absolute peach."

"Maybe tomorrow. We're not staying long."

Finally, Chloe turned her to introduce me. She had green eyes and a firm grip. I was stunned when she confirmed her name.

"You've been lost for about eighty years," I said stupidly. "No one knows where your plane went down. There are a million theories about what happened to you."

"Lost?" Amelia asked, and glanced at Chloe, concerned. "How could I be lost? I'm right here, in front of you."

"He says the strangest things," Chloe confided. "I never know when he's joking."

"Well, I'd keep him away from the champagne tonight, if I were you."

Chloe laughed, and blew a kiss as she pulled me back to the hotel. We went into a different entrance. A series of arches and staircases fell down into a darkened space below us. In the gloom, it appeared to be a huge ballroom. Columns and spires grew from the floor up to a ceiling that went nearly out of sight. We started down.

She stopped on one of the balconies and sat on the balustrade. A large stained-glass window arched over her. Darkened, the colors were hard to see, but I could make out a cat with a sword, and a greenish full moon. She saw me looking.

"Puss in Boots," she murmured. "He always scared me, just a little."

Below us, the orchestra stopped playing, and the piano went on alone, sighing over old familiar places. I leaned against a pillar and listened to it quietly for a few minutes, waiting for her to speak. When she finally did, she wasn't looking at me.

"Tell me," she said. "Something about us."

I thought about it. Cool air moved across my face, stirring the fragrance of old wood and candles. It brought the long-ago perfumes of overheated dancers and spilled drinks, but also the scent of her; clean water and oranges.

"When I'm very old, and——"

"How old?" she interrupted.

"Ninety, a hundred, or more. As old as I'll ever be."

She smiled. "I'll be younger than you," she said. "A little."

"I won't sleep unless I can smell your hair on my pillow."

She glanced over at me, interested.

"When I wake up," I went on, "I'll look around the room, afraid that all of it, all of you, was just a dream. When I see you, I'll be relieved and happy, but I'll also be sad."

"Why?" she asked, very softly. "Why sad?"

The piano trailed into silence, and there was only the whispery sound of the shadows moving around the vast room beneath us.

"I'll be sad because I slept," I said. "I'll be sad that I missed out on even a minute of my time with you."

I took her hand, and pulled her to me. She felt light and insubstantial. I smelled the oranges and salt water in her hair. After a moment, she pulled away and led me to the broad staircase that fell away to the ballroom floor below us.

Groupings of white-covered tables were gathered around plaster columns, and booths in alcoves lined the walls. All of it surrounded the dance floor at the bottom of the stairs. Deep in the gloom, I could see the orchestra. The ghostly figures sat perfectly still. Potted palms stood here and there in the dark, waiting to see what would happen.

At the far end, a single candle sparked, alight on a table, a pinpoint of yellow. Then another and another and more, until fragile light like summer stars spread across the entire room. The tiny flames glinted off glassware, the scented water in small bowls, and the jewelry of the men and women who sat in groups and watched us as we descended the steps.

The music began again, a soft, imperceptible breeze, whispering that it would wait for us, a thousand years. A solitary figure stood at the bottom of the flight, one hand on the broad marble balustrade. He gazed up at us expectantly. His dark face was handsome and inexpressibly sad.

"That's Bill Robinson," Chloe whispered in my ear. "Bojangles."

"Is this like the Cotton Club?" I asked, surprised.

"It's nothing at all like that place," she said. "Bojangles might see something here that comforts him, though. He's never left, since the day he first arrived."

He took Chloe's hand and kissed it, without saying a word. He nodded to me, and then stepped aside for a white-jacketed waiter. The second man inclined his head, and led us around the edge of the room to a table for two. He settled us with menus. Chloe set hers on the edge of the table without looking at it.

"Do you remember me clearly, now?"

"I remember you. I remember me."

"Good," she smiled. "I knew you would, sooner or later. Today's the day you were supposed to get here in the first place. Did you know? Time's a map, and this is where you should have been, all along."

"I love you," I said.

"No matter what," we said, together.

"You were stuck, and I unstuck you," she said. "You loved me, and you wouldn't leave me, so you stayed out there on the lake, caught in the moment of your drowning. You went under, over and over and over again. I couldn't leave you there."

"So you swam out to get me."

"Yes. I knew you'd listen to me, and you did. It was a Squeeze Play, a beautiful one."

She smiled, remembering it. "The problem, though," she said, "is that you're stubborn and crabby. When you unstuck, you disappeared. You were so determined to stay there, and you did. You did. You found a way to stay, but I was gone."

"You were—on the other side."

"Exactly," she nodded. "On the Train, and on my way, so to speak. It's how a Squeeze Play works—the batter is out, but the runner comes home. When you didn't come home, I had to go searching for you—again. You've been a lot of trouble, really."

She smiled at me, fondly.

"How did you find me?"

"I looked for the most stubborn man I could find. It wasn't hard."

"Thirty years later, thirty years older," I smiled. "It wasn't hard."

"Ginger helped me," she said. "Finding you wasn't hard. Getting you to remember me was hard, a little. We had fun though, didn't we? Didn't we have a fun trip? I told you a fairy tale, like I promised I would."

I reached across the table and took her hand. "You tell a hell of a fairy tale," I said. "We had fun, and this is just where we start."

"You're staying?" she asked. "Relief."

I brought her hand up and kissed her fingers. "Yes, I'm staying, if you'll let me," I said. "No matter what, right?"

She took a deep breath, and let it out.

"No matter what," she said, her eyes closed.

"How long will we be at the Shangri-la?"

336

"Not long. Until you feel like we're ready to go on ahead, to Sanctuary. We should dance, don't you think?"

She was perfectly perfect. She stood up, and offered me her hand. Her skin was warm. We turned toward the dance floor, and found our way blocked.

~ * ~

Sonny Risa answered his phone even before I heard it ring on his end.

"What do you want?" I said, without preamble.

"Good talking to you, pally!" His voice sounded jovial, and subtly different. "What do I want? I want you to stop messing around, and turn yourself in."

"Turn myself in?"

"Give yourself up to proper authority. You're an offense, is what you are! You've been a foul ball your whole life. You don't belong here."

The snow started up again, and flakes landed silently on the windshield glass and stuck. I started the motor and turned the wipers on. After a second, I twisted the knob to turn the heater on, too. I shivered, and wondered if my soaking in the lake would make me sick; my resistance was probably gone. I had a feeling it didn't matter.

"You're the proper authority?" I asked. "I doubt that, somehow."

"You don't belong here," he repeated. "Now you're running around on an expired Train ticket. You know what the real problem is, pally? You know what your problem is?"

"Tell me." I said. I felt fatigue creeping in, deep inside me. I wanted to get on the road, while I still could.

"You're practically a ghost. The only strange thing about it is that you have a heartbeat. You're a ghost with a heartbeat."

He dissolved into laughter. I got ready to hang up.

"There isn't even a name for your condition," he finally managed, and I could picture him wiping tears of merriment from his eyes. "They haven't even invented a name for it, things like you. You're a ghost who breathes and eats."

His breathing became audible. It started to get faster, until he was nearly panting on the other end. When he spoke again, his good mood had gone.

"So, here's what we do," he said. "The loser, Esteban, is gone for a little ride. The tramp, your girlfriend, the one with the child who could belong to just about anyone—except you? She's sitting tight, waiting for us. So, here's the deal. Ready for this?"

"Ready," I said. "I'm tired of this, so tired of you. Just spit it out."

"Give up the splat," he said. "She isn't yours. Guys who don't play by the rules don't get the girl, understood?"

His voice hoarsened and deepened, rising into nearly a shout.

"Give yourself up. Turn yourself in, or I'll slit the girlfriend's throat. Boyfriend Esteban can come back from the little ride I've sent him on, and take the fall for it. He'd be happier in jail, anyway, the useless prick."

"I'm on my way," I said. "See you shortly."

"I might eat her baby, though," he said, his tone suddenly quiet and reflective. "I might eat the baby all up. That's how a good story should end, I think."

I disconnected, and tossed the phone onto the seat. I put the Jeep into gear and spun the wheels getting back onto the dark highway.

~ * ~

"Telegram, ma'am. It just came."

The waiter offered a tray. A yellow envelope sat in the center it. Chloe glanced up at him, hesitated, and then picked it up. The candle on the table guttered, as if it knew something bad was coming, and the gold of it flickered on her. She regarded me for a long moment, gave a nearly imperceptible nod, and opened the flap.

She pulled out a piece of flimsy paper, the same color as the envelope. Her eyes moved and then narrowed as she scanned it. Her face drained.

"It's for you," she said. "You have to go back."

Her voice was expressionless. The air left the room. I didn't want to breathe, anyway.

"Why?"

"Mother and child in imminent danger. Stop" she read aloud. "Come soonest, no delay. Repeat: Mother and child in grave peril. Stop."

She stared at the paper until her fingers relaxed and it settled onto the table. We sat in silence. The orchestra sang softly that it was looking at the moon.

"I'll never go back," I finally managed. The voice I heard didn't sound like mine. "I'm staying here."

"You have to go," she breathed. "I'm not real, but you are. You're still real. You have to go back."

"No. Not this time. Not again."

She stood up, knocking over the vase. It spilled out its dead rose, and bled onto the tablecloth. The liquid spread and touched the telegram, turning the paper dark.

"You're still real!" she screamed. "Don't you understand that? You have to go!"

Behind her the dancers stopped, and turned to watch us. They stood and stared, shocked, faces pale, mouths parted, eyes dark. The music trailed off, and the great room got so quiet that I could hear the wings rustling in the dark rafters far above our heads.

"Real, real, real . . ."

Her voice was ghastly. She turned and ran.

"Wait, wait," I cried, and started after her.

A hand grasped my forearm. It was gently intended, but held me fast. It belonged to Bojangles Robinson. I tried to shake him off, but he stepped into my way, blocking me from Chloe's exit.

"I'll take care of her," he said. "You have to catch the Train."

"I'm not catching any Train. Let me go."

"I'm the last Gatekeeper," he said. "I have to turn you back. I'm so sorry."

"Wait, wait!" I said desperately. "I have what you're looking for. You have to let me pass!"

I scratched at the lapel of my jacket, and pulled off the single pink flower pinned to it. I tried to give him the blossom, but he wouldn't take it.

"Here's your Treasure," I said. "A pink flower. You have to take it."

"You have a different fairy tale to take care of, now," he said. "A different ending."

"I don't understand!"

I was pleading.

"Do the right thing," he said. "Do the right thing, no matter what."

His words stopped me. "No matter what," he said. "Even if it hurts, right to the very end of you. Some days, that's the only way to win——is to lose. The ball is in play. You have to advance the runner."

My arms fell to my sides. I felt the warmth of tears on my face, and wondered where they had come from.

"So, I'm never going to make it to Sanctuary?

"No reason to say 'never'. It's not a word I have much faith in."

"But not with her."

"I stay here, because I like it," he said. "I dance a little. I have a drink from time to time with the guy who plays the piano. I don't tell the future."

He took his hand back, and nodded at me, once. He seemed infinitely tired. "Go on with you, now," he said. "Time is short. You best hurry, and don't stop to breathe 'til you get where you're going."

"I remember everything, now. If I forget again, maybe I don't have to be real, too."

"Yes, you do." He turned away. "Go do the right thing. Go do what you ought to."

At the foot of the stairs, he put one hand on the newel post, and slipped out of his worn-out shoes. He left them neatly, round-heeled and side-by-side, at the bottom. He stood looking up, at the place Chloe had disappeared into, and then he began to ascend, in his stocking feet, dancing the softest of soft-shoe shuffles. The music followed him, sweet and sad, light as crumbs.

At the top, he turned around. We stood there, staring at each other. Finally, he shrugged.

"What can you do?" he mouthed. "Sometimes—what can you do?"

I shrugged back at him. I didn't know, either.

Chloe was gone, and I waited there, very quietly, to see if I could hear the sound of my own cracking. I didn't, so after a little while I turned around.

The dance floor was empty. Everyone was gone. No one sat at the tables, and there was no orchestra. The candles were dead, and only the Moon's face through the open windows gave me enough light to leave by. I didn't go back up the stairs. I walked away, to an open set of glass-paned doors at the other end of the great room.

The dark lawns were just as soft and lush under my feet as they had been. I walked across the gentle slopes of them, down toward the water. I could hear the breakers on the beach. It sounded like the sea was picking up, and just as I spotted the long line of its lights, out past the surf line, the Train's whistle gave a single long blast. The rising wind picked up the sound and spun it away.

I started to run.

-Thirty Five-

Ginger waited for me, waist-deep in the freshening surf. The waves were phosphorescent in the dark, running against me. I wanted them to pull me back, or better yet, pull me under. They didn't though, and I reached the steps where the old Conductor stood.

The windows of the passenger cars were lit soft gold, and I could sense the vibration through the water as the locomotive built steam. I started up the metal steps, and then stopped. I looked at him, standing below me.

"We have to hurry," he said. "There's a storm on the way. It won't be an easy crossing."

"You knew, didn't you?" I asked. "This whole time, you knew?"

"I'm just a train conductor, sir. I don't know anything for sure."

He followed me up the quiet aisle to the sleeper that I had shared with Chloe. After he had turned down the berth, he put a hand on my shoulder. "Best you rest for a little while," he said. "I'll wake you when we get there."

I could smell Chloe's hair on the pillow. I didn't think I could sleep, ever again. I felt the rocking of the waves as the Train began to move. Ginger went to the door, and pulled it open.

"The game is still going on," he said. "Ball in play, the runner hasn't come home, and the outcome is undecided."

He went out, into the passageway and disappeared.

~ * ~

The moon was an empty yellow balloon. The freeway ran down into the great city, a river of headlights flowing into a vast sea of neon and lit windows and flashing bulbs. The people in the cars that passed me were no more real than flickering images on a screen. I moved through an old movie.

I wanted Chloe back, and I had no way to make that happen. She had abandoned me in a strange place, with empty landscapes and empty people.

I got off at Avenue Road, and took the artery south to the heart of the city, past ivied old schools and expensive row houses and fast food joints on million dollar parcels of land. Traffic was heavy, even this late. A sign said that I couldn't turn left onto Castlefield, but I did anyway.

I found a parking place on the curb near the park a block from Nora's address, and walked back. The sidewalks were covered in melting slush. The air was warmer, here in the city. I saw the office towers lit up over the tops of the houses across the street.

Nora opened her door before I could knock. I followed her inside, and stopped in the hall. She was already shrugging on a coat. Kuba wandered out to greet me. I crouched down to see him. His long white coat had been groomed, clipped closer than I had ever seen it. After a moment, he walked away and settled himself on the floor with a sigh.

The house seemed strangely quiet after hours in the noisy Jeep. I felt as though the road was still moving beneath me.

"Kuba looks good," I said.

"He misses Esteban," she said absently, checking her phone. "He knows something's wrong."

She stared up at me, stricken, realizing what she'd said. I shook my head. It didn't matter.

"You've heard from Risa?" I asked.

"He's letting him go, when you get here," she said. "That's what he says, anyway. They're coming in on the train from Montreal. It gets in to Union Station in an hour."

"Montreal?" I asked. "What was Esteban doing in Montreal?"

Nora shrugged helplessly. I saw the dark circles under her eyes.

"He wasn't in Montreal," she said. "Not as far as I know. He went to his office this morning, same as any other day. I don't understand it, any more than the rest of this. You and I are supposed to meet the train, and then we'll get this all sorted out."

I nodded.

"Are we, Nick?" she asked. "Are we going to sort this out? Are you going to be able to end this?"

I nodded again.

"It will end tonight," I said. "When you get back here later, it will be over. I promise."

She pressed something into my hand. I looked down at the small silver token in my open palm.

"Subway," she said. "It'll be faster than driving, and finding parking at Union Station is impossible. Let's get going."

We walked to the main drag, and turned right. There were still plenty of small restaurants open on Yonge Street, and I looked through the plate glass windows at the elegant city people, laughing across glasses of wine and beer at their companions, staving off the loneliness outside. I envied them.

It was familiar, walking with Nora. Made compactly, she always moved quickly, like she meant business. I knew her cadences and rhythms, and it felt odd not to put an arm around her shoulders, strange not to have her hand at my waist. Grates steamed in the street, and the sidewalks were wet. The night city was winter-warm, and bright as day. My frozen lake seemed a lifetime and another planet away.

We hurried down cement steps, through a stainless steel turnstile, and then dashed onto the platform to catch the waiting subway before the doors slid closed. We sat on the long padded bench as the electric motors spooled up and the train moved out of the station and into the dark tunnel.

"The trip down went okay?" Nora asked. "You got here fast."

"It was okay," I said. "I made good time once I got going."

It had been about four hours since I had fallen through the ice. I thought about the bare footprints in the snow, the warmth of Chloe as she lifted me from the lake, the sound of her voice in my ear. I had never missed anyone as much. I dragged myself back to what Nora was saying.

"He got his money. He doesn't even mention it anymore. He just wants to torture us. And now, practically kidnapping Esteban. It is kidnapping, really. I don't know what else you could call it. What in the world does he want to talk to you about? Why is he doing this?"

I put a hand on her arm, ignoring her unease. "He's going to talk to me, and that will be the end of it," I said. "His reasons don't matter anymore."

"He must have a reason. Or is he such a psychopath that there are no reasons?"

"I want a promise, Nora."

She searched my face. I don't know what she saw.

"When we get there, I want you to take Esteban and go home," I said. "I'm going to settle this with Sonny Risa, by myself. I don't want you to get involved."

"I am involved."

"Not anymore."

She shook her head, and stared out the window at the passing walls of the tunnel. I leaned back on the bench and closed my eyes.

~ * ~

The Train rolled slowly into the station. I looked out the window at the empty platform. No one waited for us. Trash blew around in the eddies of air we stirred up. It was all grimy and forlorn, and the occasional little splashes of color in the scene were crude and harsh.

Ginger stood in the aisle. He tried to smile, and gave up. He appeared exhausted, and his uniform was wrinkled as though he'd slept in it.

"Do I have to get off here?" I asked, knowing the question was pointless.

He didn't answer, and the carriages finally coasted to a stop. I followed him up the aisle. I passed the pair of seats where I had sat with Chloe, and I caught her scent, a sweet ghost made of oranges and water.

At the end of the car, he shouldered the heavy door open, and the metal steps rattled down.

"Good luck, where you're going," he said. "More important, be good. In every sense of the word, be good."

"I'll do my best."

"Sometimes you don't get to hit a home run," he said. "You don't get to be a hero. Sometimes, you have to sacrifice, because it's the right thing. You have to bunt, no matter how much it hurts."

"Squeeze play—no matter what."

He nodded.

"Will I see you again?"

He laughed a little. The smile crinkled his eyes, and I noticed for the first time that he had a gap between his front teeth. I had an idea what he must have looked like as a little boy.

"You'll see me—sooner or later. You bought your ticket a long time ago. When you're ready, find a station and we'll be along. This is the Pacific Railway. We run night and day."

He put a hand on my shoulder. "Try to remember, she died for you," he said. "We don't use the word much, because it has little meaning, but she died for you, and not many of us ever get to experience that kind of love."

My mother had said the same thing, in almost the same words. I stared at him, startled, and he gave me a small smile.

"Will I see her?" I asked. "Will she still haunt me?"

He looked suddenly sad, close to tears. "I'm a train conductor, sir. I take tickets. I'm here to help you with your bags, and turn down your berth at night. If you need a pair of pants pressed, I'll take care of it."

"You don't tell the future, though?"

"I don't tell the future," he said. "I never have, and never will."

"Say you were a betting man," I persisted, "What would you back? Do you think I'll find her again?"

"I don't bet on baseball. It's against the rules."

"She's gone. I won't see her anymore." I felt a fresh stab of grief. "We were already using a second chance."

"Doesn't change what you have to do," he said softly. "Doesn't change what's right."

"I suppose it doesn't."

"You're on deck, now. You'd best be on your way."

I nodded, and went down the steps. The concrete platform felt cold and gritty and horribly real beneath my feet. I smelled exhaust fumes and garbage and frying food. I didn't look back, but I knew that the Train had faded behind me, like a dream.

I found an exit and went up the stairs, to do what I had to do.

~ * ~

The train from Montreal pulled in, blue and yellow and silver. The double locomotive passed slowly, towering over us. The diesel turbines throbbed, and made the cement vibrate beneath our feet. Nora trembled in time with them beneath my arm. I had never felt so sorry for anyone. The passenger cars followed, one by one, and she strained to see the faces in the windows and the aisles.

The steps rattled, and passengers began to disembark almost before the great steel wheels had stopped turning. People stopped to zip coats and to pull on gloves when the reality of the cold night hit them. Collars were turned up, faces were set, and they picked up the pace, hurrying to whatever warmth they were going to.

The crowd was entirely ordinary. Parents shepherded small children, made wretched by the lateness of the hour. Business types checked watches and phones, and a scattering of the elderly, most travelling alone, dragged suitcases on wheels. The cold temperatures restrained the greetings for those that were being met. A crowd jammed the bottom of the escalators. I heard a smattering of French in the conversations that passed us. It eventually thinned, and the last casual students and club car drinkers got off, in no hurry.

Tears ran freely down Nora's cheeks.

"He'll be here," I said. "He'll be here."

The enormous train sat and steamed in the cold. At last, far up the track, a figure got off and stood unsteadily. Nora broke free of me, and started running.

"Esteban!" she screamed. "Esteban!"

I followed her, more slowly. He stood very still and waited for us. Even at a distance, his face appeared haggard and slack. When Nora reached him, he took a step back and almost fell under her clutching. When I reached them, she was sobbing onto his shoulder, and he looked at me over her head. His dark eyes were circled and empty.

"You're okay?" I asked.

He hesitated, and then nodded.

"It's over," I said. "It's all over."

He nodded again, and Nora turned to glare at me. "It's not over," she said. "This is never, ever going to be over."

"It is, though," I said, as gently as I could. "It is over, now. They're done with you. He's done with you. His business is with me. He was using you to get to me. He was never after you."

"What are you talking about?" she asked, incredulous. "Using us to get to you?"

"I'm so sorry. I didn't understand it until now. I would have stopped it sooner if I had."

"Explain this," she demanded. "Explain to me what you're talking about."

I ignored her. "Can you walk okay?" I asked Esteban. "You need to get her out of here."

"That isn't good enough, Nick," she said.

"It has to be, for now, Nora. All the time we've known each other, you have to trust me, and get away from here."

"Trust you? What did you do to these people? What did you do?"

Esteban was staring at me. I nodded to him, and he managed to put an arm across Nora's shoulders and steer her toward the stairs.

"Go, Nora," I said.

She shrugged against Esteban's arm and stared at me. Her face was still wet. I had nothing else to say. She must have seen something in my face, because after a minute, she nodded too, and the two of them moved off. At the bottom of the stairs, she turned back and looked at me again. I sketched a wave. They helped each other up the stairs, moving like shipwreck survivors.

My Nora. I had loved her. I still did. I hated goodbyes, and I was saying a lot of them lately. I watched her until her feet had disappeared from sight.

I stood on the empty platform and waited. After a while, Sonny Risa stepped from behind a column and strolled toward me. He wore a long tan coat and a fedora. He moved slowly, in no hurry, and stopped a few feet away. His eyes were shaded by his hat brim and moved constantly. He didn't want to meet my eyes.

"Here we are," he said. "I told you so. It didn't have to come to this. You could have done what you were supposed to."

"Yes, it did," I said. "It had to come to this."

He held something down low by his side. When he moved, his coat shifted and I saw the baseball bat. He brought it out and held it in front of him. I saw the words "Genuine Louisville Slugger" on the shank of it. He took a step toward me.

"You broke the rules, bub. Nothing personal."

"Cumin, Turmeric, Cayenne, Blueberry . . ." I said. "A dash of each, and all together."

"Too late for that." He grinned. "A lot too late, in fact."

We stood, both of us very still, and watched each other. Beneath the hat brim, his face changed, and he appeared deeply sad, and infinitely old.

"The splat isn't real, pally," he said. "She never was. You dreamed up this whole thing. There are no happily-ever-afters, and the Turtle died a long time ago. He doesn't care."

"She is real, though," I answered. "She's real, and so am I."

He lifted the bat. His shoes scuffled on the tiles as he shifted his position.

"You have to leave her alone, now," I said. "It's the rules, you have to leave all of them alone."

"I still have business with the splat."

"No, you don't." I shook my head and took a step towards him. He moved back, a barely perceptible retreat. "This is how it ends."

"This is why you were always going to lose," he said. "You'd rather have your dreams than what's real. You're losers, pally, you and her, both. Losers."

"Everything perfect begins with an ending," I murmured, and took another step forward. "Nothing perfect ever ends."

"Game over, pally," he whispered. "Say goodbye."

"You've already lost, bad guy. You just don't know it."

"I never lose," he said, and tightened his grip.

I brought my hand up as he swung. A jolt came, and I felt my shoulder break. It vibrated, all the way to the balls of my feet. There wasn't much pain, but my arm was suddenly useless.

"I never lose," he said again, from the shade beneath his hat.

Deep inside of me, something shifted, and my body began to go into shock. We stood and faced each other. I fought dizziness.

My face felt like a hot mask, and I heard my own breath coming in red, ragged gasps. I watched his right foot in its polished black shoe slide back and plant. The next swing was wild, and I turned my body to meet it with my good arm, but my balance had gone. The bat hit the side of my head, and I heard the sound of my own cracking. A great rush of white noise washed over me, an ocean wave, and then I was looking at the tiles on the floor, up close.

I thought about getting back up, and knew I wouldn't be able to.

"You broke the rules," he said, his voice a hollow echo from somewhere up above me. "Blame yourself, pally."

He sounded strange. I felt vaguely sick to my stomach. Blood began to pool and spread on the tiles in front of my eyes, and that calmed me, somehow. I could feel it beneath my head. It was warm, like tears.

"Squeeze play, you bastard," I breathed. "Runner crosses."

I could hear my voice, but I wasn't sure if I spoke out loud. I tried again. "It was a squeeze play, the whole time," I said. "Runner's in from third, safe at home. You lose."

The most complete exhaustion I had ever felt swept over me. I was too tired to laugh, and too tired to close my eyes. The bat hit the floor in front of me, clattered loudly and then rolled out of my field of vision. His black shoes were still for a minute, and then they turned and walked away.

Later, there were the hollow sounds of shouts and running people, but I couldn't hear any of it. I saw lights. A forest of pants legs and bent waists appeared, and hands touched me. Through all the commotion, I stayed very still, and watched my own blood spreading on the tiles.

In the middle of all the moving shoes, I saw a pair of bare feet. A silver chain wound around one slender ankle, strung with a tiny bell that chimed as it came toward me. Her steps were light, heel and toes, almost a dance. They brought the fragrance of cinnamon and clean salt water.

"Chloe," I said, and then I didn't say anything else.

I felt soft sand beneath me, and I heard a train whistle, far off but getting closer. I heard the rustle of palm fronds, the rush of surf, and the beginning of music. It was soft, but it filled everything like a wind from faraway. It was a song I knew from somewhere, though I had forgotten the words.

It was a song for Chloe, and a song for me.

Reprise

"We have train to catch," I said.

"It will wait for us," Chloe murmured, absently. "There's no hurry."

She was looking up at the sky. Her face was beautiful.

I looked up, too. The snow was falling faster. Large flakes shone against the night sky, perhaps catching the reflected light from some far-off city. I closed my eyes. The brush of it on my face felt warm.

"This is how winter is supposed to be," I said. "What year is this?"

She looked at her watch.

"I think it's 1934," she said, counting. "Thirty, forty, a hundred-and-three makes—eleven? It's too dark to see for sure—but it's New Year's Eve, wherever this is. Does it matter?"

"No, not really," I said. "We have time, now."

There was a road below us, drifted white. We'd have to start walking soon, following the crumbs. It didn't make any difference if the bears found them first and ate them. We knew the way.

"Is it going to be a good year?" she asked. "Will we be happy this year?"

I closed my eyes, and made a wish.

"Happily ever after," I nodded. "I want that."

She shifted her weight and leaned against me, light and heavy at the same time. I caught her fragrance; cinnamon, oranges, and faraway. I spoke into her ear.

"*Happy New Year, then—whatever year it is. All the years—for good and always.*"

The snowflakes whirled and fell, spun close and danced as if they knew us.

"*It's snowing, but I can see the Moon,*" she said. "*How strange. Maybe it's a sign.*"

I nodded, and for a while we didn't say anything else. Then she touched my face and kissed me.

"*So there,*" she said, against my mouth.

"*So there,*" I echoed, and kissed her back.

After a long time, Chloe turned away and started walking. I took one last look back at the things I had known, the things that would go on without me, and felt a moment of sadness. Then I turned and followed her.

Behind us, the lake settled again and was quiet; the surface became a smooth looking-glass for the sky. On shore, the dark pines watched for a little while, interested, to see if there would be anything else. There wasn't, and so the forest gathered in its shadows to sleep. Eventually, the Moon took its strange light and left, and the stars came out to dance their slow, icy trails across the sky, just as they always had.

It was as if none of it had ever happened. If this was a story, it would be 'The End', but there are no ends. There are only the clean, cold nights and bright days, the turns of the kaleidoscope, the changing spills of color across everything that was and everything that will be.

The journey with Chloe was enough, and it was never over, not really.

The End

CPSIA information can be obtained
at www.ICGtesting.com
Printed in the USA
LVOW10s0151100617

537623LV00016B/57/P